In Loving Memory

of

Dianne Price

(1933 – 2013)

Wing and a Prayer

Dianne Price

BOOK TWO OF
THE THISTLE SERIES

Ashberry Lane

Other Ashberry Lane Books
by Dianne Price

Broken Wings, Book One in the Thistle Series

Published in association with Terry Burns of Hartline Literary Agency, LLC.

ISBN 978-0-9893967-6-9

Cover design by Miller Media Solutions
Cover images by Ashlee Murr Photography and iStock.com

Use of the Gaelic Biblical Texts by kind permission of the Scottish Bible Society.

Scripture used in this book, whether quoted or paraphrased by the characters, is taken from the English Revised Version of the Bible, Oxford Press, 1885. Used by permission.

Map © 2013 Mary Elizabeth Hall

Salms/Psalms 23:4

Seadh, fòs ged ghluaisinn eadhon triìd
Yea, though I walk through the valley
Ghlinn dorcha sgaàil a' bhàis,
Of the shadow of death, I will fear no evil;
Aon olc no urchuid a theachd orm
For thou art with me:
Chan eagal leam 's cha chàs;
Thy rod and thy staff,
Airson gu bheil thu leam a-ghnàth;
They comfort me.

Grace tried is better than grace, and more than grace;
it is glory in its infancy.
~Samuel Rutherford, Scottish Theologian, 1600-1661

If you are going through hell, keep going.
~Sir Winston Churchill, 1874-1965

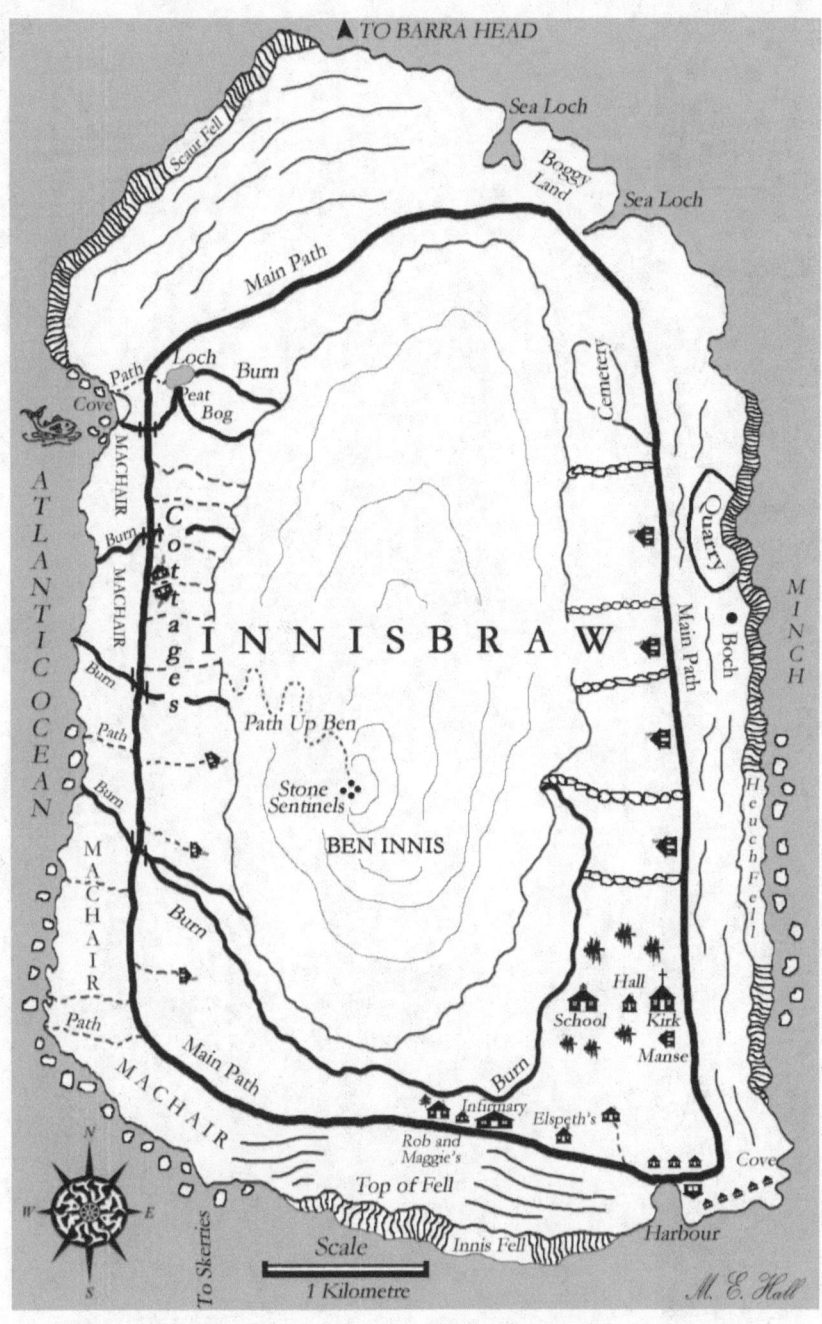

Written with some British spelling, this book also
includes a Scottish Gaelic glossary.

Dedication

To the glory of my Lord and Savior,
Jesus Christ. And as always, for True,
my best friend, husband, and the luve
of my life.

In Loving Memory

Dianne joined her beloved Savior and
her husband in Heaven one week
before her first book released. She is
probably dancing a Scots reel even as
you read this.

Chapter One

Edenoaks Air Base, England, late November, 1942

Colonel Rob Savage paused on the walk in front of the base hospital, gaze sweeping the south side of the air base.

Only 0530 and already Jeeps jounced over rutted roads, strident horns scattering bicyclists who raced each other to the chow hall. A few sluggish crewmen plodded through the main gate, heads down, uniforms rumpled after a short leave—and a long bus ride.

"Looks the same, smells the same." Rob's nostrils twitched at the odor of spent aviation fuel and smoke from Nissen hut stoves wafting palliative offerings to the bruised sky. The always present, elusive scent of fear suspended over the base turned sour on his tongue.

His bride, Maggie, swatted his arm. "It's only been six months. What did you expect?"

After a quick grin, he ticked his wildest wishes off on his fingers. "Oh, Nissen huts for everybody instead of tents, tarmac to replace those dirt roads and their potholes big enough to swallow a Jeep, and a few more hangars equipped for extensive large repairs." He laughed and hugged her waist. "A man can dream, can't he?"

"My man always dreams—then makes them come true."

The luve in Maggie's eyes stopped a breath in his throat. After looking around to make sure no one was watching, he brushed his lips across her silken cheek. The warm-honey fragrance of heather on her skin and hair spoke of their Scottish island home.

Innisbraw. The Atlantic pounding the rocky fells, sending prisms of spume high into the air, wildflowers fluttering like butterflies in a brisk sea-salted breeze, island folk smiling a greeting as one passed.

1

His yearning to return tasted sharp and clean, like a blade of spring grass.

"Where did you go, luve? You're far away."

Her pleading violet-blue eyes and plaintive question snapped him back to the present. "Home. Innisbraw."

Maggie sighed and nodded. "I miss it too." A rueful smile wrinkled her nose. "But now 'tis back to war with you." She tapped her watch. "And I'm going to be late reporting in."

Rob's answering smile faded like the sun at gloaming. "Pray for me, Maggie. I've got a bad feeling that the temporary CO may have left me some nasty surprises."

Warm fingers laced through his. "You know I will. Remember this promise from the Word: 'I can do everything with the help of Christ who gives me the strength I need.'" She squeezed his hand and mimed a kiss. Tucking errant wisps of hair into the bun above her collar, the luve of his life—his *wife*—hurried up the walk, starched hospital whites rustling.

A pang of loss brought a groan as she opened the door and disappeared inside. No more running his fingers through the mass of black hair that slipped down her slim back to below her waist. No more sitting in front of a peat fire sharing memories of yesterdays and dreams for tomorrows. No more walking across the top of Innis Fell, laughing at the pewlie gulls hitching a ride on a rare off-shore wind. His belly cramped. It would be agony not having her at his side almost every waking moment. Maggie exuded a faith he would take years to attain, and her sweet spirit understood his impetuous rush to accomplish everything immediately.

But she was right. He was back to war, where he longed to be, fulfilling his duty.

Guide me, Lord. Give me Your thoughts, Your words today.

His steps turned toward his office. A few officers he didn't recognize executed crisp salutes as they passed. Why were they smiling? They couldn't know he was their new CO—unless someone had leaked the news.

In front of Operations Headquarters, an American flag sagged on its pole, limp in the breathless morning. Hank's black bicycle leaned against the dingy white clapboards.

The familiar sight brought a stir of excitement as Rob pulled the door open.

Notices to flight personnel—some yellowed with age, some new—fluttered from a corkboard on the wall. A copy of a *Stars and Stripes* newspaper lay discarded on the empty, uncomfortable wooden bench. The same bench where those awaiting an appointment, usually disciplinary, with the CO would fidget, the odor of their sweat and fear permeating the peeling paint. The door to his old office was closed.

Major Hank Hirsch, Rob's aide since he first took command of the 396th, sat at a desk in the middle of the long, narrow room, muttering as he shuffled through a mountain of paperwork. He looked up and leaped to his feet, a grin threatening to dislodge the steel-framed glasses perched precariously near the end of his nose. "Colonel Savage!" He snapped a brisk salute.

Rob returned the salute with a smile so broad he almost choked on it.

Hank adjusted his glasses, rushed forward, and pumped Rob's hand. "Rob, you can't know how good it is to see you back. Your recovery took so long, I wondered if you'd ever return."

"It's good to be back, Hank." Rob clapped the major's shoulder.

The six months had not been kind to Hank. Salt overwhelmed pepper in his short sideburns, lines of fatigue bracketed his lips, and his once-erect shoulders slumped. He held Rob at arm's length. "You've lost some weight, but you look fit."

His voice sounded hoarse. The replacement commander must have worked him into the ground. "I feel fit. And don't worry about the weight. Maggie's on a crusade to fatten me up."

"Oh, congratulations on your marriage. General Fielding announced it at a briefing. It's been the talk of the base all weekend."

Is that why those officers were smiling? "Uh-oh, things must be mighty slow around here when that kind of news makes waves." He winked at Hank.

Hank's gray eyes sparkled, a fleeting glimpse of the man Rob remembered. "Come on, Rob. When 'the old man' finally gets hitched, that's news."

"What do you mean?"

"You really don't know?"

"No idea."

"Ever since you first took command last January, there's been a bet on how long it would take you to say 'I do.'"

"A bet?"

"That's right. I believe the pool was over three hundred dollars. Major Anderson won it."

Rob's pulse thrummed at the thought of seeing his best friend. "Den? That traitor. I'll make sure he doesn't keep a dime of that money. He'll be standing rounds of drinks at the officer's club for weeks before I'm through with him."

"Don't be too hard on him. I understand he's the one who introduced you to your wife."

"What? Is that what he's been telling everybody?"

"Sure is."

Rob suppressed a snort of glee at the thought of getting even with his old buddy. "He's lying through his teeth. All he did was dare me to ask her to dance. When I get through with him ..."

Hank checked his watch. "That'll have to wait. You have an appointment with Doc Larson right now for your physical."

"Oh, yeah, my physical." Rob's chest rumbled as he chuckled. "You're about to witness the quickest physical you've ever seen. Come on. You're going with me."

"Why me?"

"I want you to see the shape I'm in. After all, you run interference for me with Wing. I need to convince you almost as much as the doc."

⭑

Flight Surgeon Major Larson lowered his stethoscope and scribbled cryptic figures onto a chart.

Rob's heartbeat stuttered. "What's the problem? I could have run in place a lot longer if you hadn't told me to stop."

The doctor tossed the chart onto the examining table. "Twenty minutes at that pace should have raised your pulse at least thirty

4

beats over what I just recorded. What have you been doing on that island?"

Hank flipped Rob a thumbs-up and waggled his eyebrows.

"Walking, running, leg-lifts, sit-ups, more walking and running." Rob toweled off and pulled on his skivvy shirt.

"I don't understand how you can be in better physical condition than before you crashed." Larson studied the worn linoleum for a moment before looking at Rob. "A little over six months ago, you left here paralyzed from the hips down, only a breath away from dying. Am I looking at some kind of miracle?"

Rob suppressed a snort. "Miracle? If you mean instant healing, you're way off base. If you're talking about John McGrath's skill as a surgeon and the rehab plan he worked out for me, as the Brits say, 'You're spot on.'" He shrugged into his uniform shirt. "That's why so many people consider him one of the world's leading orthopedic surgeons."

Larson's face flushed. "Of course." He glanced at the chart again. "I've never been so happy to be wrong in my life."

"So I passed the physical?"

"With flying colors. I'll call General Fielding at Edenoaks Hall with the good news. He asked to be apprised of the results the minute you finished."

"Thanks. Now, if that's all, I'd better tackle a stack of paperwork." He toed into his boots. "I've got a lot of catching up do."

"A word of warning."

"Okay?"

Larson fidgeted, Adam's apple bobbing like a fisherman's float in a stormy surf. "First, I want to welcome you back to the 396th. You were sorely missed. Right now, morale is low and I understand performance has suffered severely. You have your work cut out for you. Of course, you did it once before. I'm certain you can turn this group into Wing's top performers again."

Ouch. "Anything else?"

"I want you to know how happy I am to have Leftenant McGra ... Savage back. She's a real asset to any hospital."

"Thanks, Doc. I'm glad to hear that. Of course I'm a little prejudiced, since I wouldn't be talking to you today if she hadn't called her father." Rob's tone was more gruff than he meant it to be.

The doctor's face flushed again. "I understand." He unclenched and extended his hand. "It's good to have you back, Colonel."

Hank trotted to keep up with Rob. "I've never seen Doc so flustered."

Rob grunted. "He refused to remove that large piece of shrapnel from my back—said it would kill me." He shortened his stride. "If Maggie hadn't been seconded here and contacted her father to transfer me and remove the shrapnel, I'd be six feet beneath a white cross in some military graveyard."

"Doesn't sound like Doc Larson. I've always considered us lucky to have him."

"Don't get me wrong. We are. For a while I blamed him for my being in such bad condition when I reached Edinburgh. But he was probably so overwhelmed by having the CO as a patient, he was afraid he'd botch the surgery and end up killing me."

Hank held the OP's door open. "I can't believe the RAF loaned your new wife to us again. Thought they'd hang onto every one of their experienced nurses."

Ducking his six-five frame into the building, Rob gripped Hank's arm. "Not seconded this time. It's a permanent posting." He grinned at the surprise on his aide's face. "I'll tell you all about it when we can squeeze in a few minutes."

Just outside Rob's office window, B-17s sat on hardstands in the parking lot beside the runway, the gray sky mirrored in polished Perspex windscreens. He shook his head and glanced at his watch. 0800 hours, cloudy but no rain. Why weren't they out on a strike? That would be his first question to Hank as soon as he brought in all the papers for the first briefing.

The front door slammed and his office door burst open.

Major Dennis Anderson, Rob's best friend since plebe year at West Point, rushed in, his always-ruddy face the same color as his short, unruly mop of hair. He grabbed Rob into a bear hug. "Bucko!" he shouted. "Welcome back. You look great."

Rob returned the hug, memories of the years they'd spent together threatening to tip him over the emotional edge. They hugged again, grins wide. "So do you, Den, but what are you doing here? I thought you'd be high over France this time of morning."

"Target's socked in. Storms. So the mission was scrubbed." He grabbed Rob's shoulders. "Come on. I want to see you run a few laps around the office. I've been waiting months for this."

Rob pulled away and sat at his desk, pointing to the chair opposite his. "That'll have to wait. From what I've heard, things haven't been going well around here."

"Work, work, work, that's all you think about. At least that crash didn't scramble your brains." Den plopped down in the chair.

The intercom buzzed. "Want me to hold off a while with that briefing, Colonel?" Hank asked.

"Yeah. I'll get some info from the major, then we'll look at that stack of papers. And close my office door, please. No calls, no interruptions."

Den tapped fingers on knees, right eyelid twitching.

Rob leaned back, lacing his fingers behind his head. "Doc said morale's in the tank and Hank showed me some of the worst strike photos I've ever seen. Only twenty-five percent of the bombs on target? You've been second-in-command while I've been gone. What happened?"

"Second-in-command, huh?" Den exhaled loudly and rubbed his eyes. "Who do you think was pegged to lead all those strikes? Yours truly, that's who."

"So the last commander wouldn't fly lead?"

"Wouldn't? Couldn't is the real nitty-gritty. The minute your ambulance turned the corner, Wells was on the horn recruiting an old buddy to take your place."

Rob pictured by-the-book Wing Commander Brigadier General Wells, Major General Harlan Fielding's predecessor, rubbing his hands in glee at the thought of having one of his own puppets appointed to command his star group.

Fatigue deepened the lines around Den's bloodshot blue eyes. He'd lost weight.

First Hank, now Den. What other bad news lay buried beneath piles of reports? "How well were the strikes planned?"

"Right out of the book, but don't ask how many had to be scrubbed because we couldn't get enough crews or planes into the air. The doc was right. Morale's in the tank."

How many planes, each crewed by ten good men, had they lost in the past six months? "Losses?" He steeled himself for the answer.

"So many you'll have to ask Hank for the figures."

Den was hedging, so it must be bad. He should be able to recite those numbers in his sleep. "Is that the reason you couldn't get enough planes in the air?"

"Only one reason."

"What are the others?"

"Our belated commander couldn't even find his own quarters by himself, let alone manage the protocol needed to finagle new crews out of Reassignment HQ. Wells dug in his heels and only requested replacement Forts for the 396th when Bomber Command got on his back. We often had squadrons down to three or four planes instead of seven." His eyelid twitched again. "Plus, he cut the ground crews to five men instead of the usual ten. Some planes sat on their hardstands for days waiting to be repaired and signed off as airworthy."

Rob slammed his fist on his desk and leaped up. "Five men to plug holes and replace engines? And Eighth Bomber Command cleared that?"

"They were never told. Remember, with Wells as Wing Commander, he ran the show."

"I'm surprised he didn't have a mutiny on his hands when Wing's other three groups had to cover most of the strikes." He paced, hands clenched behind his back.

Den swiveled his chair, tracking Rob. "Why do you think Wells was recalled to the States? We weren't the only group with a beef. All the pilots in Wing, including our squadrons, wrote Eighth Bomber Command and gave them the skinny. Believe me, they didn't pull any punches. Less than a week later, General Fielding booted Wells out and took over."

Rob leaned on his desk. "When was this?"

"Three weeks ago."

"What took Hal so long to get rid of my replacement?"

"He left the same day as Wells. Since then, General Fielding's been planning our strikes and finding crews, and the ground crews are back up to ten." Den snorted. "You should have heard the clapping and hooting when the general showed up at our briefing a few days ago and announced you'd be arriving to retake command today."

Maybe that explained those eager smiles he'd encountered on his way. "Why should they celebrate? I'll be lucky if I know any of the pilots still based here. I'm only a big question mark until I prove myself."

"You think the general stopped there? He spent over fifteen minutes filling in everyone there with the way you operate—planning each strike to minimize losses, flying lead plane on the hairiest missions, even your hard-nosed handling of anyone who shirks his duty. By the time he finished, the crews were so fired up they went out and bombed the living daylights out of our target. That was a set of strike photos you'd have been proud of."

Rob called Hank in and the three spent most of the day reviewing the changes to be made. After that, Rob and Den nursed another mug of coffee and caught up on their friendship. By chowtime, Rob was starved, exhausted, and overwhelmed by all he had to accomplish.

I can do everything with the help of Christ who gives me the strength I need.

Yes, with the Lord's help, he could—he would—make it happen.

Chapter Two

Rob tossed some coal into the stove and stretched his back. He'd been at his desk since 0400 studying new personnel folders in an attempt to assign cohesive crews to each Flying Fortress. A time-consuming job, but necessary. He couldn't pair an inexperienced flight engineer with a pilot who had only two missions under his belt. One of them needed battle smarts.

He studied the pictures on the wall and the flood of memories—some bittersweet, some warm—brought a smile. Several shots of his old Fort, *Liberty Belle,* with various crews. A portrait of Douglas MacArthur, Superintendent of West Point in 1911. And another of then-Colonel Hal Fielding.

Rob's smile turned to a grin. Hal had pinned the wings on Rob's US Army Air Corps uniform after teaching him to fly. No wonder Rob loved the man. He owed his flying career to Hal Fielding.

A rap on his office door interrupted a yawn. "Come on in."

General Harlan Fielding stood in the doorway, craggy face bathed in a smile. Of average height and weight, with a deceptively humble demeanor, he didn't need those two stars on his shoulder to take command of any situation. One look in his piercing, almost-black eyes did it all.

Both men clapped backs and pumped hands.

"You'll never know how good it is to see you again, boy," Hal exclaimed. He held Rob at arm's length and eyed him from spit-polished boots to tight military haircut. "Still too thin but after all you've been through, it's no wonder."

"My wife's vowed to fatten me up. You don't look any different than the last time I saw you over four years ago."

"Since when did you start spouting platitudes like a politician?"

Hal ran his fingers through his short hair. "I had a lot more brown than gray then." He pulled up two chairs and sat, pointing. "Sit yourself down before I break my neck trying to see your face. And tell me all about this new Scottish wife. I have to admit, the way you avoided females all these years, I thought you'd end up an old bachelor like me."

Rob laughed as he sat. "I hit the jackpot, Hal. God arranged for me to meet the lass He had planned for me all along. She's ... she's a miracle, that's all I can say."

"Lass? Don't clam up on me like you usually do. I want to hear every detail."

⚓

Two hours later, Rob tore off his tie and dashed from his office. "Taking thirty for a run," he shouted to Hank. Turning right at the main road, he opted for the narrow lane leading around the perimeter of the base, mind racing as fast as his legs.

Yes! With Hal Fielding commanding Wing, the 396th had nowhere to go but up. A World War I ace, Hal had more strategies under his cap than Betty Grable had posters.

Rob grinned and upped his pace. They would argue—they always did—but Hal *listened.* And he didn't need a swagger stick to stiffen his spine, or a "book" to plan strikes. Brilliant, quick-thinking, one of the best pilots in the air no matter which plane he flew—Wing couldn't ask for a better commander.

Another answer to prayer.

You're in charge, Lord, not the brass in Washington or the Eighth Bomber Command. You. He stumbled to a stop and gripped the security fence to keep from going to his knees. *Thank You for all Your blessings, Heavenly Faither. Make me worthy of Your trust. And above all, help me accomplish Your perfect will.*

⚓

His first mission since resuming command.

Rob jockeyed his B-17 off its hardstand onto the runway. His gloved fingers tightened around the yoke, stomach cramping as it had on his solo flight in a Stearman P-17 trainer.

Did he still have what it took to fly lead? *Help me do this right,*

Lord. So many lives depend on it.

His handpicked crew brought a glow of satisfaction. Only the best on base were chosen to crew the lead plane because they could expect the most attention from enemy fighters as the other Forts followed their lead on the bombing run.

He pushed forward on the controls, listening to the flight engineer call out the speed. At "one fifteen," he pulled back on the yoke and the *Bonnie Maggie* roared into the air. He tapped the copilot's knee. "Retract landing gear. We'll climb to five thousand feet and maintain till the others are in position."

First Lieutenant Lewis nodded and shouted, "Gear up."

A grinding sound came from the belly of the plane.

"How does it feel to be in the air again, Colonel?"

"How do you think?"

"Must be mighty good. If your smile were any broader, your face would split."

A weight lifted from Rob's chest. His hands relaxed. So easy, so natural, as if he'd been at the controls for the past six months instead of going through grueling therapy and learning to walk. Memories of the pain he'd suffered were fading, but the occasional nightmare still trapped him in that gut-wrenching fear of spending the rest of his life in a wheelchair. Thank God for Maggie, Elspeth, and Hugh. Not only had they taught him so much about the Christ he had accepted as a boy, but they answered every question he brought up about trusting his Saviour.

After the squadrons linked up, he pressed his throat mike. "Pilot to crew. Now comes the boring part. I'll give you a heads-up when we enter enemy air space. Until then, keep your chatter off the interphone. I need to save my hearing for when it counts."

A loud hoot reverberated through the headset.

"Should have thought about that before you signed on to fly a noisy, thin-skinned Fort, sir." The laconic southern drawl was a dead giveaway: his bombardier, Tex "Deadeye" Jeffers.

Good for him. A little levity broke up the tedium of a long wait before enemy fighters brought adrenaline levels surging.

He trimmed the bomber and engaged the automatic pilot.

Wing and a Prayer

⊶⚓⊷

Maggie plucked the last of her undergarments from the sink and draped them over the line Rob had strung near the stove. An entire day off. If only it didn't coincide with Rob's first bombing mission. Failing to control her shaking legs, she collapsed onto the cot. Memories of the terrible dream she'd had on Innisbraw—of his plane crashing and exploding—filled her with panic. *Protect him, Faither. Hold him up with the wings of Your angels. I can't bear the thought of losing him. Give me Your faith, please, Lord.*

She plucked her Gaelic Bible from the shelf. Though she knew the comforting passages by heart, reading them aloud often brought peace. She opened the Bible to a worn page in Philippians. "In nothing be anxious; but in everything by prayer and supplication with thanksgiving let your requests be made known unto God. And the peace of God, which passeth all understanding, shall guard your hearts and your thoughts in Christ Jesus." Determining to put God's promise into action, she closed the Bible and returned it to the shelf.

This was Rob's first flight. She couldn't give into such fears now. Instead, she'd wash her hair and spend the afternoon answering letters, maybe do some mending and ironing. By the time Rob finished up, her hair would be dry enough for him to brush.

Och, the pure joy and contentment on Rob's face when he brushed her hair was bright enough to bring sunshine to the dreariest day.

⊶⚓⊷

Rob winced as a German Fw 190 dove on the *Bonnie Maggie*, a bright stream of shells spitting from its machine guns.

His left waist gunner sent a steady, air-splitting barrage from his fifty-caliber gun.

The German fighter spouted a plume of smoke and nosed over into a steep dive.

"Good confirmed kill," Rob radioed the gunner.

They'd had a great bombing run, but now he had to make sure every plane and man made it home. *Thank You, Faither, for allowing me to fly again.*

13

Rob slammed the door to their quarters, tossed his crush cap onto the cot, and scooped Maggie into his arms. "There's my lass." Her sweet scent of heather, the luve shining in her eyes, and the warmth of her embrace brought a swell of elation that surpassed any he had experienced that day. He was with his Maggie, where he belonged. He kissed her face, her neck, her shiny hair, her lips—those soft lips tasting of all they had shared—and would share.

"Och, I can't breathe." She hugged his waist. "And from your smile, I'd say 'twas a grand mission."

"The best. Bombs right on target, and not a plane or crewman lost."

"What else did you expect with you flying lead?" She rested her cheek against his chest. "I know you were on heckle-pins, it being your first flight in so long, but with our Lord directing your every move, it had to turn out well."

He cupped her chin and turned her face up to his. "It was as if I'd never been away, Maggie. And I've a crew I can be proud of. Not a man grumbled or hesitated when he was needed. I'm back in the air, lass, where I belong."

She kissed his chin. "Aye. Soaring with eagles again."

He fisted a hand in her hair. Sucked in a breath. "You washed your hair and didn't tell me?"

"I've no' had the time. But you'll find my hairbrush on the pillow if you've time to brush it."

"I'd find time even if the Jerries were bombing the base."

It didn't take long to put the 396th on the path toward being the top group in Wing again. Thankfully, Maggie seemed to understand his long hours and distracted thoughts. By the time he relaxed enough to breathe again, married life had settled into a routine of sorts. Though he seldom made it back to their quarters until late evening, when he did arrive, he and Maggie made the most of their time alone.

From the first week, she taught him the dance steps to countless reels, jigs, and strathspeys, humming the melody since they had no radio or phonograph. "I want you to feel comfortable dancing whenever we hold ceilidhs on Innisbraw." She wrinkled her nose. "Besides, the exercise helps you work off tension."

On the evenings he was tied up in late meetings at Edenoaks Hall, Maggie never fell asleep before he returned to their quarters. She'd have a pot of coffee and some food waiting on the small, coal-burning stove.

She worked doubles several times a week. On the nights she was at the hospital, he spent time going over Interrogation reports, reviewing strike films and Intel information, and, as always, arguing with Wing over the need for more airplanes.

One such argument took place in Rob's office on a rainy evening a month after he resumed command of the 396th.

"How many aircraft can you put up for tomorrow's strike?" General Fielding asked.

"Sixteen."

"That's not enough."

"I've been telling you that for weeks." Rob raised his voice. "We need more planes."

Fielding brushed aside Rob's outburst with a shake of his head. "I'm talking about tomorrow."

Rob rubbed the side of his nose. Would he regret saying this? "I suppose I can have the crew chiefs make two or three cripples serviceable by morning, but I don't have crews for all of them."

"Find them. Go through your files and call back anyone remotely ready to be reassigned to duty."

Outside, brilliant pools of light lit the distant hardstands as maintenance crews readied planes for the morning's strike.

"Hal, tomorrow's target is close to the German border. I can't use crews that aren't in top shape for a run that long. Besides the flak, the Luftwaffe will throw every Fw 190 they have at us."

General Fielding removed his cap and circled the office. "Look, Rob, I know you have one of the dirtiest jobs around, but this strike needs every airplane we can put in the air. You'll rendezvous with and lead our three other groups for this mission."

"Sir—"

The general slammed his fist into his palm. "If each group has maximum numbers, we can really hammer this target." Without giving Rob time to reply, Fielding returned his cap to his head and opened the door. "I'll expect at least nineteen airplanes from the 396th in the air tomorrow morning."

Rob saluted automatically as the general left the office. He sat behind his desk and took a deep breath as he pressed the intercom button. "Hank, come in here. It's going to be a long night."

The B-17 crews, and even the ground-pounders, celebrated when bad weather over the target delayed the mission for forty-eight hours. By the time the skies cleared, Rob had twenty airplanes and their crews ready.

The 396th led the strike.

With Rob flying lead, they hammered the French target and more, including Rouen, an airfield at Bussac, and a missile site at Pas-de-Calais. Targets in Germany included Osnabrück and the oil refinery at Ludwigshafen. Two strikes against the heavily defended sub pens at Wilhelmshaven proved the most deadly. There, the group's losses were so high that Rob sat in the cockpit for a long time after they touched down at the air base, gloved fingers curled tightly around the yoke as he fought to control his grief.

Major Dennis Anderson, again his second-in-command, flew lead on short, safer "milk runs" over Saint-Lô, Niorte, Fruges, and other French targets.

The group shaped up as morale climbed and new crews transferred in. Two more B-17s arrived, the strike photos looked good, and Intel reported the Jerries were sweating. By February 1, 1943, Rob glimpsed a light at the end of the tunnel.

Chapter Three

Den Anderson tossed his A-2 jacket on top of his footlocker and threw himself down on the cot. What was with Rob? This was the umpteenth time he'd turned down a beer at the Officer's Club.

"Can't. Got a bonnie lass waiting," he mimicked, growling out Rob's reply in a throaty attempt at copying his pal's deep voice. He toed off his shoes and stared at the ceiling. Not fair—not fair at all. Who had covered Rob's rear at West Point when the Firsties picked on the teenage plebe from a hick town in New Hampshire? Who made sure the super-tall, awkward kid who habitually wore his foot in his mouth went to all the dances and parties? Who ...?

Den slapped his palm on the blanket.

Who was the best pilot, best group commander in the Eighth Bomber Command?

Who was the most honest, most loyal CAG in the whole wing?

Who was the best friend a guy could ever have?

Rob, of course.

He leaped off his cot, glanced at his watch, and tossed some coal into the small cast iron stove. Only half an hour until the other officers sharing the quarters returned—noisy, nosy nitwits—to sack out for the night.

He checked the time again before falling onto his cot, hands beneath his head.

He squirmed. Was he jealous of Maggie?

No, he'd never been the jealous type. He only wanted some one-on-one time with his pal. There had to be a way to get Rob alone.

He bolted upright. He would check Maggie's schedule, make sure she was working a double, *then* casually ask Rob to join him for an ale at the Fox's Den in Edenoaks.

17

Rob followed Den to a table at one side of the noisy pub. The ancient, half-timbered stone building was crowded with flyboys drinking and telling loud jokes. Local villagers sat as far from the Yanks as possible, nursing pints while visiting quietly or playing dominoes. A fug of cigarette smoke hung below the blackened beams, almost obscuring the nicotine-stained ceiling.

Den stared at the locals but addressed Rob. "What are your plans after the war?"

Rob took a swig of ale. "I'm not sure you want to know."

"What do you mean, bucko? Don't tell me you've finally accepted the notion of having to fly a desk someplace. We'd both rather resign our commissions than accept such a fate."

"You know me better than that." Rob drew designs in the condensation on his glass. "I'll never fly a desk for anybody, anywhere."

"Then what gives?" Den drummed blunt fingertips on the table. "You can't train pilots forever. Once this war's over, about the only job you can expect to find in the air is with one of the new commercial airlines back in the States."

"I'm not going back to the States." Rob emptied his glass with one long swallow.

Den's eyes widened. "Not going back to the States? Don't tell me you're planning to live on Maggie's itty-bitty piece of rock out in the Atlantic."

Rob leaned forward, gaze pinning Den to his chair. "It has a name—Innisbraw—and to me it means home. The minute this war's over, I *am* resigning my commission and taking Maggie back. First, I'll build the island a coastal rescue boat and then go into business building fishing boats."

Den choked on his ale. "Boats?"

"So we can lure back the local lads who've left for the service or better-paying jobs in Scotland. The island's economy's about dried up."

Den pounded his chest and cleared his throat. "You mean the guy who could never log enough time in the air is going to give up flying to build boats? You've lost it, bucko. You've absolutely,

18

positively lost it." Head in hands, he said, "I never should have dared you to dance with that leftenant."

"You don't understand." Rob held up two fingers to the barmaid. "I've found it, not lost it. When I first heard they had no rescue boat and had to rely on a small lifeboat from Barra—that's an island twenty-five nautical miles northwest of Innisbraw—I knew I had to do something. Besides, I promised never to take Maggie away from the home she loves. I need a way to make a living."

The barmaid placed two more pints of ale on the table.

Rob put some coins on her tray and took a swig. "When Maggie had to report back to duty last summer and I was stuck on Innisbraw without her, I designed a large, unsinkable rescue boat." He leaned back in his chair, straightening his cramped legs. "I can't tell you how hard it was to live without her, Den. It was like losing half of myself—or more. Designing the boat and working to walk on my own again were the two things that took up every hour of every day for months. I finished the plans just before she got leave and I was cleared for duty. We got married the day after she arrived home on Innisbraw and three days later we both reported back to duty here at Edenoaks."

"I heard things moved fast." Den stood and tossed some pound notes on the table. "But I never really knew you at all. I thought you were a born-and-bred pilot like me. I guess I was wrong."

Rob grabbed his sleeve. "I'm not about to give up flying. As soon as I have enough money, I'm going to buy myself a floatplane. I can take her up whenever the weather allows. Besides, you're forgetting we've a war to win before I build any boats, and I'm committed to seeing this through to the end. It could be years before I make it back to Innisbraw."

"Yeah, sure." Den shrugged into his raincoat. "I'll grab a ride back to base. Ciao."

⚓

Rob did not receive another invitation from Den to meet for a few ales. If he had, he could have shared his conviction that he had received a mandate from the Lord to build the rescue boat, though it probably wouldn't do any good. As far as he knew, his best friend wasn't a Christian.

Over the next few weeks, though no one could tell by their behavior on base, the close relationship they'd shared since teenagers seemed destined to die a slow death.

By February 10, the attrition rate for planes and crew was so high, Rob could put up only sixteen B-17s at a time. Plus, there were always one or two that had to abort and return to base because of malfunctions before they reached the target. He thanked God constantly for the *Bonnie Maggie*'s crew chief, Joe Arnold, who directed his crew of ten to begin plugging twenty millimeter and flak holes in her wings and fuselage the moment she reached the hardstands and kept her four Wright cyclone engines purring like well-fed lions.

In mid-February, he was ordered to London to attend the opening of Supreme Headquarters Allied Expeditionary Forces (SHAEF), headed by General Dwight D. Eisenhower, who had been designated the Supreme Commander of Allied Expeditionary Forces the previous December. Rob returned to Edenoaks filled with admiration for the savvy general and optimism that the war was at a turning point.

A month later, five brand new B-17s came from Wing over a span of three weeks.

"We're full strength again," he told Maggie the night the final B-17 touched down. "Now all I have to do is find crews for those last two. Hank is scouring the reassignment depots now."

She pulled him over to their cot. "The pressure never really eases, does it? Day after day, you face the same problems over and over again."

He wound a strand of her long, black hair around his finger. "Just one of the perks of the job. Now, enough shoptalk. Tell me what Elspeth's letter said. I haven't had time to read it."

"Much of the usual. The MacKenzies had another laddie with Alice performing her midwife duties. Shep is doing well. Learning to herd sheep, though Angus said the pup misses you. Hugh has decided to put new paint on the inside of the kirk hall if he can find any available, and the spring gales are unusually harsh this year. Tormad MacKinnon and his crew had a close call, but he managed to get his trawler back into harbour without loss of life."

"That's unexpected and grand news."

She poked his chest. "She also said that after Tormad's near-sinking, the Island Council has signed an edict officially backing your idea for a boatyard. They'll begin working on that old herring-packing shed down by the dock as soon as the weather settles and warms. It needs a new roof and some cleaning before it will be a fit place to build your rescue boat."

His heart swelled. The Lord was preparing a place before it was even needed. "More good news, though I hope they aren't going at it a bit too soon. Hitler and his gang don't seem to be in any hurry to surrender, and the war with Japan has to end before I can get back to Innisbraw."

Tears glazed her eyes. "Och, Rob, when is this horrible war going to end—all the killing and the pain?"

"I don't know, luve, it doesn't seem like any time soon." He put his fingers beneath her chin and raised her head. "Enough talk. I want to kiss my wife."

Her soft lips moved toward his. "What's taken you so long?"

She tasted so sweet. They had been married only three months, yet in so many ways his life before he met her lay veiled behind a heavy ground fog. She was his soul mate, his reason for living.

The last week of June brought the usual erratic spring weather patterns. Missions scheduled, scrubbed, and rescheduled. Frustrating, maddening, but bearable because the 396th was once again Wing's top group.

On the few evenings when Maggie and he were able to meet for supper in the chow hall, the men vied for her attention, pulling out the bench before Rob had a chance, even offering to get her another cup of tea. In turn, she questioned the lads at their table, inquiring about families and homes, and even promising to write a personal letter to the frightened wife of a navigator.

Hank kept him up-to-date on the scuttlebutt around the base, his best source of tracking morale.

"Any complaints beyond the usual?" Rob asked one late night. He spit on the toe of his dress boot and rubbed it briskly.

Hank removed the coffee pot and stirred the coals in the stove. "No complaints."

Rob shoved the polishing rag into his bottom drawer, toed into his boot, and sat back, fingers laced behind his head. "That's a first."

"Oh, a few grumbles about how hardnosed you can be if someone isn't cutting the mustard, but really they appreciate you asking them about their families and taking time to hear their answers."

"Didn't I before?"

"None were here 'before.' And if you don't want the truth, don't ask the question."

Still as honest as ever. "I really didn't?"

"Only if you were visiting the wounded at the hospital—and that's another reason morale's sky high. They can't believe the base commander would not only drop in at the hospital every day to see how they were doing, but hand-deliver a meal from a pub to a guy who can't stand the chow." He poured the last few inches of coffee into Rob's mug.

Rob bounced his knees and stared at his desk.

"Why the long face? There isn't a man on base who wouldn't fly through a brick wall for you. Just look at the strike photos if you don't believe me."

⚜

Rob stood at his office window, gazing through the foggy night at the B-17s on their hardstands, maintenance crews climbing up and down ladders beneath mist-haloed arc lights, racing to finish the last of the repairs before tomorrow's mission. He glanced at his watch.

Maggie had pulled another double, but it was almost 2300 hours. She should be finished soon.

He folded himself into his chair and put his feet up on his desk. Was Hank right? Had he changed that much? Even before the crash, he'd been close to his own crew.

But the rest of the crews? Other than a few pilots he'd known for years, they were just names with sometimes-familiar faces.

Now he felt connected to the men in all three squadrons. Same duties as before, routine unvaried, but he no longer focused on the myriad of details, rather, he prioritized the men who carried them out. His time on Innisbraw had taught him one valuable lesson— nothing was more important in life than the people with whom he shared it.

He looked at the smudged ink-blotter on his desktop. Almost every squiggle of dried ink came from blotting a letter of consolation he'd written to the loved ones of those men who sacrificed their lives. How many tears, how many ruined futures, how many shattered dreams?

Oh, Lord, be with those grieving mithers and faithers, wives and children. Hold them up in the palm of Your loving hand.

He rubbed his burning eyes and pushed aside his morbid musings with thoughts of Maggie. Before she came into his life, he'd gone from briefing to mission, from meetings to his office, from Edenoaks Hall to his quarters. Unrelentingly busy—and empty.

He glanced at his watch again, yawning. Her shift was over. Maybe he could beat her to their quarters. 0400 in five hours and he was married now. Falling asleep at his desk was no longer an option.

⁂

Maggie had a wash-up at the sink. Too late for a bath tonight. She slipped into her nightgown and took the pins from her hair, sighing with relief when it fell from the tight bun. Every muscle ached, especially in her legs and feet. She brushed her hair, turned out the bathroom light, and eyed the cot. Too small? Aye. Too hard? Definitely. Calling her name? Of course.

But she should wait for Rob.

Why was he so late when he'd be leading a mission in the morning? She rummaged through her bag, and pulled out a bottle of heather-scented lotion Elspeth had posted her. Just what she needed.

The outer door slammed.

After a sweet kiss of greeting, he lifted her into his arms. "Now that you've fattened me up, I'm going to have to start working on you. You've lost weight, and you're so tired you can barely hold your head up."

Maggie's nose went into the air and she pushed him away. "You're still too shilpit, and I've only lost a wee bit," she said, lacing her English with Scots as she always did when they were alone. "And it's no' because I'm no' eating enough. It's just all the running I do, from ward to ward and to the pharmacy and supply all day, and the long hours in the OR. There've been so many casualties this month. Mebbe there'll be a change soon. 'Tis time for things to improve."

"Well, if they don't, I'm putting my foot down. Remember who commands this air base. A few words from me and you're back to one shift a day."

How could he even think such a thing? Her hands went to her hips. "How dare you? I don't complain about your long hours, so don't find fault with mine. It keeps me busy when you're gone."

"Then we'll both cut back. It's time I started assigning more of the strategic planning to Den. In time, I'm hoping he'll realize he has what it takes to command his own group."

She put her arms around his waist and rested her cheek on his chest. "You mean it? You'll really let go a wee bit?"

He buried his face in her hair. "I mean it."

Och, he meant it now. But how would he feel the next day? The day after? She had more praying to do.

Chapter Four

His good intentions suffered a blow in July. Rob spent a long day in London where he learned of plans, with a new directive from SHAEF, to pound Germany with wave after wave of assaults.

"The AAF and RAF both are going to mount daily and nightly missions against the German manufacturing plants, and especially their fuel depots," he told Maggie when he made it back to their quarters after the final meeting. "There's something big brewing. Eisenhower has a bee in his bonnet. I don't know what it is or when it'll happen, but Hitler's going to be stung big time."

"So it's back to daily missions for you."

"When the weather allows."

"Rob, you can't expect to plan every mission and then lead it. You're losing weight again."

He tweaked her nose. "What little kettle is calling the pot black?"

She laughed. "Och, we're a fine pair, aren't we? Let's call a truce, for I know you're eating enough and you know I am. Until we can stop running at top speed, we'll just have to take a little weight loss in stride."

His right eyebrow shot up. "You mean you'll stop moving the buttons on my trousers every few days?"

"No. You don't want your breeks slipping down to your knees during a briefing. I mean I'll stop talking about it if you do."

"Okay, truce." He gathered her close. Warm, soft arms circled his neck.

"I do luve our truces."

⚓

The next night, Rob was tied up in a meeting at Wing Headquarters until almost midnight. The strike the next morning—

Operation Gomorrah—was a particularly nasty one, possibly the worst the 396th had ever faced. Though Maggie had worked a double in the operating room, he still chafed to see her and ordered his driver to "step on it."

He ducked into their quarters.

No Maggie. A crack of light glinted beneath the closed bathroom door.

"Maggie, lass!" He threw open the door.

She lay in the tub, eyes half closed. She reminded him of the Selkie, the seal who turned into a beautiful woman, in the Scots folktale she had told him again and again when he was in so much pain from his injuries.

"Och, look what's in my bathing tub," he said with a wicked grin. "A verra beautiful Selkie come all the way from the sea."

She laughed at his awkward attempt to remove all his clothes at the same time. "Who are you, calling your wife a seal?"

"Like the Selkie's luver, I'm yours forever and ever and ever."

Much later, he cradled her close in bed.

"I luve ye, Maggie, lass," he said in Scots. His heart swelled with emotion. "And I'll always luve ye."

"And I'll always luve ye." A husky whisper. She pulled him closer.

"Coorie doun wi' me, lass."

She turned and spooned her body against his.

"I can't wait to get home to Innisbraw." He rubbed his cheek against her hair. "I miss the sun on the girse and the mists on the braes and hovering o'er the glens."

"But do you miss the rain plomping down?"

"Even that. Coorying doon with you makes any storm a wonder to behold."

He had a sudden thought but kept it to himself. Hearing that he wanted to be buried at the top of Ben Innis, with the endless sky above and the sea sooking on the shore below, would only bring back her nightmares. But he had shared his wishes with their minister, Hugh MacEwan, who would see it carried out if God decided to call him home. His breath stuttered. Would that be on the morra?

It wasn't fear that left him short of breath. Just regret that he might not survive the strike tomorrow and someday return to Innisbraw—to father the eight bairns Maggie wanted.

He lifted her hair and brushed his lips across her nape. "I miss our island." Yearning tinged the whisper. "Sometimes I hear it calling me on the wind."

"Someday soon." The same yearning in her soft voice. "Someday soon, we'll go home."

Chapter Five

Rob ate three bowls of brose and drank a pot of coffee. Next came his favorite time of morning. He fed Maggie one heaping teaspoon of sweetened condensed milk—which he always found, even though it was tightly rationed—and the look of pure contentment on her face filled him with delight. He captured a mind picture of her bonnie face to replay later, before they reached the target. Her pliant lips, the luve softening her eyes. He should have planned for what followed, but like every morning, he had to urge his driver to hurry so he wouldn't be late for briefing.

As the 396th Heavy Bomber Group took off, the rumbling drone of the B-17 engines grew so loud the bottles on the shelves beside Maggie in the pharmacy juddered together. Rob would be the first to take off, leading A Squadron, followed by B and C Squadrons. Maggie counted the planes, breathing "Godspeed" for each.

Her hands trembled as she filled a tray with the bottles and syringes she needed for her wards. If only there were surgeries scheduled for the OR. At least there, she would be too busy to worry about Rob. She leaned against the counter, steadying her legs.

Unlike the RAF, the Americans did no night bombing. Daytime raids were much more dangerous, especially since the directive from Eighth Bomber Command instructing that no evasive action be allowed during the bombing run ... information Rob had withheld from her but was the major topic of conversation on base.

She picked up the tray and paused, bowing her head before locking the pharmacy door. *Heavenly Faither, I don't know why I'm suddenly so afraid. Please watch over my Rob. Keep him safe and bring him back to me, just like You have all these months. Help him make guid decisions, always praying for Your guidance. In Christ's name, amen.*

A long day of prayer lay ahead—prayer for Rob and the other men, plus prayer her faith would not falter.

The hours dragged by. Though occasionally distracted by her prayers, she administered medicaments and words of comfort to the young men in her care. She wrote a letter home for a sergeant with a wounded arm, changed dressings on suppurating wounds, and admired pictures of the fresh-faced girl back home and the baby who had never felt his faither's caress or heard his voice.

She toyed with her noontime meal, ignoring the good-natured gibes of her fellow nurses that the wife of the group commander had to put on a good appearance, not starve herself into a wraith. As the only RAF nurse on duty at Edenoaks, she often felt the brunt of their jealous teasing.

I guess it takes a colonel to cut through the red tape and get his RAF wife transferred to his own base.

She'd overheard that comment more than once. No one knew that it was her faither, not Rob, who had arranged her posting.

☙❦❧

By 1015 hours, Rob was leading a force of seventy-eight Flying Fortresses into the skies above Germany—all the squadrons in Hal's wing. The RAF had bombed Hamburg the night before, dropping over 2,300 incendiary bombs, with a loss of only 17 bombers. Other USAAF groups had bombed German soil since January, but this was the 396th's first opportunity to target an industrial city deep in the Nazi's homeland. Rob's pulse leaped. From what Hal had hinted at the night before, it could be only a few months until Berlin itself felt the power of the Mighty Eighth.

Though his gaze seldom left the instrument panel, he spent every uninterrupted moment from group rendezvous until now praying silently for the Lord's guidance.

Help me take them all home, Lord. Every man. Every plane. Every man, Faither.

He'd have to give his lads passes tonight.

Lads. Strange how the Scots crept into his thoughts when the pull of brotherhood was strong.

He keyed his overhead mike so each pilot on the strike could hear his voice. "This is Red Fox Leader to all kits. Keep your formations tight, keep 'em tight."

Black pinpricks suddenly appeared at the top of the right windscreen.

His eyes narrowed in concentration as he studied them and pressed his throat mike. "Bandits at one o'clock high. Keep 'em outside."

Bursts of fifty- and twenty-caliber machine gunfire filled the air as the German fighters moved in for the kill. Even in such tight formation, the lead plane always drew the most attention. Every gunner on the *Bonnie Maggie* fired a constant barrage from blistering-hot fifty-caliber barrels. The smoky reek of machine oil and cordite filled the cockpit.

An Fw 190 exploded close by on the left, rocking the *Bonnie Maggie* with the force of the blast.

"Keep alert. Another wave at two o'clock high. Don't let 'em inside."

The ball gunner reported a B-17 below them in C Squadron had taken some hits and was spiraling downward, smoke trailing from its engines.

"Red Fox Leader to C Squadron. Close up that hole. Tighten it up. Flak dead ahead."

Flak. Must be above the outskirts of Hanover.

He pressed his mike again. "Pilot to Navigator, how long to the IP?"

"One minute, thirty seconds, sir."

"Roger that. The flak looks dense enough to walk on. Bombardier, let me know when you have your PDI centered."

"Yes, sir."

A massive bombardment of flak darkened the sky. The *Bonnie Maggie* shook and bucked as shrapnel pummeled and pierced the aluminum fuselage and wings.

Rob flipped off the autopilot—too much turbulence. His knuckles cramped as he fought the yoke to keep the Fort steady for the bombardier. The odor of cordite and vomit, staccato of gunfire, and violent vibration, overloaded his senses. *Hold her together till we drop our load, Lord.*

The Fort trailing their left wing exploded. Hot metal pierced the *Bonnie Maggie*. A scream broke through the cacophony of machine gunfire. "Pilot to Engineer, report!"

A maddening wait, then, "Tailgunner's hit. Can't stop the bleeding. Fuselage looks like a sieve, but we still have hydraulics and oxygen."

An agonizing minute later, the bombardier reported, "PDI centered."

Rob eyed the Pilot's Direction Indicator dial on his instrument panel. When it was properly aligned, he lifted his hands from the yoke. "Your airplane, Bombardier."

Seconds later the bombardier shouted, "Bombs away!"

The sky filled with bombs as wave after wave of B-17s released their loads over the target. Black smoke and orange flames reached up from an already devastated city, the rubble burning like the fires of hell.

Rob took the controls again and the copilot toggled the switch to close the bomb-bay doors. "Red Fox Leader to all kits, climbing out and making a ninety degree turn to the right."

A huge blast shook the airplane. Rob's teeth snapped together. He gripped the yoke, watching the instrument panel.

The two fuel indicators twirled down to zero.

"Took some hits on the inboard main tanks," the flight engineer reported. "Switching to outboards, all engines."

"Get on it," Rob ordered.

A burst of flak penetrated the cockpit. Sharp pain jabbed his right shoulder and chest. Blood pooled in his right eye, but no pain. Must be a cut on his forehead. He adjusted his goggles and oxygen mask. Wiped at the blood with his glove.

"You all right, sir?" the copilot asked.

"Just a scratch."

Another blast shook the Fort. Black smoke poured from the two right engines. "Extinguishing valves set and standing by to pull charges," the copilot shouted.

"Pull both charges and feather three and four engines."

After the copilot reported the fires out, both engines off and feathered, Rob activated his overhead mike. "Red Fox Leader to Red Fox Two. We've lost our inboard tanks and on two engines, unable to keep up. You'll have to take them home, Den."

"Read you, Red Fox Leader. Want me to fly cover?"

"Negative. Repeat, negative. Take them home. Confirm."

After a long pause, Den replied, "Roger, Red Fox Leader, confirmed. Good luck, Rob, and I mean that, bucko."

Face grim, Rob banked the *Bonnie Maggie* left and quit the formation.

"We're losing about five hundred feet a minute," the copilot shouted.

"Pilot to crew. Throw out everything but the guns and ammo. Bombardier, dismantle your station and jettison everything. Get ready for bandits. We aren't in the clear yet." He tapped the copilot's knee. "Let's take her down to just above tree-top level, Mike. We'll soon be above Belgian airspace, so we could hit more flak, but if we're low enough, the bandits can't dive on us without hitting bottom."

"Bandits at one o'clock high," the turret gunner shouted.

Rob worked the controls, losing altitude as fast as he could. Wave after wave of Fw 190s streaked toward them, firing steady bursts. All the gunners shouted sightings over the interphone.

Rob tore off his helmet and oxygen mask and swiped at the blood blinding his right eye.

The flight engineer leaned over Rob's shoulder and pressed a piece of gauze to his forehead, taping it securely before wiping the blood from his eye.

"Thanks," Rob said, blinking to clear his vision.

"Navigator to pilot, the bombardier's hit," the navigator shouted over the interphone. "He's hurt bad!"

"See what you can do to help him. Pilot to Gene. Climb out of the ball turret and take over that gun for Matt. Waist gunners, try to break 'em up."

The fifty calibers barked a steady staccato.

A loud "yippee" sounded over the interphone. "Friendlies at

twelve o'clock high! Looks like our own P-47s!"

Rob looked up through the windscreen and grinned at the sight of a dozen "Jugs" peeling off to intercept the Fw 190s. *Thank You, Lord.* "How's Matt doing?" he asked the navigator.

"He's dead, sir."

No time for grief now. *Guide my thoughts, Faither.* "Pilot to crew, dump the guns and ammo. Since the cavalry's arrived, we won't need 'em anymore. And be ready to chute up. We may not have enough fuel to make it over the channel."

"We're two chutes short, Colonel, flak made spaghetti out of 'em," the left waist gunner reported.

"Roger. Send someone up here for one, and use Matt's."

"Yes, sir."

The next two hours passed in a blur of activity as Rob and Mike worked to keep the two remaining engines synchronized and running smoothly. When they passed the halfway point over the English Channel, Rob eyed the fuel gauges. Not enough to make it back to base. His forehead burned, but his shoulder and chest didn't hurt much. Must not be too bad.

He pressed his throat mike to talk to the radioman. "Get on that key and send an SOS, then bail out." He toggled the bell and sent a long warning buzz through the airplane, then turned to his copilot. "Get out of here. Keep your feet dry." The ridiculous sounding words were automatic—just something one always said when dumping one's crew into the water.

"Take my chute, Colonel. You gave yours to the crew. Let me take her home."

"I said bail out, Major! That's an order!"

The copilot hesitated, then unstrapped his seat harness before stepping down from the cockpit.

Rob nursed the engines. Had to keep enough altitude to clear the cliffs ahead.

He switched his overhead mike to Broadcast. "Army one-six-eight to niner-four-seven, Control. On two engines, almost out of fuel, just clearing the Channel. Crew bailed out over the drink. I'll try to set her down in a field."

"Roger that, Army one-six-eight. Good luck, sir."

The fuel needles hovered just above zero.

I'm in Your hands, Faither. Please help me do this right.

A few fields, but too many trees. After long minutes spent looking for a possible landing place, he spotted a church spire in the distance.

Canterbury.

He had to take her down now. Couldn't chance killing hundreds on the ground.

He dropped the nose and went to half flaps to lose more altitude.

Both engines sputtered.

He peered through the flak-scarred windscreen.

There, straight ahead, a large field surrounded by a tall hedge, one tall tree in the center. Out of fuel. Too late to change his mind now.

He went to full flaps, switched off, and feathered the two remaining engines.

A sudden image of Maggie flooded his mind.

No fear, just aching regret.

I want to hold her close one last time.

Too high.

Too fast.

Och, Lord, take care of my Maggie, my lass ...

Chapter Six

Maggie heard the first planes land a little after 1400 and began to count again. At long last, the rumbling subsided and she ran down the corridor, heart galloping.

There should have been twenty planes landing—she counted only seventeen.

Three short!

She raced outside but, in the confusion of planes taxiing to their hardstands, crash wagons, ambulances, crew trucks, and bicycling personnel racing across the tarmac, could not tell if the *Bonnie Maggie* was one of them.

She bolted inside again.

She hated to bother Major Larson. He could be a real curmudgeon and even she, his favorite nurse, had not escaped his acerbic tongue. But she had a mounting feeling of dread.

Things had been going so well. Rob would surely be promoted to Brigadier General and reassigned soon, since this was his eighty-eighth mission out of Edenoaks. "Please, dear Lord," she panted, "please let my Rob be all right." She stopped outside Larson's office door to compose herself. It would never do to allow him to see her in a state of panic. She re-pinned escaping tendrils of hair into her bun and, swallowing her fear, tapped on the door.

No answer, just the drone of his voice. Must be on the telephone. His conversation seemed to go on forever. At last. "Come."

His growl heightened her tension. She opened the door and stepped into chaos. Files and X-rays piled on his desk and spilled across two chairs. File cabinet drawers hung open. Next to the telephone, three mugs of scum-topped coffee littered the only semi-clear spot on the desk.

"Well, Leftenant Savage, are you coming in or not?"

"Of course. Thank you, Doctor." Maggie sidled through the doorway, kneading her hands to hide their trembling.

He stared at her, gaze piercing. "What is it this time, Leftenant? Still not enough sulfa to suit you?"

"Oh, no, the supplies all came in as you promised."

"Then?" Despite his fierce gaze, a glimmer of something—pity, dread, resignation—shone in his eyes.

She had never seen this look on his face. But she couldn't allow him to intimidate her now. She needed to know.

"I wonder if you've heard anything about the ... the latest count?"

"The latest count?"

"I always count the planes as they're landing—most of us do—and I'm certain we're three short." Tears filled her eyes. *Not now, Lord. No tears now, please.*

"As a matter of fact, you're right, Leftenant." He rose, came around to the front of the desk, and took her hands in his. "I expect you to be brave, Maggie."

Maggie.

He never called her Maggie.

Each breath a conscious effort.

"Colonel Savage's plane went down just outside of Canterbury."

She swallowed, throat convulsing. "Did ... did anyone see any chutes?"

"British Rescue radioed Control that seven chutes were seen over the Channel shortly before the crash." His grip on her hands tightened. "You know what that means, Maggie. The colonel would never allow an unmanned plane over land. He and two other crewmen didn't make it out." He pulled her closer.

She struggled to breathe.

"Major Anderson informed ground control that Colonel Savage's plane took fierce anti-aircraft fire over the target. He lost his inboard fuel tanks and quit the formation before it entered Belgian airspace."

The room tipped, threatening to send her crashing to the floor.

36

"He made it over the Channel and was obviously looking for a place clear of trees where he could put the plane down, but he must have run out of fuel just before he reached Canterbury." His face blurred, voice faded. "A reconnaissance plane reported the crash. The colonel's plane was almost totally destroyed."

Destroyed, destroyed.

Echoing, echoing.

Warmth bathed her head.

Her body.

Darkness.

Chapter Seven

The flight surgeon squirmed in his chair.

Maggie sat across from his desk, hands clenched in her lap.

General Harlan Fielding stood with his back against the door, cap clasped tightly beneath his left arm, expression bleak.

Doctor Larson studied Maggie's face before rising, going around his desk, and grasping her shoulder. "After hearing about the condition of the plane, I still can't believe he survived that crash. Let me tell you what we're facing." He glanced at the general.

Fielding gave a slight nod.

"We've re-inflated his collapsed lung and stabilized his broken ribs. The shrapnel's been removed from his right shoulder and chest—minor wounds. But his left shoulder is seriously broken and the ligaments holding it in place are badly torn. We've strapped that arm to his body to immobilize it."

His grip tightened.

"His right leg was broken just below the knee and his left tibia and fibula severely broken in three places, including the lateral malleolus. We've set the breaks as best we could, but ..."

Maggie held her head high.

He stepped to the window and peered out, then faced her. "It's the head injury that's the most serious. The X-rays show a skull fracture. Rob's in a deep coma. His blood pressure's so low it's difficult to get a reading, even though we've given him nothing for pain. He could never survive surgery for his other injuries."

She stared at him.

He pulled a chair around and sat in front of her. "What I'm attempting to say is ... is that the colonel is dying, and I'm so very, very sorry."

Only sounds from outside the room intruded upon the silence—

the rumble of gurney wheels, squeak of soles on waxed linoleum, far-off beep of an automobile horn.

"I know." Her voice came out a ragged whisper. "I want to take him home where he belongs."

"To America?"

Maggie shook her head. "To Innisbraw."

"He'll never survive the journey."

"But I have to take him." *Be strong for Rob. Speak up.* "'Tis where he would want to be."

"I'd feel more comfortable if we transported him to the Royal Infirmary in Edinburgh like we did the last time."

She jerked her hands away. "He's going home to Innisbraw!"

Where his heart longs to run free.

She turned to the general. "Please cut the necessary orders for both of us. My faither will be at his infirmary on the island in two days."

"Consider them cut."

Major Larson returned to his chair. "I hope you're doing the right thing."

Fielding hurried to Maggie's side. "It's right. I know this is what Rob would want. He talked about Innisbraw often, and with great longing. My prayers go ... go with you both, Maggie."

Maggie clutched at him, the sorrow on his face fueling hers. "Aye, Hal, 'tis right—but please hurry. There's so little time."

Rob survived both the Douglas C-47 military transport flight to Abbotsinch Airfield outside of Glasgow and the ambulance ride to Oban with little change to his vital signs. But Maggie knew he clung to life by a thin, frayed thread which threatened to snap at any time.

Malcolm MacNeill's fishing trawler, the *Sea Rouk,* strained against her mooring lines, as though sensing the urgency for a speedy departure on the receding tide. The sun was a white, hazy smear behind thick, grey clouds, the sea an enormous well of dark blue ink.

The skipper set up two sturdy crates next to the wheelhouse to bear the weight of the stretcher handles. "I already have permission from the British Navy to make the journey," he told Maggie in Scots. "I mind how Rob wanted to be ootside the last time, but if you'd rather, we can put him in the wheelhouse."

"This is fine. Thank ye, Malcolm."

"Och, lass, I'm so sorry." He pulled her into a tight hug.

"So am I." His heavy jacket muffled her moan. "More than you'll ever ken."

As the *Sea Rouk* wended its way around British Naval ships and floatplanes and out into the Sound of Mull, she leaned over the stretcher. "I'm here, Rob." Her Scots burr blended with the throbbing of the diesel engine beneath her knees. "We're going home, luve."

No response. There never was.

Unchecked tears streamed down her cheeks. If she tried to stop them, her heart might crumble into pieces as wee and evanescent as drops of sea mist. She reached beneath the blanket and fingered Rob's wrist.

No change. Pulse thready, almost too weak to feel, fluttering fitfully like a leaf caught in the spray of a tumbling burn.

She started as a hand grasped her shoulder.

"Maggie, lass, I've a thermos of hot tea." Malcolm squatted beside her, craggy face filled with concern. "Will you no' have some?"

She shook her head.

He got to his feet and stood with boots planted firmly against the roll of the deck. "'Tis no' like the first time you took him to Innisbraw." He squeezed her shoulder. "Courage, lass. Och, 'tis a sorry, sorry day brings Rob home to die."

His parting words echoed in her ears long after he returned to the wheelhouse. *Rob home to die, to die, to die.* She stared at Rob's dear face through tear-blurred eyes. So ashen. So still.

His lips moved occasionally but never tilted upward in that slow, provocative smile that always made her heart beat with wild abandon.

She closed her eyes and her mind filled with the picture of him painted permanently on the backs of her eyelids. So very tall and broad shouldered with long legs that often outpaced hers. Light brown hair that glinted with blonde and red in the sunshine and a forelock that always exasperated him by escaping down over his forehead. Heavy, dark blonde eyebrows above green-specked eyes, tiny lines radiating from their corners caused by gazing into the sky from the cockpit of an airieplane. His long arms enveloping her in a hug so comforting, so secure.

His hands. Och, Lord, his huge, strong hands with their long, tapered fingers, knew just how to knead a knotted muscle. His finely formed lips, full, so quick to smile, deep dimples bracketing each side. And his unconscious habit of rubbing the side of his nose when confronted with an uncomfortable situation beyond his control.

She opened her eyes and stared down at him again.

Limp strands of hair lay across the bandage covering the right side of his forehead.

She smoothed them back, mimicking one of his familiar gestures. Where was he now? She was certain he felt pain, for he moaned occasionally. Could he hear her? Could she somehow reach that place of refuge to which he had retreated and force him to hear her?

She spent the remainder of the long voyage talking to him, trying to reach deep inside his mind. She retold their last night together and how they had dreamed of going home to Innisbraw. She held his right hand in both of hers. "We're almost there, luve ... " Her voice broke. "Just hang on a while longer."

She kissed him, his lips so cold. Hot tears streamed down her face. She didn't wipe them away. She wouldn't release his hand— she couldn't.

Chapter Eight

When the *Sea Rouk* docked at Innisbraw, though it had been eight months since she had seen her beloved island, Maggie did not spare a glance at the home she had missed so dreadfully.

As soon as the boat was secured, Elspeth NicAllister, the ninety-nine-year-old woman who had been her surrogate mither, stepped across the boarding plank, leaning on her walking stick. The brisk onshore breeze plucked wisps of white hair from the braid wrapped around her head and she clutched her shawl against her chest with one gnarled hand, faded blue eyes awash with moisture.

Hugh MacEwan, minister and dearest friend, supported Elspeth's elbow. Grey crept higher through his thinning brown hair and his body sagged. No elfin smile of greeting this een—just a sorrowful sigh as he knelt at Maggie's side. He gently removed Rob's hand from hers and bent over the lad, brown eyes dark with grief.

Elspeth propped her stick against the wheelhouse and gathered Maggie into her arms. "'Tis all right, my precious lass. You're both home."

Maggie clung to her. "He made it home," she said in a hoarse whisper. "Rob made it home."

Hugh took Rob's hand, a tear trickling down his cherubic cheeks. "Our Faither in Heaven, enfold this dear lad in Your healing embrace. He's Yours, and though we can't imagine how, You luve him even more than we do. May Your perfect will be done. In Jesus's name."

Angus MacPhee, a neighboring crofter and close friend, appeared at Maggie's side, red hair rumpled in the breeze, blue eyes sad—so sad. "I thought the cairt ride would be too rough. Tormad, Mark, Malcolm, and Sim will carry Rob up the hill to the infirmary.

They'll be gentle, lass."

"Thank ye, Angus."

Elspeth reached for her walking stick. "We'd best start then. Thank the Lord it's no' plomping rain, but let's get this dear lad out of the cold wind and into a warm bed."

Maggie hadn't the heart to remind her Rob was unaware of his surroundings. "Aye, 'tis time."

⁂

Hugh eyed the crowd of folk lining the pier, shore, and path ahead. Every physically able person on Innisbraw was on hand to welcome their Rob home and to support their Maggie. Somber, tear-streaked faces peered down at Rob when the stretcher passed and heads bowed and lips moved in prayer as the fishermen carried him from the pier and up the path. Alec MacDonald, another crofter friend of both Maggie and Rob, held his wife, Morag, in his arms.

Though near stumbling from exhaustion, Maggie looked better than Hugh had expected. Thank the Lord for the lass's strong will. *Don't let my faith in Rob's recovery waiver, Faither. And thank Ye for restraining my hasty actions when I first heard from John that Rob was dying.*

Maggie must not learn of Rob's request to be buried at the top of Ben Innis. He had almost betrayed that secret by having some of the men clear a wider path from the kirkyard to the top of the ben to make The Lift, an essential part of the funeral, easier on those carrying the casket up the steep slope.

⁂

For the first time ever, Maggie regretted there were no roads on Innisbraw—just a wide sandy path around the island for folk on foot and horse-drawn cairts. An ambulance would be faster. She drew comfort from Elspeth and Hugh, each clasping one of her hands. But she couldn't be so selfish. "You can't walk that far, Elspeth. 'Tis much too hard on you."

"Nonsense. I have my stick. Though I didn't walk down to see you off when you left Innisbraw, I will see you to the infirmary the een."

Hugh squeezed Maggie's hand. "Our Rob made it this far by

the grace of God. Now 'tis time to allow Him to work His perfect will."

"Rob's dying, Hugh." How could there be more tears clogging her throat? Hadn't she shed them all? "Besides his other terrible injuries, he has a fractured skull. He's in a coma."

"That may be, lass, but our Lord has a different concept of time than we do. 'Tis a miracle our Rob is still alive. Who are we to say His divine work is over?"

Maggie looked at Hugh, then Elspeth. "You were both so certain he'd be coming back. I'm sure you didn't think it would be to ... to die."

"Of course it isn't to die! When your faither arrives on the morra, I'm sure he'll agree that where there's a breath of life, there's hope."

Startled by Elspeth's confident words, Maggie tripped over a stone in the path. They righted her and she signaled the four men carrying the stretcher to stop. "Are you trying to tell me something, Elspeth?"

The old woman bowed her head before meeting Maggie's pleading gaze. "You have so much more medical knowledge, but I know God's promises, Maggie lass. Don't stop praying." She nodded at Hugh. "We'll no' give up. Neither can you."

A tiny flicker of hope. Maggie dropped Hugh's hand and reached for Rob's. "Did you hear that, luve? Wherever you are, don't stop trying to come back." She nodded at the stretcher-bearers to continue but kept Rob's hand in hers. *Och, Heavenly Faither, take away my fear, please. Replace it with Your perfect faith. Please, Faither, I'm so afraid. Give me Your faith!*

Perhaps if she talked to Rob he would somehow know they were home.

"Wildflowers along the path flutter in the wind like butterflies of every colour, luve. I can hear the seals barking on the rocks 'neath Innis Fell." She scanned the familiar landscape. "And there's Ben Innis, tall and proud, purple heather trailing down her sides, filling the air with the scent of warm honey. And just ahead on the path is Elspeth's wee cottage, her garden ablaze with colour. Och, that rocker you always sit in is on her front entry flags, just waiting for you to stop by for a blether."

A memory of Rob and Elspeth sitting in rockers on her covered entry brought more tears.

She squeezed his hand, but couldn't continue talking lest she break down completely.

When they reached the infirmary at the top of the fell, they carried Rob into the large room he'd occupied before. Using the drawsheet, they transferred him to the bed. The fishermen who had carried his stretcher all bowed their heads for a moment before leaving the room, their young, weathered faces aged by grief.

Maggie took Rob's pulse. Still fluttering fitfully. She smoothed his hair back from his forehead and touched her lips to his. "You're home at last, luve. You're home on Innisbraw."

Hugh hugged her shoulder. "We'll leave you alone with Rob for a while. Call oot if you need us."

She pulled up a chair and sat beside the bed, holding Rob's hand. That last normal night they had talked about returning home and she had said, "Soon. We'll go home soon." She closed her eyes and pictured the longing on Rob's face as he looked at the sandy cove on the western side of the island and talked about someday watching their eight bairns ploutering about in the water. Though she struggled, she couldn't draw a deep breath.

Such agony. Her soul cried out in torment.

"Och, Lord, help me. I cannot bear to lose him. Help me to accept Your will, whatever it is. Please, Lord, please!"

Rob moaned and she opened her eyes, hoping to find him awake.

Still unconscious.

He suffered, but she could do nothing to ease his pain. Morphine would depress his already dangerously low blood pressure and then ...

She ran to the pharmacy and returned with a new bottle of saline. After setting the drip rate, she dipped a face flannel into warm water and bathed his face, taking care not to get any water on the bandage over his forehead. She would wait until the morra to change the dressing. Her faither would want to see the wound.

Her eyelids drooped, but sleep had never seemed so impossible.

Part of her wanted desperately to escape from this anguish into oblivion, but she might never sleep again.

Rob's lips moved. He made no sound.

She sat beside him once again, taking his right hand in hers, bonding them together. His fingers were cold and she warmed them with her own. Somehow, he might know she was with him. She kissed his palm and each finger, then lay her head on the bed, praying he would awaken soon.

When Elspeth and Hugh returned, she sensed their presence and raised her head.

"Och, 'tis sorry I am. You need your rest," Elspeth said. "But you also need to eat. I've made tattie bree. 'Tis in the kitchen."

"I'll no' leave Rob."

"Of course no'," Hugh said. "You can eat it here, and our Elspeth's right. You must take care of yourself. Our Rob needs you to be strong." He turned as he eyed the room. "Angus is ootside with his cairt to see if there's owt he can do. There's enough room in here, so I'll have him help me move in another bed. You can wheel it close to Rob's so you can be near him while you sleep."

"I can't sleep."

"How long has it been since you've tried?"

"I disremember. Twa nights, I suppose."

"Lass, lass, you cannot keep on like this. How can you expect to help Rob if you become ill from exhaustion?"

Tears blurred her vision and she turned away, shaking her head. "I don't know. I just know I have to be with him every second or I might no' be here when he ... when he ..." She could not say the dreadful words aloud.

⚜

Hugh gestured to Elspeth.

She quit the room.

He took Maggie's arm, forcing her to face him. "Lass, whether you want to accept it or no', this is a pivotal point in your life. If you continue on like this, your faither will have twa patients on his hands, and he needs to concentrate on saving Rob's life."

46

Tears slipped down her face as she stared at him.

His grip tightened. So fragile, that arm. "Now is the time to decide. 'Tis up to you. Either you start taking care of yourself right now or you endanger Rob's life even more. What's it to be?" She looked so stricken he wanted to relent but he did not allow his gaze to waver.

She nodded. "I'll eat and try to sleep, as long as I'm right next to him where I'll know if he ... if he needs me."

"That's the Maggie I luve. Here's Elspeth with your bree. I'll put up the blackout curtains. While you eat, Angus will help me wheel in your bed."

⚓

Maggie choked down the bree and was surprised by how much stronger she felt.

Hugh and Angus moved her bed into place.

"You gather up owt you think our Rob will need in the night so you won't have to leave him," Elspeth said. "We'll stay right here while you're gone."

Maggie put together a tray of saline and dressings and washed her face and hands in the hall bathroom. She unpinned her long hair, brushing it until it hung below her waist, her mind filled with memories of Rob's fingers tangled in her hair, a smile of joy on his face.

When she returned, Elspeth was leaning over Rob, speaking softly. Maggie could not make out the words, but Elspeth's tone was gentle and loving.

She straightened and looked at Maggie. "He's hanging on, lass. Our Rob's no quitter. He's trying verra hard—as you must."

Her firm words strengthened Maggie. "I'll try to sleep, then. He'll need no more saline for almost four hours."

After Hugh offered a prayer and they said their guidbyes, Maggie pushed her bed next to Rob's, took off her uniform tunic and shoes, and lay down facing him, lacing her fingers through his. "I'm right here, luve. I'll know if you need me."

Her heart galloped. What if he just stopped breathing? Would she know? Or would he slip away into Heaven, leaving her behind to—

She listened to his raspy, laboured breathing.

How could she lose a part of her own soul and not know?

She closed her eyes and was asleep within moments.

Chapter Nine

Morag MacDonald spent the night on the sofa in the infirmary foyer. It was no sacrifice—she had already planned to do exactly that before Hugh asked.

How could they leave Maggie alone at such a time?

Beseeching the Lord to save Rob, she lay awake half the night. She woke suddenly and rushed to the window, raising a corner of the blackout curtain. The dove-grey sky hung suspended between night and day, preparing itself for the lemon-yellow rays of the rising sun.

Walking quickly around the kitchen, she tidied up, using the task to keep from picturing Maggie hovering over her luve, wondering when he would take his last breath.

Flora MacPhee, Angus's wife and a nearby neighbor, slipped into the kitchen, finger to her lips. "I couldn't stay away," she whispered into Morag's ear before closing the kitchen door.

"I couldn't either. That poor lass. First her mither when she was only eight, and now her dear Rob."

Flora wiped at the tears lingering on her cheeks and looked around the spotless kitchen. "What can I do to help?"

"Some hot tea would go down a treat."

Morag scoured the stone jawbox, attacking imaginary stains—anything to keep busy.

Tea poured, the two women sat at the table, adding milk and heather honey to their cups.

"We have to keep praying," Morag said, stirring her tea, knowing she couldn't swallow even a sip. "I keep thinking how I would feel if something like this happened to my Graham. And it could, him being in the Army."

Flora nodded. "I feel almost guilty—my own twa lads so strong

49

and healthy and too young to be in harm's way."

Morag groped for her hand. "I've never seen twa young folk so in luve as our Maggie and our Rob. And remember how hard he worked to walk again? I bubbled like a bairnie when they were merrit and he walked our Maggie back down the aisle at kirk with no' even a limp." She squeezed Flora's fingers. "We must keep praying and praying. Surely our Lord will heal him again."

Hearing the faint rumble of Angus's cairt over the path, they emptied their un-tasted tea into the jawbox and tiptoed from the infirmary.

Elspeth and Hugh spent the day with Maggie. Elspeth sat nearby, praying, offering soft words of encouragement or making tea and more bree, while Hugh busied himself fetching whatever Maggie needed from the pharmacy or supply room.

Maggie prayed without ceasing—for Rob and also for her own strength. Hugh was right. She had to maintain her health in order to give her all for the one whose heartbeat echoed in her own breast.

Knowing how he hated not to be clean-shaven, she shaved Rob's three-day beard that afternoon.

Hugh helped change his bedding.

They were careful, but he still moaned when moved.

"Steady on, luve," she told him. "'Tis better to move a little than to lie so still."

With injuries too serious to prop him on his side, he might catch pneumonia from lying in one position so long, or an infection might take root in his wounds. But there were only three ampoules of penicillin in the pharmacy. She couldn't use them until she had to.

Doctor John McGrath arrived by trawler late that afternoon, tweed suit wrinkled, greying hair and beard unkempt from the windy sea voyage. He rocked Maggie gently in his arms, dark brown eyes, behind silver-framed eyeglasses, filled with anguish. "Och, lass, lass, I'm sorry it took me so long to get here. I had surgeries all day yesterday—war-wounded lads."

She clung to her faither, drawing strength from his warm, familiar embrace, from the smell of medicaments still clinging to his tweeds despite the long sea journey. "'Tis a miracle he's still alive, Faither. Somehow, he's hanging on." She pulled a sodden handkerchief from her pocket and wiped her eyes. "I brought all the X-rays and a complete report of the treatment he received at Edenoaks. They're in that large envelope on the clothes-press."

John looked down at the lad he'd come to luve like a son. Tears glazed his eyes as he took the limp right hand in his. "You've proven you're a fighter, lad," he said. "I just pray your body holds out as long as your spirit." He glanced at Maggie. "If I'd known he'd live this long, I'd have had you transport him to the Royal Infirmary."

"He wanted to come home. We talked about it every day, coming home to Innisbraw. I think he somehow knows we're here at last."

"'Tis possible. We don't know how much he can hear, if anything, but we're going to continue to tell him where he is and how he must fight." His gaze swept over his daughter. "Still in uniform and you look exhausted. Are you eating? Have you been able to sleep?"

"Elspeth, Hugh, and Angus were here till late last een. She made me eat some bree and Hugh and Angus brought in that bed."

"Guid. You need the sleep and we're going to assume Rob knows you're near." He squeezed her shoulder. "Go make us both a cup of strong tea. I'm going to have a look at him before I go over his X-rays and the reports you brought. On you go, lass. I'll no' leave him."

Maggie hesitated before pressing her lips to Rob's. "I'll be right back, luve. Faither's with you."

John watched her quit the room, heart heavy as a flagging stone.

Major Larson at Edenoaks had been wrong about Rob's injury over a year ago, but he was right this time. The lad had little, if any, chance of surviving such devastating injuries, no matter how strong his will to live.

John washed his hands and began his examination. When Maggie returned with their tea, he called her to his side. "Either 'tis my wishful thinking, or Rob has heard what I've been saying."

Hope bloomed in her eyes. "Och, Faither, what do you mean?"

"I mentioned your name when I was listening to his heart and the rate increased. I tried it taking his pulse and the same thing happened. Take his hand but don't begin talking until I have the diaphragm in place. The heavy wrapping over his ribs makes it difficult to get a clear reading, so I'll use his carotid." He placed his stethoscope diaphragm at the side of Rob's neck and nodded at Maggie.

"I'm back, Rob." She took his hand and leaned over him. "Remember, we're home on Innisbraw. I can hear the sea pounding on the rocks below Innis Fell."

John motioned her to stop talking. He waited a moment as if listening intently, before replacing the stethoscope around his neck. "He definitely hears you. The entire time you were talking, his pulse was elevated. When you stopped, it slowed again."

"If he can hear me, why doesn't he wake up?"

"So little is known about head injuries and the comas that sometimes ensue. One of our neurologists briefed me on what to look for. I could detect no swelling of the brain. His pupils are dilated but I would expect that after a skull fracture. The guid thing is, both pupils are equal."

"That is guid news."

He stroked his short beard. "There is one theory that could apply here. Remember, his head injury is just one of five major traumas, including both legs, his left shoulder, and ribs."

"That's why I brought him home. Doctor Larson said he could never survive surgery on his broken bones when he's in a coma."

John paced, frustrated by how little he could do. "He was spot on. The pain must be excruciating, but because his blood pressure is so low, no pain medicaments can be administered. What is a person to do when faced with pain so strong it cannot be endured? He retreats into some inner place of refuge to escape."

"Then he might wake up when the pain can be relieved?"

The hope in her voice sent a sharp stab of sorrow ratcheting through his chest. "Och, who knows? 'Tis only a theory. I need to go over everything Doctor Larson sent." He took his tea and retreated to his office, where he studied Rob's X-rays and Major Larson's report.

When he returned, Maggie lay on her bed next to Rob, caressing his cheek, telling him the tale of the Selkie and her journey from the sea.

Rob's breathing, though laboured, was deep.

John left them again, not to study, but to pray. He had never seen a stronger bond of luve between two people than the one between Rob and Maggie. But still, given the lad's injuries, the good Lord had to intervene if Rob were to live. And every prayer was vital.

There was little change in Rob's condition over the next few days. John removed the sutures from the shrapnel wounds in Rob's chest and right shoulder, but could not treat his broken bones and torn ligaments until he awakened and his blood pressure rose. Though his breathing seemed less laboured and his lungs remained free of fluid, Rob still remained in a deep coma, never opening his eyes the way some comatose patients did, even though unaware of their surroundings.

Maggie left his side only for a trip to the bathing room or for a quick bath and change of clothes. She slept beside him, fingers laced through his.

There was so little she could do for him. She couldn't turn him until his ribs healed and only his right arm was uninjured. She rubbed that arm and hand with fragrant heather lotion and clipped his nails. If he didn't awaken soon, they would have to gavage him so he could receive nutrients beyond what saline offered.

Her faither could give her no medical explanation for why Rob still clung to life. "It has to be the strong bond of luve binding you twa together," he said. "And prayer, of course."

Hugh held a prayer service for Rob every een, the kirk always full. Also, many Innisbraw folk came by each day to assure Maggie they were praying for Rob, including Angus and Flora MacPhee and Morag and Alec MacDonald, who had formed a close friendship with him during his first stay on the island.

Maggie's childhood friend, Susan Ferguson, the shy, quiet wife of Mark, one of the young fishermen who'd helped carry Rob's stretcher up from the dock, brought a handful of wildflowers she had picked on the machair. "I know how much you luve your Rob. Mark is my luve, my life, so I understand a wee bit of what you must be going through."

Maggie and she embraced, weeping.

When Susan left, Maggie sat beside Rob's bed and tried to understand all the ways she had changed since she fell in luve with Rob. Och, her faither had always said she shed more tears than a black raincloud, but weeping so often was only a small part of it. Before his crash, she had also laughed more and relished the little things she could do to make her Rob happy and comfortable. Now, her every thought, her every hope, centered on his recovery. The food she choked down to keep up her strength and the quick baths she took every een were just chores to be accomplished so she could spend her time with Rob.

⁜

After almost five weeks, Rob's vitals improved, a slight change, but significant. His blood pressure and body temperature slowly rose, and he required fewer covers to keep his skin from feeling icy to the touch. Though he moaned less, his lips moved far more. He no longer laboured for breath.

But he still remained comatose.

If only he would wake up.

John removed the tight wrappings holding his ribs immobile and they appeared to have knitted properly. The shrapnel wounds in his chest and right shoulder had also healed. A smaller bandage replaced the large one on his forehead. Not only had he hit his forehead on something during the crash, but it appeared to have been severely cut during the mission. John removed tiny particles of glass which had been driven deep into the wound.

The condition of Rob's shoulder gave John a great deal of

concern. Shoulder injuries were notorious for the pain they caused. If he lived, the lad faced several operations before he could use his arm and none of the breaks to his legs were healing correctly. It would take many surgeries and a long rehabilitation before Rob could enjoy even a half-normal life again.

But his head injury and lingering coma were the most dangerous. The longer he remained in a coma, the less chance he had of ever awakening. Major organs would cease to function and his body would fill with deadly toxins. Death was inevitable.

"If Rob doesn't awaken soon ..." he warned Maggie without specifics. "I want you to start asking him to open his eyes. Tell him how much you luve and need him. If he'll respond to anything, 'tis to something you ask."

Many times she held Rob's hand and asked him to open his eyes for her, praying God would answer her constant beseeching.

No response.

Six more days of pleading. Still, no response.

More panic-filled prayers.

More pleading.

Would he never wake up?

Chapter Ten

Edenoaks Air Base

Den Anderson threw himself down on his cot. Boy, he was pooped. Another briefing, another strike. Would this war never end? He rubbed his burning eyes and let out a deep breath. A few injured crewmen, but no planes lost today, despite a nasty combined mission to take out another German ammunition dump.

He folded his pillow, squirming to get comfortable. So much for General Fielding's promise of a commander who would lead the most perilous strikes. So far, during the weeks since Rob's crash, he himself had flown the lead plane on all the hairiest missions.

The new commander's lame excuses grated. "Sorry, I've an inflamed inner ear and can't chance the change in altitude ... Sorry, they've called a meeting at SHAEF I can't miss ... Sorry, that old football injury is acting up again."

Football injury, my patootie!

How different it would be, if only ...

He flinched at the memory of Maggie's pale, stricken face as she accompanied Rob's stretcher into the C-47 Skytrain. He should write her, but what could he say? That the Wing Commander had told them Rob was still alive but in a coma? That he understood her suffering? That some higher power—call it God, if he believed in Him—would bring Rob around?

He groaned. If only he had the faith he'd overheard Rob talk about. But why should he feel guilty? How had their God rewarded Rob and Maggie for their faith?

Den tried to erase the pictures parading before his eyes every moment he spent alone.

No use. The second he lay down, the movie projector started.

He couldn't walk out on this picture show; the script and Technicolor film occupied every corner of his mind.

The *Bonnie Maggie,* banking left on two engines and quitting the formation, him goosing his own flak-battered *Come to Papa* into the lead.

Den fell into the memory of the battle. Jumped by bandits almost immediately, he focused his attention on keeping his Fort in the air.

When the fighters gave up the chase and he was free to think again, Rob's last words echoed in his mind.

"You'll have to take them home, Den."

His gloved fingers tightened around the yoke. *Roger, bucko, that's just what I'll do.*

Once over the Channel, he broke radio silence and contacted Ground Control, reporting the *Bonnie Maggie*'s condition and warning them to have the crash wagons ready.

Come on, Rob, if anybody can do it, you can.

Scanning the runway, he lined up for landing. A few ambulances, but why only one crash wagon? Heart pounding wildly, he touched down and taxied to his hardstand. General Fielding's staff car pulled up close to the still-spooling engines. This didn't look good. Hands shaking, he ordered his copilot to shut down all systems, unplugged the radio mike, unstrapped the seat-harness, unlocked the belly hatch, and swung to the ground.

Fielding waited, face grim. "Come with me!" he barked, diving into the back seat of his car and moving over to make room for Den. Door barely latched, the car accelerated across the tarmac, dodging ambulances, crew trucks, and personnel on bicycles. "I suppose you know the colonel's plane went down."

Bile filled Den's throat. He swallowed several times, fighting to control his panic. "Where? How bad was it?"

"As bad as it gets, Major." Fielding scrubbed his face with his palms. "An ambulance and ground crews have been dispatched to the crash site southeast of Canterbury, but my driver is under orders to get there first."

"Only one ambulance?"

57

"The colonel ordered a bailout over the Channel before reporting to Control. He was almost out of fuel and was attempting to set her down in a field. As far as we know, he was the only one aboard."

Den couldn't remember much of the careening ride over winding, often single-lane country roads—mainly the constant litany running through his mind like a phonograph needle stuck in one groove: *Not Rob, not Rob, not Rob.*

But he would never forget staggering out of the car … pushing his way through a group of local farmers to get a glimpse of the broken B-17. The wreckage scattered across a plowed field littered with the massive sheared-off trunk and limbs of an oak tree.

Propellers ground into the dirt, twisted around engine housings.

Nose buried in a dense Hawthorne hedge.

Fuselage riddled with flak holes and gaping open in front of the shattered left wing.

A battered, bloody body dangling from a protruding piece of metal in that gap.

Den stumbled to a low stone wall, doubled over, and vomited.

Fielding roared to someone to stay back, and pushed aside curious onlookers, stepping over the wall and picking his way through the debris until he reached what was left of the cockpit.

"Get over here, Major, and boost me up. The colonel's still in his seat."

The wail of the ambulance throbbed through the air as they pushed their way inside. Rob sat almost doubled at the waist, harness torn loose, forehead jammed into the crushed instrument panel, chest shoved against the yoke, and left arm caught at an impossible angle between part of his seat and the mangled skin of the airplane.

Fielding placed two fingers at the base of Rob's neck. "Dear Lord, I feel a pulse." He pushed Den aside and jumped to the ground. "Medics! Medics! Over here! The colonel's alive!"

Den leaned close to Rob, trying to see his face through the dark red river of blood streaming from his forehead. "Oh, Rob, hang on, bucko. Please don't die! Hang on!"

Wing and a Prayer

A

The outer door opened. He pulled the pillow over his face, feigning sleep. Didn't want to explain his tears. Couldn't express how he felt even if he tried. *Okay, God— if there really is a God up there—listen up. They don't come any better than Rob Savage. Wake him up.*

Chapter Eleven

After a week of pleading and praying with no response, Maggie's fear heightened to desperation. Her faither would be calling a specialist at the Edinburgh Infirmary on the morra. She climbed onto Rob's bed and cradled him in her arms, kissing his cheeks and neck. She studied his pale face. "I need you. I need you to open your eyes and look at me. Please, Rob, if you luve me, if you truly luve me, open your eyes."

His eyelids fluttered.

Her heart thudded against her ribs. She rose on an elbow and watched his face. "That's right. Open your eyes."

His lips moved.

His eyes opened.

She gasped in disbelief. Had he really opened his eyes? "Rob, I'm here. I'm here beside you."

He looked at her, lips moving again.

She kissed the dimples beside his lips. "'Tis Maggie." Her trembling fingertips caressed his cheek. "'Tis your Maggie."

Recognition lit his eyes from within. "Maggie?" A hoarse whisper.

Tears flooded her eyes. "I'm here." A cry tore from her soul.

"My Maggie."

Voice so weak—but the twa most powerful words she had ever heard. She clutched him, sobbing. *Thank Ye, Faither, thank Ye, thank Ye!*

"Don't ... cry, lass." Another whisper.

She wiped her cheeks with her palms and leaned over him, hand shaking as she fingered his dear face. "They're happy tears, luve. You've come back to me."

"Never gone."

She gazed down at him, heart overflowing with gratitude and luve. "No, never truly gone." *Och, no more tears. Don't upset him. Use your training. You're his nurse.*

"We're home." His voice stronger.

She wiped her face on the corner of the bedcover. "Aye, we're home."

"Hold me, Maggie. Hurts."

She lay down and cradled him. "I know it hurts, but now you're awake, we can give you something for the pain."

He closed his eyes, uttered a long, moaning sigh.

"You can sleep. Just don't go so far away this time."

His eyes fluttered open again. "Stay ... please. Hurts so bad."

"I'll be right here. I promise." Swallowing tears, voice breaking, she buried her face against his shoulder and sang the Selkie's song—of her undying luve and how that luve would grow with each passing day. The melody and words, dredged from the memory of hearing and singing them so often, came without thought. Her mind, flooded with grateful prayers, repeated the same litany over and over: *Thank Ye, precious Lord, my Rob's awake. Thank Ye, precious Lord ...*

⋆⋌⋋⋆

John paused in the doorway, looked at Rob, and rushed to the bed. "He's awake, and you didn't come get me?"

Maggie sat up and laid a reassuring hand on Rob's right arm. "I promised I wouldn't leave him alone. He awoke a few hours ago, but he's been dozing off and on despite the pain. I've been singing and telling him the Selkie tale to let him know I'm here."

The doctor leaned over the bed. "Och, lad, 'tis so guid to have you back." He wiped his brimming eyes and polished his eyeglasses on his white lab coat.

Rob blinked and gazed up at him. "Told you ... I'd bring Maggie home." Voice so weak, words so hesitant.

The doctor didn't bother to explain the long coma. "You certainly did that." He placed a blood pressure cuff around Rob's right arm. "Let's see where we are the day." He inflated the cuff and smiled when he took the reading. "We can give you something for

61

pain. No' much, but enough to take away the worst of it."

"'Tis bad."

"The shoulder's the most painful?"

"Did ... did I lose my arm?"

"Och, no. But you did break your shoulder—verra badly." He turned to Maggie. "He can have morphine now. Start with five to ten milligrams every two to three hours as needed. That way, there won't be so many peaks and valleys."

She slid from the bed and hurried from the room.

Rob's worried gaze followed her. "Coming back?"

John patted his hand. "Absolutely. She's hardly left your side the past six weeks."

"Six weeks?"

"You arrived here on Innisbraw on the fifteenth of July. Today is the first day of September."

"September? What happened?"

"You don't remember?"

"The smell of heather and ... Maggie's voice. They kept me from the darkness."

"I mean before that."

Rob slowly shook his head.

"You crashed your airieplane returning from a mission over Germany."

Eyes pleading. "My crew?"

"General Fielding wrote Maggie asking about you. Your crew bailed out safely before the crash and were picked up by a rescue boat. None received any serious injuries." No reason to mention the dead bombardier and tail gunner. If Rob eventually remembered, fine. If he didn't, even better.

Rob closed his eyes. "Thank Ye, Lord."

He slept when the morphine took effect. For the first time since he had awakened from the coma, Maggie didn't panic when he fell asleep. This was exactly what he needed, a time free from the worst of the pain. Now, he could begin healing.

Elspeth and Hugh came by that afternoon. Tears of joy flowed when they heard the good news.

Maggie led them to the far corner of the room. "He's asleep now. I don't want our blethering to wake him."

"Don't be surprised when you hear the kirk bell ringing," Hugh said softly. "'Tis the signal the folk have been waiting six weeks to hear—and there will be a celebration of thanksgiving this een at the kirk."

"I hope you all continue to hold him up in prayer," Maggie said, voice taut with anxiety. "He has months of surgeries and painful times ahead."

Elspeth hugged her. "Of course we won't stop praying, for we know what he must endure. But 'tis with joy we look forward to the outcome. I knew our Rob would survive. I'm rejoicing to hear his mind is clear."

"His thinking is fine. He's just verra weak and he told Faither he disremembers the crash."

"'Tis probably just as well." Hugh raised his glasses and dabbed at his eyes. "It must have been a terrible thing to go through."

Maggie closed her mind against the agonizing choices Rob had faced. "Och, terrible can't even begin to describe it. General Fielding told me Rob had to have known for a long time he was too low on fuel to make it back to base."

"Why didn't he bail oot with his crew?"

"I didn't hear why until just before we left Edenoaks. The copilot reported during debriefing that Rob gave his own parachute to one of the crew to replace one damaged by flak."

"That sounds like our Rob, always thinking of his men," Elspeth said.

"Aye. 'Tis what made them so loyal."

"So, you're able to ease his pain now?"

"A wee bit. We still can't give him enough morphine to bring him complete relief, but at least the pain's dulled enough for him to sleep."

Elspeth hobbled to the bed and leaned over Rob. She studied his face for a moment, straightened, and laid her hand lightly on his arm. "Sleep well," she whispered. "The Lord has special plans for

63

you. I've known that from the first day you came to Innisbraw. "
She closed her eyes, lips moving in prayer.

He stirred, opened his eyes, and gave a lopsided smile.
"Elspeth."

"Och, I didn't mean to wake you. Go back to sleep, lad."

"Had to wake up. Bad dreams." Sweat beaded his forehead.

Elspeth moved aside as Maggie took his hand, kissing his
palm. "Just dreams, luve. They're gone now."

"Too many fighters, too much flak. Forts exploding and falling
from the sky."

"Can you get me a cold, wet face flannel?" Maggie asked
Elspeth before smoothing back Rob's forelock. "'Tis the morphine
making your dreams so dark, luve, but you need it for the pain." She
took the flannel from Elspeth and bathed his face, right hand, and
arm. "This should help chase away those dreams."

He closed his eyes. "Luve you, Maggie."

She touched her lips to his. "And I luve you."

John walked down to the manse, rehearsing his radio call. He
could have used the shortwave in his office but didn't want to
chance Maggie overhearing.

Hugh waited on a rocker on his front entry, nursing a cup of
coffee.

"Thank ye for waiting up." John squeezed Hugh's shoulder.

"Och, I never seek my bed this early. Nightly solitude is best
spent preparing my lesson for the Sabbath." He rose and opened the
door. "Come away in. You know where the shortwave is. I'll leave
you to it."

"I'd appreciate you being with me. I need all the prayers I can
get to make this work."

"You're being most mysterious." Hugh led the way to his
office.

"I'm going to contact the Principal Matron of the RAF Nursing
Service and convince her to grant Maggie a discharge."

"A discharge, is it?" Hugh switched on the Anglepoise lamp. "I
can see why you need prayer."

Ten minutes later, John connected with the very disgruntled, haughty Jones-Hilton. "I want you to know you interrupted a much anticipated late supper," she said. "I don't appreciate being called back to my office for anything less than a dire emergency, even by a surgeon of your exalted reputation, Doctor McGrath."

John mouthed *Pray* to Hugh and switched to Broadcast.

Hugh dropped to his knees.

"I apologize for the interrupted supper, Brigadier Jones-Hilton, but this is a delicate matter which can only be handled by one occupying your highly esteemed position."

She uttered a most unlady-like snort. "In other words, you've used up all your favors with Smythe. Spit it out, doctor."

Irritation burned John's stomach. "Are you aware I have a daughter serving under your command?"

"Of course. I reviewed her reassignment papers just this afternoon."

"You'll have to review them again." He switched to Receive.

Silence. Had she disconnected the call?

"I. Beg. Your. Pardon." Each word icy as a hailstone.

His body stiffened. Words distinct, tone firm, he said, "As you undoubtedly know, Maggie is on Innisbraw nursing her critically injured husband. The colonel awakened from a six-week coma last night. His life hangs by a very thin thread. Her presence is vital to his survival."

Jones-Hilton started to interrupt.

He kept his finger on the broadcast switch. "So this is my ultimatum, Brigadier Jones-Hilton. Either you grant my Maggie an immediate honorable discharge from the RAF Nurses Service, or I will resign my positions at the Royal Infirmary and Edinburgh School of Medicine as of tomorrow morning and open my infirmary on Innisbraw permanently. This is non-negotiable." He switched to Receive and mopped his forehead with his handkerchief.

Please, Faither, soften her heart. I'm no' ready to retire, but I will if she forces it. Rob cannot survive without Maggie. Please, Faither!

The slam of a desk drawer. Rustle of papers. Rapid breathing. Scratch of a pen. More rapid breathing. "Leftenant Margaret

65

Savage's honorable discharge papers have been signed and will be started through the chain of command tomorrow morning. You are a devious, despicable man, Doctor McGrath."

John swallowed to keep the grin from his voice. "Thank you, Principal Matron."

Though he continued to improve, Rob's debilitating headaches and the unrelenting, excruciating pain in his shoulder slowed his progress.

"I must start repairing Rob's shoulder," John told Maggie when she took a cup of tea into his office.

She worried her lower lip. "But can he tolerate surgery now? He's still so weak."

"If I leave it much longer, he'll never regain the use of that arm."

"Och, we cannot allow that."

"I'm going to go in and repair the worst, lad," he told Rob moments later. "'Tis only the first of several operations to that shoulder, but we need to repair the fracture and reattach some of the larger torn ligaments. 'Twill be verra painful for a week or twa after the surgery, but then you should gain some relief."

"Do it."

"You'll have to continue fighting, lad. 'Tis a lot to ask, but you can't give in to the pain and retreat again."

"I won't."

An anaesthesiologist, another orthopaedic surgeon, and an OR nurse from the Royal Infirmary in Edinburgh arrived on Innisbraw by trawler two days later.

The night before surgery, Maggie climbed onto Rob's bed so she could hold him while he slept. "I'll be at your side in the OR."

"My Maggie. Couldn't do it without you."

"You don't have to. I'll no' leave you for a second." She touched her lips to his. "Now, off to sleep. You'll need all your strength for after the surgery.

His short laugh surprised her. "Tell me the Selkie tale. I need to hear your voice."

She ran her fingertips lightly over his cheek. "There once was a verra beautiful seal who lived in the deep sea. She felt in her breast a strange yearning to journey far, far away. She swam day and night, night and day ..."

⚓

The operation took over five hours. Rob's vital signs remained steady, surprising doctors and nurses.

"We were able to accomplish more than we thought possible— even repaired his torn rotator cuff," John told Hugh and Elspeth later that day. "But urge the folk to pray without ceasing over the next few days. This particular surgery is the most painful for any patient."

The morphine couldn't keep Rob from groaning. Maggie bathed his face and told him the tale of the Selkie over and over, but five days passed before he could doze more than a few minutes at a time.

When the worst was over, fingers laced together, both fell into an exhausted sleep.

⚓

During the next several weeks, Rob made steady progress. He ate chicken broth, then some tattie bree, and drank cups of tea, but John continued the IV to keep him hydrated. Though he could have safely doubled Rob's morphine, he was reluctant to do so. The drug-induced dark dreams caused Rob to cry out and thrash from imaginary phantoms. All of his nightmares involved bombing strikes. He called for members of his crew to bail out and told his gunners, "Watch out for bandits at two o'clock high." He relived the moments before the crash, shouting, "Too high! Too Fast! My Maggie!" He awakened from each nightmare bathed in sweat.

⚓

Maggie always stood ready with a cold, wet flannel and soothing words. Perhaps the vivid dreams were somehow cathartic and would gradually move him beyond the memories of that last, terrible flight.

Late one afternoon, she shuddered at the thought of another

horror-filled night. Time to face the issue. "Would it help if you talked about your bad dreams?"

"Sorry, I can't. 'Tis all a midden of disjointed images, machine guns firing, shouts over the interphone, and bright lights coming at me from all directions—with flak so thick it turns day into night— and black smoke and fires burning below like you're over the pit of hell itself."

"You have to understand they're only bad dreams."

He looked up at her, eyes dull, face void of expression. "I'll never fly again, will I?"

His quiet question served to wrong-foot her. She wanted to pretend she hadn't heard, or even lie. She couldn't. She had promised to always be truthful. She bowed her head, shamed by her inability to meet his gaze. "No, luve, at least no' in this war."

He turned his face to the wall.

"But that doesn't mean you can't fly later, when the war's ended, just for the pleasure of it."

"So it's over for me." Voice flat. No emotion.

Her chest ached as if she'd received a blow. She had seen how much it meant to him to command the 396th, how his life revolved around his role in combating the Third Reich, in ending this terrible war.

She took his hand and cradled it between her palms. "But you're going to be much too busy. You have to build that rescue boat and get your business going."

His hand clenched into a fist. "I have to contact Hal. He'll need to appoint a permanent commander."

"He knows that. Faither and he have kept in touch."

"And?" He turned his head to look at her.

She searched his expression. Not even a glimmer of hope in his steady gaze.

"Tell me all of it, Maggie. Don't hold back now."

That shadow lurked in the depths of his eyes again, the dark shadow she had thought long banished.

How could she voice the terrible words that would change his whole future—shatter his world?

Would it be kinder to wait?

No. She felt certain he already knew.

She forced a reply. "He has decided to invalid you oot—give you what he called a 'medical discharge.'"

His eyes clamped closed. The muscles in his jaw bunched into knots. "Beats flying a desk. Hal knows I'd never do that." Voice strangled.

"That's what he told Faither."

No reaction. No shock, no burst of anger, no surprise.

This was the end of a dream he'd nurtured since childhood—a dream that kept him going when his life was devoid of luve or family. Why didn't he cry?

Or lash out in anger?

Or turn to her for comfort?

She climbed onto the bed and laid her cheek on his chest. Would he flee his anguish and disappointment by escaping into that secret hiding place he'd used most of his life? *Och, Faither, don't allow him to do that. Hold onto him, please. This is too much for him to bear when he's been through so much. Help him, please, Lord. Show him his life isn't meaningless without flying.*

She didn't try to placate him with empty words. Just held him.

Rob couldn't sleep.

Couldn't pray.

Mind muddled, he wasn't certain he believed in a God who would allow him to survive, then ground him forever.

Why had he been born? Was life some sort of cosmic joke, controlled by a puppeteer with a fiendish desire to cause suffering?

Orphaned children, fires, exploding bombs, broken hearts and bodies, dashed hopes, the agony of caring too much—or not caring enough—of loss, of despair, of hopelessness.

Couldn't fight any longer.

Hurt too much.

So tired.

Wanted to die. Just take a final breath.

Only a faint scent of heather held him back from the beckoning darkness.

Chapter Twelve

Maggie pounded on the door of the McGrath cottage. "Faither? Faither? Wake up!" *I will not cry. I will not cry.* She threw her shoulder against the warped door, forced it open, and fell into her faither's arms.

"Lass, what is it? What's happened?"

"It's Rob. He's gone away again."

"Gone away? What are you blethering about? Surely he's no' lapsed into another coma?"

"No' a coma, but he won't talk to me or even look at me. He just stares up at the ceiling, his eyes blank."

"'Tis a guid thing I'm still dressed." John grabbed his jacket from its peg and shrugged it on. He led Maggie over the cottage walk, down the path, and up the infirmary steps. "Have you tried clapping your hands, or something to startle him?"

"I even stuck him with a pin. No reaction."

"Och, there must have been brain damage from that skull fracture. How could I have missed it? I'll have to radio our neurologist."

Maggie reeled and clutched at the wall of the foyer. "It isn't physical, Faither, but something worse." A river of tears broke through her dam of resolve, filling her eyes and flooding her cheeks.

John pulled her into his arms, rocking her back and forth. "Hushie-baw, luve, hushie-baw. I need to see Rob."

She sniffled and nodded, accepting his handkerchief.

He supported her arm as they made their way to Rob's room at the end of the corridor.

John moved the bedside table and studied his patient. "Rob?"

Rob lay on his back, right hand fisted at his side, eyes open, face void of expression.

70

Her faither removed a small pen light from his pocket and turned it on, shining the light into one of Rob's eyes, then the other. "Pupils are even and no' dilated. They look normal and he's blinking, so he's no' in a coma."

She handed him the stethoscope.

He pulled down the blanket, moving the diaphragm over Rob's chest. "Heart sounds are normal. No rales in the lungs. Get me that blood pressure cuff." He inflated the cuff and took a reading. "A wee bit lower than yesterday, but no' much." He suddenly clapped his hands in front of Rob's face.

No reaction.

Pinched his right arm.

Again, no reaction.

John's sigh broke the silence. "It has to be related to that skull fracture and coma."

Maggie sat on the side of bed, picking up Rob's clenched hand. "I've told you, 'tisn't his brain. 'Tis his spirit. He's gone away again."

"Och, you said that before. What are you talking about?"

"Did you disremember Rob's parents were killed when he was a wee bairnie, that he grew up in an orphanage?"

"Poor lad."

"Or that he was never adopted because he was too tall, too quiet, too serious? He spent his first sixteen years in a place where he was no' physically abused, but never felt the luve of a family."

"Let's be having it, lass. What are you trying to say?"

She stopped trying to unclench Rob's fingers. "He told me he found a secret place within himself where he could hide when he wanted to be alone—when he hurt too much from rejection, from never belonging to a family. That's why he was so quiet, why he talked so little at the Royal Infirmary."

"Och, Maggie, how could a colonel in the Air Force—a group commander at that—perform his turn if he didn't talk?"

"I mean socially. The only thing that kept him going at that orphanage was his dream of becoming a pilot. And he's been flying ever since he graduated from West Point, an Army university in

America."

"And ...?"

"I told him about him being invalided oot last night—I didn't want to, but he asked, and I'm certain he already guessed."

John collapsed into a nearby chair. "General Fielding warned me to watch him carefully when he was told—that he might stop fighting to live." He put his head in his hands. "I thought he was raising a storm in a teacup."

"What can we do?" Maggie pressed her lips to Rob's hand, fighting the ever-present tears.

"Call Hugh and Elspeth. If this isn't physical, I've no' been trained to deal with it."

Motioning Maggie aside, Elspeth nodded to Hugh. She sat beside Rob, studying his pale face. "Och, our poor laddie. Life has dealt you another wicked blow." She smoothed his hair back from his brow. "But we've talked before about how hiding from pain is never a lasting answer." She rested her palm on his forehead and bowed her head. "Our Heavenly Faither, this lad has given up. He's tired of pain, of fighting to live, of life itself. And, I'm certain he thinks You've abandoned him. But the Holy Spirit lives in his soul, Lord, for he is one of Your children. Search him out, Faither, find his place of false refuge and speak Your words of luve. Only You can show him the life You have planned for him from the beginning of time."

Maggie felt every word go to her core.

Hand steady, Elspeth gently closed Rob's eyes. "Give him a vision, Lord, a vision of a new beginning, as You have done for so many others who have lost hope. I ask this in the name of Your beloved Son, Jesus. Amen."

Hugh led them into the foyer. "Our Rob needs to sleep so the Holy Spirit can do His work. And we need to pray that just one wee spark of fight remains to be kindled."

They dropped to their knees in front of the sofa.

Rob still slept when Hugh and Elspeth took their leave. John walked Elspeth to her cottage, said guidbye to Hugh, and returned to the infirmary for a cup of hot tea.

Maggie tiptoed into Rob's room. He hadn't moved.

His hand still lay at his side.

Fingers relaxed.

No fist.

Thank Ye, Faither, thank Ye for giving me hope.

She didn't waken him by taking his pulse, but counted his respirations. Normal for someone asleep.

His eyes moved beneath closed lids. Dreaming.

I hope You're showing him what lies ahead, Lord. He already knows how the fishermen need a rescue boat, and the lads would benefit from building boats, but I hope You give him a glimpse of what it means to be a faither—with a wife who loves him beyond measure.

She joined her faither in the kitchen. "You'll no' believe this, but his hand is relaxed. He's no' fighting the future anymore."

"Och, thank Ye, Lord." John poured Maggie's tea. "That's verra encouraging."

"It is. And he was dreaming."

"Another guid sign."

Maggie added heather honey and milk to her tea before taking a sip. "We need to talk about how to handle this when he wakes up."

"Handle what?"

"Him going away."

John grimaced "Such a strange expression, but it sums it up nicely."

"I think we should disremember it—never mention it. He took a long nap."

"What happens if he wants to talk about being invalided oot?"

"Then he should."

He reached across the table and took her hand. "Don't be too disappointed if this takes time. I'm no' doubting the Lord's ability to bring him around, but he's been through so much physically and still suffers such pain, it may take a while."

"I know." She drank the last of her tea. "I'm on my way to the pharmacy. I'll have a syringe of morphine ready on the bedside

73

table."

"You should wheel your bed into place and lie down beside him. This has been a verra trying day. If you need me, I'll be in my office."

"You read my mind."

He left.

Maggie washed her face and hands, brushed her hair, and changed into Rob's favorite white nightgown. She prepared a syringe of morphine, took a bottle of saline from the shelf, and made her way to Rob's room.

He was awake, eyes turned toward the door.

She fumbled to keep from dropping everything.

"Maggie. You're ready for bed?"

No tears! Don't let him see how happy you are. She busied herself, breathing deeply as she replaced the empty saline bottle and checked the IV site for blood or seepage. "You took a nap, so I decided to take advantage and sneak away for a wash-up."

"You brushed your hair."

"Of course. How do you feel?"

"Sit beside me and I'll tell you."

She sat on the bed, unable to suppress a hiccup of delight when he tangled his fingers in her hair.

"It's so strange." He twisted a strand around his finger. "One minute you were telling me about my medical discharge, and the next 'tis night."

"'Twas almost een when we were talking. You needed a long nap." She picked up the syringe. "And 'tis past time for your pain medicaments."

"Can we no' bide a wee?"

"You're no' hurting?"

"Nowt I can't take." He knuckled his eyes. "Had the strangest sleep. I know I dreamed, but I don't remember what about, just that it excited me and made me want to jump oot of bed and do something—don't ken what—just something."

A frisson of gratitude to their faithful Saviour sent hen's flesh coursing over her body. "Sounds like a wonderful sleep."

His fingers moved to the base of her jaw, inched up to caress her cheek. "You're going to have to help me when I start feeling sorry for myself, luve. And be patient."

"Of course I will. I ken how much flying means to you, and the minute we have the silver, you're getting a floatplane."

A tear escaped and trickled down his cheek. "Aye. Of course." He suddenly stiffened and tried to sit up.

She pressed him down. "You'll hurt yourself."

He stared at her, eyes wide. "You. When are they calling you back to duty?"

"My discharge is in the works. I'm no' going anywhere."

"Thank Ye, Lord." He pulled her close and buried his face in the hollow of her throat. "Och, my Maggie, I've been so afraid of losing you again."

"Never. You'll have to put up with me forever."

"Like the Selkie and her crofter—forever and ever and ever."

Both their discharges arrived by special post the same day. Rob read Maggie's demobilization papers, his brow raised. "I can't believe the RAF Nursing Service would give you a discharge when nurses are in such short supply."

"Faither arranged it, of course. Though I don't ken how. He must have used every argument he could think of, including me being needed here to nurse you. At least someone in command has a heart."

Rob refused to look at his own discharge. Though a letter from Den arrived the same day, he had her set it aside to read later. Quieter than usual, he lay staring out the window at the sky. Thank the Lord, his cannie Maggie gave him the time and silence he needed for his own private sorrow.

Two weeks later, Rob told Maggie he was ready for Den's letter. "I still can't focus my eyes verra well. Will you read it to me, please?"

"Are you certain? 'Tis addressed to you."

"Biddy certain. Just be prepared. Remember, Den can be a bit crude."

She took the letter from the clothes-press drawer, pulled up a chair beside Rob's bed, and began to read aloud in English.

Bucko, well, leave it to you to go out with a bang and then take the whole thing back. I can tell you, you had us biting our nails for a while. If you weren't so far away, I'd come to that island of yours and knock you alongside the head for scaring the crap out of us.

She blushed.

Just kidding, of course. The news that your demise was greatly exaggerated caused quite a celebration around here.

*You wouldn't recognize the personnel. Hank and Doc Larson are still around, along with several of the crew chiefs and a few of the nurses, but some of the old flight crews have gone on, probably drinking exotic cocktails on some Pacific island, dreaming about the rain and fog and the good old days at the (**CENSORED**).*

You'll be mad as a wet hen to hear you've achieved hero status. Your name is mentioned with reverence and awe and everybody looks at the new commander and wishes the one and only Colonel Rob Savage was piloting the lead plane. Of course, they didn't know the real you. Ha ha. It doesn't help that the new CO flies his desk like a gen-u-ine ace but has only led a few milk runs, despite Wing's prodding and threats to have him replaced.

We're still slamming some of the same old targets and a few new ones. Can't say more or you'll receive a letter full of holes, thanks to those tight-*&& censors. (Hope they choke on their black ink.)

Maggie held the letter close to his face. "I don't understand. What does an asterisk and twa ampersands mean?"

"Don't even try. Just Den getting away with swearing."

"Och." She picked up the letter and continued reading.

One of these days, I'm going to show up on your doorstep loaded down with an armful of medals to pin on you. Wing put you in for the Silver Star and another DFC, plus a third Purple Heart to add to that drawer-full of medals you already have. Didn't know I was keeping company all that time with a real twenty-four carat hero.

Well, briefing is at oh-dark-thirty, so I'd better sign off. Say hello to that beautiful wife of yours and follow her orders so you can start building those—ugh—boats. You realize I'll never forgive you for stealing her away before I even had a chance to meet her. Ciao, Den.

She folded the letter and replaced it in the envelope.

Rob ran a finger over her bonnie face. "Sorry it fashed you, but that was pretty mild for Den. Must have realized I'd want you to read it too. After this war's over, we're going to have to fix him up with some bonnie Scots lass who'll show him life as a bachelor isn't as guid as he thinks."

She pinched his cheek. "You don't look fondly back to the guid auld days when you could kiss a lass guid-een on her door flags and walk away, free and single?"

"I've got what I always wanted." He pulled her close, kissed her deeply, smiling when he raised his head and looked into her eyes. "I'm the luckiest man alive. I have it all and then some."

His sincere words earned him another kiss.

His lips moved slowly beneath hers as he expressed his luve.

When she finally pulled away, they both gasped for breath. "Och, luve, just think, on the morra's morn, you'll have surgery on your left leg and, in a few weeks, on your right. Then we can get you ootside in a wheelchair." She kissed the tip of her finger, and touched it to his lips. "You really should try to sleep. Faither's scheduled your surgery for 0800."

"I'll have plenty of time for sleep afterward. All I want tonight is to feel you close and show you how much I luve you."

"You show it every day."

"Never enough. Never nearly enough." He buried his face in her hair and nuzzled her ear before his lips sought hers again.

Maggie assisted John as three partially healed breaks were re-broken, set, and aligned with metal pins to keep them stable. They cast his leg from above his knee to his toes. Such a long, difficult, physically demanding surgery, but she'd never seen her faither do better.

Rob awakened to find John and Maggie smiling down at him.

Licked his dry lips. "How'd it go?" Words slurred.

"Verra, verra well," John said. "Barring unforeseen complications, that leg should be every bit as strong as it was before."

"That's no' saying much. That's the ... one I limped on, remember?"

"Och, only after running over fifteen kilometres and climbing up the rocks from the strand. You're an impossible man to please."

"Just joking. Thank ye for ... all you've done."

John's smile revealed his good humour. "I know you didn't mean it. I've been around you long enough to know how much you luve to tease."

Rob tried a grin. Mouth wouldn't cooperate. "That's me sorted, then," he mumbled before closing his eyes and giving in to sleep.

No jokes when he came fully awake. Severe pain for several days. He tried hard not to moan, knowing how it upset Maggie. The constant, unrelenting pain wore on him and though he tried, smiling and talking took too much energy.

After a week, the worst over, Rob scratched at the cast nonstop. "There's an itch down by my ankle," he said, "and it's driving me daft. I think it's time to have Angus bring Shep back, if he can bear to part with him. I miss my dog."

Maggie chewed on his words. "He's been asking me to tell him when you've recovered enough. Perhaps it would be better to wait till you're walking well again. We don't want him knocking you over."

"But I miss him."

"Och, I know you do. Let's wait a while longer, at least until your right leg's been operated on. Then, we'll bring him here where he belongs."

"All right." He sighed, obviously disappointed. "I was hoping his tongue might be long enough to reach this itch."

"Och, Rob! I'd offer to bring you a twig to scratch with, but it could break the skin. Why don't I get out your plans for the rescue boat? That should keep your mind off the itch."

"Don't think I can focus that well yet, but we can try." At least he didn't argue.

She brought the plans and a pile of specification sheets he had written the year before. "Can you read it?" She helped him hold the first spec sheet.

"Still a bit blurry, and when I'm in a hurry, my penmanship suffers. Hand me the plans. Mebbe I can read my printing."

She unfurled the first sheet and held it up so he could see.

He studied it carefully. "Och, I can't wait to start building her. It's too bad we have to go through another winter without a rescue boat for Innisbraw."

"Well, this should be the last winter we do, and knowing you, you'll be down at the shed on crutches trying to lay the keel."

"You may be right. Since I won't have to report back to duty next summer, I can't wait to get started."

He still grieved about being invalided oot, but tried so hard to hide it, she sometimes forgot. *Please, Faither, take the pain from his heart and fill it with joy that he has a new life here on Innisbraw.*

Late the following day, as Maggie tucked in Rob's bedding, Malcolm appeared in the doorway, carrying a large box. John followed the skipper, an I've-got-a-secret grin tilting his beard.

"Malcolm, we got something in the post?"

"Patience, lass." John handed her a knife to cut the twine.

Malcolm placed the box on Rob's bedside table. "I promised Hugh I'd take him his post. He's waiting on a shipment of used hymnaries for the sanctuary and they came the day."

Rob tapped the box. "You can't wait to see what's in it?"

"I'll be back later this een." He tipped his cap and walked out, rubber boots squeaking like excited mice on the waxed floor.

"Hurry on, lass," John urged when Maggie fumbled with the twine.

"Och, 'tis so awkward, and besides, this says 'tis from the Royal Infirmary. Shouldn't you open it?"

John took the knife with an impatient "humph," cut the sides of the box, and unwrapped the packing paper, tossing it on the floor.

Inside lay a large, slightly tapered box made of dark wood with a cutout pattern on the front and dials on the right side. "'Tis a Pye wireless radio and it couldn't have come at a better time."

Excitement brought her heart thumping. "'Tis so bonnie."

"You'll notice the dials are a wee bit worn and there are a few scratches, but the auld woman who sold it to my head nurse said she'd had it since long before the war. She's moving in with her auldest lad's family and they already have a wireless."

Rob shot Maggie a smile. "Now you can have that music you've been dying for. And we can listen to the news since I can't make it into John's office to listen to the shortwave."

Maggie threw her arms around her faither and planted a noisy kiss on his cheek. "I can't thank ye enough!" She giggled like a young lass, rubbing his stiff beard-prickles from her lips. "It will fit on the clothes-press and there's a plug on the wall."

Her faither's bushy eyebrows rose. "I'll move it over there if you'll let go of me."

Maggie fidgeted until he had plugged in and turned on.

He rotated the dial.

Her expectant smile faded at the sound of static.

"Are we too far away from Scotland for any reception then?" Rob asked.

"They put up a new relay station in Glasgow last year. Wait, just wait." John turned the dial farther to the right.

They all jumped when a burst of music filled the room. He turned down the volume. "That must be American music." His face puckered like he'd sucked a sour apple. "And what are they singing? I want to hear the news."

"That's *I've Got a Girl in Kalamazoo*." Rob's laugh sounded like it came from his toes. "That *is* American music!"

⁓⁂⁓

Rob ate more than usual, happy for the company when they all took their supper in his room that een so they could listen to the BBC Forces Programme. Malcolm slipped in quietly during the news broadcast, just in time to hear that two hundred twenty-nine B-17s had just bombed Schweinfurt, Germany, on their second raid over the city.

"They were out to destroy their ball bearing plants," Rob said.

John eyed him with amazement. "That many planes just to stop some ball bearings from being manufactured?"

"Without ball bearings, the Nazi war machines would grind to a halt. I just hope our losses weren't too high."

"Is there any way of finding oot?" Maggie asked.

"That'll be classified."

A musical programme followed. "Presented for the enjoyment of the thousands of Yank troops stationed in England," the moderator announced with pride.

Rob studied Maggie's face while she listened to "April in Paris" and Artie Shaw's rendition of "Stardust." Bemused smile, faraway look in her eyes.

Malcolm never stopped grinning, but John showed little animation until the last tune. He finally tapped his toes to the syncopated rhythm of Duke Ellington's "A Train."

⁂

Rob underwent surgery on his right leg two weeks later and a second shoulder surgery three weeks after that. Though successful, both surgeries left him in pain for days. The cumbersome metal and plaster brace John rigged for his shoulder interfered with sleep, but he gritted his teeth and carried on, praying constantly for the courage to get through this with the least possible complaining. He would do anything needed to have unhindered mobility when this ordeal ended.

Once John cut back on the morphine, nightmares seldom interrupted what little sleep he could manage, but he often lay awake for hours, fighting gelid thoughts of a future without flying, threatening to encase him in icy darkness like a loch 'neath a smothering blanket of snow. Only prayer and concentrating on Maggie's soft breath, light as the murmur of a far-off burn, brought solace from his grief.

Chapter Thirteen

A bright surge of laughter woke Rob from a light sleep. He rubbed the scar on his forehead and reached for a glass of water.

"Did you have a nice nap?" Maggie asked, laughter trailing her through the door. She took the glass from his hand and lifted his right shoulder so he could drink. "Don't want you slubbering all over your covers."

A wave of excited voices wafted down the hallway.

Her smile widened. "'Some of the womenfolk have brought Yule decorations. Sorry we were so noisy."

Surely, he heard her wrong. "Yule decorations?"

Her laugh reminded him of sleigh bells. "Don't act so surprised. 'Twill soon be what you Americans call Christmas. Scotland, as well as the other Western Isles' kirks, don't celebrate the season openly, but Hugh says 'tis the birth of Christ that led to His sacrifice on the cross, so on Innisbraw we always do." She sat beside him, smile fading. "I thought you'd be pleased. Remember all the ribbons and tinsel in hospital and the chow hall at Edenoaks?"

He mentally kicked himself. Time for another uncomfortable revelation from his past. "I've never seen many Yule decorations."

She frowned. "Why?"

"Och, Newton had a Christmas tree in the village square, and ribbons on some front doors, but the orphanage never had the silver for such things."

"But surely you bairns made paper decorations."

"Not that I can remember. Mister Pointer read the story of the Christ Child's birth from the Bible on Yule Een, and everybody got a cup of hot cocoa made with evaporated milk—a yearly treat—but that was all. I've luved the taste of evaporated milk ever since."

"When rationing ends, I'll order some Cadbury's cocoa and tins of evaporated milk."

"Probably won't taste the same. You know how we men are, always dreaming about the guid auld days."

She smoothed the forelock back from his forehead. "Then I've made you dreariful, no' happy." The light in her eyes winked out.

"No." He took her hand. "I've always wanted to see how the Yule was celebrated where silver was no' so tight. Tell me about these decorations."

"You're certain?"

"Biddy certain. Come on. What had you all laughing like a crib full of hens?"

She leaped up. "I'll no' tell you, I'll show you." She raced from the room and returned moments later, arms laden. She dropped everything on his bed and held up the first item. "This is one of the garlands they made from branches of fir trees around the kirk. They've strung holly berries for a bit of colour."

He fingered the soft needles, bringing it close so he could inhale the biting fragrance. "Where do they put them?"

"Around doorways and over windows." She laid the garland down and showed him a stack of cut paper.

"Those must be snowflakes."

She held up several different shapes. "Aye. They're cut from used, ironed paper. We'll Sellotape them to the windows." She picked up a red bow. "And these have been used for years, carefully laid aside in a dark place so the sunlight won't pull the colour from them." Her eyes sparkled again.

"Thank ye for showing me, luve." He pulled her close for a kiss.

⚓

Several days later, Rinait MacPhee, Angus and Flora's only lass, brought him a bright red woven scarf. Her face matched the colour when she shoved it into his hands and fled the room.

"What's the matter?" Rob asked. "I didn't get a chance to thank her. She worked hard on this."

"Och, Rob, surely you ken the lass fancies you."

"What? I'm almost auld enough to be her faither. Don't talk daft."

She framed his face with her palms. "You'll never believe how braw you are, luve. Half the lasses on the island and a few of the grown women are smitten with you."

He stared at her, mouth open. "You have got to be kidding. I just turned thirty and I'm a verra happily merrit man. Come on, Maggie, awn up. You're kidding, right?"

"I'm serious. 'Tis the way of life, luve. Lasses always take a fancy to what they can't have."

"Women." He groaned. "I'll never understand them."

"I don't care if you understand women, as long as you understand how much I luve you."

"I mean it, Maggie. Just thinking about it puts me in a fash."

"Why? Because someone finds you attractive? And stop rubbing that scar on your forehead. It won't go away and it makes you even more braw. If I'm no' bothered by how the lasses feel, why should you be? You're verra guid-looking, you've a fine body, you're kind and giving, and you have put yourself in harm's way countless times to protect others." She stepped back. "There, I've said it. Have I committed the unpardonable sin, or do you still luve me?" Splotches of red coloured her cheeks, her blue eyes sparkled like moonlight on the Minch, and her chest rose and fell rapidly.

He groaned. "Och, Maggie, you're driving me daft. And there's no' a thing I can do about it!"

She tumbled into bed next to him and smothered his face with kisses. "You can kiss me."

⚓

Rob fretted. Yule was only days away and he had nothing to give Maggie. John assured him that Malcolm could pick up a gift in Oban if Rob would tell him what to buy. He thought long and hard before deciding.

Malcolm delivered it the night before Yule Een.

"Thank ye, Malcolm. Someday I hope I can repay you for all of your help."

"Och, 'tis my pleasure. I'd give tuppence to see her face when you give her this."

"No' a chance. This is for one of those private moments."

"I hear they're having a Yule party here on the morra's een. Sim and me are laying over, so we'll see you then."

"See you, Malcolm, and thank ye again." Rob looked down at the small box, pulse racing. Pray God Maggie liked it.

The following day the infirmary buzzed with activity when womenfolk brought more garlands, ribbons, and sweets. As they decorated Rob's room, he lay back and soaked in their happy blether.

Morag MacDonald placed candles on his bedside table. "Made these myself to sweeten your dreams. 'Tis said the scent of heather is soothing to the soul." She lit the candles before she left the room.

Their fragrance brought to mind the scent lingering on Maggie's hair and skin from the soap Elspeth made.

Maggie came in, buried behind an armload of dried flowers. "Bridget MacNab dropped these off. They're from her garden and they've been hanging to dry from her clothes-drying racks so she could brighten your room for the Yule."

"I've never imagined a luve like our folk express. I had no idea it even existed."

She arranged the flowers so he could see them from his bed. "Are you ready for your first trip in the wheelchair?"

"More than ready, but I'm afraid 'tis going to take five grown men to lift me. These casts on my legs must weigh a hundred stone, and I can't help much with my arm trussed up like a cuddy in the traces."

"Mebbe no' five, but Angus and Malcolm are just waiting for the word. And I have to say, you look verra braw in your new dressing gown."

"I appreciate John finding one during rationing and giving it to me early. I was dreading going to the party in that one I borrowed from the infirmary last time I was here. It didn't even come to my knees."

"It was a wee bit short."

"Thank ye for wearing your hair down." He nibbled on her

fingers. "I won't need any sweets this een. I'll just feast on you."

She leaned over and kissed him—long and hard. "That's not till later."

Teasing minx.

Her blue eyes danced and her lips were so inviting he had to fight himself to keep from pulling her into bed. Her glorious hair cascaded down her blue sweater to below her waist. Clad in a long, grey-blue plaid skirt, she looked so bonnie, so warm, so luving.

"Are you ready? Everybody is here."

"I'm ready."

The transfer into the wheelchair brought several groans, but the pain diminished as Maggie pushed him down the hall to the foyer. A large peat fire glowed in the fireplace. Yule decorations brightened the large room. Elspeth, Hugh, Malcolm, and Alice Ross—the island's postmistress and midwife—sat on the sofa.

The chairs pulled in from around the infirmary were all occupied. The MacPhee family, Alec and Morag MacDonald, fisherman Tormad MacKinnon and his Anna and wee Kaitlin, and Mark and Susan Ferguson all smiled greetings.

One auld brother-sister pair, Christina and Fergus MacCrae, he had not seen since his return to Innisbraw. The woman, body and limbs terribly crippled in an accident when she was a young lass, sat in the homemade chair Fergus had fashioned to accommodate her twisted spine.

Rob asked Maggie to wheel his chair closer, nodded his greeting to Fergus, and cradled one of the woman's misshapen hands in his own. "Fàilte, Cairistiona, Nollaig chrìdheil," he said in the Gaelic, her only language. He looked at Maggie. "Please translate for me. I don't have enough of the Gaelic no' to offend her."

"You have made this a truly grand night with your presence," she translated from his Scots after he spoke the words.

Christina's clouded blue eyes twinkled as she withdrew her hand and poked his arm with a bent finger. "Don't waste your sweet words on a wrinkled old prune like me." Her smile faded and she raised a twisted hand to his cheek, patting it awkwardly. "May our loving Faither continue to heal your body and spirit. You are in our prayers every morning and een."

After Maggie finished translating, Rob had no words. This sweet auld woman had suffered more pain, both physical and emotional, in her lifetime than anyone he had ever known. He wanted to ask her how she could live with the constant pain, her childhood dreams shattered, without giving up—but now was not the time. Though well into her eighties, her beauty still shone beneath her finely-lined, pale skin. He imagined how hard it had been to never feel the caress of a luver or husband, never cradle her own bairnies, never walk through the wildflowers on the machair or down the path to visit a neighbor. Thank God she had her younger brother who saw to her every need and had acted as her sole caretaker since their parents died.

Paddy McDonald, the island's only Irisher, had bought and refurbished the howff the year before. He and his musical lads stood by the front door, instruments at the ready. John signaled and they began a rollicking tune on the bodhran, penny whistle, pipes, guitar, and button accordion. Everyone rose to greet Rob and wish him a Guid Yule.

Overcome, Rob choked back tears.

A helper at the orphanage had once told him not to worry about finding a family of his own, that the Lord was preparing a very special family and he had to be patient. He wished he could thank her for her prescient words. Though it took years of loneliness and longing, his childhood prayers had finally been answered. He had a family.

Angus stepped outside and returned with a magnificent blue merle Australian shepherd wearing a large red ribbon around his neck.

"Shep!" Rob called.

The dog froze for a moment, sniffing the air. Then he bounded to Rob's side and licked Rob's face and hands, whining and wagging his plumed tail so fast it blurred.

Rob buried his face in the shepherd's fur. "Och, Shep, 'tis so ... guid to see you."

The dog looked up at his master's face, licked his chin, then circled and lay down at the foot of the wheelchair, heaving a deep sigh.

Rob rubbed the side of his nose. "Sorry to take him back from you, Angus, after all this time."

The crofter grinned and shrugged his shoulders. "Och, he's a fine dog, even if he was whelped with a long tail instead of a bob. I was just remembering how the pup followed you everywhere when you were learning to walk. 'Tis a bond made in Heaven itself."

The festivities began in earnest. Elspeth told a story in the Gaelic about the traditional Yule Een celebrations of years long past, with Maggie translating the words Rob did not yet understand. Anna MacKinnon and Susan Ferguson sang a Yule carol. Graham MacKay played "Silent Night" on the pipes. Hot, spicy tea and plates of scones, shortbread, sair heidies—small, iced sponge cakes—and tablet appeared from the kitchen.

Maggie sat beside Rob, feeding him bites of sweets and helping him balance his mug. Someone, either Maggie or Morag, had even made him coffee.

He didn't eat much. The medicaments for pain diminished his appetite. But this was his first ever genuine Christmas party and he didn't want to miss a thing. He dropped his right hand to his side and snapped his fingers.

Shep's wet, cold nose pressed into his palm.

A lump choked his throat. Was there any finer feeling?

As the hour grew late, Hugh read the story of the first Yule from the book of Matthew. They all sang carols, ending with "Auld Lang Syne" in the Gaelic, and everyone joined hands as Hugh offered a prayer for the coming year.

By the time they all said their guidbyes and departed, Rob, limp with exhaustion and the throbbing pain in his left shoulder, sagged in his chair.

When John, Malcolm, and Angus retired to the kitchen for another cup of tea, Maggie pulled on her coat, wrapped two blankets around Rob, and wheeled him out onto the broad, stone-flagged entry, closing the door so quickly she almost trapped Shep's tail.

A cold, clear night.

"Let me turn you to see the Aurora Borealis."

Rob gazed at the dancing horizon, undulating waves of intense green and purple and teasing glimpses of yellow filling the sky.

"Being a member of this family of Innisbraw folk is a heavy responsibility," he said, rubbing Shep's soft ruff. "I've never seen a more luving, more serving group of people in my whole life. I doubt they exist anywhere else."

She kissed his cheek. "Then you're right where you belong."

"Pray God I'm worthy."

"Don't start that, Rob Savage."

He looked up at the sky, awash with stars. "I wish you could be up in the air with me on a night like this. 'Tis magical, especially when you're flying over countryside dotted with sma' villages. The stars above and the lights below sparkle like a thousand candles lit by the hand of God."

"We'd best get you inside. You didn't eat much the night so I know you're hurting." Her voice sounded thick, as though she were fighting back tears.

"Och, 'tis the morphine. Kills my appetite."

"I ken that. But I can also tell you're in pain. This is your first time in a wheelchair, and 'twas far longer than Faither and I expected. I don't want you to suffer all the night."

The pain in his shoulder stabbed with each beat of his heart, but he didn't want to miss a moment of this special een. He glanced up at the sky one more time before looking out at the Minch. "I can hear the sea sooking on the shore. 'Tis a soothing sound. I never in a million years imagined I'd be living on a wee island and thinking it was a bit of Heaven."

Another spasm of pain. His fingers tightened around the arm of the wheelchair.

She took the handles and pushed the wheelchair toward the doorway. "I'm giving you a shot of morphine before you're transferred to bed. You're going to need it."

He didn't argue.

By the time the three men had Rob back in bed, exhaustion drained the last of his energy.

Maggie settled Shep onto a blanket in the corner and bathed

Rob's face, right arm, and hand in cool water before climbing up on the bed and cuddling him. "Is it any better, luve?" she asked, soft fingers stroking his cheek.

"Much better." He pulled her closer. "You can't imagine how much the night meant to me. Having Shep back, the music, the fellowship—all of it."

"I'm afraid it was too much or your shoulder wouldn't be hurting, but you're mistaken if you think I don't ken how much you enjoyed it. It's been a long time since I've seen you smile so much."

His fingers sought her hair. "Sing me to sleep, Maggie, like you have so many times."

She nestled her cheek against his chest and sang the Selkie's luve song. The final words of the Selkie tale echoed in his mind.

"And they lived on their wee island in the sea, forever and ever and ever ..."

He sank into the soft, downy feathers of sleep.

Chapter Fourteen

"How much longer do I have to wear this contraption?" Rob scowled at the brace holding his arm out from his side. "I'm thinking having it on is what caused the pain last night."

John sat on the side of the bed. "It wasn't the brace, but being out of bed so long. Don't disremember, your shoulder's been patched with metal plates and screws, and you've most likely built up scar tissue around the work we did. Having your arm immobile hasn't given you the opportunity to break down the scar tissue with exercise, but in about twa weeks we can get rid of the brace and start some therapy. By the time your shoulder's in guid shape, you should be through the final surgery on your left leg and be ready for crutches."

"How long are we talking about before I can start leading a normal life?"

"Och, I don't know, lad."

"How about a best-case, worst-case scenario. Can you do that?"

John steepled his fingers. "So far, you've made an amazing recovery. I'd say, barring complications we can't foresee, six to nine months before you're in the same shape you were in before the crash—no' an outcome I'd have predicted a few months ago."

"So, you're saying in six months or less, I can start building muscle and endurance again?"

"That sounds about right."

Another six months. He could do that—but not nine. "I can handle that, though I was hoping the timetable would be a bit shorter. I hate to see Innisbraw go any longer without a rescue boat, but Maggie may be right. I could be on crutches laying the keel."

"I expect you to accommodate yourself to my timetable when it

91

comes to therapy, no' yours." He used his *doctor's* voice.

"You give the orders and I'll follow them. I might question them occasionally, but you're the commander here." Facing his faither-in-law, Rob gave a sharp salute.

That night, Rob called Maggie over to the bed before she left to have her bath. "I hope I didn't ruin your Yule by hurting so much. I gave John his gift this afternoon, but I haven't had a chance to give you yours."

"Since when have you had an opportunity to go shopping?"

The delicate arches of her raised eyebrows reminded him of wild rose stems bending 'neath morning dew. "Santa had a helper this year. Och, I disremembered, he's Faither Christmas here. Anyways, he had a helper."

"And just what did this mysterious helper bring?"

"Bathe yourself, then you'll see." He tapped the tip of her nose. "Get to it, lass."

"Well, my Faither Christmas didn't need a helper, but he left a present for you too."

"Did he? I thought bringing Shep back was my present."

"I already gave him to you once, when he was a wee pup. 'Tis something else, but if I'm to bathe myself first, you'll just have to wait." Soft fingers trailed his cheek before she hurried out.

He lit the heather-scented candles on his bedside table with the cigarette lighter Morag had thoughtfully left behind. Matches would have been difficult to manage one-handed. He turned out the bedside lamp and waited for his Maggie, eagerly watching the doorway.

At last. She slipped inside, wearing his favorite white gown and a smile radiant as a summer's full moon. Her hair spilled down her back, sparkling in the candlelight like a fall of dark, cascading water. "Guid Yule." She handed him a large box tied with a red ribbon.

He patted the bed. "Up you come."

She sat beside him.

He placed a small box in her lap. "Guid Yule to you." He pulled her close for a kiss. She smelled even sweeter than the candles.

Shy, hesitant smile. "You go first. I hope you're no' disappointed."

"Don't ever say that. Owt from you will be a treasure."

"'Tis just something I made."

"Then, even more the treasure." He untied the bow, opened the lid, and pulled out an ecru sweater with finely executed stitches. "You knit this for me? When?" He held it up and looked at it in the flickering candlelight. "The blackout curtains are closed so turn on the lamp, lass. I want to look at the designs. I've never seen owt like this."

She snapped on the lamp. "'Tis called a gansey, a fisherman's sweater, with cable and seed and purl stitches. This is what our fishermen wear to keep warm in winter. I thought you could wear it when you're working in the shed."

"Working? Never. 'Tis much too fine to wear to work."

"But that's what it's for. 'Tis made of wool I spun before I left Innisbraw—before nursing school. The wool comes from Innisbraw sheep. You can't hurt it. It's practically indistruct—"

He silenced her with another kiss, heart swelling with gratitude. His Maggie loved him enough to spend hours knitting him this bonnie sweater.

"Then I'll wear it to work with pride. When did you make this? I never saw you knitting."

"I took the yarn and needles with me to Edenoaks and worked on it when you were at those long night meetings with Hal. You almost caught me a few times. Once you came in so quietly I had to hide it 'neath the mattress on our cot." That teasing smile. "I feared you'd feel the needles poking through that thin pad they called a mattress."

He held the sweater to his face and inhaled deeply. "I thought so. It has the slight reek of peat."

"That's from dipping the wool in peat water and onion skins to give it that natural colour. Do you mind?"

"You know how I luve the sweet, smoky reek of peat."

Her laugh sent candle flickers dancing. "'Tis a guid thing we

93

no longer use the auld way of dying wool to get that colour."

"And what was the auld way?"

"I'm no' sure you want to hear."

"Maggie ..."

She wrinkled her nose. "Men's urine."

He stared at her in disbelief. Slowly, grimace turned to grin. "You're right. I wouldn't want to go around reeking like a bed pot." He brushed his lips across her flaming cheek. "Now, 'tis your turn."

She eyed the small box in her lap.

"Leave the lamp on. You'll need it."

She opened the box—and drew in a deep breath. Inside lay an intricately woven Celtic ring with a small area of solid gold, four letters engraved into the smooth surface. She held it up to the light. "M.H.B.S. No' our initials. What does it mean?"

He took her right hand and slid the jewelry onto her ring finger. "Mind, heart, body, and soul—all the ways I luve you."

Tears transformed her eyes into glittering stars. "'Tis so bonnie. Every time I look at it, I'll remember this een—and your luve."

"Och, Maggie, my Maggie, how I luve you."

Two weeks later John removed the wire cage elevating Rob's left arm and replaced it with a soft sling to wear when not exercising his shoulder.

Rob celebrated by eating three large bowls of tattie bree and four pieces of bannock.

"I've never seen an appetite like yours," John said. "But then, I've never had a patient as tall as you. The average man is about five-eight."

"Six-five isn't really all that tall." Rob sipped his coffee. "I had a classmate at the Point who was over six-seven."

"'Tis tall enough. Now, the main reason I wanted to see you is to give you the approximate timetable you can expect for the next few months."

Rob ducked his head. "Does this mean you're going back to Edinburgh? I feel guilty keeping you here so long."

"I've done what I wanted to do, lad, including treating many of the island's folk. But you're right, I must get back to Edinburgh. You and Maggie will continue with the therapy on your shoulder." He pulled a small calendar from his pocket. "Let's see, this is January 15. I'd say we plan on the mids of February for the final left leg surgery. Your right leg will be healed by then and, if the bones have knit properly in your left and I'm able to remove the pins, we should have you up on crutches by early spring."

"My shoulder will be up to it by then?"

John nodded. "You realize that shoulder will always be the weakest of your joints, the most easily re-injured?"

"You've told me that."

"Remember you may require additional surgery sometime in the future."

Rob suppressed a groan. Another surgery. "I hope it's after I'm walking again."

"It should be years away. Just something I can't rule out completely."

⚓

John's departure brought changes. Elspeth resumed teaching Rob the Gaelic, the ancient language of Scotland which was spoken by everyone on the island. And every day, one or more of the islanders dropped by for a visit.

Alec MacDonald walked into Rob's room without Morag, who had always accompanied him.

"Coos give you the mornin off?" Rob grinned at the thought of a guid blether with a friend.

Alec threw himself into a chair with a grunt. "Och, this isn't a social visit. Is Maggie no' about?"

"Since 'tis no' raining, she's oot pulling up some of the dead plants in her garden at the cottage. You look like you just took a bite of green apple. What's wrong?"

"'Tis those U-boats. I just got a message from the RAF radio operator at Benbecula warning us to double our guards on the shore every night. Their patrol planes have reported more sightings of U–boats much closer to the western shores of the Hebrides than usual."

Och, Rob had forgotten all about the crofters who patrolled the western shores of the island every night, searching the sea for even a tiny blink of light that could mean a German U-boat had surfaced. It wasn't right that Barra and other larger islands to their north had an armed, trained Home Guard while Innisbraw, with its population of few more than two hundred, had been deemed too small.

He pulled another pillow beneath his head so he could sit up higher. "Can you do that? Do you have enough men?"

"Of course no'. We'll have to lengthen the hours they spend on guard from four to at least six. 'Twill mean most of our crofters going around sleeperie all the day." He ran a hand over his face. "At least 'tis still winter so they're no' as busy."

"But why would the Jerries want to invade a sma' island like Innisbraw?"

"The lad who called didn't think they would, but he was under orders to warn every island."

"If only I could help." Rob slapped the bed.

"Just warn Maggie about the blackout curtains. The infirmary's on the Minch side of the island, but who knows? They could sneak around the south end of Innisbraw and into our harbour if they could find a way around the rocks 'neath the sea."

"I know it doesn't help now, but as soon as I'm able, add me to your list of guards."

Alec got up and stretched, back popping. "You just get well. I didn't mean to fash you, but I did promise to tell everybody on the island, so I'd best be on my way."

Maggie, working at the soil caught beneath her nails with the blade of a small paring knife, came into his room soon after.

He shared the news and gazed out the window. "This explains something that's had me puzzled."

"What?"

"Why I've been hearing twa airieplanes crossing the island every night instead of the usual one. The Isles of Benbecula and Tiree must have doubled their air patrols."

"Airieplanes? What airieplanes?"

"You haven't heard them, then?"

"No' a sound." She put the knife on the bedside table and took off her shoes, climbing onto the bed. "I don't want you fashed about this. There's no reason to think they'll shell us or try to land on our shores. We have nowt of value for them to destroy."

Surely, she was right, but the poor crofters, slogging through the pishing rain and gale-force winds when they should be abed.

Sleep came hard that night. *Och, Faither, protect this sma' island, please. Life is hard enough for our folk without having them in a fash about being invaded.*

Chapter Fifteen

Though eager for the final surgery on his left leg, Rob had a new worry—Maggie. She acted sleepy, often needing a nap in the afternoon. This lengthy ordeal was too hard on her. Good thing John returned to the island on the fourteenth of February, accompanied by his medical team.

"It isn't like you to be so tired," Rob said to Maggie, using his commander's tone. "Have you been sneaking around and treating patients you haven't told me about?"

"Och, no. And I'm no' tired, just sleeperie." She sat on the bed and took his hand. "There's something I need to tell you, but I'm a bit afraid how you'll take it."

"What is it, luve?"

Her hand trembled.

His stomach cramped.

"You're no' sick are you? Och, Maggie, tell me now. We'll face it together—whatever it is."

She ducked her head, bright spots of colour staining her cheeks. Her body shook. "You're going to be a faither." Her breathy whisper resounded like a shout.

"You're biggen? We're going to have a bairnie?"

"Aye. Faither confirmed what I've been suspecting for over a month. We're going to have a bairnie."

Maggie was biggen. "Over a month? Why didn't you tell me?"

"I wasn't certain ... and we didn't plan on having one so soon."

He slipped his left arm out of the sling and pulled her into his arms. "Och, Maggie, Maggie, we're going to be a family, a real family." Tears filled his eyes as he smothered her face and hair with kisses. "I luve you so much."

She buried her face against his chest.

After all the years of fearing he would never have a family of his own, the Lord had finally deemed it time. "I know when our bairnie was conceived," he choked, rubbing his cheek over her hair. "On Yule Day, right after we exchanged presents."

"Our Lord had a present for both of us."

"The greatest present He could give." He stiffened. "You can't do any more lifting, and you need to get more rest and—"

She stifled his words with her palm. "Women have been birthing bairnies for centuries. 'Tis a perfectly natural occurrence, and it doesn't require any special changes in the way we live."

"This isn't just any bairnie. 'Tis ours. Please promise you'll take care of yourself."

"All right, Faither." She kissed the tip of his nose. "I'll be a guid lass."

He let out a whoop of joy. "Faither! I'm going to be a faither!"

⁕

Rob's surgery took longer than expected and John ordered Maggie out of the OR when her stomach rebelled. She waited outside in the hall, pacing and looking at her watch until her faither came out.

"He's doing fine." He removed his mask and cap and scratched his beard. "It took longer than anticipated because we decided to replace the pin in his ankle with one we'll leave in permanently. That leg has been weaker since he injured his back that first time and it needs all the support we can give it."

Her hands clenched. "Will he be able to walk?"

"Of course. And run. Cold weather may stiffen it a bit, but knowing Rob, that won't slow him down."

Thank Ye, Lord, thank Ye. She threw her arms around him. "What wonderful news. He went into surgery in such guid spirits, I couldn't bear to dash his hopes of living a normal life."

"You won't have to." He returned her hug, then held her away. "Now, little mither, we're about to take him back to his room. He'll sleep for a while, but I know your face will be the first he wants to see when he opens his eyes."

Price

During the first week of April, smoke drifted in through the open window. "Maggie, do you smell that?" Rob lifted his head from the pillow. "Should we sound an alarm?"

Maggie flashed a teasing smile. "They're only burning the heather on Ben Innis, so you've nowt to worry about."

"Burning it? But why would they do that?"

"They burn the auld bushes every April to give the new green shoots room to grow and our men an opportunity to gather the long, auld branches for cottage thatch. In Scotland, they burn their heather-covered bens in strips so the capercailie chicks will have the auld growth for cover and the adults can eat the new, tender, green leaves."

"Capercailie?"

"'Tis a kind of grouse, large, and said to be verra tasty. 'Tis hunted all over the Hielands."

"But isn't burning the heather dangerous? Our soil's so peaty, couldn't it put the whole island afire?"

"They keep a close watch on it. 'Tis done every year, so you'll just have to get used to it."

Burned to promote new growth. Was this what the Lord had done for him? Allowed testing in the fiery furnace so he could grow spiritually?

By the middle of the month, Rob felt like he was taxiing down the runway, ready for wheels-up. The old transfer bars were installed on his bed, and with only one short cast on his left leg, he pulled himself in and out of the wheelchair with little help.

Though his shoulder still ached after a difficult bout of therapy, it strengthened daily. Spirits soaring, he chafed to use crutches but followed John's written orders, spending as much time as the weather allowed out on the entry, going over the lists of lumber, hardware, and other supplies needed to build the rescue boat.

Every night, when he and Maggie cuddled in bed, he touched her swelling belly and marveled that their bairnie was growing larger and stronger. The first time he felt movement beneath his palm, he choked up and kissed her belly. "Our bairnie. Our wee bairnie."

⚜

On the tenth of May, John returned to Innisbraw with a new set of metal crutches. "These are lighter and stronger than the auld wooden ones," he told Rob. "Also, they have wide bands that encircle your arms rather than padded rests beneath your armpits. These will put less pressure on your shoulders."

"When can I start?"

"No' so fast, lad. I need to remove that cast on your left leg and then you'll have to practice walking on the parallel bars. When you can manoeuver yourself to my satisfaction, I'll give you the crutches, no' before."

Once the cast was removed, though still weak from so much time spent in bed, Rob worked diligently on the bars. Unlike after his first crash, it was only a matter of strengthening his pale, wasted legs, not learning to walk. And his knees and left ankle only ached after bending them.

By the time John returned to Edinburgh four days later, Rob could use the crutches with ease.

The next Sabbath, Angus took them in his cairt to services at the kirk for the first time since their return to Innisbraw. With Maggie's pregnancy obvious, teary eyes and smiles followed them as they made their way up the aisle toward their pew.

Rob tucked his dressing gown more securely over his pyjamas—och, worn not only in public, but in the house of the Lord—and averted his eyes anytime somebody looked at him.

Hugh took his place at the lectern, elfin smile accenting his round cheeks. "Maggie, will you please translate what I am saying into Scots so Rob can understand every word?"

She shot Rob a smile and nodded.

"Dearest folk of Innisbraw," he began in the Gaelic. "Today we rejoice in the return of our Rob and our Maggie. Though he has been through far more than any mortal should ever have to endure, our Rob has persevered. He asked me yesterday to convey to you his deepest gratitude for your prayers, both for he and Maggie. And now they eagerly await the birth of their first baby." He paused for a moment.

Maggie caught up in the translation.

Hugh looked directly at Rob. "I wish to say something to you, Rob. We celebrate your return to our midst and thank our Lord for bringing you back to us alive and for healing your broken body. But we also want to thank you for choosing to become a member of the Innisbraw family, and for showing courage and an intrepid spirit when faced with unimaginable pain. It is with grateful and glad hearts we welcome you into our family, Rob Savage. You are truly one of us and we are all richer for it."

Chapter Sixteen

Shep pressed his nose against Rob's leg, tail thumping on the entry's stone flags.

"What is it, lad? Hear a creature you're wanting to chase?" Rob picked up the sketch of a gift he planned to make for Maggie and slipped it into his dressing gown pocket before she could return from the kitchen. He didn't get much time away from her watchful eyes.

Shep whined and nosed his hand.

"Och, 'tis the gloamin'—most likely a rabbit seeking a guid hiding place before night. See how dark the water of the Minch—"

The rumble of cairt wheels interrupted his musings.

Shep leaped to his feet and dashed for the path as Angus pulled up in front of the infirmary.

Why was Malcolm seated beside the crofter? Rob grabbed his crutches and made his way out to the path.

Two large boxes rode in the back of the cairt.

"Hoy, ye!" he hailed.

"Hoy, yersel'!" they called in unison as they climbed down from the bench.

"Didn't expect delivery on those used tools I ordered so soon, or did Maggie order supplies I don't know about?"

"No supplies, and I don't think these boxes have your tools in them." Malcolm walked to the rear of the cairt and hefted one box. "Too light."

"Who are they from?"

"The return address is Edenoaks Air Base, England."

Rob's grin evaporated. Edenoaks. Just what he needed, another reminder of all he'd lost. "Sorry you rushed them up here. Just some auld things to put into storage."

"Are they now?" Malcolm eyed the size of the boxes. "Are you biddy certain? Could be you have a friend at this Edenoaks who's sent you a present. Mebbe you should open them and have a keek before we put them in the storage room."

"Don't need a keek."

"Best no' put anything in storage till you know what it is," Angus said.

"Blast it for a soldier, I don't want a keek!" Instant remorse clenched Rob's throat. Och, why had he lashed out at two friends who had come out of their way to do him a favor? "I'm sorry, Angus, I didn't mean to talk to you like that. 'Tis just some things from the past." He tightened his hands on his crutches. It wasn't fatigue making them tremble.

Malcom stared at him, open-mouthed.

Angus shuffled his feet. "'Tis all right. They're your boxes. If you want them in the storage room, that's where we'll put them."

Remorse turned to shame, shame to guilt. He beckoned them closer. "I owe you both an explanation."

They looked as if they were about to protest.

He held up his hand. "Please. Hear me oot." What should he say? How much should he tell them? Despite the pain he would face, he had stepped way over the line this time.

Malcolm nodded. "'Course, lad."

"I've dreamt of flying since I was a lad, and I spent the last twelve years of my life eating, sleeping, and breathing flying." He took a deep breath and plowed on, voice thickened with tears. "Because of my last plane crash, that part of my life is over forever." He looked up at the sky, fighting to control his grief. "'Tis hard to give it up. Those boxes contain everything I collected over the years. Manuals on Air Tactics, pictures of my auld airieplanes and crews, uniforms, letters from auld friends who had died—all reminders of what I've lost. I want to disremember it. 'Tis all in the past." He lowered his gaze.

Malcolm squeezed Angus's arm. "You know that cooling shed behind John's cottage?"

"Aye, 'tis where the wee burn runs through, where he keeps things what have to be cold, like milk, butter, and such. We have one jest like it."

"I'm certain he has a few pints of ale in there. Be a guid lad and fetch three. Some things a man has to give up should be sent on their way properly. We're going to toast Rob's past."

A glow of warmth infused Rob's body. "Malcolm, my friend, that's the best idea I've heard in a long time."

Angus returned in a flash.

The three men sat on the entry railing, opening their ale.

Rob raised his bottle. "Here's to friends and comrades, past and present."

"Slàinte mhath," the other two men said in unison before taking a swig.

"Here's to never knowing if you're coming back in one piece, but never quitting," Malcolm said.

They repeated the old Gaelic toast.

"Here's to a war those Krauts will never win," Angus exclaimed. "Slàinte!"

Maggie appeared in the infirmary doorway when they were down to the last swig.

Rob raised his pint. "Here's tae us!"

"Wha's like us?" Angus shouted.

"Gey few, and they're a' deid!" Malcolm roared, finishing Robbie Burn's age-old toast.

They gave a hearty "Slàinte" and drained their bottles.

Maggie's smile made Rob's breath catch as she hugged his shoulder. "What's all the shouting about? I heard you from the kitchen."

"Just friends hoisting a pint. Bless Malcolm for thinking of it."

"Would these friends care to share supper also? There's galore."

Angus leaped to his feet. "Och, Flora will dunt me on the head for being late to our own supper." He looked at Malcolm. "Where do we put the boxes?"

Rob winked at the skipper. "Put them in my room if you will. I misspoke before. There's some clothes I know I can use."

"Your room it will be." The skipper grinned as he and Angus

each lifted a box and carried it into the infirmary.

Maggie poked his chest. "You got boxes in the post and didn't call me?"

"'Tis the rest of my things from Edenoaks. We'll go through them after supper."

⚜

Once Maggie finished the supper dishes, Rob grabbed his crutches and pulled himself to his feet. "I know we usually spend our eens oot on the entry, but I'd like to tackle those boxes. I could use some clothes. Wearing pyjamas and a dressing gown to kirk fair fashed me, and I've been looking forward to using my binoculars—if they packed them."

Once in the room, Maggie studied Rob as he eyed the boxes. She took his face between her palms and looked into his eyes.

That dark shadow of pain bloomed in their depths.

"You don't have to do this now. Only when you're ready."

He groaned and placed his hands over hers. "Och, luve, twa dear friends just taught me a verra important lesson. What I had for the past twelve years should be celebrated, no' shoved into a storage room and disremembered. There are no words to express how much it hurts to say guidbye to it, but now I realize I don't want to disremember it all. There's too much guid in there to bury forever. I'm ready."

They spent a long time sorting the contents of the first box into piles: one, the things he would store—flight manuals, dress raincoat, crush caps and official correspondence—and two, clothing he might want to wear.

Rob palmed his log book and slipped it into his dressing gown pocket when Maggie was busy piling clothes onto the bed. He couldn't bear to have it lost somewhere in the storage room, but didn't want to fash her.

She smoothed the creases from his A-2 leather bomber jacket. "I know you'll wear this. 'Tis your favorite."

"A guid thing I was wearing my sheepskin-lined jacket on that last flight. I'll remove the eagles from the shoulders and 'twill be perfect."

"Here's your denim breeks. And what about your dress blouses

106

and breeks?"

"I might use the ETO jacket, I suppose, and twa pair of the breeks and a couple of shirts." He eyed his dress blouses, one with a silver eagle on each shoulder, his silver pilot's wings, US Army Air Forces pins, and theater, combat, and decorations ribbons—what everybody in the military called "lettuce." He fingered the Eighth Army Air Forces patch sewn onto the left shoulder. "Let's put those into storage. They're of no use to me now. The blouse with my pilot's wings we'll keep here to wear when peace is declared."

She sat on the bed and rested her head against his arm. "No words can express how sorry I am, luve. I know how much you miss flying."

"I do miss it—verra badly—but I've a new life now. 'Tis time to move forward."

They finished unpacking the second box the following morning. Rob held up a picture of Den and him taken in front of the *Bonnie Maggie*. "I'd like to hang this in here, if you don't think your faither will mind."

"Of course he won't. What about those other framed pictures, the ones of your planes and crews?"

"They used to hang in my office. I'll need an office of some kind at the shed so I'll hang them there."

"And all the letters?"

"Let's find a box and put them in one of those drawers in the clothes-press." He picked up a pile of letters bundled together with string. "These are from Senator Keyes. You might want to read them sometime. Without his endorsement, I'd never have gotten into West Point. Even with his help, it was hard getting permission for a student from a wee village in New Hampshire, especially an orphan."

"Shouldn't you write him? He may have heard about your accident and be in a fash."

A pain shot across Rob's chest. "I thought I told you. The Senator died just before I got my wings. He'd no' been well for over a year."

"Och, Rob, I'm so sorry."

"Somebody from his office called with the news a week after I sent him an invitation—the only one I posted—to the pinning ceremony." He untied the string and shuffled blindly through the envelopes, thoughts filling with memories of the man who had toured the orphanage during an election year and taken an interest in an extremely tall, shy, tongue-tied twelve-year-old who dreamt of flying.

Maggie's touch brought him back to the present.

"His letters were always filled with words of advice and bits of Washington gossip he thought I might find—" He looked at her, mind blank. "I disremember the Scots word."

"What is it in English?"

"Gossip that's entertaining, is as guid as I can come up with."

"Then the word you're looking for is 'shortsome.' You speak Scots so well, I forget 'tis no' your native tongue. Do you miss speaking English?"

Bless Maggie for diverting his bleak thoughts. "No' at all. I'm back to dreaming in Scots."

She sent him a teasing glance. "And what are you dreaming about?"

He growled a laugh and hugged her. "What do you think, bonnie Maggie?" He lipped her throat.

"Och, you're single-minded man."

"Mebbe, but I've no' heard you complaining."

"As I've heard your American nurses say, 'don't hold your breath.'" She raised her lips to his.

⚜

A visit from Hugh broke Rob's afternoon routine of exercise, a nap, and more exercise. "I thought I'd share the coming Sabbath's lesson. I know there are words you still struggle over in the Gaelic and I don't want you missing anything."

"Och, 'tis thoughtful, but I don't want you wasting your valuable time with the likes of me."

"'Tis my duty and pleasure to see that every Christian hungry for the Word is fed. And you're no' the only one I see, for I also visit all the folk too sick or frail to make the journey to kirk." Hugh reached into his jacket pocket and brought out an obviously new Gaelic Bible. "I hope you don't mind me bringing you a wee present. We can use it together the day."

Rob took the Bible and read the cover aloud. "An Bìoball Tiomnadh Aosda 's Nuadh—The Auld and New Testament Bible." He opened the cover and blinked back tears as he read the words Hugh had penned.

Fir Rob, ma brither in Christ. Mae yer life be lang an ful o' God's peace. Beannachd.

"Hugh, I have no words to say what's in my heart."

"Words are no' needed."

"Thank ye, brither." Rob cleared his throat. "I'll treasure this always."

On the sixth of June, John radioed from Edinburgh that a massive Allied Force had struck the Normandy coast in France. "If the invasion's successful, Germany's domination of Western Europe will be broken. I'll send you copies of the Edinburgh newspaper, *The Scotsman*, as soon as 'tis oot on the morra. From what I can gather, the RAF and your American Army Air Forces began the attack by bombing all the German coastal defenses and those larger towns inland." He hesitated. "I imagine the 396th took part."

Rob fought to control his excitement. "I'm sure of it. I've known for over a year something big was in the works. If this invasion is successful, France, Belgium, Holland, and Denmark could all be liberated."

"Pray you're right." John coughed. "Before I sign off, there's a favor I'd like to ask."

"Owt, you ken that."

"I'd like you and Maggie to move into the cottage."

He couldn't mean it. "But that's your cottage and we're doing fine here. I'm hoping to start on our own home the minute I finish building the rescue boat."

"You haven't begun laying that keel, have you?"

"Och, of course no' but my legs are getting stronger every day.

Shep and I are taking long walks together. I shouldn't be on these crutches much longer."

"I'm glad to hear that. Now, please do as I ask and move into the cottage so you'll be settled before Maggie births my grandbairn."

"But you'll need it when you come in August."

"I'm no' able to spend my usual three months on Innisbraw this year—that's my main reason for wanting you to move in. All the war-wounded have forced a major renovation of the Royal Infirmary and they'll no' let me leave for that long. I'm hoping to take a week's holiday sometime in July, but that's all I can manage. I don't want the cottage vacant so long."

Rob searched for an answer. True, the McGrath cottage had fallen into disrepair, but he felt guilty imposing on John's generosity. He had a sudden, disquieting thought. "Does the cottage have a radio? I don't want to be cut off from everybody with Maggie biggen."

"Already taken care of. Malcolm will be bringing a radio, both transmitter and receiver, in a few days. All Maggie has to do is find a place for it in that sma' cottage. The radio is large, remember, about half a metre wide and a metre tall. It'll have a Mains-powered battery charger and Malcolm will get it all set up and ready to use. If you have trouble with the Pye radio, you can hear the BBC Forces Programme on the shortwave at eight-oh-four and eight-seventy-seven kilohertz. Just make certain 'tis out of the way so you don't trip over the cables."

"Then we'll move in on twa conditions—you allow me to make some repairs, and I pay for all the flour, sugar, tea and other supplies Malcolm delivers when we've the need."

"You have the silver?"

"Of course. Most of the pay I've received since coming to the UK is sitting in the Bank of England in London, drawing interest. I'll write them for a withdrawal."

"Then, aye on you paying, but no repairs till you're off the crutches."

"Major repairs, aye."

"And you'll no' be climbing ladders until next spring, at the earliest."

"If the thatching needs repairing, I'll hire it done. Deal?"

"Deal."

"Thanks for calling about the invasion, John. It gives me hope that this is the beginning of the end for Adolf Hitler."

"Amen to that. Before I sign off, how's Maggie?"

"She's wonderful—never been bonnier."

"Keep an eye on her. If it looks like 'tis going to be a difficult birth, radio me at once. I'll get there as quickly as I can, even if I have to hire one of those airieplanes that land on water."

So John was worried Maggie might die like her mither had when birthing Calum, Maggie's younger brother. Rob pushed back his own panic at the thought. "You know I will. Alice says though she's wee, Maggie looks like she was made for birthing bairnies."

"Pray God she's right."

"Pray God," Rob said fervently.

Several times that day, Rob sent up a petition to the Lord that Maggie would have no trouble delivering their bairnie and that the wee bairnie would be healthy, whether lad or lass.

Maggie really had never been bonnier. Her skin glowed with health and even her hair shone more than usual. She seemed to fear he might find her swelling belly unattractive, so he constantly told her how bonnie he found her.

Back during his years at West Point, though Den had dragged him to almost every party and dance, he always felt awkward and shy around girls. Many tried to engage him in conversation, but his tongue twisted around his words until he gave up trying to talk and they drifted away with pouts and backward glances of disbelief. His experiences in the military were much the same and, though he took a few dates to the cinema, the women soon tired of his awkwardness and grunted replies and, much to his relief, took up with other flyboys who were more fun.

He found his voice when he met Maggie. Now, she was the focal point of his existence and, though it didn't seem possible, every day he luved her more.

Maggie cuddled next to Rob on the entry bench, face turned up to the gradually darkening sky. Gloaming—her favorite time of day. High, wispy clouds played a game of chase while the sun hopscotched across the tops of the waves one last time before slipping below the horizon.

The scent of the sea on the breeze—so clean, so invigorating, that smell. Her smile turned to a soft laugh when Rob cupped her belly in his huge palm and parted her hair to run his lips across the back of her neck.

"'Tis so quiet," he whispered, "only the sound of the sea sooking on the shore—like all the birds and wee creatures are too spent to give voice when the day dies."

"Or just grateful to settle into their burrows and roosts with full stomachs."

He chuckled and rested his chin on her head. "My practical Maggie."

"'Tis called 'nesting' when you're biggen."

"Are you ready to listen to your faither's news?"

"Only if 'tis guid. I don't want to ruin the een's magic."

"'Tis verra guid." He pulled her onto his lap.

She rested her cheek on his chest and listened with growing excitement while Rob told her of the Allied invasion. Och, why hadn't she pressed him for information earlier in the day? She didn't want to remind him of all he had lost, but curiosity overcame caution. "Will the newspaper list the air groups that took part?"

"That should be classified, but I know the 396th was involved. We were getting briefings at SHAEF that something really big was in the works even before I left. We were going to start hitting their synthetic oil refineries in Romania, finally bomb the interior of Germany, and that was just the beginning."

"So, being the top group in your wing, you would have led that mission."

"Possibly even other wings."

She studied his face. Not the grief she expected. He looked excited.

"There must have been over a thousand B-17s in the air that

day." He turned his face to the dark grey sky as though seeking a fleeting glimpse of that staggering sight. "That would have been a wonder to behold. I wish I could have seen Hitler's face when he heard the news."

"Do you really think the war may be over soon?"

"I don't know about 'soon,' but we've definitely turned the corner."

The war in Europe might have been grinding slowly toward a bloody climax, but for those living in the Outer Hebrides, it was far from over. A radio call from Alec the following day brought the chilling reality home for Rob.

"I just got another call from Benbecula about keeping our coastal guards on alert," the crofter said. "A British destroyer escorting a sma' convoy of merchant ships loaded with supplies for the military units at Benbecula and South Uist spotted a U-boat close to the surface nearby. They opened fire but the U-boat slipped 'neath the water. It took over twenty DCs dropped from the destroyer and a refitted, armed trawler before the sea biled and they heard explosions and saw an oil slick."

Rob winced. "How close were they to Benbecula?"

"No' far from the coast of Baile a' Mhanaich, where they were to drop anchor and off-load. The young officer who radioed me said the U-boat was most likely planning to torpedo the destroyer and trawler before taking oot the merchant ships."

"We can't expect them to just put up their hands and surrender. I'm thinking they must see the handwriting on the wall and are going to throw everything they have at us to keep from losing this war."

"You mean after what happened at Normandy? Hugh told me John radioed him with the news."

"He radioed me too. I don't know what to say, Alec. I still can't imagine why they would attack us, but all we can do is keep a sharp eye oot every night."

Rob turned the radio to Receive and sat back in John's chair.

Maggie was napping.

No reason to worry her with Alec's information. She had enough to think about with the impending move and her advancing pregnancy.

Chapter Seventeen

The second week of June brought luminous white clouds—ethereal, lofty peaks and valleys—transformed into new shapes with each changing stream of stratospheric wind. Frothy, rain-fed burns slowed their hectic pace and shallowed, revealing smooth pebbles buried in sandy bottoms. Budding catkins and leaves competed for space along willow branches, and new heather leaves, tender and fragile, turned their pale green surfaces to the weak sun.

Those folk with small crofts took advantage of the rainless spell and forked over kailyard gardens for summer crops and singled plots of neeps, their aching backs forgotten at the thought of boiled fresh greens for supper. Crofters with more land hitched cuddies to ploughs, turning vast areas into neat furrows for oats and barley.

The fever to work hit Rob as well. Balancing awkwardly on one crutch, he'd scraped and repainted the entry door, its surrounds, and the window frames on Maggie's childhood home, then wedged a wooden shim beneath the lower hinge on the warped door to keep it from dragging when opened. No' much to show for so many hours of sweaty work.

He hobbled across the path and stood looking out over the dark blue Minch. *Thank Ye, Faither, for the bonnie sight of sea and harbour.* An intangible connection anchored him to this island. Its ancient past of plaid-clad warriors battling invaders pulsed through his body with each beat of his heart. Its craggy rocks and emerald girse, thatched stone cottages, and rushing burns were as familiar as his own skin. Home. Such a simple word for the overwhelming emotions it evoked.

A shaggy cuddy trotted up the path, Lachlan MacNab on the cairt bench waving a greeting.

Rob hurried across the path to open the gate. "'Tis guid to see you, Lachlan. I wasn't certain you'd have time for me."

The slim, broad-shouldered young cow-crofter looped the reins over the brake handle and jumped down. "Sorry I'm late. Had a bull jump the dyke. Took me a guid bit of time catching the cannie beastie."

"No problem. From what Alec said, you've a fair talent for repairing thatch."

Lachlan ground the toe of his boot into the sandy path. "Och, I wouldna say that. There's others handier than me."

"And them all too auld to scale a ladder." Rob laughed. "Come away in and see what you think. I've noticed what looks like rot."

A grin of agreement creased Lachlan's ruddy cheeks. "Let's take a keek."

They walked around the cottage, Rob pointing out several areas of dark thatch.

"That's rot, all right."

"Can you patch it without taking the whole thing down and starting over?"

"Och, aye. I've been replacing parts of our own thatch since Bridget and me merrit. I'll just take my cairt down to our croft and load up what I need. Be back in a tick."

While Lachlan worked on the roof, Rob checked the pipe and boiler system connected to the fireplace to heat the water for the kitchen and small bathroom and found them in good condition, considering their age. As much as he sweated, he'd be dripping wet with the fireplace burning on a rare warm summer day. But how could he complain? Unlike most of the folk on Innisbraw, the cottage had electricity for lamps and plumbed water.

He stepped outside, ducking beneath the low lintel just in time, and leaned against the dyke, watching Lachlan work.

The crofter scaled the ladder carrying a huge bundle of long heather branches mixed with willow twigs over his shoulder. Once atop the thatch, he wound a length of supple reed around and around the lower quarter of the bundle, then poked the end of the sheaf into the waiting space. He grunted, sweat flying, as he shoved until it was wedged tightly. Good thing he was young and strong.

When the radio arrived, Malcolm and Angus had it set up and ready to use within the hour. Maggie radioed her faither to tell him all was well and thank him.

With Maggie into the sixth month of her pregnancy, Rob refused to allow her to do any of the heavy cleaning. He hired Flora and several crofters' wives to scour the inside of the cottage from top to bottom. It took them two days but, when they finished, even Rob admitted the tiny cottage had charm.

"I'm going to put up fresh lace curtains I put aside before the war," Maggie said as she looked around the spotless interior. "See how the worn floor flags nearly glow? And I have several bed covers I've pieced over the years. They'll brighten our bedroom."

"You're fair happy about this, aren't you?"

"Of course. It's no' like moving into our own home, but the infirmary is too big to be cosy."

He had to tease a smile from those bonnie lips. "You realize we're going to have to build a large home for ourselves if we're going to have room for our eight bairns."

No smile. Instead, tears inched down her rounder-than-normal cheeks.

He wiped one away with the pad of his thumb. "What did I say, luve?"

"You can't really want eight bairns, and I don't blame you. I'm only six months pregnant and already as big as Ben Innis."

He guided her to a rocker and pulled her onto his lap.

"I'll hurt you."

"Maggie Savage, stop bubbling."

She sniffled and looked up at him.

"How many times do I have to say it? Your body has never been bonnier." He laid a palm across her belly. "You're carrying our bairnie in there. You only look big in front because you're so sma' the bairnie has to pop out somewhere. Come on, awn up." He rubbed the tip of his nose against hers. "'Tis only logical."

A tremulous smile tilted the corners of her mouth.

"As for eight bairns, I've always told you it sounds like a

perfect number." He kissed her forehead. "Now, I don't want to ever hear another word from you about how you're afraid I don't like the way you look. You're my bonnie Maggie, and your belly is bonnie." He nibbled her earlobe.

She nestled closer. "I'm sorry, luve. I don't know why, but the slightest thing makes me cry."

"'Tis called being biggen. I understand it's been going on since Adam and Eve had their first bairnie." He settled back and began rocking. "This is verra nice. Let's spend the night here."

"The bathing tub is wee compared to the large one at the infirmary."

"'Tis sounding better and better."

※

They spent their first night at the cottage. The large bed, though not long enough for Rob's legs, was wider than the hospital bed they had been using.

"'Tis a guid thing we like to coorie doun," Rob murmured, at the edge of sleep. "I never did like cold ankles and feet."

"Then wear what you Americans call 'socks.'" She covered a yawn.

He fisted his fingers in her hair. "I'll just smoorich my lass instead."

※

Alec and Morag helped move their belongings over from the infirmary the next day.

After they'd left, Rob suggested they use some of the handsel gifts they had received at their wedding ceilidh.

Maggie shook her head. "They're for our own first home. We'll wait."

Rob still went next door to the infirmary to exercise his legs and shoulder, but living in the small cottage satisfied him more than he had imagined possible. He could sit before the hearth and watch Maggie at work in the kitchen. He often rocked in front of a glowing peat fire, watching her prepare supper or knead bread for the morra.

Only one problem fashed him—none of the four windows in

118

the cottage opened. "I'm going to have to change that," he said to Maggie. "I'll have Malcolm look for some used hardware in Oban. I've used sashing and counterweights before so you could slide the windows up, but on this side of the Pond, the windows push open. No matter how I go about it, we're going to have windows that open so we can hear the seals barking on the rocks and the sooking of the surf—and I'm no' about to go without the warm-honey scent of heather when it starts blooming."

Maggie put down her knitting. "Do you really know how to make windows that open and close?"

"You've disremembered I helped the director of the orphanage build his new house the last year I was there. His lad, Bill, had a sma' lumber mill and took the time to show me how to do all sorts of things."

"But you were so young."

"Doesn't matter. I've always enjoyed working with wood."

"You're certain you won't hurt yourself?"

"I'm biddy certain, Mither Savage."

The Pye radio brought hours of pleasure. They bundled in sweaters and jackets and spent every een on the entry flags with the door open so they could hear the news and a music programme called "Music While You Work." During the broadcasts of American comedy shows, Maggie giggled like a young lass at Charlie McCarthy and Bob Hope's humour, but Jack Benny's droll wit often left her quizzing Rob for answers to questions about what Benny meant and why everyone in the studio audience laughed.

By the middle of July, with windows refurbished and Maggie's garden flourishing, Rob felt like a real married man with a home and the wife of his dreams. If only he could convince Maggie he could walk all the way down to the shed every day on his crutches without hurting himself.

"It's no farther than I walk around here all day," he said. "I'm working on a surprise, so you can come with me, but you can't come into the shed."

"A surprise? What for? My birthday isn't until December."

"I know. I missed it last year, but 'twill be different this time. Anyway, this is no' a birthday gift, so you'll see when 'tis time and no' before."

Instead of Elspeth coming to the infirmary, Rob made his way down to her cottage every other day. They sat on her stone-flagged entry, she with her tea and he with his coffee and scones, as she taught him the Gaelic, the sound of the sea sooking on the shore and the occasional bleat of one of Angus's sheep a familiar, soothing background.

"'Tis a difficult language," he said. "Probably the most difficult I've ever studied."

"Harder than German?"

"And French and Italian too."

She patted his hand. "You're the quickest learner I've ever had. In another six months, you'll be speaking, reading, and writing the Gaelic like 'tis your own."

"Then what language will I dream in?"

"Whatever language you use the most—more than likely Scots. Are you dreaming in Scots now?"

"All the time."

"I said you were a quick learner."

"I just hope I'm quick when it comes to being a faither."

"Och, Rob, whatsomever are you blethering about now?"

"I haven't been around wee bairns since I was young. I want to do it right, but I don't have an example to build on. I never knew my own faither or mither, them being ... being killed when I was only a wee bairnie."

"You've told me. But you've a kind heart. You'll do fine, never fear."

"I don't think my men at Edenoaks considered me kind. Anything but. I could be fair strict."

"With guid reason. You were making certain your young lads did their turns properly so they would stay alive. And being a faither isn't all hugs and kisses. Your bairns will also have to be trained in so many things." She placed a gnarled hand on his knee. "Tell me this. Were you unreasonable in your dealings with the young lads at

Edenoaks?"

"I'm sure they thought I was."

"That's no' what I asked."

Fingers tapping on his thighs, he considered her question. "I don't think I was. I did push them to their limits but I never asked them to do owt they hadn't been trained well for."

"Then, what's your worry?" She ducked and swatted at a swarm of midges.

"I don't know how to be a faither to a wee lass."

Elspeth slapped the arms of her rocker and laughed. "So that's what has you so fashed. Lasses are no' so different than lads in most ways. There is only one thing you have to remember with a lass, and that is if she has a faither she respects and luves and who respects and luves her, she'll know what to look for in a man and no' go off all whittie-whattie when she grows up."

"It scares me to death I'll do something wrong. I'm so big; what if I hurt her?"

She wagged a finger. "Stop borrowing trouble. You have your bairnie half grown and it isn't even birthed yet. As for having a lass, I'm certain you don't have to worry about that for a while. I'm thinking this bairnie will be a braw lad."

Rob swallowed a choke. "Is that just an educated guess or are you telling me a truth?"

"Look at the way Maggie carries this bairnie, Rob, all oot in front."

"What difference does that make? She's so wee there's no place else for it to go."

"Och, you men are so ignorant about a biggen woman. When someone as wee as Maggie is carrying a lass, she'll gain weight all over, no' just in front. Perhaps 'tis an auld grandmither's tale, but in my ninety-nine years, I've seen it proven many more times than no'."

"And this is why you say 'tis a lad?"

"'Tis no' the only reason, but I'm a bit tired. All this blethering has worn me oot."

She did look tired. He pushed himself from the rocker and

121

leaned over to kiss her cheek. "Thank ye for the lesson, Elspeth, and your reassuring words. I didn't really care at first, but now I hope it is a lad. That way I can practice before I have to face faithering a lass."

She patted his cheek. "Och, on you go then. If ever there was a lad destined to be a guid faither, 'tis you."

"I pray you're right."

"As you should, lad. 'Tis only fitting."

Chapter Eighteen

John arrived on Innisbraw the next Friday. He walked around the cottage with Rob and Maggie, smiling and nodding. "Now it looks like it used to, lived in and luved. Thank ye."

Rob smiled. "'Tis I who should be thanking ye. I hate to think of you bedding at the infirmary this week."

"Those box-beds are too sma'. Besides, I'll be over there most of every day anyway. I should have listened when Elizabeth told me to add an office when I was building this cottage, since that's where I spend most of my time."

"You'll take your meals here," Maggie said. "'Tis far easier than having to cook for yourself at the infirmary."

"Of course I will. Now, I can't help but notice how well you're walking on those crutches, Rob. I think it's time to turn you loose with a walking stick for the week I'm here. If you do well, you can try walking without it."

"That's grand. I hoped you'd say that."

"I'll have to be satisfied with how you're getting around before I'll allow you to walk alone. And watch Shep, there. Make sure he doesn't trip you. A fall could set you back."

His warning didn't dampen Rob's enthusiasm. "I understand."

The doctor wasn't finished. "And even when I do allow you to go walking on your own, there's to be no running or climbing rocks for at least six to eight weeks. That left leg will need some babying for a while."

Rob found walking with a stick much easier than with crutches. He still favored his left leg, but it took less effort to get around quickly. Would the limp improve or be with him for the rest of his life, deterring his running?

123

John and Maggie spent a great deal of time preparing the infirmary for the doctor's long absence, freeing Rob to work on his surprise for Maggie. He savored the walk down the hill to the shed. The weather was perfect, filled with sunshine and breezes so warm he no longer had to wear his A-2 jacket on the jaunts. The swell of the sea and the sound of it crashing onto the rocks of Innis Fell exhilarated him. How could he have dreaded living on an isolated island?

Wildflowers clung to precarious perches among the rocks, and the shrill keen of Pewlie gulls filled the bracing heather and sea-scented air. Thank the Lord, Maggie had brought him home instead of taking him to the Royal Infirmary. Gazing out at the vast expanse of sky and sea may not be as satisfying as flying, but it deserved a close second.

The used woodworking supplies he ordered came by post and he began his project in earnest. Planing the wood down to a satiny finish soothed him. The soft swish of the plane had an almost hypnotic quality.

He chafed to begin the rescue boat, but he had another three months before he could start laying the keel. He flexed his shoulder. No pain. Just stiff. A month ahead of schedule with his rehabilitation, he would do nowt to delay a complete recovery.

⚓

By the time John packed for his return to Edinburgh, Rob's limp had greatly improved.

"You can walk on your own now, as long as you promise me you'll take care," the doctor said as they waited for Angus's cairt for a ride down to the dock.

"I'll no' do owt I shouldn't. 'Tis a promise." He waited on the infirmary steps while Maggie saw her faither off. When she returned, her warm smile made his pulse race. He led her inside and tossed the stick into the infirmary supply room.

"You'd best watch oot. I'm on my own twa legs at last."

"Och, there's no stopping you now."

He removed the barrette from her hair. "Let's celebrate." His dimples deepened as he pulled her into his arms.

She gasped. "I can't breathe."

He turned her so the bulge of her belly had more room. "Better?"

"Much better."

He savored her sweet lips, her warmth, the scent of heather on her skin and hair. Regret and a stab of anger brought a flush of heat. "I wish I were stronger and could carry you over to the cottage, but at least I can put my arm around you while we walk."

They settled into a comfortable routine. While Rob met with Elspeth for his Gaelic lessons, continued his therapy at the infirmary, or worked at the shed on her present, Maggie enjoyed her garden and knit, wove, or sewed things for their bairnie. They took long walks together, holding hands and losing themselves in the bonnie nature surrounding them. Each Sabbath, they attended services at kirk, then took a basket dinner to one of their favorite nearby spots, a small natural cove on the southeastern strand where a large patch of marram grasses bent in the ocean breezes, and shore birds pecked for tender morsels on the shore. Puffins often rode the gently rolling surf, their comical faces eliciting giggles and chuckles.

They never tired of the view. The deep blue Minch turned to bright turquoise as it neared the shore and shallowed. Great- and lesser-backed gulls rolled and dove above the sea, while red-breasted mergansers rode the swells, ignoring the oyster-catchers with their bright red beaks and raucous *pik-pik-pik* calls.

Common orache and pale mauve sea rockets cluttered the drift line just above the shore, and scattered among the clumps of marram grass, sea sandwort, silverweed, and birdsfoot trefoil vied for the warming sun. The sandy soil lay carpeted in sea pink and thrift.

Occasionally, they sat with her back nestled against his chest for hours, scarcely saying a word but many times they talked non-stop. They shared stories about their childhoods and long winter days spent in school. Every Sabbath, Rob found it easier to share more of his lonely past. Though he tried to put a humorous spin to his memories, cannie Maggie couldn't be fooled and always dragged the painful truth out of him, word by halting word. Facing what he had buried for so long often made his eyes sting, but on their long walks up the hill to the cottage he always found his spirits lifted, as though burdens he hadn't even known existed had been removed by simply digging them out of their dark hiding places and exposing them to the light of Maggie's understanding. Time and again he questioned why God thought him worthy of such a blessing.

⁂

Though Maggie did understand and even gave him new insight into the cruelty of bairns who had never been taught better, she could never come up with a reason in her own mind for the adults in his village being so cruel, especially after hearing that most of them regularly attended one of the two churches.

How could Rob be so tender and loving now when he had not grown up with a family who unconditionally accepted who and what he was simply because he was their lad?

The morning after one particularly heartbreaking afternoon, she radioed Hugh while Rob was working at the shed and poured out her grief and anger.

"I'm thinking you've forgotten one verra important bit of doctrine you've been taught," the minister said after a pause. "We all have auld sin natures, lass, and they can lead us astray from the path of righteousness if we're no' vigilant, especially if we have many others around us with the same inclination toward evil."

"You mean the entire village he grew up in was evil?"

"Och, of course no'. You mentioned that man at the store who made sure Rob had a piece of sweet tucked into his cheek when he left. I'm certain there were many others in that village who felt sorry for the orphans, but oft-times Satan veils the minds of the guid to what is happening in their mids."

Maggie shared Hugh's insight with Rob that een and was relieved to learn it brought him new understanding. Only one thing marred her happiness over the next few weeks—catching him gazing up at the sky, hands clenched, a palpable yearning on his face.

They had both looked forward to Maggie's younger brother's time off from the boarding academy he attended on the Isle of Harris, but John radioed that Calum would, once again, spend his six-week summer holiday apprenticing on a fishing trawler.

Even without Calum's visit, the summer passed too quickly. By the middle of September, the days were often cloudy with a brisk onshore wind delivering a warning of the winter to come. Though they still took walks together, Maggie wore a heavy sweater and Rob his A-2 jacket—and their steps were slower. She was nearing the end of her pregnancy and he didn't want her to get worn out.

But when alone, he pushed himself, Shep trotting at his side to keep up with his master's long stride. Thank God the limp had disappeared. Almost time for him to start running again. He couldn't wait for the opportunity to build strength and stamina.

The seventeenth of September, the BBC War News reported that the blackout was to be changed to a "brownout," allowing as much light as a full moon, with blackout restrictions going into immediate effect if there was an air raid. This news didn't affect the island much. Everyone still put up their blackout curtains, but those who had to visit a toilet outside began using partially hooded torches, if they had number eight batteries, or a paraffin Tilly lamp turned as low as it would go.

The last Sabbath of the month, instead of the long walk to kirk, Rob talked Maggie into a short, slow stroll across the fell. She enjoyed the morning, watching the seabirds floating in one place against the brisk wind, and the view of the deep blue Minch stretching toward the horizon, waves like white horses galloping in frenzied abandon across the crests.

For dinner, she ate only a few spoonfuls of the haddie bree.

"Are you feeling poorly?" Rob asked.

"No' at all. You know I always eat more at tea or suppertime." She glanced out the window as she took their bowls to the jawbox to rinse. "Angus's cairt just pulled up at the gate." She reached for her apron strings.

"He's brought your surprise from the shed." Rob untied her apron and patted her bottom. "Into the bedroom with you while I bring it in."

"But I have to greet him. 'Tis only mannerly."

"Och, quit your stalling. Into the bedroom and don't keek. Keep the door closed till I tell you to open it."

She poked his chest. "Then, hurry. You've teased me long enough."

"Patience, wee mither." He nuzzled her ear and closed the door with a firm click.

A few minutes later, the cairt creaked away, the clop of hooves growing fainter.

Maggie waited, tapping her foot, hand gripping the door latch.

At last, Rob called, "Oot you come, lass." He stood in front of the fireplace and, next to her rocker, a large wooden cradle reflected the firelight.

Her breath caught. "Och, Rob. 'Tis so bonnie." Smooth wood, tight joints, the soft curve of both rockers. "You made this? It's the most wonderful present I've ever received." She hugged him.

He pressed a kiss to her hair.

"'Tis so smooth." She stooped and ran her fingers over the wood, setting the cradle rocking.

"You think 'twill do, then?"

"'Tis perfect. I was thinking we were going to have to use one of the drawers in the clothes-press. I have all the bedding ready. Help me prepare it for our bairnie."

He placed a firm pillow in the bottom before Maggie tucked in a soft linen sheet and topped it with two of the blankets she had woven. "'Tis ready." He pulled her close and nuzzled her cheek. "You're so bonnie you've been driving me daft all the morning. And I do give the best backrub on Innisbraw. You've said so yourself."

She kneaded her aching back. "That sounds wonderful."

They made their way into the bedroom where Rob helped her out of her skirt and sweater, petticoat, and woolen tights and settled her on the bed. "On your side, luve. I'll sit beside you."

He rubbed her tight muscles.

It felt so good, she moaned. "Aye, right there."

He gently kneaded the tight muscle until it loosened, and moved on to another.

She relaxed, eyes closed, near to sleep.

A gurgling wrench tweaked the inside of her belly.

She gasped.

Wetness.

Rob stiffened. "Did I hurt you?"

"No, it's just ..." She rolled over onto her back and clutched his hand. "My water just broke. 'Tis time."

"Time? You mean the bairnie's coming?" He jumped up. "I'll go fetch Alice."

"No." She moaned. "Don't leave me alone, please." An urge to strain caught her unawares. "Don't ... go, Rob." She panted while a spasm racked her belly. "'Tis too late."

Chapter Nineteen

Why couldn't he split into two people? Run for Alice *and* stay with his Maggie. What would help her more? Alice was having trouble with her shortwave radio and, since he hadn't done any running yet, he didn't know if he could get down the hill to her quarters behind the post office, and back again in time.

"Get towels!" Maggie cried between contractions.

He raced into the bathing room and returned with an armful.

"Put them 'neath me."

He rolled her and covered the soaked bedding. His hands shook. What did he know about childbirth? "Shouldn't I boil water?"

Caught in the throes of another contraction, she shook her head. "No time." She groped for his hand. "Take off my under-breeks."

Rob removed them and grabbed her hand as she strained.

Her belly drew up into a hard ball and relaxed for a moment before contracting again. Her face was soon blotched with red and covered with perspiration.

Och, Lord, what should I do?

Every time she strained and tightened her grip on his hand, his stomach cramped.

His pulse raced and blood pounded in his ears as she suffered longer. *Help her, Faither, please help her.* He dabbed at her wet forehead with a corner of the sheet.

After fifteen minutes of hard labour, she arched her back and drew up her legs. "It's coming. Help our bairnie." She took several deep breaths. "As soon ... as the head's born, help the shoulders oot ... one at a time."

He knelt on the bed, heart constricting when Maggie let out a hoarse cry.

A tiny head emerged, facedown.

He reached out and gently guided one shoulder, then the other. He cradled the head and shoulders in his palm as another contraction racked Maggie's body, and the bairnie slipped into his waiting hands. With a sob of relief, he lifted it up and cradled it awkwardly in his arms. "'Tis a lad. A braw lad!"

The bairnie squirmed, arched his back, gasped one breath, another, and let out a lusty cry.

Maggie closed her eyes and slumped back.

Rob's breath froze. "Maggie? Maggie! Don't leave me!"

She looked up at him, tears wetting her cheeks. "Put him across my belly." Such an exhausted whisper.

Rob did so, then swiped a sleeve across his own eyes. "He has your black hair and he's so braw, but there's something wrong—there's white streaks all over him."

She turned the loudly protesting baby over onto his belly and pulled a corner of the bedcover over him. "Now you can boil some water. You have to tie and cut the cord. Then you'll have to bathe him." Loud and clear. No whisper this time. "That white all over him is called vernix. It kept his skin from wrinkling while he was in the womb."

Rob stood rooted to the spot. "I can't bathe him. I might drop him."

"You didn't drop him just now when he was so slippery. On you go—boil some water—just a wee bit." Definitely not a whisper.

He ran into the kitchen, put a small amount of water in the teakettle, and set it on the hot part of the stove, adding enough peat for a good fire. His hands shook so badly he dropped the peat twice before he got it into the stove and had to take time for a wash-up before returning to the bedroom.

"Now, the umbilical cord. Get some of that string and the scissors from the left drawer in the aumrie. Wash the scissors in soap and water and pour the boiling water over the blades, then bring everything in here." She spoke over the lad's cries.

Rob followed her instructions.

131

When he returned, she uncovered the lad and turned him onto his back. "I'll hold him so he doesn't wriggle while you tie the string tightly around the cord just above his belly. When it's secure, cut the cord just above the knot."

His hands trembled and his body shook. Fingers clumsy, as if clothed in heavy gloves, he tied two tight knots—just to be sure— and reached for the scissors.

"That's right," Maggie said as he positioned the blades. "Now, cut."

He closed his eyes and pressed the blades together. He opened his eyes. He'd done it.

She covered their son again. "Now, bring in that tin basin from the kitchen about half full with warm water—no' hot—just so you can put your hand in it and feel neither hot nor cold."

He couldn't move. "I'll drop him. I know I will, and he's rouping so hard."

"No, you won't. 'Tis normal for him to have greetin' match when he's born and he doesn't like being on his back. Our Robbie needs to be cleaned off. On you go."

With his back a little straighter, head a little higher, he raced for the kitchen. Robbie. He had a lad named Robbie. And this lad would grow up surrounded by a family who loved him. When he returned with the basin of water, she told him to get a flannel.

Why did she keep asking him to leave?

"And soap?" He paused in the doorway.

"No soap."

He stumbled into the bathing room and returned with the face flannel and a clean towel from the hanging rod.

"Guid." She uncovered Robbie and picked him up, then scooted over on the bed. "Put the basin beside me on the bed. Now, take him from me and cradle him in your left arm with his head resting on the inside of your left palm and the rest of his body over the inside of your arm, holding him firmly. Perfect. Now, dip him into the water and bathe him with the flannel, first his face and head. Be sure to get all the wrinkles around his neck clean."

Rob cradled his son on his arm and slipped him into the water. He could do this. He had to do this.

132

The bairnie still cried, tiny chin quivering.

"Hushie-baw, wee laddie. 'Tis all right, Faither's got you." He gently washed the tiny face, head, and neck, then wrung out the cloth with one hand and bathed his lad's body.

Maggie handed him the clean towel. "Hold this in front of your chest with your chin, lift him out of the water, and wrap it around him."

The bairnie stopped crying as Rob blotted him dry.

Reality hit like a ray of blinding sunshine. He had a son!

He couldn't help grinning like a daftie. "I think he needs a hippen. He just got the towel and my shirt wet."

"They're on the clothes-press. And bring the pins. I'll do it. You can watch. This time."

Rob sighed with relief as he fetched the cloth. He removed the basin from the bed and watched as she folded the hippen and pinned it around Robbie.

"There's a gown in that top drawer, luve, and a blanket in the bottom one. Our lad needs to be bundled up. Being born was a traumatic experience for our wee Robbie. He needs to be swaddled verra tightly."

Rob brought the items.

She dressed Robbie in his gown and wrapped him securely in the soft blanket.

How did she …? But Maggie was a nurse. Of course she knew all about birthing and taking care of bairnies.

He eyed the soiled blanket and sheets. "Shouldn't I help you clean up and change the bed-clothes? I'm afraid the towels didn't help much."

She laid Robbie beside her on a clean spot on the bed.

And strained again.

Och, Lord, what was wrong? He leaned over her. "What's the matter?"

"I've more work to do."

He couldn't breathe—he couldn't. "There's surely no' another bairnie."

She barked a short laugh. "I have to deliver the afterbirth. It might no' look guid but 'tis perfectly natural."

Take a breath before you end up on the floor. She's all right.
"Och, Maggie, what's the afterbirth?"

"'Tis the placenta—the sac—our lad's been living in the past
nine months."

"Can I help?"

"Press on my abdomen." She panted. "Move your hands down
verra gently, no' too hard."

He pushed lightly on her abdomen and a few minutes later,
watched amazed, as a the mass slipped from her body.

She lay back, breathing heavily. "Just put one of those towels
over that midden. We'll change the bedding soon." Long, deep sigh.
"I'm going to rest a bit and hold our lad."

"Our lad." Tears blurred his sight. "I can't believe I'm a
faither—that we're a family—a real family." He sat on the bed
beside Maggie.

Her hair lay tangled and damp with perspiration and her face
was streaked with dried tears, but she had never been bonnier.

An intense feeling of tenderness washed over him. He cradled
her and Robbie, kissing both their foreheads. "Och, Maggie, thank
you for our lad." He strained to speak around the tears in his throat.
"This is the most wonderful thing I've ever experienced." He
touched his lips to hers. "I luve you," he whispered, "forever and
ever and ever."

Somebody pounded on the door.

Och, what now? "I'll catch you right up." When he opened the
front door, Hugh and Alice stood on the entry flags.

"Rob, have you hurt yourself?" Hugh said. "There's blood on
your face and your shirt's a midden."

"We have a braw lad, Hugh."

Alice rushed past him and into the bedroom.

"A lad!" Hugh exclaimed. "How's our Maggie?"

Rob grabbed him into a hug. "She's grand. Och, Hugh, she was
so brave. I didn't know what a woman went through giving birth."

"I've been told it can be verra hard." He smiled at Rob. "Why
didn't you go for Alice? I met her on the path, coming to check on
Maggie."

"There wasn't time. When wee Robbie decided to be born, he was in a hurry."

"Impatient like his faither, is he?" He took Rob's arm. "Go away in and sit before you fall. Your legs are shaking like saplings in a blowsterie wind."

Rob collapsed into his rocker. "I don't mind telling you, I was fair terrified. I didn't know what to do, but Maggie walked me through it. I caught our lad in my own twa hands." He shivered at the memory. "'Twas the most wondrous thing I've ever done."

"Your wee lad is fortunate indeed to be born into this family." Hugh fingered the cradle beside his rocker. "It seems your hands have been busy at other things. Is this the present you've been working on in the shed?"

"Aye. We just got it ready and Maggie's back was aching and she lay on the bed so I could rub it, and then she said 'och' and it was too late to go for Alice."

"Well, from what you've told me, you've all three come through this in grand condition." Hugh ran his hand over the cradle's smooth side. "This is a fine cradle. You've a talent for working with wood, there's no doubt of that."

"There's something almost spiritual in helping a few pieces of wood take shape into something you can use."

Alice came out of the bedroom, her arms filled with soiled bedding.

Rob leaped up. "Maggie?"

"She's in grand shape and you did a fine turn. Now, wash that blood off your face and show Hugh your new lad. Maggie's heard him out here and she's on heckle-pins to show off your wee bairnie."

"You're certain Maggie's all right then?"

"She's fine, just verra tired. But I must warn you about your next bairnie. The second usually comes faster than the first so I'm thinking you'll never be using my services." She beamed at him. "Your bairnies are going to be in too much of a hurry."

But they wanted eight. He had to watch Maggie go through agony seven more times?

Alice's laugh was as gruff as her voice. "You did everything right, so don't look so afraid. I'm taking these linens down to my place to wash. On you go now, get that blood off and show Hugh your braw new lad."

Rob washed his face, then beckoned to Hugh.

Maggie lay on her side with their lad cuddled in the crook of her arm, crooning a lullaby in the Gaelic.

Overcome with luve, Rob froze for a moment, burning the picture into his memory. He tiptoed in and leaned over, kissing her cheek. "My Maggie."

Her smile so filled with luve. "No' a man in a hundred could have done what you did. You're going to be a wonderful faither."

"I've brought Hugh in, since Alice told me to. If you'd rather we stay ootside ..."

She grinned up at Hugh. "Come you here and meet Robert John Savage, our firstborn."

Rob moved aside and Hugh leaned over the infant.

He fingered the baby's fine black hair. "Just like yours, Maggie. But I'm thinking he has a look of Rob about him too."

"Our Robbie does. He has a dimple on each side of his mouth when he moves his lips."

They were both daft. "Och, he looks just like Maggie."

"Haud yer wheesht!" Maggie exclaimed. "He has your lips and eyebrows and the shape of his face is like yours, just as I would have it."

He knew that tone. He ducked his head and nodded.

Maggie reached for his hand. "Make Hugh some coffee, and I could use some tea," she said, voice gentled.

"I've no time for coffee," Hugh said. "I've the bell to ring. It's been too long since the bell has heralded the birth of a new bairnie on Innisbraw!"

"You ring the bell when a bairnie is born?"

"Aye. Four rings for a lad and five for a lass."

Rob couldn't help a wee tease. "What do you do if 'tis twins?"

"Thank the guid Lord, that's never happened since I came to Innisbraw. I'm thinking that would cause a rare fankle." He leaned over the bairnie. "I'd like to say a wee prayer before I take my leave." He placed his palm on Robbie's brow as they bowed their heads. "Our faithful Heavenly Faither, we thank You for the safe delivery of this precious lad, Robbie, and we thank You that You have ensured him a happy home by bestowing him on loving parents who are dedicated to fulfilling Your will. Bless this home and those who dwell in it. In the name of Christ our Saviour. Amen."

After Hugh slipped out, Rob changed his shirt, pulled a rocker into the bedroom, and held his lad while Maggie sipped her tea.

"If he has his faither's appetite, I'm going to have to eat and drink all day just to make enough milk." That mischievous smile was back.

"Och, what can I fix you to eat? I'm a terrible husband. I forgot all about it."

"Nowt right now. This tea tastes so guid I'm thinking I'll take a wee nap before I give our Robbie his first feeding."

"Are you certain? I'm no' a cook as you well know, but I can inbring a jeely piece."

"I'm too tired to eat now. Besides, as soon as the bell rings, you'll find yourself with so much food you won't know what to do with it all. Almost every woman on Innisbraw will be at our door with a dish or bowl of something from her kitchen—no matter how bare her own food presses."

The thought made his stomach growl while lifting one responsibility from his aching shoulder.

Less than an hour after the bell in the steeple rang out its joyous message, the food began to arrive. All the women voiced their congratulations but no one stayed or asked to see the bairnie, though Morag, Flora, and Susan Ferguson did ask what they were naming their new lad. The kitchen was soon so inundated with food, Rob carried most of it out to the cooling shed so it wouldn't spoil.

Shep turned in circles, nose in the air, tongue lapping, as if tasting the tantalizing aromas.

At gloaming, the last cairt gone, Rob dished up a plate for Maggie and took it into the bedroom.

She was changing Robbie. "You'd best bring me several

hippens, and he'll need a fresh gown and blanket. He's soaked."

Rob handed her some hippens, a gown, and blanket, and sat next to her on the bed, afraid to hear the answer, but needing to ask. "Is that normal? He was just born."

"Completely normal. He'll go through a stack of these, gowns, and blankets every day, but I wouldn't use rubber hippen covers even if the War Department hadn't banned them. They give a bairnie the rash."

While she changed the lad, Rob examined his son. "He has such long hands and feet. And he's so shilpit. Are you sure he's all right?"

"He's perfect. He's just an extremely long bairnie. Alice lifted him and said he weighs over nine pounds."

"Over nine pounds!"

"That's a braw weight. 'Tis no wonder I was so big."

Rob touched the tiny hand. A frisson passed between them. So soft. Silken as milk pods dotting the girse in autumn.

The bairnie made a fist around his faither's finger and tried to bring it to his mouth, moving his head from side to side, making sucking sounds.

Maggie bundled him into the clean blanket. "I can't believe he's hungry so soon." She unbuttoned her nightgown. "On you come, wee Robbie. Your supper is ready."

"But you need something to eat first."

"I'll eat later. I'm no' about to turn down a hungry lad."

Rob watched as she coached their son. Once he latched on tightly, he sucked heartily, making little mewling sounds.

Rob's heart swelled with luve. Surely there was no more beautiful sight on this earth.

One tiny hand escaped the blanket and began to wave around.

He smiled down at his Maggie and his Robbie. "'Tis a miracle," he breathed, "a miracle like none other."

❧❧❧

Early the next morning, Rob radioed John with the news of the birth of his first grandbairn. "He's so braw, John, you wouldn't believe it. And I'm afraid he has my appetite. Maggie says she's never seen a bairnie eat so much when only a few hours auld."

138

"Then Maggie's all right?"

"She's grand and such a brave lass. I couldn't believe how well she did."

"And without a midwife. How are you, Rob? Did you come through it all right?"

"I've never been so scared in my life, but Maggie helped me. It was like trying to fly a B-17 if I hadn't soloed a trainer. It was a miracle, John, that's all I can say. A miracle."

"You've made me a verra happy man. I can't bide long, but I'm coming to Innisbraw a week come the morra. Tell Malcolm I'll be at the dock in Oban at 0600. I can't wait to meet our new Robbie."

⚓

Over the following days, Rob only left the cottage while mither and son napped. He began running, slowly at first, until he built up his stamina, Shep prancing and cavorting at his side.

The night before John's impending arrival, Rob awakened to the drone of an approaching airplane. It sounded a lot lower than usual.

Maggie stirred, but didn't awaken.

He slipped out of bed and pulled on his denims and shoes before creeping out of the cottage, Shep at his heels.

The roar intensified as he reached the front path. He looked up in time to see the vague outline of what looked like a bomber passing overhead. It couldn't be. He had to be mistaken—after all, it was the mids of the night. But even if his eyes deceived him, he had heard that distinct kind of rumble hundreds of times while standing on the flight tower, watching his planes return from a strike led by Den Anderson.

The plane sounded as if it were headed southwest and climbing fast. But why had it been so low? *Och, Lord, what's happening?*

Chapter Twenty

Gaze raking the leaden western sky above the inky sea, Rob hurried down the fell path. A flash of light lit up the darkness close to shore.

Had the plane crashed?

"Och, Faither, please no!"

A loud rumble.

A brilliant burst of blinding light.

He dropped to his knees, pulling Shep to his side. Did the ground shake or was it his legs?

Several more loud rumbles.

The far-off drone of airplane engines were soon lost in the clamorsome wind. The light on the sea dimmed and winked out.

Reality hit like a punch in the belly. That patrol plane had bombed a German ship or U-boat—right off the shore of Innisbraw!

He rubbed the quivering shepherd's ruff. "'Tis all right, lad, there's nowt to fear." Hen's flesh peppered his bare chest and arms. *Nowt to fear?*

The distant war now threatened his home. His family.

He staggered to his feet and trotted up the path toward the cottage. The night skies this far north still held a hint of light, even this late in September. He would finish dressing and find out what had happened, even if it meant walking to Alec's croft.

He opened the cottage door, surprised to see a lamp burning in the bedroom. Och, if a U-boat had found its way into the harbour, he'd just provided a target for their deck guns. He pulled Shep inside and closed the door.

"Rob. Is that you?"

He stepped into the bedroom.

Maggie lay in bed, cradling their lad to her breast. "What are you doing up long gone the turn o' the night," she asked, "and with only your breeks and shoes on?"

It would frighten her, but she had to know. "I heard an airieplane again, and this time I saw it pass overhead." He sat on the side of the bed and gave her a quick kiss.

"Och, your lips are cold. I thought you needed the watterie. Don't tell me you've been ootside."

He told her everything he had heard and seen. "Since you're awake, I'm thinking of raising Alec on the radio."

She lifted their lad and laid him across her belly, gently patting his back. "You're certain the airieplane didn't crash?"

"The explosion was too big and I heard its engines after. If it was a U-boat, they must have caught her still on the surface and dropped a load of bombs right on top of her, then went to full power so they wouldn't be caught in the blast. And I didn't see any tracers from the sea or sky, so I'm thinking they got a direct hit. There won't be much left of whatever they bombed."

She shivered. "What are tracers?" She put the bairnie to her other breast.

"Tracers are what you see at night when large guns are fired from a plane or boat. From what I saw, I'm thinking whatever they were after was on or verra close to the surface."

"But you don't know if it was a ship or a U-boat?"

"I'm almost certain it was a U-boat. A ship would have burned longer and I'm certain those last rumbles were torpedoes exploding."

The bright sheen of tears filled her eyes.

A stab of guilt. He should have been holding her. He toed off his shoes and lay down beside her, spooning close. "In a way, what happened the night is encouraging. It shows the air patrol is doing their turn and doing it well."

"But it was so close to Innisbraw."

He glanced at his watch. "'Twill be light in about twa hours. Alec won't know owt till the guards on the shore report in, so I'll wait till then to radio him. Who knows? It could have been one of our own men who called in that air strike."

Now that they were all awake, Maggie made tea and coffee

while Rob burped Robbie and walked the floor, cradling his lad close to his heart.

Please, I beg You, Heavenly Faither, keep my Maggie and Robbie safe.

He laid the sleeping bairnie in his cradle and walked into the kitchen, drawn by the aroma of freshly brewed coffee.

"Put on your shirt and socks before you get pneumonia." Maggie handed him his mug.

"Och, I'm no' cold," he grumbled, heading for the bedroom.

The radio in the tiny lounge came to life at 0700, just as the sun coloured the eastern sky. Rob dove for it.

"Rob. I didn't get you out of bed, did I? Over."

"No, Alec. I was getting ready to dial you up. Over."

"Then you've already heard what happened? Over."

Rob rubbed his eyes. "Nobody radioed us, but I did hear that plane pass over the island last night and saw the light and heard the explosion when it bombed that ship or U-boat."

"Och, I should have known an auld Air Forces man wouldn't sleep through that. I've just finished talking to the RAF at Benbecula and it was a U-boat, though Lachlan MacNab, the man we had guarding that cove, didn't see or hear anything till that plane roared overhead. Like to skeered him to death, especially when those bombs exploded. He threw himself behind a big rock, sure he was a dead man."

"Is he all right?"

"Other than shame-faced for no' seeing that U-boat, he's no' hurt."

"Did they sink the sub?"

"They did. It was a miracle them getting there before it could dive. Since Benbecula has so many airieplanes, Tiree's only doing weather information gathering now. A Halifax spotted what looked like a sub surfacing, but since they didn't have what it would take to sink it, they had to pass the information on to the closest patrol plane from Benbecula. It was one of those Flying Fortresses covering the Atlantic. It crossed Barra east to the Minch so they wouldn't give themselves away, then crossed Innisbraw back to the

Atlantic and found themselves almost atop that U-boat sitting right there on the water."

"There's a bombardier at Benbecula who should be getting a medal for that," Rob said. "He didn't have any time at all to line up and pickle those bombs."

"Pickle?"

"Just American slang. Somebody once said the Norden bombsight is so accurate it can drop bombs into a pickle barrel, so dropping the bombs has been called pickling ever since."

"Och, something so dreadful happening close to our shores puts me in a fair fankle. That's why I called you."

"What can I do?"

"You're the only one of us who's had any experience dealing with the Germans. I'm calling a meeting of the guard at the kirk hall the day at 1500 and I'd like you to be there. Over."

Rob flipped the switch back to Broadcast and leaned forward.

Maggie pushed her way in front of him. "Absolutely no'!"

What had her in such a fash?

"Have you gone daft, Alec MacDonald?" Her voice rose. "Rob's only been on his feet a wee while. There's no way he can walk across that shore in the dark without falling and hurting himself, and us just heading into the stormy months. Over."

Rob tried to push her aside but she flipped the switch to Receive and held her ground.

"Don't fash yourself, lass." Slow and reasoned. "I don't expect Rob to join the guards now. I just want him there to give us his thoughts on how we can make better use of the men we have. Over."

Maggie flipped the switch again and retreated to the bedroom, shoulders stiff.

"I'm back," Rob said, "and I'll be there." Rob signed off and went after Maggie.

She stood at the small bedroom window, staring out at the Minch through the lace curtains.

Och, what a midden. He put his arms around her. "I'll just go and have a listen to what they have to say." He rubbed his cheek

143

across her hair. "I don't want you in a fash over this."

She whirled, throwing her arms around him. "I'm so sorry," she cried, voice muffled against his chest. "I don't know what came over me. You're a grown man. I had no right to act like your mither."

"But you're right, my legs are in no condition to handle the machair or shore yet, especially in the dark o' night." He ran his lips over her forehead. "And it felt guid having the one I luve looking out for me."

Two blue eyes peeked up at him. "Then you're no' fashed with me?"

Surely, the long kiss he gave her was answer enough.

Chapter Twenty-One

Wind-whipped rain lashed against his face as Rob hurried down the path toward the kirk. Would this be a wasted trip? Trained in aerial combat, he knew nothing about guarding an island against an attack from the sea.

A memory slowed his steps. "Defense against an enemy is using logic in the face of long odds," he recalled hearing at a lecture during Tactics as a firstie at the Point.

That bit of information had helped him save many a plane and crew over the years.

He skirted the kirk and climbed the stone steps to the kirk hall, removing his soaked A-2 jacket and stomping the wet sand from his shoes before opening the door.

The crofters who gathered in the hall came well-prepared. Those who had schooling brought detailed logs of every night, including where they had concentrated their efforts and why.

Rob listened as they read excerpts which they thought might give him a better idea of how they guarded the island. He studied the nautical chart laid out on a table, taking special note of the depth of the sea as it approached the jagged shoreline. He pointed to the large cove toward the northwest of the island. "So this is where you station twa men?"

Alec nodded. "We thought it best since it offers such a wide strand for the German's beaching their boats. And the water's shallow so far oot, they wouldn't chance upsetting in the surf."

Rob studied the map carefully, the way he would a bombing route proposed by Wing. If only he had his plotting magnifier. He leaned closer, eyes narrowing as he checked the fathoms. "I see that, but even after it deepens, if you use this legend at the side of the map, you have to go oot three-quarters of a nautical mile—that's over a kilometre—before you reach water deep enough to hide a U-boat without grounding her on the bottom."

"That's why she'd have to surface," Gordon MacLeod said. "And if she did, we'd have a chance of seeing her."

"Over a kilometre oot, even if the rain's pishing down?"

They crowded around and watched Rob run his finger across the map.

He tapped a spot. "What about here? There's a deep undersea valley less than half a kilometre from shore starting here and running south."

"But the twa coves along that spot are sma' and the surf strong," Alec said. "Surely they'd choose a place with calmer seas to come ashore."

Rob rubbed the side of his nose, spotting a flaw in their reasoning. "I've been to those coves—granted, it was almost twa years ago—but I doubt they've changed that much. Though the surf is higher than that large cove south of Scaur Fell, I'm thinking the Jerries wouldn't have a problem landing a boat right here." His finger stabbed the southernmost cove on the western shore.

"But look at the rocks on the south side, man!" Michael Nicholson stepped forward. "Innisbraw's lost many a trawler cutting that corner of the island too close trying to make the harbour afore a gale."

"The rocks on the shore will give you men guid cover and they'll no' try a night landing in any cove in any kind of gale." Rob straightened and kneaded his aching back. "They use rubber boats—inflatables—and they're too hard to control in a skailwind."

Alec's face flushed. "Then we're wasting our time keeping a look-out in the winter?"

"No' at all. I'm just thinking you need to keep your men positioned the way you've been doing during a pishing rain or skailwind. Though you wouldn't see them until they were close in, that wide cove would give them a better chance of making shore, even from far oot."

Alec let out a long breath.

Rob bent and tapped the map again. "But on a cloudy night, or one with a skifter and no' much wind, I'd concentrate my men on that southernmost cove where the enemy wouldn't have to surface until he was close to shore. I don't know much about U-boats and the like, but I do know a wee bit about how the Jerries think, and they're fair cannie."

"But we've never done it that way." Michael thrust out his chin.

Rob raked his gaze over the skeptical faces around him. "How many of you agree with Michael?"

Feet shuffled, bodies twitched. No one spoke.

"I don't bite," Rob said. "If you've a better plan, I'd like to hear it."

Silence.

So some still considered him an incomer. Well, that was their problem, not his. He had one last, very important point to make. "If you check with Lachlan, here, I'm thinking you'll find that's exactly where they sunk that sub last night."

꧁

Rob's news about the sinking of the U-boat and his meeting with the shore guard made John enjoy his visit more than usual. Nothing could compare to holding his first grandbairn and breathing in the milky, new-bairnie scent. This was his Maggie's lad. How had the time passed so quickly? Just yesterday she was this sma', her wee head covered with the same black hair, same blue eyes staring up at his face.

He braved the spells of drenching rain and squalling winds, spending a few hours every day at the infirmary, handing out medicaments to islanders with sore throats or long-term ailments, and bringing some of the bairns' inoculations up-to-date.

The two men spent hours talking quietly while Maggie and the bairnie slept, but John's visit was short.

Rob saw him off at the dock early Tuesday morning.

"Don't try to do too much running, lad." He gave Rob a warning look. "Listen to what your body tells you. You're still too thin. Eat plenty of meat."

"The womenfolk are still bringing food. They say they'll keep cooking for us till Maggie gets her strength back."

John clapped him on the shoulder. "I know you're worried about the U-boats, but we'll just have to keep praying. I can't imagine why they'd ever come ashore here."

"You're most likely right. Have a guid trip back. We're looking forward to a longer visit next time."

"I'm leaving here with a light heart. Wee Robbie is healthy and so are you and Maggie." John removed his glasses and wiped his eyes. "And I know mither and lad are in luving hands. You're a fine man, Rob Savage. As I've told Maggie, I couldn't be any prouder if you were my own flesh."

"Thank ye, John. I'll try to live up to that."

Maggie ignored Rob's gaze as they made their way down the path. Elspeth, who had been suffering from a cold, had sent word by Angus that she was finally well and eager to see the new bairnie.

Now, the following Saturday, Robbie was on his first outing— a visit to her cottage.

Rob's forehead creased. "You're certain this isn't too soon— too much?"

He was asking for the second time? "Och, stop mithering me. It feels grand to be ootside. And the sun is finally shining after all that rain." She took a deep breath. "I hate being cooped up like a broody hen all day."

"Are you certain you and Robbie are warm enough?"

What a persistent man. She swatted his arm. "I'm biddy certain. Besides, here we are."

Elspeth waited at the top of the steps.

Shep bounded up and nudged her hand in greeting.

"Here's our Shep," she said, patting his head. "Come for a bite of scone, have you, lad?"

Rob whistled and Shep ran back down the steps to his side. "I'm afraid the Savage males always come begging for food, Elspeth. My apologies for Shep's bad manners."

"Och, he's a fine dog. Up you come. I want to see our braw Robbie before he's auld enough to walk."

They followed her into the cottage.

Shep took his usual spot on the rug in front of the hearth.

Elspeth sat in her rocker and held out her hands. "I'm ready."

Maggie stifled a laugh. So Elspeth suffered a bit of impatience too. She removed Robbie's blankets and placed the squirming bairnie in her arms. She motioned Rob back as the old woman pulled up the lad's gown and examined his long legs, smiling as her arthritic hands caressed his slender feet. "I'm of a mind you may no' be the tallest in your family, Rob, when this lad grows up. Just look at these hands and feet."

Rob nodded.

She picked the bairnie up and put him over her shoulder. "He's a strong one. See how he already holds his head up?" She ran her fingers through his fine, black hair. "He has your colouring, Maggie, but I see more of Rob in him."

"I do too," Maggie said, shooting Rob a warning glance.

"He's a guid mixture of the both of you." Elspeth lowered the baby to her lap and studied his face. "You've a bright future ahead of you, wee laddie. You'll make your mither and faither verra proud someday."

Maggie's laugh broke through. "I don't see how we could be any prouder."

"I understand." Elspeth covered the lad with one blanket. "Rob, if you'll take wee Robbie, Maggie and I will go into the kitchen to inbring an early tea. I've fresh scones and shortbreads."

Rob picked up his son and cradled him in his arms. "That's guid. Here I was scolding Shep and 'tis me that's starving."

Maggie put her arm around Elspeth's waist, savoring the warmth of their unique, loving relationship. "He had a big breakfast only twa hours ago, but I'm one to talk. Robbie's nursing so often, I'm about to oot-eat Rob."

The three friends spent another hour discussing Robbie's birth, the sinking of the U-boat, and the need for even more prayer to protect their tiny island.

"Were they trying to put a boat ashore?" Elspeth asked Rob as he zipped his A-2 jacket.

"I don't suppose we'll ever know, but if they were, they were so quiet about it. Lachlan didn't hear a thing. You know how sound carries over water, especially at night. It could have been for reconnaissance, to see if we have any guards posted, though why they'd want to land here at all has me in a swither."

Rob squeezed Maggie's elbow as they walked back up the path. "Our Elspeth's a real treasure. I only pray we'll have her for a long time."

"We most likely will. Her faither passed at ninety-four and her mither at ninety-eight. She still amazes me with her stamina."

He pulled Maggie to a stop.

"What's the matter, are your legs hurting?"

"No' a bit. I was just thinking about how blessed I am and I can't take another step till I express my thoughts." He paused for a moment, smiling down at her, then bent to brush his lips over her cheek. "I have the one lass in the entire world our Lord knew was perfect for me, a strong, healthy, braw lad, and a fine dog. I have friends who are more family than most folk ever dream of having, and I live on a wondrous island with endless sea and sky." He swallowed the tears clogging his throat. "Was there ever a man so undeserving, yet more blessed?"

Maggie smiled up at him, eyes soft with luve. "Undeserving in your eyes only. Don't disremember, God looks on the heart. You've already paid a higher price than most with the pain you've suffered. You've been tested and you've no' faltered. 'Tis guid to be grateful for all you have, but don't question God's wisdom. He knows who will be faithful, no matter what."

"I don't want to fail Him. Or you and Robbie."

"You won't. You're too stubborn, remember?"

Cannie, cannie lass.

He threw back his head and laughed. "Aye, much too stubborn."

Chapter Twenty-Two

A break in the stormy weather offered Rob an opportunity to begin training in earnest. He ran early every morning, often before the sun's first rays stabbed across the dark waters of the harbour like beacons from a hundred lighthouses. For now, he avoided the rocky descent to the base of Innis Fell across from the cottage and stayed to the path leading down to the dock and around to the western shore—past the fishermen's cottages, the kirk and manse, and four large cow crofts. When the path turned south, he doubled back behind the crofts' dykes. Curious Hieland coos rushed to the dykes at the ends of their coo gangs, pushing and lowing in their haste, stretching out long tongues and blowing steamy gusts when he didn't stop to offer a tasty branch or handful of long girse.

He skirted the lower flanks of Ben Innis, Shep at his side. Even when they flushed a bird or small creature from the heather or prickly gorse, the dog never gave chase.

Rob focused on his goal: get in good enough condition to cover the path halfway around the island, run up the steep western slopes of Ben Innis, and down the eastern side to home. He lengthened his run every day, if only by a few metres.

Maggie swept the cottage floor flags, heather broom flying, alarming memories fueling her energy. After Rob's first crash, she'd been appalled by his weight loss. Stubborn, impatient man—overdoing it again and dropping weight. She yanked the door wide and attacked the pile of sand, sending a cloud of debris over the entry flags. The minute she finished the breakfast dishes, she'd have her say and he'd better listen.

Half an hour later, he returned.

"You're doing too much running."

151

He grunted.

She ignored it. "I have no complaint about your appetite, but you're dropping weight every day."

"Just fat, Maggie. I'm building muscle."

She put Robbie over her shoulder, patted his back until he burped, and settled him at her other breast. After Rob's first injury, even before he could walk, he had snuck in leg-raises when he should have been sleeping. Trying to change this stubborn man's mind was as fruitful as batting her head against a stone dyke. "Why are you doing this to yourself? I could understand your need to get into shape before. You wanted to be fit for duty. I know you and you wouldn't be doing this if not for a specific goal." She glanced at him out of the corner of her eye.

Lips set in a firm line. Jaw muscles clenched.

He often talked about the importance of using logic—why couldn't he use it to analyse his own actions?

He leaned forward in his rocker. "I've already ordered all the air-dried lumber I'll need from Bill Pointer, the friend I was telling you about who owns a lumber mill in New Hampshire. I want to be in the verra best possible shape when I build the rescue boat and after that, our home. There's a lot of hard, backbreaking work in both projects, so I've got to be up to it physically."

Hmm, a large flaw in his reasoning. "Will you be using only your legs and increased lung capacity, then?" *Talk your way out of this one.*

"Well, no. I'll have to start working on my upper body strength also, especially my left shoulder and arm."

"When?"

"As soon as my legs are in shape and I don't limp every time I get tired."

Her patience slipped another notch. "Haven't you learned anything in the past twa years? I thought you finally understood that muscles need time to rest. Working them every day in the same way is counter-productive."

"I'm in a hurry. I want this to be the last winter Innisbraw fishermen have to lay their lives on the line every time they go oot."

Her silence made him squirm.

He added peats to the fire before going into the kitchen and washing his hands. He returned, rubbing the side of his nose. "So, you're thinking I should work my upper body one day and my lower the next?"

"It isn't important what I think. 'Tis whatever you decide is best to accomplish what you want to do."

"But I enjoy running."

"I know you do. Why else would you go out with the rain plomping down and the wind blowing? You just go too far, is all."

"You sound like every teacher and flight instructor I've ever had." He stabbed his fingers through his hair. "Since you can't all be wrong, I must be a kilometre off the mark."

"Och, Rob." She put Robbie into his cradle and knelt on the rug in front of Rob's chair, taking his hands and looking up into his face. "You're a verra special man. You'll do owt, go through owt just to help others—don't say a word until I'm finished—but you have to learn to take care of yourself too. If you don't, you'll be in no condition to help others when they need it. Can you no' see what I mean?"

Her cannie question caught him unprepared. "My ... mind understands but the rest of me is so impatient to get it done, I can't seem to stop myself." He leaned over and kissed her cheek. "I'm sorry to get you so fashed, Maggie, I truly am."

"All you need to do is plan an exercise schedule—one you'll enjoy, one you'll carry oot—instead of running all over the island, wearing yourself down. Now, tell me what sort of special strength you'll need for building the boat."

A safer subject. "There will be a lot of lifting and carrying when I get the lumber and have to move it from the dock and stack it in the shed, and again when I fit the timbers and boards into place on the boat. But even before that, I'll have to loft the plans."

She looked at him, brow creased.

"I need to set aside at least a quarter of the shed floor and draw a detailed, life-sized plan of the boat on the floor. That way I can size each piece of lumber to the plan before I put the boat together. That'll cut down on mistakes since I'm a novice boat builder, though all boat builders do it."

"You'll be kneeling or squatting to do that?"

"Aye."

"So, we have kneeling, squatting, lifting, carrying. What else?"

"I'll need to plane the wood smooth, though I'm hoping to get a used electric planer, and I'll use a drill, maul, hammer, screwdriver, level, sander, saw—again, hopefully an electric one— och, that's all I can think of right now."

A safer subject?

She had him. Maggie used his favorite reasoning tool better than he did.

That was him finished, then. "I guess what I really need is a whole-body workout."

"We should radio Faither and get his ideas on this. He or one of his therapists should know what you need to do."

At least she didn't gloat when she bested him.

"I hate to bother him."

"He's so interested in your rescue boat, you know he'd luve to help."

⚓

John was not only eager to help set up an exercise regime for Rob, he sounded delighted to do anything he could to keep him from losing any more weight. As Rob detailed the work he was planning to do, the doctor asked questions. The sound of his scratching pen came over the radio.

One week later, a large envelope arrived by post; inside was a complete plan for the gradual strengthening of every muscle Rob needed, not only to build the rescue boat and house, but to retain his meagre body fat.

If you continue to lose weight when following this plan to the letter, let me know. You could have a problem with how you metabolize food. That would have to be addressed and corrected immediately before you begin burning muscle mass.

Rob didn't like this one bit. He had to cut back his running to four times a week and the distance by almost half. But, he had to admit, the more weight he lost the harder it became to maintain the schedule he had set for himself, so he reluctantly gave in and started implementing the entire regimen John sent.

By the end of November, he began to see some results. Not only could he run more easily, he didn't tire as quickly, and his arms, shoulders, and back strengthened daily. Though he didn't regain any of the weight he had lost, he didn't lose more, so Maggie no longer nattered about how thin he looked.

When he wasn't exercising, he worked on a china cabinet he was building for Maggie's birthday in December. He also continued his lessons in the Gaelic with Elspeth, and even spent time on the design for their home.

"One thing we definitely need is a shower," he told Maggie one afternoon after coming in muddy from a short trip to the shed in the rain. "The tub is fine for a guid soak but I'd rather take a quick shower after a run or workout."

"There's no' a single shower on Innisbraw, and only a few large bathing tubs. You'll be setting a precedent here."

"Is that guid or bad?"

"'Tis guid, of course." She gifted him with a smile. "You've said yourself, when the war is over they should finally lay the sea cable to bring telephones to our island. Just think, telephones and showers and a boatyard. Innisbraw will soon belong to the twentieth century, especially when they provide electricity to the rest of the island."

Change. Usually good, but sometimes bad—very bad. "Just as long as we don't lose the closeness we have here. No progress is worth that."

She set aside the hippens she was folding and put her arms around him. "We'll never lose that, for it comes from the souls of our folk. It will just mean life will be a bit easier, and that can't be a bad thing."

How could a few soft words turn his world from dreichy grey to sunny yellow? He pulled her close and kissed her. Her warm, pliant lips, sweet as heather honey, brought a tingle of excitement. He'd waited six weeks for this moment. "How long before Robbie wakes?" He nuzzled her ear. "'Tis already gone 1600."

"He should sleep for at least twa more hours." A throaty whisper as soft fingertips caressed his cheeks.

More tingles.

He pulled the barrette from her hair. "Then smoorich with me, lass." He picked her up and carried her toward the bedroom.

"Shouldn't we at least wait till the een?"

"I can't wait that long." He laid her on the bed and, fingers fumbling, unbuttoned her sweater. "I've been wanting you all day."

"All day?"

"Since you met me at the door with a cup of coffee when I came in from my run."

"I was in my dressing gown and hadn't even brushed my hair."

He started on her dress buttons. "There's nothing more fetching than my lass with her hair tangling down her back and her cheeks rosy from sleep." He groaned, nibbling her neck.

"You're impossible."

"And you like it. Come on, awn up."

"I don't like it."

He sat back, mouth open.

"I don't like it," she repeated, unlacing his shirt. "I luve it."

Chapter Twenty-Three

The war in Europe appeared to be escalating toward a bloody climax. Paris had been liberated the previous August. In October, Aachen was the first German city to be captured and secured by the American 1st and 9th Armies. The news from the Pacific Theatre, however, was not as encouraging. Sections of Tokyo smoldered after the first B-24 raid on Japan, but battles raged on the Palau Islands after nearly ten weeks of intense fighting. Even though United States forces landed on Leyte Island in the Philippines in October, the US Fourteenth Air Corps abandoned its airbase in Liuchow, China, the same week. Japan was digging in, fighting to the death.

Rob wrote Bill Pointer in New Hampshire, asking for an estimated delivery date for his lumber. After the reply came, he stood on the path in front of the post office and tore open the envelope. He skipped the usual greeting and update on Bill's family and scanned the rest of the letter.

Sorry, Rob, but all merchant ships, large and small, have been commandeered for war-related purposes. President Roosevelt has made several radio broadcasts rallying Americans to sacrifice even more to defeat Germany and Japan. Your lumber is already cut to your specifications and stacked to dry in our shed. I promise to give your shipment top priority the minute peace is declared.

Stunned, he stared at the letter until the ink blurred. How long would that be? A few more months? Years, even?

Och, he should have known about the merchant ships since the same had happened in the UK. He was boxed in—couldn't get the lumber he needed anywhere in Europe because of the war. And Bill was the only one he knew who had access to the perfect mix of hardwood trees and didn't use a kiln to dry his lumber.

He stuffed the letter into his pocket, called Shep, and broke into a run. He passed the howff and the weaving shop, almost oblivious to the black, louring clouds suddenly releasing a deluge of rain. Within moments, he was soaked to the skin, but ignored the snell wind driving the icy torrent against his head and body. He ran blindly, senses tuned only to frustration, disappointment, and guilt at failing to fulfill his promise to build a rescue boat over the coming months.

Being invalided out of the Army Air Forces had been a most crushing blow, but the shattering of the dream that kept him going after the first B-17 crash was just as devastating. When the pain was so severe he wanted to die, he had concentrated on that goal. But he had failed—not only the fishermen, but the Lord who had given him the mandate.

The Lord.

Och, forgive me, Faither. I've failed You so many times in my life but this is the verra worst. I've another hurdle to overcome, one I canna control, and I don't know what to do. Help me, Lord. I know I don't deserve it, but please help me do Your perfect will.

He stumbled. Was this war his fault? Of course no'. Could he stop the U-boats from destroying so many supply boats? Again, no. But what could he do if building the rescue boat was no longer an option for the immediate future?

His breath came in ragged bursts as he slogged along the wet, sandy path up the southwest side of the Innis Fell.

Steam rose from Shep's drenched coat and his tongue hung limply from the side of his mouth.

They'd run around the entire island.

By the time they reached the cottage, Rob's left leg throbbed. Limping so badly each step required Herculean effort, he shivered in the cold wind blasting from the north as he opened the door.

The kitchen and lounge loomed dark and vacant.

"Maggie?"

No answer—and the cradle was empty.

Where had she gone with Robbie?

He hobbled down to Elspeth's cottage and rapped on her door.

158

No light. No welcoming footsteps. Not home.

He collapsed on her top entry step, hugging Shep's neck. "Where are they?"

From the moment Robbie had been born, Shep had appointed himself Robbie's guardian. When the dog was not out running with Rob or taking a quick trip around the croft yard, he lay close beside the cradle, not moving until ordered to.

He grabbed Shep by the ruff and looked into his eyes. "Find Robbie, Shep. Find Robbie."

The dog lifted his nose, scenting the air before taking off down the path, toward the harbour.

The harbour?

Rob's heart leaped into his throat.

Had Maggie grown tired of living with him and taken Robbie to Edinburgh to stay with John? The idea was ridiculous but, like a strange bump in the night bringing a vision of a burglar, it needed to be investigated.

He followed Shep, no longer able to control his limp, mind groping for reasons for her to leave.

He upset her by his refusal to accept praise.

And he still had trouble sharing everything with her—perhaps that was it.

Shep passed the pier and continued down the path.

All the old insecurities that had plagued him since childhood—the fears of being alone, no family, no one to hold him, to luve him—welled up inside. It was bad enough to fail with the rescue boat, but so much worse to fail Maggie.

How should a husband behave? He'd never spent any time with married couples before coming to Innisbraw. Was he doing something wrong?

When he was five, a couple adopted him, but then returned him to the orphanage a year later with no explanation. Yes, Maggie had chosen him, but who was to say she didn't wish she could return him?

But wouldn't she have said something? Wouldn't she have pushed him away or shown her displeasure? *Heavenly Faither, I don't know what I've done, but I'm such a failure.*

He couldn't go on much longer. Shep would soon get so far ahead, Rob would lose him in the gloaming. Soaked through to the skin, teeth chittering, he forced himself on.

The dog turned into the lane leading to the kirk. No light in the sanctuary.

He stumbled after the dog, across the girse toward the manse, where a tiny glint of light shone at one side of a blackout curtain.

Shep climbed the stone steps, shook himself vigorously, and sat on the top step, flanks heaving.

Rob stumbled up the steps, so exhausted he didn't have the strength to knock on the door. He collapsed next to Shep, gasping for breath.

The dog licked his face.

"Find ... Robbie," Rob panted.

The shepherd raced to the front door and scratched at it, barking.

Rob staggered to his feet just as Hugh opened the door.

"My word!" Hugh exclaimed. "Shep and Rob, it's wet and cold oot here." He closed the door and made his way to Rob's side. "Have you hurt yourself? You're shivering. Come away in, I've a guid fire going."

Couldn't waste time getting warm. "Maggie. Can't find Maggie and Robbie."

"They're in the chaumer." Hugh put his arm around Rob's back. "The meeting's almost over."

Rob's legs gave way. He went to his knees. "They're here?"

"Of course. They're at a Women's Aid Society meeting. Maggie said she left you a note."

A note? "I didn't see one." But he hadn't looked, either.

Hugh ran back into the house, returned with a knitted hap, and tucked it around Rob's shoulder. "You're wet through to the skin. Should I get Maggie then?"

"Don't do that. I've been a daftie, Hugh, thought she'd grown tired of me and left."

"Tired of you?" Hugh shook his head. "This is going to take some explaining. I hate to keep you out in the cold another tick, but we'd best go around to the kitchen door. I'm no' sure you want Maggie to see you like this."

"You're right." Rob groaned.

Ordering Shep to follow, Hugh helped Rob around to the kitchen door and pulled him and Shep inside.

Rob went to the stove and huddled over it, shivering convulsively, while the dog plonked himself down in a corner, panting.

Hugh poured Rob a mug of coffee, and after rummaging about in his aumrie, held up an unopened, dusty bottle of whisky. "I've been keeping this years for just such an opportunity." He added a stiff shot to the coffee. "This should warm you."

Rob sipped the dark, bitter brew. At least it was hot. He never drank anything stronger than ale and felt the burn of the whisky all the way to his stomach. He looked down at his clothes.

His shoes and denim breeks were soaked and muddy, and he hadn't even had the good sense to put on his A-2 jacket when he went for the post, so his shirt clung to his skin like lime to a wall.

He'd really done it this time.

"I'm sorry about your floor, Hugh. I'll clean it up."

"Blethers. We've got to get you into some dry clothes."

"No, I'll just go oot the kitchen door and cut through the girse to the cottage. Are they going home in Flora's cairt?"

"She picked them up along with Elspeth so I'm certain she'll be taking them home. But you're in no condition for such a long walk."

"I'll have time if I hurry. I'll make it up to you about the floor, Hugh. If you'll get Shep some water, we have to be going."

"Rob?" Maggie stood in the kitchen doorway, Robbie over her shoulder. "I thought I recognized Shep's bark."

He groped for a chair and sat, head in hands. *Whatsomever she says, I've got it coming.*

She handed Robbie to Hugh and knelt before Rob. "Have you hurt yourself? You're soaked." She took his icy hands in hers, rubbing them.

He was too embarrassed to meet her inquiring gaze.

"Why didn't you wait at home for me? You shouldn't have come all this way when you're so wet. You're freezing." She turned to Hugh. "Could you have Morag hold Robbie, then draw a tub of water? No' too hot, just enough to take out the chill."

Rob forced himself to sit up straighter. "I'll bathe myself at home. If I'm a daft enough to go running with the cold rain pishing down, I can wait to get warm."

Maggie wouldn't release his hands when he struggled to stand. He sat again.

"Faither warned you no' to get chilled. Remember, your left lung was damaged when you broke your ribs. Now, you're going to get out of those wet clothes and into a hot tub. When you've stopped sheevering, we'll talk about going home."

How could she look at him with such luve? "I'm a fool, Maggie. A complete fool. When you weren't home or at Elspeth's, I thought I'd lost you, pushed you away."

Her mouth opened in surprise. "Then you're no' here to see us home? What are you saying? Lost us? How could you lose us?" She looked up at Hugh. "Do you know what he means?"

"I don't think he found the note you left him."

She looked up at Rob, eyes dark. "But I left it in the bathing room, knowing you'd need to bathe yourself after your run."

"I didn't go into the bathing room because I'm a fool."

"Start the tub filling, Hugh, and ask Flora to take Elspeth home, then stop at our cottage and gather up a complete change of clothes for Rob. She helped with the laundry before Rob hired Anna again so she'll know what he needs. Och, and have her bring his leather jacket. Since he's no' wearing it, she'll find it on a peg by the door."

Rob hung his head, so humiliated he couldn't even voice a protest. When had he ever done anything so daft?

She got up and held out her hands. "On you come, luve, I'll help you. You're shivering so hard your teeth are chittering together."

"I can do it." But could he? He was so tired it took effort to raise his head. He took a deep breath and forced himself to stand.

She hooked her arm through his and they shambled into the

bathing room. She helped him undress and climb into the tub.

The hot water felt so guid. Why couldn't he stop shivering? He lay back and closed his eyes. The shivering finally stopped, but a single spasm shook his body as he pictured her blue eyes, filled with luve and concern.

Maggie knelt beside him. "Are you warmer?"

He nodded.

Hugh knocked on the door and handed Maggie a pile of clean clothing. "When you're ready to go, just call oot. Flora and I are in the kitchen having something hot to drink. She's enjoying holding wee Robbie and she says to tell you that, though the rain has stopped, 'tis still windy and cold ootside—and Shep lapped up twa bowls of water."

"Thank ye, Hugh. We'll be ready to go in a few minutes." Maggie pulled the plug and held up a towel. "Oot you come then. I'll dry you."

He felt helpless as a bairnie when she toweled him dry and helped him dress. "I'm a real bother." He averted his eyes as she laced his shirt. "I don't know why you put up with me."

"If you don't know that by now, you never will." Voice subdued. And sad.

He wanted to pull her close, but his arms dropped to his sides. "What I'm trying to say is, I'm sorry, Maggie, sorry for this whole midden."

She pulled his gansey sweater over his head and held out his jacket. "We'll talk about this later. I want to get you home and into a warm bed."

"I'm no' sick."

"No' yet, and I'm going to do all I can to keep it that way."

His fingers fumbled with the jacket zipper.

She pulled it up. "I'll get my coat and Robbie's things, and we'll go home."

Rob followed her into the chaumer where Morag was tidying up after the meeting. She eyed him with a glimmer of amusement. "Isn't it just like a man to go oot in the plomping rain and get soaked? My Alec's forever dripping water all over the chaumer's

stone pavers from his wet clothes no matter how many times I tell him to leave them on the entry flags."

If only it were that simple.

Chapter Twenty-Four

Shep, exhausted for once, curled at his master's feet, nose tucked beneath his tail feathers.

Though Maggie and Flora chatted about the meeting, Rob couldn't say a word on the ride home. When they arrived at the cottage, he forced himself to thank Flora. "I don't know much about sheep, but whenever Angus needs help with owt, promise he'll let me know."

She nodded, eyes lowered. "I will, though it was no real bother."

He took Maggie's elbow as he opened the door, but only as a polite gesture. Getting warm and a few minutes' rest in the cairt had helped immensely, though his legs still ached and he couldn't stop limping. Outwardly, he felt much better, but inside, his stomach churned. He pulled the blackout curtains and turned on the lights.

Maggie laid a protesting Robbie down in his cradle.

Rob helped her off with her coat. "I'll add peats to the fire while you nurse our lad. If you don't start soon, he'll be rouping so hard he won't have the breath to suck."

"You should be abed." She removed Robbie's extra blankets and settled him at her breast.

"There's nowt wrong with me. I was cold, is all. I'm fine now."

"You're limping, so you're no' fine."

"'Tis just that left leg." Aching to put his arms around her, he couldn't, not until he knew she didn't resent him. What could he do—or say? She hadn't left him, but could he have sensed her unease, perhaps subconsciously?

He stirred the embers, added several peats to the fire, limped into the kitchen, and filled Shep's food bowl.

"Come sit in your rocker, Rob. We need to talk."

165

His stomach cramped again. "I should bring in more peats."

"Later. We need to talk now."

That rocker looked inviting but he couldn't sit so close to her without reaching for her hand. He stood in front of the fire, feeling awkward and more than a little sick.

"Surely you're no' still cold?"

He shook his head.

"What's wrong? Something's happened the day but you won't tell me what. Talk to me, Rob, please."

He stared into the glowing fire and pretended it was the smoking peat and not tears burning his eyes. "I'm ... I'm sorry if I'm no' the man you deserve, Maggie. I understand if you regret our marriage as I don't know how to be a guid husband."

She laid their loudly protesting bairnie into his cradle at the side. "I don't understand." She put her arms around his waist and rested her cheek against his back. "What's brought on all this daft talk?"

"I'm just one big failure as a man, Maggie, and I'm sorry it's hurt you. I never wanted that."

Maggie ignored the cries of their hungry bairnie and grabbed Rob's arm, pulling him around. "I don't know what you're blethering about." She curled herself against him, but her breath caught when he didn't embrace her. "Talk to me. Right now. What's happened?" She stepped back and dropped into her rocker.

Heartbroken.

This sounded like the Rob she had first known, the man who so feared getting close to anyone, who had spent his entire life without luve and was so desperately lonely. Heart plummeting at the pain on his face, the agony in his eyes, she swiped at the tears on her cheeks. She leaned forward and grabbed his hands. "I don't know what happened the day," she said, talking loudly over Robbie's frantic screams. "But I do know that if you won't tell me, something might be broken between us—something that cannot be mended. You once told me you would luve me forever. I can't believe you didn't mean it. Luve is shown by sharing our hearts with each other."

Rob closed his eyes. His knees folded, face resting in her lap. His hands groped for hers. "Och, I meant it, Maggie, and I'll always mean it, but you're too fine, too guid for the likes of me." He mustered the courage to meet her tear-filled gaze. "I've failed the Lord, the folk of the island, and I've failed you—especially you."

Hurt confusion clouded her face.

Och, would he never learn that leaving her in the dark about his disappointments only made things worse? He closed his eyes for a moment, searching for the words. "I ... I got a letter from Bill Pointer in the post the day. He can't ship the lumber for the rescue boat till after the war ends. All the merchant ships have been taken over by the American government."

She worried her lower lip. "Is that what has you in such a fash? But what has this to do with you failing me?"

"Och, Maggie, I'm ... I ran the path around the island after I read the letter and when I didn't find you here, I thought I'd done something to make you leave me." He dropped his gaze. Such pain in her eyes. All his fault.

Soft fingers caressed his cheeks. "I can't imagine what made you even think that. Have I ever pushed you away?"

Never. He shook his head.

Robbie's cries had stopped.

"Our lad has rouped himself to sleep, but before I wake him to finish his feeding, I need you to get up and hold me close while you tell me everything. You've been verra quiet the past few weeks but I thought you were thinking about your plans for the boat. Have you disremembered how guid it feels when you share your fears?"

She was right. He couldn't keep his fears and disappointments festering inside until erupting into a full-blown panic.

He got up and sat in his rocker, pulling her onto his lap. "I ... I've been wanting to get into shape so I can join the shore patrol." He rested his cheek against her hair. "But I know how fashed you were before I went to that meeting, so I've kept my fears of the U-boats to myself. That bombing off our shore made me realize how close the war is, Maggie, and with the Jerries feeling the end near, they're apt to try owt."

"All the folk are worried about the U-boats. That's why Hugh spends so long praying about it every Sabbath. And I agree that you should join the patrol if that's what you want." She squeezed his fingers. "But you have to promise to dress warmly and have a nap every afternoon. Is that why you've been so quiet?"

"That and wanting to get to work on the rescue boat." He grunted. "Must be a burden being merrit to somebody who wants everything done yesterday."

"But why would you even think I'd want to leave you?"

"I suppose it was feeling like I've failed at everything, so I must be failing you too." His arms tightened automatically. "Are you certain you're no' wishing you hadn't chosen me?"

"It breaks my heart to hear you ask that. I'd choose you a hundred times over." She pulled away and smiled up at him.

The pressure in his chest lifted and he couldn't help returning her smile "You would? I haven't failed you?"

"As usual, you're expecting too much of yourself. 'Tis just this terrible war. As soon as it's over, you'll build your boat."

He gazed at her. "Would a wee kiss help say how sorry I am for fashing you?"

"No. But a verra long kiss might."

He held her, smoothing wisps of hair back from her face, caressing her shoulders, whispering words of endearment as he nuzzled her cheek. He couldn't remember being so tired, but his stomach no longer cramped and the weight on his chest was gone. Why had he reacted so violently to that letter? Hadn't all those old fears been put to rest, especially after the long Sabbath afternoons Maggie had spent peeling back the layers of his buried past? *Och, Lord, thank You for my Maggie, and please help me share things with her so this never happens again.*

Maggie sighed as she lifted Robbie from his cradle, woke him, and put him to her breast. Would Rob ever overcome his painful past—or had it buried itself forever in the recesses of his mind, waiting for the moment he let his guard down?

He lifted the empty peat basket from the hearth and limped into the kitchen for the box beside the stove. Such a strong man, determined to protect others, no matter the cost to himself. Yet so vulnerable.

Hot tears burned her eyes. Somehow, she must protect him from his fear of failing those he luved.

Help me recognize his needs, Faither, before they overcome him. Hold him up. Guard his heart against the de'il's sly whispers.

"Are you hungry?" she asked while he washed the peat-black from his hands.

"Gleg as gled."

"Then I'll put this sleeperie lad in his cradle and fix you some supper."

"What about you?"

"They served an early tea at the meeting and I ate far more than my share."

"I can heat up that guid chicken bree we had for dinner. And while I do that, I'll tell you what I was thinking the day while I ran up the fell toward home."

"I won't listen if you're going to talk about failing again."

"This is before I knew you were no' home. Once I got it through my thick head there is nowt I can do about the delay, I realized there is something I can do to fill my time until the war ends." He broke a slab of peat into smaller pieces, dropped them into the kitchen stove, and put the bree on to heat. "I was praying while I ran, no' understanding why God's plan had to include me getting invalided oot before the war ended if I couldn't even build the rescue boat instead of bombing the de'il out of the Jerries. But it suddenly hit me. You know how I was going to build the rescue boat and then our home?"

It wasn't the bombing he missed. He still grieved about no' being allowed to fly, even if he never talked about that. "Aye."

"Well, since the war—especially in the Pacific—looks like it could go on for a while, I've decided to spend the wet winter months designing our home, and then build it next spring and summer. Unless something unexpected happens, like Germany and Japan putting an end to the fighting suddenly, we could be living in

169

it by the time the weather turns next fall."

Och, what a surprise! "I luve it. Where do you want to build?"

He dished up a bowl of bree and brought it and a handful of bannock to eat in his rocker. "If you agree, I'd like to put it next to this croft but farther away from the path to give you room for a large garden oot front. Do you think the Island Council would approve?"

"Of course. The Donald deeded all the land on the island to the folk of Innisbraw over a hundred years ago. They'll be pleased you want to spare the low ground for the sheep and coo crofts and choose the top of Innis Fell instead. It sounds perfect."

He dipped a piece of bannock into the bree. "This will be our home for the rest of our lives so we want to plan it right." He ate two pieces of bannock, spooned the bree into his mouth, and got up for another bowl.

"You really want to build it large enough for eight bairns?"

"Of course." He came back in and sat down. "And I want to add twa rooms just for us—a place for you to do your spinning and weaving so you can leave your loom up all the time, and an office for me so I can do some work at home."

So much money. "Do we have the silver for all of this?"

That deep, rumbling chuckle she luved. "I didn't spend even a fraction of my pay for years. I saved it all and it's been earning interest. I can use the tools I have to buy to build the house for boat building too, but there is one wee problem."

"What's that?" Robbie stirred and she rocked the cradle with her foot.

"I don't know the first thing about building a stone house. The one I helped build in America was made of wood." He began to eat again, but slower.

"Wood? How did the folk stay warm in winter and cool in summer?"

"They had a wood-burning stove and fireplace. Wood burns hotter than peat. In summer, they just kept the windows open to the breeze."

This was one fear she could take care of right now. "There should be no problem with a stone house. The stones are from right here on Innisbraw—from the quarry on Heuch Fell. Besides, putting up the walls of a house here on Innisbraw is never a one-man job. Every able-bodied and available man on the island will help."

"Would you be upset if I used the same type of slate tiles that are on the infirmary?"

"Of course no'. But those you'll have to get from Wales."

He finished the bree and went into the kitchen to rinse the bowl. His limp was better, but he hadn't eaten as much as usual.

"You only ate twa bowls. Are you certain you're no' hurting?"

He grabbed two shortbreads. "Thanks to my having my head full o' mince, I ache all over, but it hasn't affected my appetite." He broke off a piece and put it in her mouth. "I'm just excited about building our own home."

"No more hiding your heart from me, Rob, my luve."

He placed the remaining shortbread on the table, pulled her to her feet, and held her close, molding his body to hers. "Our own home, Maggie." He removed the barrette from her hair and pulled up a strand, inhaling. "Just pray I can find everything I need to build it."

Chapter Twenty-Five

Though it was probably too early for a blether, Rob interrupted his run a week later for a stop at Alec's croft. He found the crofter in the coo gang, forking grass hay from his cairt into large piles.

The long-horned Heiland coos lowed plaintively, impatient to begin their morning meal. Their pungent odour smelled earthy and surprisingly pleasant.

"Och, Rob, you've saved me dialing you up on the radio the mornin." Alec's smile appeared forced. "'Tis a guid thing the rain's no' pishing doon or you'd be soaked again."

"From the way that sky's louring, I'll be cannie to get home before it starts." Rob leaned against the wooden fence, well out of the way. "What's this about you dialing me up? More trouble with the U-boats?"

A heifer, blowing a cloud of steam and rolling her eyes, licked Alec's waxed jacket sleeve with her long, rough tongue.

Using his hip, he steered her toward a pile of hay and slapped her on the rump before tossing his fork into the cairt. "No' this time. Benbecula called last een and told me there've been fewer sightings the past few weeks. Said we can go back to patrolling with fewer men if we've a mind."

"After sinking that sub on our shores? I came by to tell you to add me to the patrol. If my legs are strong enough to run, I can handle the machair and the rocks."

"Are you certain?" Alec ran a hand over his stubble-studded chin. "Wouldn't do to set you back. Though we could use you, we could, for I'm no' cutting even one man. Like you, I can't forget them bombing that U-boat less than a kilometre from our shores."

"I'm biddy certain."

"You'll need a black cap to cover your light hair. And a waxed

172

jacket and breeks to keep you dry. And boots, of course."

"Malcolm gave me some auld boots one of his crew left behind. He was no' as tall as me, but taller than most, so they're serviceable though tight. I'll make slits at the toes and cover them with tape. And I'll use John's waxed jacket and pants. They're short in the arms and legs but I'll wear my denims and A-2 jacket under them. Maggie's knitting me a cap with some black yarn Elspeth gave her. I have my binoculars but I'll need a weapon. Edenoaks didn't send my pistol in the boxes they posted."

"I've a fine sharp knife or a guid fork. You can take either one."

A knife or wooden haying fork? A knife would be a good weapon for fighting in close, or disabling a man from the back, but useless against anyone armed with a gun. A fork gave one more reach and could easily be driven completely through a man, but its long handle was vulnerable to being snatched or batted from one's hand and, like a knife, offered little defense against a gun.

"Neither sounds verra guid, but I'm thinking I'll go with the knife. With my left shoulder still being weaker, I could drop the fork. A knife is easier to hide if taken by surprise."

A skailwind drove rain against Rob's peat-blackened face, stinging like pellets of hail, as he trotted toward Colin Stewart's croft just before the turn of the night. A bad dream had wakened him, threatening to close his throat and drenching him with sweat, but it was so hidden in the dark, nebulous folds of his mind he couldn't grasp it. He slogged down the sodden path, concentrating instead on Alec's partnering him with Colin Stewart. He'd met Colin, a sheep crofter, while recuperating on the island almost two years before, when Maggie needed protection from an insane auld woman.

Though they had spent less than an hour together, Colin had explained the best way for the wheelchair-bound Rob to use a shotgun. The crofter was intelligent and solid—someone Rob could trust to cover his back in an emergency.

Colin waited in front of the recessed door of his cottage, clad in waxed clothes and rubber boots, a hooded torch trained on the stone flags at his feet and shotgun beneath his arm. The sheep crofter put out a beefy hand and grasped Rob's, his greeting warm and hearty. "I'm fair pleased you're able to join us. I see you're dressed for the cold, wet weather and you've blackened your face and hands, but where's your weapon?"

"I've a knife tucked into my belt. I'm no' sure I can handle a fork since my left shoulder isn't strong enough."

"A knife! Och, we all have knives, but that's no' enough." Colin pulled another shotgun from the darkness beside the door. "You remember how to use this, don't you? I know you didn't have to fire it before, but it's all loaded and ready to go." He pulled a handful of shells from his jacket pocket and handed them to Rob. "Just in case we have visitors the night."

Rob pocketed the shells. "Thank ye, Colin." Armed with a shotgun and a knife, he should be able to handle himself if a U-boat tried to put an inflatable ashore. "Do I still shoot from the hip?"

"If you don't have time to raise it and take aim, that's what you do."

Rob tucked the shotgun beneath his arm. "What part of the shore do you patrol?"

"Since my croft is so far south, we'll cover the last twa coves on the south side of the western shore."

Rob turned the narrow beam of his own hooded torch on the ground as they walked across the rocky girse toward the machair.

Colin grunted. "From what you said at that meeting, I doubt we'll see owt the night, what with the wind and rain."

"I doubt it too. I checked from the fell and it looks like 'tis almost full tide. Those waves will be high on the rocks, but I brought my binoculars."

"That's guid news. I took over this spot from Lachlan. He's reid faced he didn't see that U-boat, but he didn't have binoculars and he was alone that night."

"You'd best brief me before we get too close to shore, though with this blowsterie wind I doubt anybody could hear our voices." Rob stepped around a rock jutting up from the ground. "Or that whistle you're supposed to use to warn the radioman."

"Och, you're right about that. On a night like this, we pair up and send one man to warn Duncan MacKenzie—he's manning the radio this shift. If you're the runner, you make for that large rock in the middle of the machair almost to that cove by Scaur Fell. You ken the one I mean?"

"Isn't that a far piece to run if we see something, especially having to ford all the burns along the way?"

Colin's shoulders shook in silent laughter. "Mind what you told us at that meeting? Alec took your advice about where a U-boat could surface in the wind and rain. On a clear night or one with a wee wind and light rain, he has four of us at that southern cove and the radio nearby. 'Tis only when 'tis windy with the rain blowing a gale, like the night, he puts the radio closer to that wide cove up north."

When they reached the shore, they hunkered down behind a large rock to the left of the southernmost cove and turned off their torches.

Rob pulled his binoculars from beneath his waxed jacket and trained them on the sea. The rain instantly beaded on the glass, obscuring anything he might have seen in the darkness. He took out his handkerchief, wiped the lenses, and replaced the caps. "These won't work the night, but from the sound of those waves it doesn't make any odds-on. Nobody could land an inflatable in that surf."

"Well done, lad. I'll go over to that other cove while you stay here. See you at the grey 'o the mornin."

The relentless wind and rain continued for weeks until Rob wondered if the shore watch they kept during the winter months was worth the effort.

His body adjusted to rising before midnight, but he missed cuddling with Maggie and waking before her to spend long, precious moments fingering her soft, black hair spread across the pillow and watching her sleep soundly until the first stirrings from their lad's cradle awakened her. That first glimpse of her startlingly violet-blue eyes always sent his heart galloping.

Though he usually arrived home early enough for Robbie's

first feeding of the day, and they often napped together, he still felt like the six hours he spent on patrol robbed them of something precious that could never be recaptured.

But what if the poorly armed crofters couldn't repel a landing? If he wasn't part of the effort, he'd never forgive himself.

Chapter Twenty-Six

The day before Maggie's birthday, Rob spent hours at the shed, waxing the finish on the china cabinet until it glowed in the overhead lights. He stood back and eyed the cabinet critically, running his palm over the satiny finish one last time. Not bad for bits and pieces of recycled lumber from the pile against the shed's back wall.

Maggie would luve displaying her mither's china.

He threw an old sheeting over the piece and pulled his A-2 jacket over his gansey. On the morra's afternoon, he and Angus would deliver it in the cairt. Head ducked against the rain, he ran up the hill toward the cottage, heart beating faster. But it always raced when going home to his Maggie.

She stood at the stove in the kitchen, stirring something that smelled so good his mouth watered. She turned and smiled, cheeks rosier than usual, tendrils of ebony hair escaping her barrette and curling about her forehead.

He hung his jacket on its peg and took her into his arms. "My Maggie." He kissed her cheek.

"My Rob." She placed her hands on both sides of his face and reached up on tiptoe to kiss his chin. "Och, you're wet and cold." She grabbed a tea towel and pulled him down so she could wipe the rain from his face and hair.

The moment she finished, he scooped her up into his arms and carried her to his rocker so he could hold her on his lap and nuzzle her neck. "I know 'tis long gone 1700, but I've been verra, verra busy."

"I've never been so kittled up about a birthday in my life. Can't you give me one wee hint about what you've made?"

He buried his face in her heather-scented hair. "No' a queek.

You'll have to wait till the morra's afternoon."

She peeked at Robbie who was asleep in his cradle. "I'd better spoon up our supper now. 'Twill be dark soon and you'll have to be on your way."

Her pensive words brought a stab of guilt. "This is the last een I work the early shift. Then, 'tis back to the turn o' the night with Colin."

She dished up beef collops and skirlie, one of his favorite suppers.

The beef strips were fork-tender and the oatmeal and onion skirlie fried to perfection. The crisp crust of the pan bread offered a perfect complement to the flaky insides. He sipped his second mug of coffee. "That was grand." How could she make such simple ingredients taste so delicious?

"Did you get enough? You only had three helpings."

He groaned. "I'm so full, I can hardly breathe. 'Tis guid you knew I was such a big eater before we were merrit, or I would have skeered you off before now."

"No chance of that. You know I only worry when you don't eat. I hear our lad stirring. You'd best hold him now while you can."

He pulled down Robbie's covers. "On you come, lad, let's be having you." He lifted their bairnie out of the cradle and sat in his rocker, placing the lad in his lap.

Robbie stared up, smiling, tiny fists pumping. How he'd grown. Black hair curled around chubby cheeks and dimples danced beside his lips. He followed every movement with his dusky blue eyes, especially fascinated by Shep, who received Robbie's first genuine smile. Shep was so devoted to the lad, there were mornings when Rob hated to take the animal for his run. But he was bred to be a working dog and needed the exercise.

Rob lifted one tiny hand and leaned over to kiss it, grinning when Robbie grabbed for his chin. "Did you have a chance to make a list of things you want in the new house?" he asked after Maggie took the lad and sat down to suckle him.

"Aye, but I'm thinking the list may be too long."

"I told you to write down everything you've ever wanted in a home. I may no' be able to make it all work, but I'm going to try."

"Are you certain about 'closets' being built into the walls? I know you said I should include them, but I've never had a home with in-built closets before."

"Each bedroom should have a closet big enough for everyone's clothes. That way, we won't need clothes-presses in the rooms for storing things, or hooks along the walls."

"It seems like such unnecessary finery."

"Och, Maggie, it really isn't. With the clothes oot of sight, you can hang those bonnie pictures you luve on the walls. And I'm thinking we should have a closet by the front door for coats and jackets."

"Another closet?"

"Aye, and one in the bathroom for towels and such."

Her laugh tinkled like a burn tumbling over polished stones. "You've gone daft over closets."

"Mebbe, but remember, for every closet, that's once less clothes-press or aumrie I have to build or try to find to buy. But the main room I want you to concentrate on is the kitchen. Be sure you have plenty of bunker space for making bread and baking. And I want to build a sma' box at the back of one bunker with a light in it so it's warm for proofing your bread."

"You're going to spoil me. What's wrong with using the top shelf on the stove like I do now?"

"You're no' thinking ahead. With eight bairns coming and going and slamming doors, your bread will collapse like a punctured tyre."

"Our bairns will no' be slamming doors."

He swallowed a smile and raised an eyebrow. "Really? Who's talking daft now?"

"They'll no' slam doors or I'll skite their lugs."

His hands covered his ears. "Och, another generation made to toe the line with the threat of a punishment that's barbaric."

"If you tell them that, I'll skite yer lug."

He laughed and leaned over to nibble her earlobe.

"You're giving me hen's flesh." She raised Robbie to her shoulder and patted his back. After a loud burp, she settled him at

179

her other breast. "How are we ever going to furnish our home? We'll need beds and tables and chairs and ever so many things. With the war lasting so long, there's no chance of buying what we need in Scotland and having it shipped here. Even that dreadful Utility Furniture made of plywood is no longer available—and only newly merrit folk or those bombed oot were allowed to buy it."

"Och, I wouldn't fret about that now. There's still a large stack of auld lumber in the shed. If I run short, I can use driftwood from the shore. I can make the bed frames so all we'll need are the mattresses. I'm sure we can find the other things we need somewhere in the Western Isles."

"Do you suppose someday we could have one of those refrigerators like we have at the infirmary? It would be a wonder, no' having to worry about food spoiling, or going ootside to the cooling shed for milk and meat and such."

"I'll order it as soon as the war's over." He toed off his shoes and pulled on his waxed breeks and rubber boots. "And I want to get you a washing machine with a wringer. I know Anna's helping you with the washing, but I'd like you to be able to do it any time you want, no' wait for her to be here on Mondays and Thursdays."

"Och, with all these betterments, what would you have me do all day? Sit and tweedle my thumbs?"

"I can think of all sorts of interesting and productive things." He waggled his eyebrows.

Her face coloured. "Rob!"

Shrugging into his waxed jacket, he eyed her. "I'm sorry, luve, I was just teasing you."

"Are you sure?" She peeked at him, eyes wary.

"I'm the one with both feet in my mouth, remember?" He took Robbie from her and nuzzled the lad's cheek before handing him back. "I'm away, then." He pulled on his black knit cap and tucked his knife into his belt beneath his waxed jacket. "I'll cover my skin with peat-black from the pile ootside. I'm on the south side of the island again and I'll be by myself this time so I don't want to be late. Colin's Ruth is feeling poorly and he doesn't want to leave her alone."

She laid Robbie in his crib and melted into his open arms. "I

180

don't like it when you're all alone oot there. Please be careful."

"You know I will be, and with this wind and rain, there's no reason to be fearful. The sea's too rough for anybody to try a landing the night." He sat in his rocker and pulled her onto his lap so he could hold her close while they kissed. The sweet scent of heather lingered in his nostrils as he hung the binoculars around his neck, picked up the shotgun and torch, and left.

It seemed like a miracle when the sunshine broke through the dark clouds the following day, flooding the island with a soft, bruised-lemon glow. Rob sent Maggie to Elspeth's early in the afternoon. "Don't keek out her front window. And stay in her kitchen. I'll catch you up when we're finished."

"Aye, Faither." Her saucy, teasing smile brought a bark of laughter.

He swatted her bottom and sent her down the path, Robbie bundled in her arms. When she was out of sight, he went into the cottage and emptied the old aumrie, stacking the dishes and everything from the lower cupboards on the kitchen table. A glance out the window above the jawbox revealed dark, louring clouds, heavy with incipient rain. Pulling on his jacket, he took off at a run down the hill, Shep at his heels.

Angus pulled up in his cairt just as he reached the shed. The crofter doffed his bunnet in greeting. "I brought an auld bedcover. If Maggie's present is as nice as that cradle you fashioned, we don't want to scratch it."

"Thank ye. That was a guid idea."

The piece was so heavy they struggled to get it into the cairt. Angus ran his callused fingers over the smooth wood. "'Tis a wonder of an aumrie. I'm afraid Flora will be wanting one and I could never fashion it together, or do the fancy carving you put around the top."

"'Twasn't easy. The wood was so auld it wasn't soft enough for a knife. Had to use a chisel."

"You're spoiling it for the rest of us men, you ken."

"Och, you all do your own things for your wives and you know it. Those dry-stacked stone dykes around your croft are a wonder to behold."

Angus ducked his head. "Well, I do enjoy working with stone."

Rob patted the side of the cairt. "I'm thinking we should wrap it in the cover and lay it down on its back so it won't tip over."

They wrapped it securely before gently easing it down and climbing onto the bench.

The crofter slapped the reins and the horse took off at a sedate walk. "I'm using Jack. He's aulder and slower than Feona."

"Another guid one, you."

They rode in companionable silence, Angus puffing contentedly on his pipe. When they arrived at the cottage, they moved the old aumrie into the spare bedroom. It took up so much space there was little room to manoeuver between the two box-beds, but the tiny cottage offered no other choice.

The new aumrie made it through the doorway with only a fraction of an inch to spare.

Rob released the anxious breath trapped in his lungs. Though he'd measured the space several times, he'd had horrible visions of being unable to fit it through the opening. He returned the ragged bed cover to Angus and clapped him on the shoulder. "I'll be over next week to help you fix that byre roof. I owe you much more work than that, but at least it's a start. Thank ye again, Angus."

"'Twas my pleasure. See you at kirk on the mornin."

Rob waited until Angus drove off before arranging the dishes in the new aumrie. Maggie would most likely change everything to suit herself, but he wanted to show her how nicely the large platter and bowls could be displayed on the top shelf. The thin groove near the back and railing at the front edges of the shelves would keep the china from being jostled off by a careless bump. The wide counter above the covered shelves would be a good place for her mither's china cup, a bunch of dried heather, and bits and pieces of things Maggie treasured. He left the boxes and tins from the old aumrie on the table for her to organize to her liking.

Finished, he washed his face and hands, put on a clean shirt, and turned his steps to Elspeth's. A chuckle rumbled in his throat when he recalled his horror upon hearing there were no automobiles on Innisbraw. He'd disremembered dreading the thought of having to walk everywhere. Now, he realized how much he enjoyed this lifestyle, even when the winter storms rolled in, one after another.

Drops of rain spattered his face as if the clouds had read his thoughts.

Maggie and Elspeth stood on the covered entry. "Don't be getting into a fash," Elspeth said, "we just came oot. I couldn't abide this lass's pacing back and forth and jumping at every wee sound since we heard Angus's cairt go by."

"No' kittled up, are you, luve?"

"No' at all. I'm always so busy since Robbie came, 'tis hard to sit still."

"I see." He kissed her flushed cheek. "We could stay and bide a wee, if that's what you want."

She stomped her foot. "Rob Savage. I've waited long enough."

He took Robbie from her and pulled the blanket over the bairnie's head. "Then we'd best be away. We're going to get wet." He took Elspeth's hand. "I'll ask Angus to drop you off after Sabbath services on the morra so you can see what has this lass in such a fankle."

"I wouldn't miss it for the world."

They hurried up the path, heads lowered against the now-driving rain. When they reached the cottage, Rob made Maggie cover her eyes as he opened the door and led her inside.

"Down," he said to Shep, pointing at the hearthrug before unwrapping Robbie's outer blanket and hanging his jacket and Maggie's coat on their hooks to dry. Would she be disappointed after all the anticipation?

"What are you doing?" Maggie asked.

"Redding up a bit."

"You're drawing this oot a'purpose!"

He put Robbie over his shoulder and took her hand, leading her to a spot in front of the aumrie. "You can have that keek now." He held his breath.

She opened her eyes and stared.

His heart dropped like a just-released bomb when she took one long look, let out a gasp, and buried her face in her hands, shoulders shaking. He laid the protesting bairnie in his cradle and returned to her side, drawing her into his arms. "It's so hard for me to put into words how much I luve you, I thought I'd try to show you instead."

She looked up at him, tears trickling down her face. She threw her arms around him. "Och, Rob, 'tis so bonnie I can't believe it. You really made this?" She looked at the cabinet again, smiling and weeping at the same time. "I can't believe you could have made this glorious aumrie just for me. I'm overwhelmed, luve."

He held her while she wiped her cheeks with the backs of her hands and ran her fingers over the smooth surface of the wood.

"How could you get such a lovely shine? And the luve knot carved at the top, and the Gaelic words you've carved around it. 'Tha mo grath agaidh gu brachd'—'Our luve is eternal.'" She rested her cheek against his chest. "I'll treasure this for the rest of my life."

He kissed her, salty tears the perfect counterpoint to her sweet taste. Maggie was pleased. If only he wasn't on patrol at the turn o' the night.

Chapter Twenty-Seven

Rob walked out the front door of the cottage just before midnight, thoughts filled with watching Maggie suckle their lad in bed—the sooking sounds of a hungry bairn, her soft crooning and regretful sigh when she realized he had to leave. He still felt her breath on his cheek as she touched her lips to his. Och, this never got any easier.

He stopped on the last stone flag, suddenly aware of the light wind on his face. The storm had blown over, taking with it the howling winds and pounding rain and leaving behind only a pale moon, coyly hiding one moment, then bursting from behind a high cloud to bathe the sky with a teasing glance before disappearing again.

With no rain to obscure it, a light high on the fell would be obvious to anyone watching from the sea. He adjusted the waxed-cloth hood over his torch until only a tiny slit remained, latched the gate behind him, and walked down the path, apprehension cramping his stomach. If the Jerries wanted to put an inflatable ashore, a night like this would be ideal—especially with low tide only two hours away.

He hesitated for a moment. Should he go back inside and radio Alec about increasing the guard at the south cove? Better not. It would make him late and put Maggie in a fash. He had already wakened her once by thrashing and calling out in the mids of another bad dream. With a nursing bairnie, she needed all the sleep she could manage.

He'd walked this way so many times, it didn't take him long to make his way down the fell and across the path to the machair. *Heavenly Faither, give me guid, clear judgment the night. And whatever happens, may it be Your perfect will.* He stopped before reaching the rocky strand and studied the sea through his binoculars.

Black as Maggie's hair all the way to the horizon.

Nearing the western shore, he took several deep breaths to calm his thudding heart. Keeping the light trained on the ground, he turned the torch off and on several times to warn Colin of his approach.

Three flashes blinked ahead and to his left.

Guid. Colin was waiting.

Rob ducked down and picked his way carefully across the scree, dodging smaller rocks until he reached the large one they used to screen them from the sea.

Colin squeezed his shoulder as he hunkered down beside him, leaning close so he could be heard over the surf crashing upon the rocks lining the southern shore at their left. "There's three of our best-trained lads behind those rocks on the other side of the cove, and Michael Nicholson behind me."

Another squeeze to his arm confirmed Michael's presence.

"Six of us?" Rob spoke into Colin's ear. "What about the rest of the shore?"

"Alec had a call from Benbecula just gone dark. They picked up several radio signals from U-boats heading south, so every able man on the island was called to patrol, trained or no'."

"Several signals?"

Colin squeezed his shoulder again. "Get those glasses oot, Rob. This could be the night."

"Where's the radio?"

"About twa hundred metres nor'east of us and we'll no' have to run to signal the radioman. Nobody's better than Michael at sounding like a Pewlie startled oot of sleep."

Rob propped the shotgun against the rock, readied the binoculars, and pulled his black cap further down over his ears. He'd better have enough peat-black on his face and hands to block out his light skin. Crouching and raising the glasses, he moved them over the sea in front of the cove, then lowered them until he could just make out the slight shimmer of waves lapping at the shore. He blinked his eyes to clear his vision and repeated the motion.

Och, Lord, please keep the moon behind the clouds if they do try to put a boat ashore the night—and don't let me be wrong. If

186

they land at that large cove by Scaur Fell, those lads could be in real trouble.

After an hour of crouching, Rob's left leg cramped. He handed the glasses to Colin and sat on the scree, massaging his calf and stretching his leg.

Michael bent over him. "Let me pull on it. That sometimes helps."

The cramp eased, but were they all dancing at shadows? Why would the Jerries land on Innisbraw? A scantily-populated island with no industry, no large fishing fleet, no geographical importance, no—

He swallowed an oath. Of course! Innisbraw was the last barrier between the Atlantic and the southern Minch. If heavy artillery could be put ashore here to take out the air patrols from Benbecula, the U-boats would have a much easier time reaching the Inner Hebrides and coast of Scotland without being bombed from the air.

He pushed Michael's hand away and crouched, leaning his back against the rock. Surely the RAF at Benbecula was aware of what he had been so slow to realize. Why hadn't they formed a Home Guard on Innisbraw, men trained and armed well enough to repel a landing? He groped for Michael's arm and pulled him close. "Do you men know what to do while you wait for a bomber from Benbecula if they do try a landing?"

"We've been practicing sneaking up on them in the dark and taking them oot before they can reach the machair."

"You'll have to kill them. Are you ready for that?"

"We're ready for whatever it takes," Colin said quickly. "They'll no' harm our women or bairns."

Rob pressed their shoulders. Did they realize how hard it would be to take a life? Did he? Dropping bombs from several thousand feet insulated him from the carnage left behind on the ground. He'd had no training in hand-to-hand battle armed only with a knife. But when he flew a P-47, he never hesitated firing his fifty-caliber machine guns when he had a German Ju 88 fighter-bomber or Messerschmitt Bf 109s in his sights.

Aye, there were pilots in those planes, but they were the enemy and trying just as hard to knock him oot of the sky. Only one kill occasionally returned to haunt his dreams. He'd been close enough to see the young pilot.

Rob fingered the haft of the knife tucked into his belt. How would he feel if he had to slip that sharp blade into a man's back? He took off his waxed pants and jacket and kicked them aside. If he needed to move quickly, they were bulky and his denims and dark brown A-2 jacket were almost invisible.

Colin was still using the binoculars.

Rob, trained to look for anomalies, crouched beside the crofter, scanning the sea, eyes narrowed in concentration.

The moon flickered for a second, then ducked behind a racing cloud, leaving one tiny crescent exposed.

His breath froze. What was that?

188

Chapter Twenty-Eight

Without the plomping rain and skailwind, the temperature must have plummeted. Maggie shivered as she tucked Robbie into his cradle. Best add more peats to the fire. She slipped into her dressing gown, stepped into her warm baffies, and turned on the lamp in the chaumer. Mebbe the wash hanging from ladders suspended from the rafters was dry.

She smothered a laugh with her palm, picturing Rob attempting to avoid a damp slap in the face when manoeuvering around the lad's wet hippens, blankets, and gowns. He'd take a step, duck, another step, duck again, like the long-legged storks she'd seen outside of London. He never complained, but summer couldn't come soon enough for her. The thought of time spent outside in the sunshine and the sweet heather scent of newly gathered clothes and linens filled her with longing.

Rob. He must be freezing on the shore. At least she'd have a warm fire awaiting him. She stirred the embers, added several peats to the fireplace, wiped her hands, and stood on tiptoe to feel the hem of a blanket. Dry. Guid. She'd make some tea and fold the washing while it steeped.

⁂

Colin stiffened. The crofter ducked down and silently handed Rob the binoculars.

He slowly raised them above the rock and adjusted them, pressing his face against the padded eyepieces.

"About fifty metres oot, dead centre," Colin whispered.

Rob studied the dark shape coming steadily closer. He caught the glint of water lifted by an oar and pressed Colin's arm as he ducked his head behind the rock, leaving the glasses where they were. "Tell Michael to send the signal, but take care moving about."

He had just pressed his eyes to the glasses again when Michael gave several short throaty whistles, then one long keening one, letting it die out as though a gull had been startled and flown away.

The black shape on the water hesitated, then resumed its movement toward the shore.

Within moments, Rob could decipher the outline of an inflatable with several dark shapes huddled inside.

They would beach soon.

He ducked down again, groping for Colin and Michael, who moved in close. "What about our men on the other side of the cove?" he whispered. "Do they know to wait till they see us moving?"

"Aye," Colin said. "That's what they've been told."

"We wait till the Jerries are busy pulling the boat ashore, then crawl across the sand slowly, using the rocks for cover. No guns, Colin, just knives. We don't want that U-boat to hear us and dive before the plane gets here. Try to take them oot withoot a struggle."

Both men acknowledged with a touch.

As the rubber boat neared the foreshore, what sounded like an argument carried over the water.

Thank God he still remembered his German. He strained to make out the words, putting a finger in his left ear to drown out the pounding of the waves on the rocks to his south.

It *was* an argument, something about when to send the signal. Signal for what? For the U-boat to dive?

Nervous sweat ran down his cheeks, but he couldn't wipe it away without disturbing the peat-black.

Moonlight flickered for a second before dying.

He studied the dark outline of a large rock closer to their target. When the boat scraped on the sand and the Germans began talking again, he moved, squeezing behind the rock, quickly followed by Colin and Michael. They huddled together, listening.

How many were in that landing party?

He peeked around the side of the rock, then tapped Colin's arm five times, praying he understood. Colin returned the taps. There was another argument among the Germans, this time about how far up to beach the inflatable.

The man pulling the front of the boat dropped his rope and barked out an order. "Sei ruhig!" the German hissed, then ordered the others to pull the boat farther up the shore to leave room for the one that would follow.

Twa boats!

Och, Faither, be with us all! If we can keep them from signaling, the U-boat will still be on the surface when the plane ...

Time to move. He memorized the positions of the men pulling the boat, tapped Colin's shoulder, jerked out his knife, and dropped to his hands and knees, swallowing a gasp when the sharp scree scraped into his flesh. Pray God Colin and Michael were fanning out behind him, and the three crofters on the other side of the cove were also on the move.

He lowered himself to his belly and slithered across to the smooth sand very slowly, keeping his head down so they wouldn't see the whites of his eyes. He headed toward the man who had been issuing orders. If he could somehow take him alive, and make him talk ...

A few loud grunts, a muted groan and gurgle.

Rob rose to his knees and launched himself at the figure standing frozen at the front of the boat. He grasped the man's face from behind, covering his mouth with his left palm as he brought the knife up and held the blade against his throat. "Frieren!" he hissed in German, pressing his knees into the backs of the man's legs until he collapsed against the bow of the boat. Rob jerked him over onto his back and kneeled beside him, quickly covering his mouth again.

Shocked eyes stared from a pale face. So young.

Had Rob made a mistake about who was in charge? He leaned close, showing the lad his knife. "I'm going to take my hand away from your mouth," he rasped in German. "If you make a single noise other than answering my questions, I will slit your throat from ear to ear. Verstehen?"

The lad only continued to stare up at him.

Rob pricked the side of the German's throat with the point of the knife. "I said, understand?" he repeated, forcing a grin as though enjoying himself.

The lad nodded, Adam's apple bobbing convulsively.

Rob slowly removed his hand, the blade of the knife pressed against the pale throat. "What is your rank and name?"

"Leu ... Leutnant zur see ... Verner Rolf."

He'd made no mistake. This was a junior officer.

Colin kneeled beside him and said, "Twa of the Germans are dead and twa wounded." The crofter trembled. "No injury amongst us but Murdo Murray's bitten hand."

"Guid work, you. Have five of our men move around aside the boat. I doubt they can see this far, but they might pick up some movement. I've got to get some information oot of this officer."

The lad's eyes widened at his words.

"Sprechen zie Englisch?" Rob said.

"Nein."

Rob had seen better liars but let it pass. "What is the name of your Kapitan?" he growled in German.

Again the Adam's apple bobbed.

"I'll not repeat every question, Leutnant Rolf. The next time you hesitate, you're dead."

"Oberleutnant zur see Heinz Ginger."

"And this signal you're supposed to send? What is it and when?"

The officer's eyes closed. He was surely weighing his own life against betraying his countrymen. "Three flashes of light, a pause, and then three more. We are to send the signal when we are certain it is safe to send the other boat."

Rob stared into the lad's eyes. Was he telling the truth? The shame he saw in that terrified gaze was the answer he needed.

"How many men on the other boat?"

"Zehn."

"Arms?"

"Zehn maschinengewehrs."

Ten machine guns! "What kind of ammunition?"

"I do not know."

Rob nicked his throat with the knife again. "No more lies! Ammunition?"

The lieutenant licked his lips. "Hartkern."

Rob's breath caught in his throat. Ten machine guns armed with metal-piercing shells could easily knock a low-flying patrol plane out of the sky. "Colin," he whispered as loudly as he dared.

The crofter bent beside him.

"Look for a signaling torch in the boat, probably in the bow." While he waited, he glanced up at the sky, breathing a prayer of thanks when he saw only dark, roiling clouds. He pulled up his cuff and looked at the softly-illuminated hands of his hack-watch.

A little over six minutes since Michael had sent the signal to Duncan at the radio. Surely, Benbecula would have several patrol planes in the air after issuing a warning to Alec. If only one were close.

He'd like to wait and send that signal to the U-boat the second he heard the plane, but every minute he waited was fraught with danger. If Oberleutnant Ginger feared his landing party had been compromised, he would either open fire on the shore or more likely, submerge as quickly as he could.

Colin thrust a large torch into his hands. "This is all I could find. But you wouldn't believe the long-guns in that boat."

"Each of you men grab one of the guns and start moving the wounded and dead up onto the machair. Even if they can somehow see you walking bent over, they'll think you're being careful no' to be spotted by the islanders."

Help me get this right, Faither. So much depends on it.

He raised the torch and turned it out to sea, steadying his hand as he turned it on. Three blinks, a pause, and three more blinks. "You had better not be lying," he said, staring into the pale face below him.

And that plane had better come soon. Armed or no', if that other boat lands, we're all dead.

"Kill me!" the lad suddenly blurted. "Do it. I'm a coward and a traitor to my fatherland." Silent tears slipped down his cheeks. His body shook.

Rob stared out to sea. "The war's almost over. A few weeks or months in a camp and you can go home. I'm sure your mutter and

193

vater will be very happy to see that you have survived."

"Nein. They will be—"

Rob clamped his hand over Roth's mouth and strained to listen. Hard to hear over the surf, the drone of airplane engines in the distance forced him to his feet. He clamped the knife blade between his teeth and removed his belt, wrapped it around the officer's wrists, and pulled it tight. "Crawl up that small bluff ahead and keep crawling until I tell you to stop. It is a little late to sacrifice your life for nothing." He took the end of the belt, hafted his knife, and nudged Roth to his knees.

Tremors ran over the lad's body as he crawled. It was slow-going over the sharp scree. They scaled the small bank and reached the sandy edge of the machair.

Relief lasted only one deep breath. The air suddenly filled with the roar of airplane engines and staccato of large guns firing.

"Keep going!" Rob barked, looking back over his shoulder as he prodded the lieutenant on.

Bright tracers lit up the sky as the guns on the U-boat's deck and those from the nose, waist, and both turrets of the diving aircraft exchanged fire.

Don't let them down that plane.

A small explosion erupted on the sea.

Rob concentrated on the sound of straining engines as the bomber executed a steep, banking climb.

Several enormous, prolonged explosions overpowered Rob's senses. He pushed his prisoner down and covered his quivering body with his own. The ground beneath them heaved.

Chapter Twenty-Nine

Maggie bolted up in bed, clutching the covers. She snapped on the lamp, leaped up, and rushed to Robbie's crib.

The bairnie slept soundly, arms thrown wide, chest rising and falling with each normal breath. He'd kicked off his blankets.

She pulled them over his bare feet and tucked them in. Returning to the bed she picked up her watch from the table. 0215. She'd been up till after 0100.

What woke her from sleep if it wasn't their lad?

A sudden feeling of dread brought hen's flesh coursing over her body. Rob!

She turned off the lamp and groped her way to the window, lifting a corner of the blackout curtain.

Dark. No stars, no moon. She strained for an unfamiliar sound, but heard only the pounding of her own heart. Not even a breath of wind 'round the cottage stones.

Fingers numb, she dropped the curtain and fell to her knees beside the bed, burying her face in the sheet. *Faither, please be with my Rob. I'm suddenly so afraid and I don't know why. Keep him safe, Lord, please keep him safe.*

❦

The ground beneath Rob and the lieutenant heaved and shook. An image of shattering metal and devouring fire flashed before Rob's closed eyes. More explosions, each more muffled than the last. Torpedoes.

A few minutes later, only the roar of the surf on the south shore nearby filled the eerie silence.

Rob sat up and looked out at the sea, fearing that second boat may have been close enough to shore to survive the blast. He swept the glasses back and forth. Nothing but dark water.

The young man beside him sobbed and moaned. "Mein Gott, mein Gott."

Colin and Michael appeared out of the darkness. "Are you all right?" Colin asked, dropping to his knees beside Rob. "We didn't know if you left the shore in time."

Rob moved his jaw and yawned to clear the ringing in his ears. "We're fine. What about the wounded Germans? Any of them serious?"

"Both," Michael said. "One has a sooking wound in his chest and the other lost a lot of blood, but we finally got it stopped."

"Why?" Colin suddenly cried. "Why would they want to land here? What have we ever done to them?" He put his head in his hands, shoulders shaking as he rocked back and forth. His clothing reeked of the sharp, metallic scent of fresh blood.

Rob didn't know what to say. Colin Stewart was a man of the land—a gentle, kind-hearted man who had never experienced the horrors of war. Hugh would have an answer, but there was much to be seen to first.

The five crofters somberly gathered together and lifted the wounded Germans, taking turns carrying them toward the infirmary, their steps illuminated by hooded torches. They left the dead where they lay, too drained to even think of carrying them. The young lieutenant, hands still tied, stumbled beside Rob, head down.

Alec and Hugh met them as they reached the main path.

"Any wounded?" Alec asked quickly.

"None of ours," Rob said, "but these prisoners need medical attention or they're going to die. And somebody has to tell the rest of the guard to cover that large cove and no' to stop watch till the grey o' mornin. There could be more U-bo—"

"I got another radio message from Benbecula. Twa destroyers sunk another U-boat just south of Barra so I doubt there are more, but I'll find somebody to make the rounds and pass on your message."

Hugh hugged Rob. "Was it bad?"

Adrenaline spent, so drained he could not speak aloud, Rob whispered, "'Tis war, Hugh."

196

Despite the glowing warmth from the peat in the infirmary fireplace, Maggie shivered. Even the cup of hot tea Morag thrust into her hand could not thaw the fear, spreading like the crust of ice on a frozen loch, crushing the breath from her lungs. Where was Rob? Had he been nearby when the U-boat was bombed?

"'Twill do no guid to worry." Morag patted her arm. "'Tis just as I told you when we knocked at your door and found you already awake. Alec received a radio message that some of our shore guard called in an airstrike against a U-boat close to our shores—and that we should prepare the infirmary in case there are wounded."

Maggie took a sip of tea, forcing herself to swallow. "You're certain they didn't say where it happened?"

"Only that it wasn't at that large cove near Scaur Fell."

Tea sloshed over the side of the cup, filling the saucer. Maggie's fingers trembled as she placed the tea on the mantle. "What could be taking so long?"

"'Tis a long walk, and in the dark." Morag grasped her elbow and led her to the sofa. "I'm thinking now we have the examining rooms ready, we should spend time on our knees in prayer."

Their prayers were cut short by voices outside.

Maggie leaped up and raced to the door, flinging it wide, not caring about the danger of escaping light.

A group of men staggered across the entry flags, carrying what looked like two bodies. Maggie dashed outside, her gaze sweeping each face as it reached the light from the foyer: Alec and Colin, struggling to carry a man in a German uniform; Duncan and Michael bearing another unconscious German. Murdo, Hugh, Gordon ...

Drops of dark red blood spattered the wooden floor. Her knees buckled. She gripped the door latch.

There, toward the back of the group. Rob!

She rushed forward and fell into his arms with a sob of relief.

Tremors shook her body. Hers—or his?

The throb of his heart beneath her cheek, his fingers tangled in her hair, his strong arms gripping her close, the taste of the sea on his lips. Her Rob was safe. "You're no' hurt?"

He rubbed his cheek against her hair. "I'm fine, luve. But we have twa prisoners with serious wounds." Voice raspy, words slurred with fatigue.

She took his hand. It trembled beneath her fingers. "Let's get you inside where 'tis warm."

He gripped the arm of a lad in a German uniform and followed her into the foyer.

The bright glow of the lights revealed some of the terrible things in which he had taken part. Smudges of peat on his face, hands black with peat and dried blood, eyes bloodshot and dark brown with fatigue—and that same shadow of inner pain.

Morag brushed past, carrying a tray of hot sweetened tea. "Oban is sending a floatplane as soon as 'tis light enough to land," she said. "Och, you can't ken how guid it is to see you all alive."

⚜

Rob forced himself to stop staring at Maggie—his luve, his anchor in the mids of madness. "Murdo has a bite wound on his hand, and it wouldn't hurt to check this lieutenant's neck. I nicked him with my knife."

Maggie winced, then straightened, face filled with resolve.

Rob held the young officer's arms while she pushed his chin up and examined his neck. "He can wait. Take the badly wounded into the examining rooms. I'll do what I can till the airieplane arrives."

Rob held her back. "Where's our lad?"

"Flora's with him. Alec radioed Angus the moment the shore guard contacted him about the bombing of the U-boat. Morag and Flora came to the cottage. He'll be fine. Just like his faither, thank the Lord."

The moment the wounded were carried away and Maggie gathered what she needed from the pharmacy and supply and hurried off to see to their care, Rob pulled Alec over behind the admitting desk at the back of the foyer and leaned against the counter. He needed an answer to the question that had been haunting his thoughts on the long walk to the infirmary. "The next time you talk to Benbecula, I want you to put a question to them."

"What's your question?"

198

"I realized just this night why Innisbraw is so important to the U-boat commanders." Rob's eyelids drooped with fatigue as he reminded Alec that Innisbraw was the southernmost barrier between the Atlantic and southern Minch. "I want you to ask them why there was never a Home Guard set up here, one trained and well-equipped, like they have on Barra, South Uist, Benbecula, and the rest of the islands to the north. If the Jerries take over our island and place machine guns, especially those with armour-piercing shells, in strategic places, they could wipe out every patrol plane crossing our shores."

"Machine guns? How could they get them ashore?"

"By an inflatable launched from a U-boat."

"But the guns you men took from that boat the night didn't look like machine guns."

"There were ten machine guns on a boat that was to follow the one we captured, and ten men to use them."

Alec stepped back, obviously shaken. "No one's said owt about a second boat landing."

"It didn't land. Our prisoner told me about it. I sent the signal Leutnant Rolf was supposed to send, telling the U-boat commander it was safe to launch the second boat. It didn't make shore because it was sunk by the B-17, either by one of their fifty-caliber machine guns, or it was caught in the explosion when the bombs hit."

Alec groaned and leaned against the desk. "How were you able to communicate with him?"

When would this night, with its endless questions and answers, be done?

"I took five years of German, twa in high school and three at West Point, so I understood everything they were saying to one another while they were beaching the boat. I was going to debrief you. We haven't had time."

"Thank our omniscient Lord for your guid schooling. I'm going to use John's radio and contact Benbecula now. Is there owt else they should know?"

"The U-boat was commanded by Oberleutnant Heinz Ginger." Rob rummaged through a drawer and pulled out a piece of paper and a pencil. "I'll write it down for you. It may help the Brits identify which sub was sunk, though I'm certain Rolf will be interrogated when he reaches Oban." He licked the short lead and began writing.

Alec rubbed his unshaven chin thoughtfully. "When the idea of an Innisbraw Home Guard was first posed years ago, it was decided that the large rocks on the sea bed, especially the skerries no' far from our southern shore, would keep the U-boats from attempting such a perilous route. I'll be most happy to inform those in charge of Benbecula that they made a serious error in judgment, one that could have resulted in all our folk being killed or taken prisoner."

⚓

The German with the chest wound died before Maggie could cut off his clothing. She sprinkled sulfa powder into the other prisoner's deep shoulder wound, bound it tightly, and hooked up an IV with saline and another with plasma.

He had lost so much blood it was doubtful he would survive.

But he looked so young. Even if he was the enemy, she hoped he would live. She stripped off her gloves and left the examining room to get Murdo and the other prisoner.

Rob sat on the foyer sofa, staring into the fire, while Morag poured more sweetened tea for the crofters, many sitting on the floor, their backs against the wall.

The German lieutenant sat in a chair, staring at the floor. Someone had tied his legs to the chair but his unbound hands clenched a cup of tea. It looked untouched.

The fire had warmed the room quickly and waxed breeks and jackets cluttered the floor around the crofters, their faces still smeared with peat—some spattered with blood—and their eyes glazed as though they looked inward, examining their own souls. Several had killed men this night. Was her Rob among them?

She knelt in front of him and looked up into his face.

Eyes bleak, he smiled weakly and fingered a lock of her hair. "I'm sorry you had to see any of this," he said, voice hoarse. "How are your patients?"

"One died almost immediately. The other—I don't know. 'Tis doubtful he'll survive." She clasped his grimy hands and squeezed them. "I know you're no' wounded, but how are you—inside?"

"Sad. Verra sad. This is a heavy burden for some of our menfolk to carry the rest of their lives."

"Are you one of those men?"

His gaze shifted to Colin Stewart, who sat slumped against the wall, hands fisted in his lap. "No, but I somehow managed to be in charge the night, so the blood is on my hands as much as theirs."

She framed his sooty face with her palms. "Would it be better if those invaders had been the victors?" She stared into his eyes.

✦

Maggie's quiet question broke through his desolate thoughts and he blinked rapidly. "No. We could have lost many more than just the six of us on the shore. With the machine guns they had on that second boat, they could have taken over the island, giving their U-boats easy passage into the Minch. Thank ye, my Maggie. I'm so tired, I let the darkness take over."

She sat back with a fleeting smile. "Then I'll ask your help in treating your prisoner. He doesn't look fearsome, but I don't want to be alone with him, and I need to treat Murdo's hand. A human bite can be dangerous."

Alec and Hugh entered the foyer from the far hallway. "Oban radioed," Alec said. "Their Halifax floatplane just took off so we'd best get the patients ready to transport to the harbour."

"Only one patient, and him closer to dead than alive," Maggie said. "The one with the chest wound died." She stood and smoothed her skirt. "But I need to treat this prisoner's neck. It will only take a minute, and then I'll see to Murdo's hand."

Rob pushed himself to his feet. "Hugh, if you don't mind, I'd like you with us when Maggie sees Leutnant Rolf. I don't know if the lad's a Christian, but he knows he betrayed his country with the information he gave me and he's desolate. I'll translate for you."

"Of course. I've radioed Arthur to ring the kirk bell in an hour, calling the folk to prayer."

"I'm no' sure they should gather together in one place yet," Rob said. "No' till we hear from Benbecula that it's safe."

"I've just spent time with them on the radio," Alec said,

201

"giving them your message. They'll send someone later to talk to all of you involved the night and they said twa destroyers and several armed, refitted trawlers will be patrolling from Barra south to our shores. They also said they'd add an extra airieplane to the air patrol."

Rob watched Maggie clean two small punctures and tape pieces of gauze into place on Rolf's neck.

The prisoner sat on the examining table, eyes averted. He refused to answer any of Maggie's questions, which Rob translated into German. She gave him a tetanus shot when he wouldn't tell her if he had been protected, explaining to Rob that the supply of the antitoxin was getting low.

The German looked up when Rob began translating Hugh's soft words of comfort, many taken directly from the Word of God. Tears glazed his eyes when Hugh reminded him that Hitler's violence upon the innocents of Europe was responsible for this war, not the actions of those recruited to fight it and that regardless of how hard either side fought, the outcome depended upon God, not man.

"Ich ... I am not Nazi," he said haltingly in broken English. "I only serve or mein mutter und vater ... zey be put in ... uh ..." He looked up at Rob. "Gefangnis?"

"Prison." So the lieutenant did speak some English.

"Ja. Prison."

Hugh patted his arm. "Rob, tell this lad his mither and faither will be very happy to see him when this war is over, and he will have a lifetime to help rebuild the devastation wrought by a madman."

Even before Rob finished translating Hugh's words, the lieutenant began to sob. "Danke shoen," he said brokenly.

An hour later, the dead had been recovered, the prisoners transported to the waiting Halifax, and Murdo's minor bite wound treated and a shot of tetanus administered.

"I'm going to send these men home to their crofts," Hugh told Rob, "and I suggest you take Maggie home to your bairnie. Our folk need reassurance and time spent with our Lord. I'll visit you men one at a time later the day."

"I'm fine, Hugh." Rob's attempt at a smile failed. "I don't know about the rest, but Colin needs your help."

"You all do. Now take your lass and go home where you belong."

After everyone had gone and Maggie finished cleaning the examining rooms, she found Rob standing in front of the fire, staring into the smouldering embers.

Was he reliving everything that had happened that dreadful night?

"'Tis time to go home," she said, handing him his jacket. As soon as he zipped it, she put her arms around his hips and steered him toward the door.

Rob walked outside.

Fleeting clouds chased a weak sun.

He inhaled deeply. "'Tis guid to smell the clean scent of the sea. I'll have to wash before our lad sees my face." He grimaced.

"You're so exhausted, I'm surprised you're able to talk or walk. I'll feed Robbie while you bathe and then we'll smoorich in bed." She tucked her slim fingers into his back pocket.

"If I don't fall asleep in the tub first."

Rob couldn't eat a bite after he bathed, but he did drink several glasses of water and a cup of coffee before holding Robbie. He inhaled his lad's innocent scent and relished the feel of his healthy body pressed close to his chest. *Thank ye, Faither, for all You did the night. Please be with our menfolk, especially Colin, and cleanse their souls from all they saw and did the night.*

Once the lad fell asleep in his faither's arms, Maggie put him in his cradle and doctored the puncture wounds on the heels of Rob's hands. "How did you do this?" She dabbed a glass wand covered with tincture of Merthiolate on the gouges.

"Och, 'tis nowt," Rob grumbled. "I had to crawl over sharp stones on the shore." The warm fire made his eyes smart. He laid his head back and rubbed his lids.

She lifted his robe and examined his knees. "Just some bruises.

Your denims must need mending."

Her face was a blur when she looked up.

"Och, come to bed, luve, just a short nap. I'll never get you to our bed if you fall asleep here."

The only thing keeping Rob awake since they arrived home was the thought of cuddling with Maggie, but he was asleep only seconds after his head hit the pillow.

Maggie nestled against his warm body, giving thanks to the Lord for saving him—and their island.

She slept briefly, startled awake when Rob jerked and mumbled something in what sounded like the German he had spoken in the examining room. He'd been suffering from bad dreams for weeks and what had happened the night would not help. *Och, Faither, take away his bad dreams so he can rest.* She reached for her clothes. *And heal his mind and soul so what he's seen and heard the night doesn't haunt his thoughts.*

Hugh visited the cottage that een.

Maggie disappeared into the bedroom to suckle Robbie so the two men could have some privacy. The low murmur of voices coming through the closed door went on for over an hour as she sat on the bed holding their lad in her lap, talking to him softly, tickling his belly and nuzzling his neck. When he yawned deeply, she crooned an old Gaelic lullaby, smiling down at his wee, bonnie face.

Later that night Rob shared what had happened on the shore. She didn't interrupt with questions when he hesitated, but she did lace her fingers through his when he revealed how he felt when he held the blade of the knife to the young German's throat.

"I wasn't certain I could kill him," he admitted. "He was just a lad following orders. I was so desperate I don't know what I would have done if he hadn't answered my questions."

"But our gracious Heavenly Faither made certain you wouldn't have to face that decision."

He kissed her bare shoulder. "That's exactly what Hugh said. I can't believe all the Lord did the night. He even made certain the moon remained behind the dark clouds when we needed that." He chuckled. "Can you imagine, Maggie, when I was still in high school and deciding what language to study, even then the Lord was guiding me? If I hadn't learned German there and taken advanced classes at the Point, what happened the night could have ended verra differently."

"Are you going to be all right then?" She trailed her fingers over his cheeks. "You had bad dreams when you slept earlier."

He rose up on one elbow and looked down at her. "It'll take time, but I'm no' sorry for what I did, or for the death of those men. We live on an island far from the major fighting, but every victory against the Wehrmacht, no matter how small, brings this rotten war closer to an end."

Maggie rested her cheek against his bare chest. *Please make this the last of it, Faither. No more blood and death—please.*

Chapter Thirty

What a fankle. Rob's birthday was in three days—only eight days after hers—and Maggie couldn't think of anything to give him, but one present. Malcolm had bought a dozen carpenter pencils, rationed and almost impossible to find, for lofting the rescue boat plans. What a paltry gift compared to the bonnie aumrie Rob had made her.

Only one possible solution remained: Tormad MacKinnon had given her the name and shortwave call sign of an Oban small-boat builder who struggled to keep his business going in the face of all the shortages. Since it was so early in the morning, she should wait until Rob went off later to help Angus repair his byre roof, but every minute counted.

The moment Rob left the cottage for his run, she radioed the man and inquired about any special tool Rob could use.

"Such a list would fill pages. It depends on what kind of boat he's going to build and how large." He sounded old and tired.

His flat London accent reminded her of Will, the English orderly who had befriended her at her last RAF posting. Could she play on his sympathy? Voice breathless, she said, "I don't know and if I ask him, he'll want to know why. Please, please can't you help me? I'm desperate."

The clack of ill-fitting dentures set her own teeth on edge. "Wait a bit, missy. There is one tool every boat builder needs. It's a wooden-soled plane—those with metal soles are too hard on the surface he'll be planing—but they are rare nowadays."

"Where can I find such a plane?"

"I have several around here. They've been used, but you'll not find a new one, what with the war and all."

"Are you willing to sell one?" *Please, Faither, please.*

206

A snort. "Willing? Every pence is so scarce, I'd sell me own mum, God rest her soul."

"Can I have somebody pick it up?"

"That would work, so don't get your knickers in a twist."

She giggled at one of Will's favorite phrases and they settled on a price—probably too high, but worth it.

An hour later, Maggie rushed out to the path to greet Angus. "Rob's just bathed after his run. He's getting dressed." She handed him an envelope. "Please tuck that into your pocket and give it to Malcolm when he docks the een. He'll find instructions for picking up a birthday present for Rob, as well as a list of things we need, pound notes, and our ration books."

"Birthday present, is it? Well now, I'll see it done and haud ma wheesht."

She waited until Rob left for Angus's croft again on the ninth of December before bundling Robbie up for the walk down to the post office. What did a plane look like? Could she carry it home?

Alice lifted it onto the counter. "Och, whatever that is, 'tis heavy."

Dismayed, Maggie eyed the heavy, awkward-looking hand tool. She wrapped it in a towel Alice loaned her and carried it, along with Robbie, up the hill. The thought of a strong, hot cup of tea spurred her on. Panting from her heavy burdens, she plonked Robbie into his cradle and slid the plane and pencils under one of the narrow box-beds in the spare bedroom, then collapsed into her rocker, too exhausted to put the kettle to boil.

The early winter's gloaming shadowed the entry flags when Angus's cairt pulled up at the gate and Rob climbed down. He limped toward her, only a brief flash of white teeth visible in his dirty face.

She gripped his arm and led him to the open door. "Oot of those reeky clothes. Just leave your skivvies on."

Angus carried two large boxes to the door. "Thank ye for your help, Rob. Couldn't have finished it so soon withoot you."

Rob pulled his shirt over his head and flashed a tired grin. "Ye're verra welcome." He waited until the crofter left, toed out of his shoes, and stripped off his denims. "Sorry for all the dirt, lass, but we finally got the byre roof repaired. It was a fair midden of rot and such."

Her heart ached. As usual, he'd done too much. She kneaded his shoulder. "You can move those boxes into the kitchen after you've had a bath."

"Best do it now or I'll forget."

"Then, come away in. You'll need twa tubs of water to get clean."

He dropped into his rocker.

She'd leave his clothes on the door flags for now and she'd wash them on the morning. Sabbath or no', they were much too reeky to leave for Anna. She hurried into the bathing room to draw his water.

How well he had adjusted to island living. In America, he had enjoyed all sorts of fineries unavailable here, yet he never complained about the hard work involved in simply staying alive. At Edenoaks he had seldom walked since he had a personal driver, Jeep, and staff car. Now, he walked everywhere and seemed to enjoy it.

If only they already lived in their own home.

He'd be in that shower in a tick.

Rob stood at the sink, drinking glass after glass of cold water. Och, he was always causing more work for Maggie. Wee Robbie's birth increased the washing several-fold, yet she never mentioned the hours she spent gathering up the reekies and finding a place to hang them after Anna had them washed. It being winter, the pull-down racks hanging from the rafters were always filled with hippens and Robbie's gowns and blankets and, knowing Maggie, she would never leave those fouled denims till Monday.

She shooed Rob off to bed early when she found him asleep in his rocker. "You're no' used to such work, and you have to get up afore the turn o' night for guard duty." She handed him two APCs and a glass of water. "Off to bed."

"I'm fine, just sleeperie."

"Bed, Rob. Now."

He nuzzled her cheek. "I luve it when you're in a fash. It makes your cheeks even rosier, and your eyes sparkle like crystals o' frozen night mist. Come to bed with me, luve. I want to smoorich."

How could he say he never put his luve into words? "I've a few things to do. The morra's your birthday, remember?"

"You've merrit an auld man," he said, following her into the bedroom. "I'll be thirty-one on the morra."

She stepped into his open arms, savoring his warm embrace, smiling when his chest hairs tickled her cheek. "You're still only six years aulder than me."

"But just think, when I'm one hundred, you'll be just a youngster of ninety-four."

"Och, to bed with you. Auld men like you need their rest." She laughed and pulled him down so she could kiss him. His kiss so soft, so filled with luve, her resolve evaporated and she tumbled into bed with him.

Her work could wait till after he left for guard duty.

Rob whistled under his breath as he hurried across the machair to meet Colin. Maggie was nursing their lad when he left their bed, her face filled with the same contentment he felt after their een of smooriching. Since the British Navy patrolled the shore, concern about another U-boat attack no longer cramped his stomach with dread. And so far he hadn't wakened Maggie with bad dreams about that night in the cove with Michael and Colin.

Colin. Back on guard duty, a bit quieter mebbe, but he'd never been one to blether. *Give him peace of heart, Faither. He's such a guid man.*

Maggie put Robbie into his cradle before she sorted the supplies she had ordered and put them away, bemoaning the lack of storage space. As soon as she was sure their lad was asleep, she got out her baking ingredients. What she lacked in birthday presents, she would have to make up for by cooking all of Rob's favorite foods. She steamed a clootie dumpling, baked sweet scones, and took the clotted cream she had set to curdle the day before out to the cooling shed. With the paraffin near gone, she couldn't use a Tilly lamp and using only a hooded torch to show her the way over the rough girse took longer. She shivered as she stepped back inside the cottage.

She washed the dishes, brought Rob's dirty clothes in from beside the door and set them to soak in the tub, then nursed Robbie again and tucked him into his cradle. Yawning, she added more peats to the fire and let Shep out for one last time. When he returned from his wanderings, she settled him on the hearthrug and crept into bed, longing to return to the times when Rob would be there to warm her icy flesh.

There was frost on the ground the next morning, a rare occurrence on an island surrounded by salt water. Rob crept into the cottage, greeting Shep with a whispered welcome and rubdown. He washed his sooty face and hands, brought in a large pile of peats, added some to the fireplace and stove, set the water to heat for Maggie's tea and his coffee, and quickly shaved before peeking into the bedroom.

Maggie sat up in bed and stretched.

His pulse leaped. What a bonnie sight.

Robbie stirred in his cradle, eyes still closed, fist to mouth, sucking.

Rob sat on the bed and pulled Maggie near for a kiss. "Guid mornin," he whispered.

She burrowed against his chest. "Guid mornin."

"How did you sleep?"

"As if I died." She escaped his clutching hands and hurried into her dressing gown and baffies. "How was your night?"

"The usual. Robbie's finally stirring. He slept late."

"Och, he woke up late for his last feeding, then fell asleep before he'd finished one side."

Rob picked up the squirming bairnie. "I'll change him while

you get some tea. The water's hot."

A grateful purr.

By the time he had Robbie changed from the skin out, the bairnie was out of patience and protesting loudly. Rob handed him to Maggie, who immediately put him to her breast.

Frantic wails quieted to eager slurping.

"Your coffee should be ready by now."

"Where's your tea?"

The bairnie sucked so avidly, one could hear each gulp hitting his empty stomach.

"In the kitchen steeping 'neath the cosy. You can bring it in with your coffee."

This was what Rob missed when he pulled a later shift on the shore. Nothing warmed his heart like sipping his first cup of coffee while watching their hungry lad suckle. He leaned back in his rocker. "This is living."

Maggie caressed his arm and smiled. "Happy birthday, luve."

Oh, it was that. "I'm no' accustomed to having my birthday remembered. 'Twill take some getting used to."

"You'd best get used to it, then. You were either recuperating from your wounds or going to war before. From now on, December 10 will be Rob's day."

"All day?"

A delightful laugh. "Aye, all day."

He licked his lips. "Then I have a suggestion for how to celebrate."

"That comes much later. We'll have a special tea early this een and then you get your presents."

"Presents? I hope you didn't get in a fash. I can't think of a single thing I don't already have."

"Just a couple of small things you need. I'll say no more."

"Wait a minute. I didn't make you wait till after supper, wife."

"Well, if you're a verra, verra guid lad, I might give them to you just before tea, but no earlier."

And she called him stubborn. He laughed and drained his coffee mug. "Will you be after more tea?"

"Later." She handed him Robbie. "Your lad's been such a piggy, he needs a verra large burp."

Rob walked Robbie around the cottage, trailed by Shep, until the burp was oot. Once their bairnie was settled again at Maggie's breast, he went into the bathing room and shut the door. He emptied the tub and ran hot water, then scrubbed his denim breeks. Sweat trickled down his cheeks.

Why would any man envy a woman's work? Everything they did was so tedisome and hard.

When the rinse water ran clean, he wrung out the breeks and draped them over the towel rod. He'd hang them over the drying racks later. The sark and socks didn't look clean but they were old. He emptied and wiped the tub and went back into the living room.

Maggie and Robbie were fast asleep, the lad still at his mither's breast.

Kneeling, he studied their peaceful faces. How had he ever existed without them?

Maggie stirred and smiled up at him.

He gave a tender kiss before he whispered, "Back to sleep with you. I've a suspicion you were up after I left last night. Those boxes I brought in last een are empty."

Her sleepy smile earned her another kiss. She tried to stand. "I need to bathe before kirk and I have to get your clothes clean first."

"Already done."

"Och, luve, you didn't. 'Tis your birthday."

"What odds-on does that make?" He picked up the sleeping lad and laid him in his cradle. "I'll hang my clothes from the drying rack and run your bath water." Grin wicked, he added, "Then I'll wash your back the way you like."

"It's your day, no' mine."

"Then let me spend it doing what I enjoy." He leaped up. "Just stay there by the fire till I finish. 'Tis cold in the bathing room."

Tub full, he helped Maggie out of her dressing gown and nightgown and watched her pin her hair on top of her head. Och, he couldn't wait until een.

She stepped into the tub and he knelt beside her, soaped the face flannel, and ran it over her graceful back.

"Mmm. That feels so guid."

He tasted the back of her soft neck.

"So does that." She unlaced his shirt.

His breath quickened.

⚜

After Sabbath services, Rob ate three bowls of chicken bree, then stood at the window above the jawbox and watched frenzied whitecaps, listening to the muted boom of waves crashing high on Innis Fell. The weather was unusually cold and clear and, though the sun shone, the little heat it gave off quickly dissipated in the blowsterie winds. Thank the Lord, John had plenty of peats stacked. It took the fireplace and kitchen stove burning at capacity to keep the cottage cosy on such a cold day.

Maggie finished nursing their lad, handed him to Rob, and picked up her knitting.

He sat in his rocker and laid the lad on his knees, watching the expressions on his face.

The bairnie cooed and blew bubbles of saliva, tiny lips pursed, bright blue eyes staring up at his faither.

His occasional fleeting, toothless grin taxed Rob's self-control. He wanted to grab up his son and kiss him from head to toe. The laddie often wore an expression similar to many that appeared on Maggie's face—a soft half smile with a faraway look in his eyes, as though imagining something very pleasant.

"He's surely the bonniest bairnie in the world. And look how strong he is. When he grabs my fingers, he looks like he's ready to pull himself up."

Needles flying, Maggie worked to the end of the row and laid down her knitting. "No' for a while yet, but he is strong. The other mornin I found him at the head of the cradle. Somehow, he pushed or wriggled himself all the way up there."

Rob uncovered one kicking foot. "I'm thinking Elspeth may be right. Those are the longest feet. If he keeps growing as fast as he has, he's going to be taller than me when he's a man."

"Och, I hope no'. Finding clothes and shoes for you is enough of a fankle."

"Aye, and instead of his feet and ankles hanging off the bed like mine, the poor lad will have his legs out of the covers all the way to his knees. Let's hope he marries a lass who likes to coorie doun as much as you."

"Just listen to us. Our lad's only ten weeks old and we've already got him merrit."

"He just soaked my breeks." Rob held him up.

"I doubled his hippen. 'Tis all the milk he drinks. 'Tis a good thing I've plenty, for he wants to eat all the time." She scooped Robbie up and took him into the bedroom.

Rob followed her. "Speaking of eating, I could use a buttery."

She pinned a fresh hippen on the bairn and reached for a clean gown. "Don't have too much. Remember, we're having an early tea instead of a late supper."

"Guid. I don't know what you have in the oven, but my mouth's watering just smelling it."

"Don't keek. 'Tis a surprise."

"Another surprise?"

"Just put Robbie in his cradle. 'Tis time for his nap."

"I think I'll go oot and throw a stick for Shep. He didn't get any exercise this mornin."

"Wait and I'll bring you a buttery with jeely."

"Better make that twa or I'll never make it to supper—och, tea."

"We're eating in less than an hour. One is all you get."

Maggie peered through the window as Rob threw a stick down the path for Shep to fetch and raced the dog. She smiled. Rob's agility amazed. Och, he still limped a bit after running too far, but only eighteen months before, he'd been a breath away from death. His body so badly broken it seemed impossible he could survive, let alone live a normal life.

What no one had considered was Rob Savage's indomitable will and determination. *Thank You, Lord, for that.*

She set the table with china from her new aumrie and checked the supper in the oven. Almost done. Slipping into her coat, she waited until Rob's back was turned before running out to the cooling shed for the butter, milk, and clotted cream. After sneaking back in, she retrieved Rob's presents, set them on the table beside his plate, pulled the clootie dumpling from its hiding place, and started water to boil for tea and coffee.

Rob came in fifteen minutes later, face wet as Shep's lolling tongue. He hung up his A-2 jacket and went into the bathing room to wash.

She waited by the door until he came out. "Close your eyes. I'm no' tall enough to cover them."

He smiled and closed his eyes.

She took his hand and led him to the table. Would he like her choices? "You can keek now." His wide grin when he spied the plane erased her anxiety.

"I had Malcolm looking all over for one but he said there wasn't a single one for sale in Oban. This is exactly what I wanted. Where did you find it?"

A warm flush washed her cheeks. "A verra nice auld man I talked to on the radio was willing to part with it after a bit of sweet-talk."

"Och, poor man. He didn't stand a chance." He examined the tool carefully. "Someone's taken verra guid care of this. He even sharpened the blade." He hefted it in his hand. "A guid fit. I'm going to enjoy using this." He put the plane back on the table and picked up the box of carpenter's pencils and smiled. "Do you think this will be enough?"

What had she been thinking, buying so many? "You said you had to draw the entire boat plan on that rough wood floor and I—"

His long arms pulled her close. "I'm only teasing. You're right. I'll go through all of these pencils just lofting my plans."

His fervent kiss erased her doubts.

When he lifted his head, tears glistened in his eyes. "These are my verra first birthday presents given to me by someone who luves me. Thank ye, lass, from the bottom of my heart." He sat in a chair and pulled her close. "I keep forgetting how it almost breaks your neck having to look up at me. And I want to hold my woman." He framed her face with his palms.

Another kiss. Soft. Tender.

⚜

Shep nosed between them.

"Your timing could use some work, dog." Rob pushed him away.

"He knows your other present is ready to take from the oven."

"Smart dog."

She picked up two hot pads and opened the oven door. "The joint is ready."

"Joint?" He leaped up. "Beef joint?" He took the hot pads from her. "Here, that looks heavy, let me lift it oot." His grin widened as he lifted the pan out of the oven.

A large joint of beef, surrounded by tatties, neeps, and carrots swimming in pan juice, filled the roasting pan.

"Where did you get such a treasure?" He set the pan on the back of the stove.

"Alan and Ishbel MacCrae butchered a coo last week and when they heard how much you hate mutton, Alan was eager to have you try some of his beef. Morag told me how to cook it and gave me some of her root vegetables since I didn't plant any last spring."

"Alan sounds like a man after my own heart."

"Go get the platter and large bowl from the aumrie, luve. A birthday tea calls for guid dishes."

His mouth watered as he spooned out the vegetables and transferred the meat to the platter. He took a large knife from the aumrie drawer. "This will be my first attempt at carving. Bear with me." After finishing his third large plateful, he said, "We're going to have to get that refrigerator as soon as possible. One with a freezer compartment." He wiped his mouth with his napkin and leaned over to kiss her. "That was the best beef I've ever tasted, lass. Thank you for a birthday I'll never forget."

"It isn't over yet." She got up and filled his mug with coffee.

A familiar, tantalizing aroma rose from the steaming mug.

"Am I dreaming, or is this the special coffee John finds in Edinburgh?"

"A birthday gift from Faither."

"Then, pour your tea. The beverages might be a bit unorthodox, but I'd like to propose a toast."

She poured her tea, sweetened it with honey, and added milk.

He raised his coffee mug and touched the rim of her tea cup. "Here's to the Savage family, no longer a dream in a lonely lad's heart, but the real thing—a real family with twa people who luve one another, a braw lad, and a guid dog. Slàinte mhath!"

Chapter Thirty-One

Very early the following morning, a radio message came in from Maggie's faither. "Young Graham MacDonald's been admitted to the Royal Infirmary for injuries he received in battle. They're no' life-threatening but, like Rob, he's going to need months of therapy."

"Och, Faither, do Morag and Alec know?"

"No' unless the Army's notified them. The lad insisted they no' be told before, but since I'm bringing him home to Innisbraw on Friday, you'll have to prepare them for his arrival."

She pressed her fist to her lips, fighting panic. Only three years younger than she, Graham had been a lifelong friend—so bright, so loyal, and so committed to his role in the war. Like Rob, really. "How bad are his injuries? Will he be crippled?"

"'Tis too early to tell. Depends on how hard he's willing to work. He took a bullet in his left femur and it broke the bone in several places, damaging muscle and soft tissue. I've inserted a Kuntscher rod into the medullary cavity of the bone, but there's nowt more we can do for him here. I'm sorry to add to your turns, but therapy is all that can help him now."

"I'll tell them but I'll take Rob along with me. He's had more experience at this than I have. 'Tis going to be so hard on them, him being their only bairn."

"Aye, and like Rob, Graham was making a career of the Army, and that's all up in the air. If he hadn't suffered such damage to major muscles, he could be back to duty in weeks, but now ..."

"Has he been told what he faces?"

"Of course, but you know Graham. 'Tis guid Rob's around since they're so much alike. Graham and he have never met, but Morag must have filled her letters to him with news of Rob, for the lad's most eager to meet him. I'm thinking 'tis a bit of hero worship."

"He's always had a keen mind. He couldn't have chosen a better hero."

"I couldn't agree more. We'll be arriving with Malcolm on Friday een. You know what to do to get the infirmary ready. I'm certain Morag and Alec will want to spend their nights there, at least for a while."

"How long can you stay, Faither?"

"Through Ne'erday. I'm determined to spend the Yule and see in the Ne'er with that grandbairn of mine."

"Wonderful. You won't know him, he's grown and changed so. He's even smiling now."

"'Tis going to seem like a month instead of only three days till I see all of you. I'm sorry to have to burden you with this, but I know Rob will be a help."

"He will that. Take care, Faither, I'll have everything ready." Maggie paced the floor, impatient to share her news with Rob.

After an hour, impatience turned to anxiety. Rob had not returned from patrol and Robbie had already been fed, bathed, and returned to his cradle. Rob had never been this late.

But surely she would have heard if something had happened.

Shep got up from the hearthrug, stretched, and trotted to the door, tail wagging. Seconds later, Rob opened the door, a smile on his sooty face. "Sorry I'm so late, lass, but Alec gathered all the guard on the machair for a meeting." He wiped his palms on his breeks, ruffled Shep's fur, and gave her arm a quick squeeze.

"A meeting? Whatever for at this time of mornin?"

He peeled off his waxed jacket. "'Tis grand news for a change," he said, tugging off his rubber boots. "Benbecula notified him that after that last attempted landing on Innisbraw, the Royal Navy and RAF are setting up permanent patrols of our shores, and the Army's sending a platoon of thirty-six soldiers here to do the guarding, day and night." He dropped into his rocker and rolled waxed breeks from his legs. "They're even setting up twa Nissen huts to house them and another sma' one for cooking. The Army will boat in whatever food and supplies they need." His smile widened to a broad grin as he got up and hung his rain gear on their pegs. "Until they arrive, Alec's cutting our hours back to four instead of six. Starting in about a week, you'll have a husband in your bed all night, every night."

"That's splendid news." She hugged him, resting her cheek against his sweat-dampened shirt, imagining long nights of spooning and ... She pulled back, hand flying to her mouth. "Och, I wish I had guid news for you."

"What is it, lass? What's happened?"

She told him about Graham. "I hope you'll go with me. I can't face Morag and Alec alone with such news."

"Of course I'll go, though you'll have to wait till I have a cat's lick." He headed for the bathing room, talking over his shoulder. "In person is a much kinder way of learning something like this than by wire or letter."

She followed him and sat on the edge of the tub. "After Sabbath services, Morag said she hadn't heard from Graham for several weeks. She was verra concerned."

He splashed water on his soapy face. "We'd better plan on getting over to their croft before the next post arrives." He checked his image in the mirror. "You never know, the Army could notify them of his injuries at any time."

"Do you suppose you could go over and ask Angus if we could borrow one of his cuddies and his cairt? Their croft is a long walk from here, especially with Robbie."

"Guid idea. I should shave but I'll just put on a clean sark." He dried his face and hands and stripped off his shirt. "Has our lad suckled?"

"He finished just before Faither radioed."

"Guid. He won't be rouping." He unsuccessfully tried to tie the laces at the neck of his Jacobite shirt. "Och, you'll have to help me again. I never can do this."

She straightened the laces and tied a neat bow. "And you never will. Your hands are too large and the laces too sma'."

"No sma'er than my shoelaces," he grumbled, pulling a fisherman's sweater over his head and running his hands through his hair before shrugging into his A-2 jacket. He looked at Maggie, eyebrow raised, then grabbed her and kissed her soundly before leaving to get the cairt.

When he drove the cairt up to the dyke, Maggie bundled Robbie in several blankets and put on her heavy coat.

The air was still unseasonably cold.

She pulled the outer blanket over the bairnie's face as she let Shep out, closed the door, and ordered the dog to stay.

Rob helped her up, took his seat, and gathered up the reins. "Angus gave me a quick driving lesson and put Jack in the traces. He's so auld, I shouldn't get into too much trouble."

"You'll do fine." She rested her head against his arm.

As Maggie delivered the news, Morag broke down and sobbed while Alec held her, his face betraying grief—and fear.

Rob took his arm. "Why don't we go oot and see how those coos of yours are doing?"

Maggie took Alec's place, patting Morag's back and offering words of comfort.

Alec lifted his jacket from its peg. "You've only seen my coos and heifers. I've been wanting to show you my young bulls. They're oot in their coo gang."

Rob studied Alec as the two men walked toward the pasture.

Only Rob's senior by about fifteen years, Alec appeared to have aged a great deal during the past few months. Serving on the Island Council, heading up the patrols, and taking care of his large croft must be too heavy a burden. Threads of silver invaded his thick, black hair, and his usually erect shoulders sagged.

Rob rested his elbows on the top rail of the wooden fence. "I wanted to talk to you alone."

Alec studied the ground. "I thought as much. Then, 'tis worse than what Maggie said?"

"No. Everything she said is true. I just want to explain what Graham's facing."

Moisture filled Alec's blue eyes as he looked up at Rob. "Will our lad be a cripple?"

"'Tis unlikely. He should recover completely."

"What do you need to talk to me about then?"

Rob sighed. Why did he have to be the one to explain the painful work ahead? Because he'd been through it. "I said he should recover completely. Whether he does or no' will depend on how hard he's willing to work to get there."

"Work? I don't ken what you're saying."

Rob gestured at one of the young bulls which eyed him with friendly curiosity. "I don't know much about coos, but if they're like most large animals, if they break a leg, they just lie there till they die."

"Aye. They struggle for a while, but that's what they finally do." Alec lowered his head again and shuffled the toe of his boot over the ground.

"Some folk aren't all that different, yet others can't be held down. They'll go to any lengths to regain their mobility."

"Graham's no' a quitter."

"I'm sure he isn't. But as his faither, you're going to have to keep prodding him to get up, even when the pain's so bad his groans tear you up inside. He's facing the hardest work he's ever done. You ken I'm speaking from experience."

"I do." Alec met Rob's piercing gaze. "No' a one of us thought you'd live, let alone walk again, and here you are, running by our croft four days a week and doing your share on patrol."

"It's a lot to put on your shoulders, Alec, but he's your lad and a lad looks up to his faither. You're going to have to set a fire under him that can't be put out. Are you up to it?"

Determination hardened Alec's gaze. "If how hard and long he works affects the ootcome, I'll no' let up on him till he can run as well as you."

"Then your lad's future is certain. He'll come through this strong and mobile as he ever was." He squeezed Alec's shoulder. "But there's one thing all the folk on Innisbraw must do. They must hold Graham up in prayer every day."

Alec smiled for the first time since greeting them when they arrived. "Aye, they do that, and thankfully, they will that."

222

Hugh called a prayer meeting that een. "You know what we all must do," he announced before the prayers began. "Like you did for Rob, you must pray to our gracious Lord to hold Graham up when he's in so much pain he would falter and give up. Be diligent. Be faithful. Follow our Lord's example."

After the prayers ended, many of the folk asked Rob to help Graham. "I'll do owt I can."

Rob stood with Morag and Alec late Friday afternoon as they watched Malcom put the *Sea Rouk*'s gangplank in place.

John was the first to reach the dock. He clasped Rob's shoulder. "Thank ye for being here. The lad's in pain and exhausted."

"'Tis a hard trip. We need to get him up to the infirmary quickly—no time for blethering with the folk who have gathered."

"Aye, and we'll need some strong lads to get him off the dock. I see Angus's cairt on the path."

Angus and his son Edert stepped forward, along with two other crofters. "We're here to help," Angus said.

John motioned to Rob. "I'm thinking 'tis time Graham met you. It may help him through this."

Morag and Alec hurried over the gangplank, but Rob held back until John motioned him aboard.

Morag knelt beside the stretcher weeping softly, Alec beside her, arm around her shoulders.

Rob knelt beside them, reaching for Graham's hand. "I'm Rob Savage."

The lad looked at him. Pain and fatigue etched his haggard young face.

"Shall we get you ashore now?"

A weak nod.

Rob signaled Angus and the others they were ready.

The stretcher passed between rows of Innisbraw folk who had come to welcome Graham home. No one attempted to slow them with greetings, but their bowed heads showed Rob they were all praying for the lad.

Once they had the stretcher in the cairt, with Feona in the traces, the ride went quickly. When Maggie came out of the infirmary to meet them, Rob leaped down and drew her aside. "Hurry things up as much as you can, luve. The lad's verra tired and in pain."

She nodded and stepped to the back of the cairt. "His room's all ready," she told her faither. "Let's get him inside. He'll have Rob's auld room."

They lifted the stretcher and carried it up onto the entry and into the infirmary. The door at the end of the long hall stood open. John went ahead and directed them to put the stretcher on the edge of the bed. He placed himself on one side and Rob on the other. Maggie put her hands beneath Graham's head and neck and on the count of three they lifted him up and had him lying in bed before he could tense his muscles.

Rob moved back and allowed Maggie and John to take over.

She smoothed the sheet and pulled up the bedcover while John leaned over Graham.

"You're home, lad. I'll give you a little something for pain, and then off to sleep you go. There'll be time for visiting on the morra."

Graham mouthed his thanks.

As Rob turned to leave, he heard his name and stopped.

Graham held out his hand.

Rob retraced his steps and gripped the lad's hand.

"Thank ye," Graham whispered. "I couldn't have held on much longer." Tears glazed his blue eyes.

"I know. I felt the same way after all those hours on the *Sea Rouk*." He tucked Graham's hand beneath the blanket. "As John said, off to sleep you go. You'll feel a lot better on the mornin."

The lad closed his eyes with a sigh.

John beckoned to Morag and Alec. "He's made the journey better than I expected. Just needs a guid night's sleep. Maggie's got the room opposite this one made up for the both of you. Let him sleep. 'Tis what he needs most right now."

Rob found Robbie asleep on the sofa in the front foyer. His heart melted as he picked up his son and placed him over his shoulder, holding the tiny head close to his cheek.

The bairnie gave a sleepy, toothless smile.

"Back to Willie Winkie you go, wee one. Faither's got you." He paced the room, patting his son's back, thanking the Lord over and over for such a blessing and adding another fervent prayer for Graham's speedy recovery.

Maggie went home with Rob and Robbie while John spent the night at the infirmary in a vacant patient room. After they had eaten a late supper and Robbie was tucked in for the night, Rob held Maggie on his lap in front of the glowing peat fire. "If Graham has the same experience I did, he'll feel much better soon." He unclasped her barrette and pulled her close, inhaling her sweet scent.

"He's always been such an active lad." She nestled against his chest. "Of all the lads on Innisbraw, it was always thought he would go the farthest and accomplish the most."

"That's in his favor, as long as he doesn't get too down about his military career. He shouldn't count himself oot yet—I'm sure the Army hasn't." He rested his chin on the top of her head. "You can help Morag through this. Alec knows what he has to do, but I'm sure her mither's heart is breaking."

"She was terrified when he volunteered for the Army the day he turned eighteen, but I know she was proud too. Thank ye for your help, luve. 'Twas exactly what he needed."

"I was fortunate enough to have experience with the same circumstances is all."

She stiffened. "Rob. Accept a compliment for once."

"All right, lass, you're verra welcome."

"That's better." She returned her cheek to his chest. "I think you twa will get along well. You may be nine years aulder, but you're a lot alike."

"Poor lad."

"Och, there's no hope for the likes of you."

Was there a hint of laughter in her grumble? He chuckled and leaned down for a kiss.

Chapter Thirty-Two

Innisbraw erupted into a roar the next morning. A large merchant boat pulled up to the dock, its railing lined with soldiers. Alec's warning to keep to their customary Saturday routines and not interfere with the military men debarking had fallen on deaf ears, the folk being starved for excitement. Groups of celebrating folk gathered on the path along the harbour, standing five to six deep.

A holiday feeling electrified the air. Faithers hoisted young lads and lasses to their shoulders. Crofters' wives wept and waved wildly, undoubtedly celebrating the end to interrupted sleep, bad dreams, and the fear of losing their men.

Alec pushed through the throng, through the babble of excited voices. Old men, clad in patched tweed breeks held up with wide braces over heavy sweaters, drew contentedly on their cuttie pipes and reminisced about memories of the Great War. Their wives, many wearing aprons over faded cotton dresses, gossiped behind raised, work-gnarled hands, holding their shawls close against the brisk, cold breeze.

Young lasses practiced smiling provocatively at one another, hands on hips, but ducked their heads and blushed fiercely the moment the line of soldiers approached. Lads lengthened their strides, trying to march alongside, eyes sparkling at the thrill of impending danger, as the disciplined lines of soldiers passed by in their grand uniforms, real guns over their shoulders. Many times the sergeant leading the group raised his whistle and gave a shrill blast to warn a lad out of the way. Several collies, on the loose from their crofts, nipped at any heel they could find while herding the group of soldiers up the path like a flock of errant sheep.

Local crofters, hired for the morning, tossed duffle bags, tents, cots, and other provisions high into their cairts before slapping the

226

reins and clucking to their cuddies. They soon caught up with the lines of soldiers marching up the hill to Innis Fell toward their destination: the centre of the machair above the western shore.

The Savages watched the activity from the high fell path in front of the cottage. Rob eyed the commotion, shaking his head. "You'd think 'tis a special holiday."

"'Tis." Maggie hugged his hips and laughed. "We finally have real soldiers with real guns to guard our shores, no' crofters armed with knives and digging forks."

"I didn't expect them to take this path to the western shore. 'Tis shorter, but there is the climb."

"Och, what's a wee climb to fit lads?"

"We'd best get out of the way behind the dyke since they're already past Elspeth's cottage." He called Shep to join them and latched the gate. "No bowfing, lad. There's enough noise." He pulled Robbie's blanket up to shelter the lad from the clouds of dust stirred high by marching feet.

Maggie poked him in the ribs. "You're smiling, so I'm thinking you're as kittled up as I am."

"'Tis a stirring sight."

The first line of marchers passed, led by their sergeant who held a whistle clamped between his teeth. The Tommies did not turn their heads, but many side-eyed the family, a few glances registering surprise. Most likely wondering why a fit-looking, fairly young man wasn't away at war.

Shep trembled and nosed Rob's leg when he caught the scent of the collies still herding diligently.

"'Tis all right, lad," he said, stroking the shepherd's silken ears. "They'll be off in a tick."

The last rank of four marchers passed.

Maggie ducked her head. "They all look so young. I hope they're well-trained."

"Don't worry, luve. They surely are."

"And did you see those guns? What are they—do you know?"

"Enfield rifles."

"Just think, as soon as they've set up their camp, you won't have to risk your life standing guard."

"Best of all, you'll have a husband in your bed all the night."

"Aye, all the night." She wrinkled her nose and smiled up at him, the brisk breeze swirling black waves about her flushed cheeks.

His right eyebrow rose. "Do I see a hint of a promise, wife?"

"Mebbe."

Teasing, bonnie lass.

She took Robbie from his arms and scooped up a basket covered with a tea towel. "We're away then."

He brushed his lips over her cheek. "The cairts could be along any minute, so keep to the side of the path," he warned as she headed next door to the infirmary and he inside to bathe and shave. After four hours on patrol, he'd only had time to wash his face and hands and gulp down a cup of coffee before the merchant boat arrived.

After he dressed and slipped into his A-2 jacket, he ordered Shep to stay and took off at a run down the path to Elspeth's cottage. His lessons in the Gaelic had been sporadic since his nightly guard duties started, and he was eager to spend time with his dearest friend.

He kissed her cheek in greeting. "You've had a guid view of all the excitement."

"'Tis past time they realized we could be in peril." Her gaze probed his. "How are you, lad?—and I don't mean your body. Have you been able to turn over to our Lord what happened that night?"

Elspeth was the one person on the island not easily placated with a glib answer. He helped her to her rocker, leaned his back against the entry railing and told her everything he could remember about his role in the U-boat sinking. "So it's going to take some time, but war's like that. After a while, the mind pictures fade and take their places among all the rest that have gone before."

"That young German lad, the one in command, still bothers you, doesn't he?"

"That's me sorted, eh? If he'd been aulder, I don't know if I'd feel the same, but it made me realize we aren't the only ones Hitler

228

has to answer for. Many of his own folk—the ones who are fortunate to survive—have had their lives ruined by his evil."

"I've already added Verner Rolf to my prayers." She picked up her Gaelic Bible and motioned him to the other rocker. "I've decided to use the Word of God in our lesson this mornin. I'm thinking the Lord's Prayer is something you should learn in the Gaelic. There's so much comfort to be found there, especially in the words, 'Dèanar do thoil air an talamh, mar a nithear air nèamh—Thy will be done on earth, as it is in heaven."

He settled into the rocker.

She tapped his knee. "Of course, we ken that will never happen until He comes again and establishes His reign here on earth, but if we pray for His perfect will in our lives, we will be doing our part in preparing for His return."

As always, Elspeth's practical Christian principles strengthened Rob's resolve to do his best. After an unusually productive lesson, he went up to the infirmary for his upper body workout, which had also been hit-and-miss for the past few weeks. Busy concentrating on the count as he lifted weights, he didn't realize John was standing in the rehab doorway until he spoke.

"Your left shoulder appears to be coming along verra well indeed." The doctor's beard tilted with a broad smile.

Rob returned the weights to their shelf and wiped his face with a towel. "Haven't been as faithful with them lately, but since I'm only missing four hours' sleep for another few nights, I'm meaning to get back on schedule."

"Someday, I want to sit down with you and find out exactly what happened that night. Maggie radioed me with the news of your success against the raid and the sinking of the U-boat, of course, but I'm certain she didn't tell me everything."

A worm of guilt burrowed deep into Rob's belly. He hadn't shared his experiences with John but, since the doctor had been so busy after bringing Graham to Innisbraw, there hadn't been an opportunity. This morning was no exception. "If they ever get around to that debriefing they talked about, I'll see if you can sit in. The Lord was working verra hard that night, John. And He's continuing to work, bringing comfort to our men who had to take a life. It isn't something they'll ever disremember, but they seem to be handling it better now."

⚜

John winced at the memories of the mutilated bodies he had treated, many—despite his skill—unsuccessfully. "Mebbe this war will soon be over and we can all look forward instead of back on what we've seen and done."

"Mebbe soon." Rob stared off into the distance.

"Maggie has a maskin pat of tea and a pottle of coffee in the kitchen. Let's go have some."

"You'll no' have to twist my arm. She brought some scones too."

"Och, don't tell me, you're gleg as gled so soon after breakfast."

"Haven't had time for breakfast." He followed John into the kitchen.

"It wouldn't matter, lad, it wouldn't matter a bit. I'm delighted to find you looking forward to food."

Rob poured a mug of coffee and took two scones. "Give me another week. A few nights of uninterrupted sleep will have me feeling like a new man."

"You mean that lad of yours is already sleeping the night through?"

"Och, that's different. Lying there in bed and holding our lad is one of my greatest pleasures."

"That's guid to hear." John grinned like a daftie, but he didn't care. "I held that braw grandbairn early this mornin. He smiled at me, lad, he really did."

"'Tis enough to melt you into a puddle, isn't it?"

"I teared up like some auld eejit."

"He does that to me too. If my men in the 396th could see me with Robbie, they'd think me aff the knot."

John leaned forward, smile fading. "Hearing you say the 396th reminds me. Graham asked if you were going to be around the day. He wants to talk to you."

Rob swallowed his last bite of scone and drained his mug.

"What about right now?"

"That's what I like about you, lad, you don't waste time."

"I've never been able to figure out if that's a vice or a virtue."

"In this case, 'tis a virtue. Come you on. Morag will want to use the kitchen to prepare Graham's dinner soon."

⁎⁂⁎

When they reached Graham's room, Morag had just finished straightening his fresh bedding. Apparently the lad had asked his mither to help him bathe and shave, evidence of his military discipline.

"I'm glad you're here," Morag said to Rob. "Our lad's been asking for you."

"Why don't you take this opportunity to make the lad his dinner while I get a little work done in my office?" John said.

Morag shot Rob a grateful smile. "Have a guid visit." She followed John from the room.

"Well, I see I was right," Rob said, smiling at Graham. "You look better than you did yesterday."

Graham cleared his throat, but when he spoke his voice was still unnaturally husky. "I had my first night's sleep with only one ... bad dream."

Rob pulled over a chair, turned it backward, and straddled it, resting his arms on the back. "Bad dreams, is it? About the war?"

Though her lad resembled Morag—same narrow face, same dimpled chin—he was obviously a tall man like his faither, though very thin and unnaturally pale. His black hair was cut short and his eyes were the same startling blue as his parents', but inside their depths lurked the despair of a young man who had experienced and seen too much and couldn't forget no matter how hard he tried.

"Why did I get to come home?" A cry from a tormented soul. "Why did I live when all my men were slaughtered like ... like ...?" He closed his eyes and turned his face to the wall, fists clenched so hard his knuckles blanched white as whale bones tossed up on the shore. "I'm no better than a one of them. An entire rifle platoon wiped oot in seconds—thirty guid men, and we didn't even have time to deploy our mortars for smoke cover. Our orders took us

231

right into an ambush. The blood. All that blood."

"I've lost up to eighty men on a single bombing strike." Rob's voice was deliberately stern. Graham didn't need pity. "I didn't see the blood they shed, but I did watch their planes go down in flames and knew they were dying in agony. My own plane, and a few others, made it back to base with the crews alive."

Graham pushed his head further into the pillow.

Rob got up and paced to the window, lifted the curtain, and studied the cloud-bruised sky. "The bad dreams fade and then go away after a while, but it does no guid to feel guilty about coming home." He dropped the curtain and returned to Graham's bedside. "All of us who served and survived have to leave that in God's hands, or the life He spared is wasted and destroyed by guilt—and that pain is worse than any bullet from a German machine gun."

Graham lay still.

Rob sat down again and leaned forward, hiding his own sorrow behind a rigid façade. "But that wasn't why you wanted to see me. Give over. I've things to do."

When Graham turned his face, instead of anger at Rob's hard tone and seemingly heartless comments, there was relief. "I ... I have some questions I want to ask, but I'm no' sure I should."

"I said give over. I'll answer if I can."

The lad still hesitated.

Rob gave him time.

"I was just wondering about this ... this therapy John's been talking about. What's it like?"

A good change from death and destruction. "'Tis work, plain and simple—so much work you'll be sweating like you've run ten kilometres in the summer clad in your heaviest winter clothes. And 'tis painful. I don't know how it will be with you, but mine hurt—verra badly."

"Work and pain. Owt else?"

Rob stared at Graham intently. "You'll want to quit. Time and time again you'll tell yourself it isn't worth it, but it is. You can't let yourself give up, no matter what."

Graham returned his stare. Determination sculpted his lax face into granite. "If you could do it with twa bad legs, I'm no' about to give up with one."

"Then you'll do grand." Rob pushed aside his reticence to talk about the lad's military future. Time to face it head on. "I understand you want to make the military a career."

"I did once."

"You've changed your mind?"

"I'm thinking the Army won't be wanting me now."

"Why no'? In a few months you'll be fit enough to return to duty."

"Doing what? Working at a desk somewhere, writing useless reports? You opted oot."

Rob hadn't anticipated this turn in the conversation. He took a deep breath to quiet his racing heart. "My case was different. I did one thing and did it well—I flew airieplanes." *Och, so hard to say aloud.* "That's the only reason I was a career man, so I could fly. Didn't matter if it was fighters or bombers, I flew them. I only wanted to fly."

"How could you give it up?"

The most painful question of all. "I ... had to. There's no way they could be sure I was physically fit to fly a B-17 into combat without endangering myself and my crew. I think they were wrong, but I wasn't in charge of Eighth Bomber Command. Plus, I could never fly a desk."

"I don't want that either." Graham's fingers shook as he ran them through his thick, black hair.

"But my problem isn't my legs. It's my shoulder. My left will always be a bit weaker than my right." Rob looked at the lace curtains billowing in the sea breeze, praying silently for the right words. "So I had to change careers. Innisbraw needs a coastal rescue boat and I'm going to build and command one."

"Need a partner?" Graham asked suddenly. "I'm thinking my faither could use me around here. He's aged a lot since I was home on leave."

Rob masked his surprise. It had never occurred to him that Graham would seriously contemplate leaving the service. "I'd never turn down an offer like that, but your command might order you

233

back when you've recovered." He stood and replaced the chair. "And you need time to think this over. I'm biddy certain your folk would welcome having you home to stay, but you must do it because 'tis right for yourself."

"I don't know what's right anymore." Red blotches stained Graham's gaunt cheeks. "I know the Army needs me, but so does Faither. I feel like I'm being torn in twa."

"That's all the more reason to bide on any decision." Back to his official tone. "Don't even attempt to make up your mind now. Just work on getting your leg back into shape. You'll need that no matter what you decide to do with the rest of your life."

The keening cry of a gull pierced the silence.

The lad seemed to consider his words. "That's me sorted, then. I will that."

⚓

Rob attacked the salt-encrusted grime on the outside of the cottage's front window while Maggie swept the entry flags.

A low drone caught his attention.

He shielded his eyes with a hand and searched the sky.

An RAF Catalina flying boat circled the harbour for a landing.

"That'll be the men come for the debriefing. Better put water on for tea, while I fetch your faither. He wants to hear what happened, if they'll allow it."

"Why have they waited so long?" She tossed down her broom. "It isn't fitting—making you go through it again when you're trying to disremember."

He scrubbed at a smear in the corner of the glass. "They've been busy making sure we're protected."

"And about time too."

"I believe you're gaw." He laughed, flicking the rag at her bottom.

"Of course I'm gaw. How can you take it so lightly?"

"Because I know how the military works. It's taken countless calls and letters—in triplicate—to get them here. Don't take it oot on the poor de'il they've sent, luve. He's only following orders."

"It's still wrong." She picked up the broom and stalked into the cottage, nose high.

Alec soon accompanied two airmen who eyed the cottage with interest. The RAF Group Captain was obviously cought off-guard by Rob's height, and he appeared even more uncomfortable when Alec informed him that not only was Rob an American, but had been a B-17 heavy bomber group commander invalided out after being wounded. The "Groupie" was probably dying to know how an American colonel happened to end up on Innisbraw with a wife and son. But the officer graciously accepted the tea Maggie offered, said it was fine if John listened as long as he didn't interrupt, and asked Rob to sit across from him at the small kitchen table. He began the interrogation by asking Rob to tell in his own words everything that had occurred from the moment he arrived at the shore, and to please speak slowly so his aide could make a written record.

After waiting days to have it behind him, Rob found the debriefing anticlimactic. His long experience in interrogations helped him give a concise, exact accounting of every action, every word, every impression. He worried about lapsing into Scots but the familiar routine helped the English flow. He did omit being unsure he could kill the German lieutenant. Too personal that, and it had no bearing on the outcome.

When he'd finished with the description of the arrival of the Halifax from Oban and the departure of the prisoners, Rob sat back, swiping his sleeve across his sweating forehead while the aide finished writing his last words.

Chapter Thirty-Three

Alec was a gentle faither. Despite Alec's good intentions, his son needed a hard taskmaster. With his experience as flight leader and group commander, Rob was the ideal candidate. Graham responded immediately to the militaristic attitude Rob took with him. The lad, trained to obey a command with no questions or hesitation, soon looked to the "Colonel" for orders.

Careful not to step over the line, Rob always consulted John or Maggie before asking the lad to do anything and was quick to praise a good job, much the way he had behaved with his own crewmembers. He found himself enjoying his new role. Graham, intelligent, articulate, and eager to excel, seemed a kindred soul.

With the New Year approaching, the topic of conversation around the supper table at the cottage concerned how to celebrate Hogmanay.

"I must have missed it last year," Rob said. "All I remember is the Yule gathering at the infirmary."

"We haven't had an island-wide celebration since the war started," John said. "Some folk get together with neighbors. Ever since the blackout, we've curtailed festivities like first-footing."

"What's first-footing?" Rob asked.

John leaned back and laced his fingers over his belly. "'Tis when a stranger, preferably tall and dark-haired, knocks on a cottage door just past the turn o' the night on Ne'ers Day. When the folk ask him in and he steps over the threshold, he presents them with a bottle of whisky which they open and share with him. Having a first-footer stepping over your threshold is said to bring luck throughout the year."

Rob chuckled. "No' many strangers on Innisbraw."

"Och, you can pretend he is."

When Maggie started to speak, John raised a hand. "Now for some guid news. I've been in contact with Calum, and he'll be spending Yule and Ne'ers weeks with us this year. The fisherman he's been working for every school holiday is dry-docking for repairs, so the lad will be free."

Maggie's face flushed with pleasure. "Och, Faither, that's wonderful. I've missed him terribly."

Unable to curb his growing enthusiasm, Rob said, "With our own family growing and so many folk wanting to see Graham—and Calum, since he'll be home—why don't we ask Hugh if we can use the kirk hall? That way, there'll be room for all the folk. Even some of those British lads no' on patrol might like to come."

"Guid one, you," John said. "Graham's coming along well. A cairt ride over to the kirk hall and spending the een in a wheelchair shouldn't hurt him a bit."

"I've a Women's Aid Society meeting on the morra." Maggie's eyes sparkled with excitement. "I'll ask Hugh. If he agrees, we women can begin planning a real Hogmanay ceilidh."

John looked down at Robbie, nestled in his arms. "What do you think about that, wee laddie? Your first ceilidh."

The bairnie smiled and blew bubbles.

~*~

"It will be guid to see Calum again," Rob told Maggie when they were alone later that night. "He should be almost finished at academy."

"Aye. He'll sit for his Highers this year even though he's no' going on to university. I'm thinking he wants to prove to himself that he could if he wanted."

"So he's still bent on fishing for a living?"

She grimaced. "I'm afraid so. Faither's been trying to tell him what a hard life he's chosen, but 'tis all he's ever wanted."

"Well then, in a few years, we'll have to build him his own trawler."

Her eyes sparkled like moonlight on a loch. "What a grand idea."

Rob and Colin looked toward the dark outline of the Nissen hut, used by the soldiers for cooking and eating, looming up from the centre of the machair. The Tommies had done a grand job getting it set up and supplied, and they were also doing well restricting the light from the Tilly lamps they were using in their temporary tents—though the men not on guard were probably still fast asleep on their cots this early in the morning.

"Och, I canna believe this is our last night on guard." Colin sighed, handing the binoculars to Rob for his turn. "It's been hard on Ruth, having me gone so many nights for so long. She's sorry we didna stay on Mull instead of coming to Innisbraw in nineteen and thirty-six. Auld neighbors have written they have a Home Guard there."

Rob adjusted the glasses and swept them over the cove. He'd been wanting to ask Colin if he suffered any bad dreams or guilt over the German he had knifed to death, but still didn't think the time right. "Have you heard from your lad or lass lately?"

"Aye, though we're both a bit fashed with Martin's latest post."

"He's no' been wounded, has he?"

"No, but he has decided he likes the sea more than sheep crofting. He's talking about transferring from the merchant fleet to regular Navy when the war's over."

Distressing news. Martin was Colin's only lad. Who would carry on when Colin grew too auld to take care of the croft? "What about your lass, Betty? Mebbe she'll meet some sheep crofter at that croft she's working on in the Borders and bring him home after the war."

Colin snorted. "You sound like you've been reading her posts. Ever since she joined the Women's Land Army, young as she is, she's been threatening to do just that. And according to her last letter, she thinks she's found him."

"You don't sound too happy about it."

"Och, those Borderland lads are too Sassenach by half—comes from living so close to England."

A dark, blurred shape appeared on the horizon.

Rob stiffened and put out a hand. "Take a keek. 'Tis far oot and looks like one of ours, but you're better at recognizing ships."

Colin took the glasses and raised them, adjusting them quickly. The binoculars shook as the crofter studied the shape of the ship.

Was he afraid of another attack?

After a time, he lowered the glasses with a sigh. "Aye, 'tis ours—one of those destroyers they have patrolling."

"I doubt the Germans will ever attempt another landing on our shores." Rob pulled back his cuff and checked his watch. "Our last patrol will be over in an hour, then it will be up to others to keep our island safe."

"Have you ever killed a man?" Colin asked suddenly. "I know I did what had to be done and it wisna a sin, for we are at war, but I still have dreams about that knife slipping in so easily ... and the blood, so much blood."

Rob raised the glasses but he was not seeing the dark sea, or slight flush of pale grey lighting the sky as dawn approached. Instead, he was watching a Messerschmitt Bf 109 burst into flames in front of him, and reliving the unforgettable sight of the young pilot jerking back and forth like a puppet on strings. "I've killed a lot of men, mebbe thousands with all the bombs I've dropped." He lowered the glasses and knuckled his eyes. "But the ones I dream about are the pilots I shot down when I was flying P-47 fighters. You get so wrapped up in the chase, rolling and banking, climbing and diving, trying to get that Swastika-marked plane in your sights long enough to take him oot before he gets you. Even after you land and go through debriefing you're still caught up in the chase." He handed the glasses to Colin. "'Tis only in your dreams they haunt you. But it fades after a while. I've learned to spend some time with the Lord each night before sleep. The wartime dreams seldom come anymore."

"Then I'm more blest than you as I have only one bad dream to disremember."

⁂

On his morning runs, Rob noted how the respite from the gale-ridden weather benefited more than just the folk living on Innisbraw. The other Nissen huts went up quickly and the tents, which had been temporary quarters for the thirty-six soldiers assigned to guard the island's shores, were dismantled and barbed-wire fences were erected to keep out inquisitive islanders. Uniformed guards, armed with STEN submachine guns, became a common sight along the edge of the machair. Day and night, each squad took its turn patrolling.

How had the young soldiers adjusted to the lack of piped water or electricity? Even on the American air base he had commanded, the crews complained about everything: the lack of privacy, boring food, delayed mail. Did the Brit lads grumble among themselves, especially when queued up at a crudely-built outside latrine, shivering in the cold wind as an unexpected rain trickled freezing drops inside their upturned collars?

⚔

Rob installed his old trapeze and transfer bars on Graham's bed, and the lad quickly mastered transferring himself to the wheelchair.

"I can't wait for the Hogmanay ceilidh," he told Rob. "'Twill be guid to get oot of here for a few hours. I ken I won't be able to dance but I can watch."

Rob grinned at the lad's youthful enthusiasm. Had he ever been so young and eager for fun? He couldn't remember.

This lad had folk who luved and supported him—he had a family. Rob's background was so different. Perhaps it was a blessing, making the present all the more precious.

The thought surprised him. Too busy living a life he had never dreamed possible, he rarely dwelt on his lonely past anymore.

He eyed Graham's smiling face. "Ready for some arm and shoulder exercises?"

"You're worse than a warrant officer in a fair fash."

"That wheelchair's going to get auld mighty fast. You'll be begging for crutches but you won't get them until your arms and shoulders are built up."

"Aye, sir," Graham sighed. "Arm and shoulders it is. Show them to me again, will you?"

"You've been doing them for over a week, soldier. I give the orders, you do the work."

Graham picked up the hand-held weights and did a bicep curl. He groaned. "Like I said, you're worse than a warrant officer stiffening his spine with his swagger stick."

"'Tis a guid thing you said that with a smile, mister, or I'd have to confine you to your quarters for Ne'ers."

"I was smiling. I was smiling!" His sober face belied his words. "Did you have to confine your men to their quarters very often?"

"No, but I did confine a lot of them to the base."

"What got them into trouble? Refusing an order?"

"Och, that's a serious enough offense to get you a court-martial, especially if it occurred on a mission." Rob grinned at the memory of inebriated or hungover crewmen trying to stand at attention while he gave them the evil eye. "It was more likely for starting a fight in one of the pubs at Edenoaks, getting mouthy with a senior officer, or always being late for oh-dark-thirty briefings." He handed Graham a towel. "Time to work on your triceps."

Graham wiped his hands and took the lighter weights. "What was your least favorite duty at the 396th?"

A quick, easy answer. "Writing letters of condolence to the relatives and luved ones of my men who were killed in combat. Some of my squadron leaders couldn't do it."

"And your favorite?"

Another easy one. "Leading all three squadrons home safely after a successful strike."

"Wasn't it hard making so many decisions every day for so many personnel? Mither wrote me that you had almost a thousand people under your command. I had trouble leading a rifle platoon."

"A commander never does it alone. You have to delegate authority or you can never get your primary turn done. There isn't enough time to organize strikes and assign plane crews if you have to oversee the personnel in the chow hall, for instance, or the ground crews. And my aide took the heat off me every day by performing an unbelievable series of duties." Rob held out his hand for the weights. "That's enough work on your triceps. It's time to get up on the bed for your favorite exercise."

"Modified sit-ups. Ugh!"

"Aye, but I can't stress their importance enough. I felt like you do, but when I finally began using the crutches, I didn't have a single backache."

Graham wheeled himself over to the bars and made a smooth transfer.

Once he was lying down, Rob removed the pillow.

"When do you think I can begin using crutches? I'm more than ready."

"Och, I don't know. I do know John won't let you until he is biddy certain you're ready. You'll probably have to work on the parallel bars first, like I did, and it's a guid thing too. 'Twas hard enough to walk with those sticks after the bars. I don't want to think what would have happened if I hadn't been ready."

"How did you bear it so long? I understand that after both of your crashes, it took months before you could even walk with crutches."

How *had* he stuck it out for so long? "I'm no' sure, for it was a combination of so many things. I'd have to put Maggie's support at the top of the list, and John's skill as a surgeon. Of course, the prayers of all the folk are right up there." He grinned. "You haven't known me long, but you'll find out in time I'm about as stubborn as a bull determined to join the heifer in the next coo gang. You tell me I can't do something and I'll kill myself proving you wrong."

Graham grinned back. "Sounds like me. My only problem is finding the common sense to stop doing something daft before it really does kill me."

"Och, you're describing me too. Let's pray you find a lass like my Maggie. If she didn't have the patience of a saint, she'd be long gone and I'd be truly dead."

Graham fidgeted. "I used to be smitten with Maggie." Boyish, lopsided grin. "I thought she was the bonniest lass I'd ever seen, even if she was aulder than me." His already ruddy cheeks flushed bright red. "I suppose I still think that, but since she's spoken for, I've had to broaden my search."

"You'll find her. And you're right, you ken. Maggie's the bonniest lass I've ever seen too, and I've been a lot of places." Rob straightened and gave a mock frown. "Enough stalling. Get with those modified sit-ups, soldier."

"Aye, sir, after just one last question. Sir, if I may?"

"Snap it out."

"What are you going to wear to the ceilidh?"

Now that was a surprise. "Wear? Why does it matter?"

"You've already got your lass, but I haven't."

Rob swallowed a laugh. "I think your full dress uniform would be a guid choice."

"It's no' too much?"

"I'll most likely wear my uniform pants and shirt and A-2 jacket, providing Maggie approves. I don't have any guid mufti. Your uniform's a fine choice. You'll be fighting off the lasses." He pinned Graham with a hard stare. "Now get to work on those sit-ups."

⚜

Even the howling gale descending upon Innisbraw on New Year's Eve did nothing to diminish the turnout or the spirit of the revelers, especially since all of the crofters were now free to attend.

Angus rigged a tarpaulin over the back of the cairt so his passengers wouldn't get wet. Rob wore what he usually wore to kirk—his dark green uniform pants with a dark green uniform shirt, tan tie, and dark green ETO blouse.

He felt a little foolish wearing his old uniform to a ceilidh, but Maggie insisted on the ETO. "You can wear your leather jacket in the cairt, but 'twill be much too warm inside. Besides, that short blouse looks so guid on you." Maggie, stunning in her pale blue sweater and long, royal-blue wool skirt, had pulled her hair back and tied it at the nape with a wide ribbon.

Calum arrived late that afternoon and appeared to have grown over thirty centimetres in two years. He was still very slim and his resemblance to Maggie as strong as ever. He and John wore dark blue tweed suits with crisp, white shirts and colorful ties. Robbie was even dressed for the occasion in pale blue trews and a sweater Maggie had knit.

The party was in full swing when the Savages arrived. They exchanged hugs, kisses, and handshakes with those folk they hadn't seen for a while.

Robbie bounced up and down in Rob's arms, not at all intimidated by the noise and confusion. His blue eyes sparkled in the overhead lights, and his head turned constantly as he took in all of the bright decorations adorning the hall. He was especially fascinated with the children.

Kaitlin MacKinnon, now three, took it upon herself to amuse the bairn. She brought him a bright red bow and even tried to feed him a piece of scone.

"I'm so sorry!" her mither Anna exclaimed. "The lass has never seen such a wee bairnie before. She's always putting things in her dall's mouth. She must think he's a dall."

"'Tis all right," Rob said. "He likes the attention."

Maggie took the bairnie from Rob. "This laddie needs a fresh hippen. Why don't you go over and rescue Graham. He seems a bit whalmed by all the attention from the lasses."

Rob laughed. "'Twas what he wanted. I knew the uniform would do the trick. I'm no' about to interfere."

"You're just afraid Rinait will see you."

His smile vanished. He didn't find her teasing remark amusing. "I'm no' going near that lass. She sent me luve blinks every time I went to kirk after you went back to duty at that RAF base."

"Why, Rob Savage, I'm thinking you're afraid of a wee slip of a lass of fifteen. Shame on you."

"No' afraid, just leery."

"You've no call. It looks like she's only got eyes for Graham."

"So it does. But I'll no' save a man who doesn't need rescuing."

Maggie gave a quick smile and took off to change Robbie.

Rob made the rounds of those lads in uniform and shook their hands, welcoming them to Innisbraw and thanking them for their service. Several eyed his military clothing, but no one said anything.

A few of the older lasses cast inviting glances at the soldiers, especially Anna MacLeod, who had blossomed into a bonnie young woman. It wouldn't be long before the Brits were included in the festivities.

He spotted Calum at the refreshment table and joined him. "A lad after my own heart. What's guid?"

Calum swallowed a mouthful of cake. "'Tis all guid. After the food at academy, these sweets go down a treat."

Rob took a plate and dished up a large spoonful of clootie dumpling, piling it high with clotted cream. "I know this is guid. My Maggie made it."

They ate in companionable silence until the music started and Calum went off to find a partner for the reel. While he ate, Rob watched the Brit soldiers heading toward Graham. They all saluted the captain and several eyed the pretty, red-haired lass at his side with hopeful smiles, while their sergeant engaged the captain in conversation.

Graham's dour look made it clear he didn't enjoy having his time with Rinait interrupted.

Rob stacked his empty plate on top of the others on the table and walked across the room to join a group of fishermen enjoying a lively discussion.

"I'm telling you, after the war, Scotland's government is going to have to change the fishing rules," Tormad MacKinnon was saying. "Those large trawlers are ruining the Minch and, with the U-boats, we can't use our smaller boats in the Atlantic like we used to, even with the skerries causing so many ticklers."

All the men nodded.

Malcolm MacNeill draped an arm over Rob's back. "Well, in time, Rob here will have that rescue boat built so it won't be so dangerous for us here on Innisbraw."

Thomas Campbell asked, "When are you figuring to start that boat, Rob?"

"The minute the war's over. The lumber's ordered. They just can't ship it yet. That was a delay I hadn't considered."

Mark Ferguson leaned closer, brushing his red forelock off his sweaty forehead, his young, weathered face florid from the heat in the hall. "Any idea of when that'll be?

"Not long now, at least in the European Theatre. I read in the Edinburgh *Scotsman* that General Patton's on a counter-offensive through France, heading for Bastogne. I don't see how the Germans can hold out much longer. Of course Japan may be another story."

"How quickly will you complete the boat once you start?" Thomas asked. "It's really awful having to go oot knowing there's no help nearby if you get into trouble."

"I figure it will take me over a year, mebbe less if I can find some local help."

"If you're working during a force seven gale or above, count me in," Tormad said.

Thomas and Mark also agreed to help if the weather was too bad to take their trawlers out.

"That will be grand. The keel beam and stern post are going to be too heavy and awkward to handle alone, even with a windlass. I'll take all the help I can get."

"'Tis the least we can do," Mark said. "Having our own rescue boat will be the answer to a heap o' prayers."

Maggie slipped through the group of men and grasped Rob's arm. "Enough man talk. Elspeth's holding Robbie and I want to dance."

Rob kissed her cheek. "Then on we go, lass." He nodded to the others and led her out to the middle of the floor where they were soon doing a stately strathspey. Though awkward at first, this was one of the dances Maggie had taught him at their wedding ceilidh, and he soon relaxed and enjoyed himself.

Paddy and his lads played a slow tune next.

Rob took Maggie into his arms.

She rested her cheek against his chest. "Mmm, this is my favorite way to dance."

He nuzzled the top of her head. "Mine too. I like having you in my arms."

"I only wish they knew a Glenn Miller tune, then it would be perfect." That teasing smile, those dancing eyes. "I forgot to tell you that you definitely don't have to worry about Rinait anymore. Seems she has a new conquest."

Unwilling to pass up a chance to tease his lass, he asked, "Och, and who would that be?"

"Graham, of course. She hasn't left his side all een."

"I was right. 'Tis the uniform—'twill do it every time."

Chapter Thirty-Four

Alec drove his cairt along the western path, turning his gaze to the pale blue heavens. Only the first week of March and already what the folk called the "steady weather" was blessing them with clear skies. Following an unusually cold and wet winter, the weak rays of sun brought a smile to his face and energized his flagging spirits. To his right, several crofters ploughed portions of the machair for crops of barley, rye, and oats. Most likely they were taking advantage of the break in the rain to plant an early crop while there was still a good chance of more showers to water the young seeds. A Tommy led a shaggy cuddy ahead of a crofter guiding a plough. Not a surprising sight. Many friendships had sprung up between the islanders and the lads who patrolled the shore.

He clucked to his cuddy and guided the cairt over the rough machair to the sentry standing guard at the gate to the Army compound. "Ian, lad, they still have you planted like a stump in a field?" He doffed his bunnet and grinned at the young Tommy. "I'll need some help carrying this load."

Ian propped his rifle against the fencepost and licked his lips. "What have you brought this time, Mister MacDonald? Last week's shortbreads were better than my mum makes, and her taught to bake by my grannie from Kircaldy."

"Butchered a bull. Some nice joints here. 'Twill add some muscle to that tall frame of yours."

"Beef? Lord luve a duck! I'll whistle up cook and his helper while you keep guard. Don't want any of those bonnie lasses of yours invading the camp and spreading good cheer." He grinned, waggled his brows, and raced off to the cook's hut.

At loose ends after the house plans were completed in

February, Rob eagerly accepted Angus's offer to teach him how to cast peat. He inhaled deeply as they climbed the brae-side of the fresh water lock. "There's no' as much smell to the bog when you're up close—mainly newly turned earth."

Angus puffed on his pipe. "You've got to burn it first and then there's no sweeter smell, 'less 'tis the reek from a smoke o' tobacco."

Nothing could compare to the aroma of burning peat, but saying so might sound quarrelsome. "Which pit will we use? There are so many."

"Yonder a bit, closer to the rise of the ben."

They skirted countless pits, exchanging greetings with men wielding spades in a seemingly tireless rhythm of dig-lift-release. Angus led him to the edge of a broad pit. "We share this with Tormad. He says he's happy to include your family." He handed Rob a casting spade. "'Tis going to be short, tall as you are, but I've never seen one longer."

Rob stepped on the blade. A bit of stooping, but not too bad.

The crofter tapped his pipe on the ground and carefully ground out the glowing embers. "Till you learn how, 'tis best to work in twas, one to cast and one to lift."

"I'm ready. Show me what to do." The tuskar, a long-handled, spade-like peat-iron was simple to use until it came to easing the large rectangle of chocolate-coloured peat off the little hook-like flange attached to the blade and into the hands of the lifter.

Angus had to help several times to keep the peat from breaking into pieces.

Rob stared at his hands. Why was he so clumsy? After a frustrating hour, he developed a rhythm, casting a piece and releasing it into Angus's waiting hands.

Angus laid each piece along the top of the pit. "In twa weeks the peats should be dry enough to stack into cas bhic. If you dinna ken the Gaelic word yet, that means 'little feet'. 'Tis three peats set on edge with another across the top. Then, sometime later this simmer, we'll carry them oot to the path and haul them in my cairt to our crofts."

Rob massaged his aching back. "How much do we have to cast

to last both our families through winter?"

"Och, working hard and each doing our own casting over a thousand peats a day, the both of us should have enough in about twa weeks."

Bite your tongue, Savage. But two weeks? Will my back hold out that long?

⁎⋏⁎

Only Maggie's nightly backrubs, and the shame of giving up when every man on the island accepted the task as his duty, kept Rob going until he cast the final peat. He found it easier to kneel and stack the casbhic. Now knowing the backbreaking labour that kept a fire burning in stove and fireplace, he'd never take a glowing peat fire for granted again.

On the twentieth of the month, he brushed off his wet knees. After over two weeks of hard, manual labour, it was a relief to spend his days in the shed. He fashioned the rest of the used lumber into a large bed frame and kitchen and dining room tables and chairs.

When that ran out, Alec offered a stack of rough lumber he kept in the loft of his coo byre. "I only use it for fence repairs and I can use driftwood for that."

Certain the crofter was using the lumber as a way to thank him for helping Graham, Rob almost refused. But what if their roles were reversed? He accepted the offer with a hearty handshake.

He ordered slate tiles for the roof of the new house from a small family-run quarry in Llanberis, Wales. Welsh might be a Gaelic language, but it didn't sound at all like Scot Gaelic. It took two frustrating days to work his way through family members until he reached a grandson invalided out of the British Army who spoke English. After all the hassle, the slates still might not arrive before they were needed.

He started work on two rocking chairs, using a boiler he had bought to steam and bend the wood for the rockers. Countless radio messages and letters to friends and relatives of some of the Innisbraw natives resulted in a trawler-load of used lumber from Lewis, Harris, and North and South Uist, the largest islands in the

Outer Hebrides.

Malcolm executed a bit of magic and found a large, used, stone jawbox and a bathing tub, basin, and watterie in a partially-burned, abandoned manor house in one of the more affluent areas of Oban. "All they need is a bit of scouring and a new seat for the watterie and they'll do," he said, when refusing payment.

⁓⋏⸲

Now that Graham was on crutches and getting around well, he often kept Rob company while he worked. Rinait always followed him to the shed, hanging on every word Graham said. It was plain to see the lad was just as smitten.

"I hope she's mature enough for Graham," Rob said to Maggie one een. "He's a bright lad with a promising future."

She stopped her spinning wheel with her hand and separated the clump of wool she was working with. "Och, she's a guid lass. Not wanting to go on to academy, she doesn't have schooling as guid as Graham's, but she is bright. She does all the weaving for her family and is a big help to Flora around their cottage. She'll make a fine wife."

"Admit it, Maggie, you're an unabashed romantic."

"You're one to talk."

He settled a sleepy Robbie into the crook of his arm. "I'm no' a romantic. I'm a realist."

"You're the most romantic man I've ever seen. As for being a realist, you'll get no argument from me as long as you add the word 'optimistic' to the front of it."

"There is a bit of a dreamer in me, but I do know how to face facts."

"Och, you do?"

"Aye." He grinned. "Fact one, the menfolk on the island have all the stone cut for our house and have it moved to the building site next door. Fact twa, I'll finish the rockers in another three days. And fact three, we'll start on the house in one week." He laid Robbie in his cradle and knelt by her side. "But fact four is even more important. You're the bonniest lass in the world and I want to kiss you till your toes curl."

She laid the spindle down and rested her forehead against his.

"See? You're the romantic one."

Rob looked up when Graham hobbled into the shed—alone. "Where's Rinait?"

"Visiting Elspeth. Something about doing a weaving using auld designs."

Rob put down the plane and brushed off his denims. "Let's go over to Paddy's for some coffee. I'm fair parched."

They took a table along the wall and blew on their steaming coffee. Graham averted his eyes and displayed a sudden interest in the worn table edge, rubbing and fingering it with twitching fingers. "There's something I need to talk to you about."

"Therapy getting you down?"

"No. Och, 'tis as hard as you said it would be and hurts like the de'il, but I'll soon be using a walking stick instead of these crutches." He raised his eyes and met Rob's gaze. "Nowt can stand in my way of getting around on foot."

Something had the lad in a fash, but if it wasn't the therapy, what? Could he and Rinait be having problems?

Watch your words, Savage. You're the last one to offer advice. "Och, we're a lot alike. I felt the same myself." He took a large swallow of coffee. "So what brought you here the day?"

Graham's cheeks flushed. "'Tis Rinait." He shifted in his chair and raised his cup but set it down without taking a sip. "I'm ... fair smitten with the lass."

"And how does she feel?"

"The same."

"Then, what's the problem?"

"Rinait won't be sixteen for twa months and I'm twenty-twa."

Familiar ground. "Maggie's six years younger than I am. It might be well to wait a year or so, but your lass is more mature than most. Maggie told me she's helped her mither around the house since she was a bairn."

"Six years? That makes you around ... thirty. You don't look that auld."

"Och, I'm thirty-one and an auld man compared to you. When I

251

was twenty-twa I was teaching flying to green Air Corps cadets." He squirmed beneath Graham's close scrutiny.

"Don't you miss it—the flying, I mean?"

"Aye, I miss it." How could he voice his feelings about such a tender subject? "It was all I thought about when I was a lad and about all I did from the time I was twenty-one." He got up and walked to the window.

High, dark clouds smeared like wet peat grime across the pale spring sky.

"But I wouldn't trade what I have now for what I had then even if I was offered a lifetime of nowt but flawless takeoffs, smooth flights, and perfect landings. When you're merrit and have a family, you'll ken what I'm on about." He cleared his throat as he lowered his gaze to the harbour water, choppy beneath a brisk breeze. "I'm hoping to buy a floatplane one day. It won't compare with the fighters I flew in the war, but at least I'll be in the air again."

Graham settled into his chair. "I still don't know what I want to do for the rest of my life. I always wanted to be in the Army and thought I had a lifetime career. But something's changed. I'm seeing this island and our folk in an entirely different way than when I was a lad. Then I couldn't wait to get away to see the world, meet new people, and live in exciting places. Now I'm beginning to see how real our folk are—no' boring and tedisome to be around—but caring and luving. I'm no' sure I want to leave."

"Well, Innisbraw hasn't changed, and I'm certain the folk here are the same." Rob turned and met Graham's gaze. "I'm thinking you may have just grown up. I know this island and its folk got under my skin from the beginning. I've been a lot of places and I couldn't wait to get back here to stay. 'Tis home."

Graham emptied his mug in a few hasty gulps. Did he need confirmation that it was all right for him to resign from the Army and stay on Innisbraw?

Och, Rob wasn't Graham's faither. The lad would have to seek advice from kin.

The door of the howff burst open and Hugh rushed up to their table. "Maggie needs your help, Rob. Elspeth's had a fainting spell and won't allow Gordon MacLeod to carry her to the infirmary."

Rob leaped to his feet. "Where is she?" He pushed Hugh to the doorway.

"Sitting in her garden. Our Faither had his eyes on her, for Susan Ferguson was walking with Gordon on their way home from picking up their posts and saw Elspeth lying on the ground. She sent Gordon to find Maggie. Rinait had gone inside to fetch a skein of wool and came out at Susan's shout."

Alec's cairt waited outside. The crofter scooted over and made room for Hugh and Rob.

"Maggie's with her?" Rob asked the minister.

"Aye. She couldn't raise Angus so she radioed Alec. She's afraid it could be a heart attack—or even a stroke."

Chapter Thirty-Five

Rob's belly twisted into ropes. Not Elspeth. Not so soon. *Faither, please hold her up in Your luving hands. We still need her here!*

The moment Alec pulled the cuddy to a halt in front of Elspeth's cottage, Rob leaped down from the cairt and vaulted the low stone dyke.

Maggie sat next to Elspeth, holding a bed-quilt around her shoulders.

Rinait, Susan, and Gordon stood beside her, faces tight with anxiety.

"Rob, thank the Lord you're here!" Maggie called.

He dropped to his knees beside her, his gaze raking over Elspeth's ashen-grey face and drooping eyelids. "What's this I hear about you not allowing Gordon to carry you to the infirmary?" His hand gently grasped Elspeth's shoulder. Like a bird's wing, it was, all bone and skin, with little flesh.

She opened her eyes and tried to smile. "Och, I just had a bit of a stumble and sat down for a rest."

"Susan found you unconscious, so 'twas more than a stumble," Maggie's shaking voice and tear-stained cheeks revealed her fear. She took Rob's arm and mouthed *hurry*.

He motioned her aside, scooped Elspeth into his arms, and stood. Maggie weighed no more than a hatchling, but Elspeth was much lighter. He cradled her close to his chest as Hugh rushed to hold the gate open. "Have Alec run you and Hugh up to the infirmary in the cairt," he told Maggie as he started up the path. "I'll carry her there."

"I'll no' break like a basket of eggs," Elspeth grumbled against his chest.

"Save your breath." The words sounded harsh so he leaned

over to kiss her forehead.

"Just a wee stumble," she said with a sigh. "I was redding up my garden for spring."

The cairt passed them, Hugh and Alec on the bench, Susan, Gordon, and Rinait standing in the back.

"If that's all it was, I'll have you back to your cottage in a tick. But I meant it when I said to save your breath."

"Stubborn lad."

He was stubborn?

At least she stopped trying to talk and closed her eyes.

Please let it be only a *stumble, Lord. No' a heart attack or stroke.*

The onshore wind whistled around his ears as he climbed the infirmary steps and hurried across the entry flags.

Hugh held the front door open. "Maggie said to take her to the first examining room. She wants to run some tests."

Maggie stood beside a machine sprouting tentacles like a sea creature.

Rob laid Elspeth on the padded examining table and pulled the blanket around her. "Is there anything I can do to help?"

"You can wait in the foyer with the others while I run this EKG." She patted Elspeth's arm. "We women prefer being undressed in private."

EKG—some sort of test for the heart. Though reluctant to leave, Rob joined Hugh, Alec, Susan, and Gordon, who were deep in prayer on their knees in front of the sofa, Rinait nowhere in sight. He prayed fervently, mind pictures of all that Elspeth had done for him interrupting, twisting the folds in his stomach until he winced from the cramps.

He'd seen Elspeth for the first time as he was being carried down the pier after the long trip from Oban to Innisbraw on Malcolm's *Sea Rouk*. He had been so tired, so overwhelmed by the thought he might never walk again. But when she knelt beside his stretcher, clasping his cold hand in her warm one, offering such a sweet smile of welcome, he had been drawn to that warmth like a moth to a flame.

She never stopped believing he would walk again. After a few months, her teaching from the Word infused him with his own faith. And all the lessons in Scots and then the Gaelic, her stories about the history of Innisbraw, had planted the idea of a rescue boat in his mind.

Tears slipped down his cheeks. She was the grandmither he had never known, the constant source of courage and faith that had brought him through that second plane crash alive and, eventually, strong again.

I know I'm being selfish, Faither, but I cannot abide the thought of losing her now. I want her to see the rescue boat launched, to know it's all come true because of her faith and prayers. Please let her bide here on earth a while longer, Lord, please.

⚓

Maggie tore the paper strip from the EKG machine and studied it, forcing her trembling fingers to still as she looked for signs of a heart attack.

Normal. It looked normal.

Och, if only Faither were here. I'm no' a doctor.

Elspeth studied her from beneath drooping eyelids.

"I can see no signs of a heart attack," Maggie said, "but I'm no' finished yet—and don't tell me it was a simple stumble."

"'Twas a stumble but I felt verra weak before that."

"What do you mean? Weak how? Your whole body, just your legs?"

"All over. My belly's been uggit the past few days and I admit I haven't eaten much. I thought some time ootside would help."

Maggie's fingers palpitated Elspeth's belly. "Does that hurt?"

"No. Just feels empty."

"Have you been drinking plenty of tea?"

"Nowt sounded guid, even tea."

Maggie pulled up a pinch of skin from Elspeth's arm.

The pinch stayed peaked for quite a while before collapsing.

"Och, you're dehydrated. I'll get a saline IV going before I check your eyes and muscle coordination." She asked Elspeth questions as she worked, mainly to divert the aulder woman's

256

attention from the long needle, but also to keep her own heart from beating out of her chest. She couldn't lose Elspeth now. This was the woman who had stepped into her mither's shoes when Elizabeth McGrath died in childbirth. She never could have survived raising Calum without Elspeth's patient help and encouragement.

All Maggie knew about being a wife and mither came from the wise counsel of a woman who had never even been merrit.

She shined a light into Elspeth's eyes. "Track my finger." She moved her finger out to the sides, then drew it closer to Elspeth's nose.

Normal pupils, only those sagging eyelids, but that could be caused by fatigue, and they both sagged, no' just one.

"Squeeze my hand. As hard as you can."

Elpseth's grip was steady.

"Guid. Now use your other hand."

Also good.

Moving to Elspeth's feet, she placed her palms beneath her soles. "Now, press down as hard as you can."

Nice pressure.

"That's guid."

One last test.

She got a rubber mallet from a drawer, raised Elspeth's knee, and tapped the rubber against a reflex point.

The knee jerked. The other responded the same.

No' a heart attack, no' a stroke.

Relief overwhelmed Maggie and she sat on the examining bench before her legs collapsed. "If I only knew why your stomach has been uggit."

"Och, I know why."

"Why didn't you tell me?"

"You didn't ask."

Maggie pulled the blanket up to Elspeth's chin. "I'm asking now."

"Many of the folk have been singling their early neeps. They know how I do luve boiled neep greens, so they've been dropping them off by the basketful. They tasted so guid and fresh after all the canned beans and boiled cabbage, I'm afraid I ate too many."

Laughter and tears mingled as Maggie hugged her beloved friend.

Neep greens indeed.

⚹

Rob did not find the answer amusing. "You mean she fainted because she ate too many neep greens?"

"No. She fainted because her stomach was too uggit to tolerate even liquids. She's verra dehydrated. I'm going to give her another bottle of saline before I have you carry her back to her cottage."

"She can't be left alone."

"Of course no'. The womenfolk will take turns staying with her for several days and nights. 'Twill fash her but that's the way it shall be."

Susan and Gordon walked oot the door, smiles creasing their faces.

How could they dismiss something like this so easily? Didn't they realize how close the island had come to losing the one who held them up in prayer—who kept them bonded together into a body of folk intent upon helping one another?

"May I see Elspeth?" Hugh asked.

"Of course. She'll be here several more hours. She's sleeping, but your prayers will help her to recover her strength."

The moment Hugh left, Rob grabbed Maggie and pulled her onto his lap, pressing her face against his heaving chest. "So close," he whispered gruffly. "I cannot bear the thought of losing her."

Her thoughts seemed to mirror his. "I can't either." She clutched Rob's shoulders.

This day they had heard the prelude to a heartbreaking dirge.

One day, Elspeth's long sojourn on earth would be over. One day, the Lord would call her home. One day—pray God—a long time from now.

Chapter Thirty-Six

They broke ground for Maggie and Rob's new home on Monday, the ninth of April. With Elspeth strong enough to stay alone now, Maggie readied herself to see the men at work. Once on the site, she balanced Robbie on her hip and leaned over the croft dyke as the men lay the footprint of the walls.

Rob ruffled Robbie's hair and planted a quick kiss on Maggie's cheek. He unfurled the excavation plan on the dyke beside her and referred to the measurements as stakes were driven and towie cord strung.

Though many of these men had built their own cottages, they all shook their heads at the size of the house.

"'Twould make three or more of mine," Angus said, "but Flora and me only had three bairns and you're building for eight."

Maggie blushed at the sly grin he shot her direction.

"Are you certain about this entry measurement?" Alan MacRae asked. "'Tis a verra large one, and you've got it raised off the ground a guid twa steps."

Rob crossed his arms in a way that meant he was growing impatient.

He'd better get a tight rein on that, as he'd be answering many questions over the coming days.

"Raising it and bringing the roof oot over it will give the bairns a dry, flag-stoned, guid-sized place for play when the rain's pishing down."

Arthur MacNab looked at the plans. "I never heard of twa doors leading in and oot of a hoose except at the manse. Why did you put a door coming oot of the left side?"

"That's the room where Maggie's washing machine will go. 'Tis a middlin' sma' room, but if our feet are muddy, we can come in that way and no' foul up the living room."

Hen's flesh coursed over her body. No' only was her Rob saving her having to scrub the floor so often, she would have a washing machine.

Arthur tamped tobacco into his pipe. "Living room?"

"That's just another name for chaumer, but since it's going to be so large, I'm using American words instead of Scots."

The following morning, men lay the footings below the frost line. They stacked the stones like bricks, in staggered rows, then trowled lime to seat each stone. The men worked silently, not talking unless necessary.

When Rob joined in the work, he found out why. Handling the large stones took so much effort there was no breath left for idle blethering.

They worked until late afternoon.

As soon as the men went home to their cottages, Maggie rushed over for a look. "I can't believe it. The walls already reach my waist." She ran her hands over the darker-coloured corner stones, fingering the tight joints. "There'll be no wind sneaking into this home."

He took hold of her elbow and led her toward the cottage, kneading his shoulder and trying not to limp. Opening the cottage door, he wiped a sleeve over his gritty forehead. "I'm so dirty. I need a bath."

"'Tis already drawn." She disappeared into the bathing room and returned, holding out her hand. "Twa APCs, and don't say they're no' needed."

"You'll get no argument from me." He swallowed the aspirin and drank a glass of water in several hasty gulps.

"Bathe yourself and I'll give you a rubdown. You're no' accustomed to this kind of labour. You'll be sore on the morra."

"Aye, but it'll pass soon enough. By the time our home is finished, I'll really be in shape to start the rescue boat."

He slept poorly. His left shoulder and leg ached despite the hot bath, aspirin, and rubdown. The thought rankled, but he'd best take it easier on the morra.

Maggie nestled closer in her sleep. Her silken skin, soft as a lover's whisper, brought a shiver. He plucked from the pillow an ebony tress and brushed it across his cheek.

The following morning, he limped over to the construction site, stopped, and stared at the number of men gathering there—at least thirty or more.

Before he could voice his surprise, Angus pulled him aside. "I see you're limping. We've all had a blether and you have nowt to prove to us, Rob. The stone work is too heavy this soon after you being hurt and all. You can mix the lime. 'Twill still be a lot of work but you will not have to do all that lifting."

And he'd tried so hard not to limp. "I want to do my share." His chest tightened. "But you're right. The lifting was a bit much."

"We've work galore for you to do. Besides mixing the lime, you'll have to cut the wood for the window and door frames and fit them into place afore the day's spent. Don't fash yourself."

Rob mixed up several buckets of lime to get them started. Once the larger stones for the window sills were fitted into place, he cut and mitred the wooden frames, checking them with a spirit level before cementing them in. Though he worked up a sweat, he didn't strain his shoulder and leg.

As the day waned under louring skies, the men gathered around him, explaining the scaffolding they would build the following morning to enable them to work on the first storey.

"It helps that you're going to have what you call the living room coomceilt," Arthur said. "With a steep slope, we won't have to build the walls up so high all the way around." He arched and stretched his back. "The only added turn will be cutting the top stones at an angle so they lay flat for the roof."

"Och, I'm sorry to make more work."

The wiry crofter brushed aside the apology. "Don't put yourself into a fash over that. Gordon MacLeod is a master cutter. He'll have the turn done before you know it."

Angus eyed the fruits of their two-day labour. "The way we're

261

going, we should have the ooter walls finished before the Sabbath."
He drew on his pipe, smiling.

"I can't believe it," Rob said. "There's no way I can thank all
of you enough for working so hard. I just wish you'd accept some
silver for your labour."

"'Tis nowt," Lachlan MacNab said with a grin. "O'er the years,
you'll do your share when some of the folk need help repairing or
putting up new cottages. That's the way of friends on Innisbraw."

A radio call from John interrupted their peaceful Thursday een.
"I just heard on the wireless—your President Roosevelt died the
day."

Stunned, Rob sat before his legs gave way. "Och, what
dreadful news. I may no' have agreed with the man's politics, but I
admired the way he inspired people and listened to his military
advisers. To lose him now, with an ongoing war, 'twill make a fair
fankle of things."

"Vice President Truman will be sworn in. Surely he's capable
of taking over."

Rob snorted. "That'll be quite a task for a man who once sold
hats for a living."

"Well then, we'll just have to pray for the Lord to ensure his
rapid education."

A big task. Anxiety hoarsened Rob's voice. "Aye, pray verra
hard."

By Saturday een, the outer walls stood, windows and doors
were framed, and the chimney and firebox were completed.

"What comes next?" Maggie asked as they walked around the
new house.

"The roof—if the slates ever arrive. 'Tis not a conventional
way to build a house but I want to take advantage of the guid
weather before we start on the interior walls. We'll frame for the
roof on Monday."

This cloudy but rain-free weather wouldn't hold forever. Those
slates had to arrive soon.

On Wednesday een, Rob stood in the cottage yard, studying the black clouds swirling around Ben Innis's monoliths. The roof was framed but the slates still hadn't arrived, and the air was heavy with the odour of incipient rain. Didn't look guid. Even if the slates came on the morra, rain would flood the ground inside the walls of the house, turning the place into a muddy morass of sand and peaty earth, slowing the work on the inside floor and walls.

Rob paced the cottage as gale-force winds and rain lashed the island for the second day. Indeed, had the slates arrived by train in Oban, Malcolm's trawler would have been unable to sail in such high seas.

Maggie put down the hippens she was folding and hugged Rob, stopping him in midstride. "You can't do anything about the storm, luve."

"Och, I know that. I'm just afraid the slates will never arrive, and that quarry's the only place still doing business despite the war."

"They'll come. You should be taking advantage of the time for a bit of a rest."

"I took a keek at the inside of the house this mornin. 'Tis like a small loch in there."

"It'll dry. Besides, what does it matter if there's a delay? We have the cottage."

Impatience gnawed at his insides. "Once things start happening to slow down a building schedule, they usually keep on happening. I want to be in our new home as soon as we can."

Maggie slipped her fingers inside his back pocket. "Our lad's down for a nap. Could I interest you in a wee smoorich with your wife?"

The storm blew out as quickly as it had begun. The slates finally arrived aboard the *Sea Rouk* on an overcast, calm Saturday een. Several men with strong cuddies trundled the heavy bundles of slate down the pier to their cairts.

When they arrived at the building site, Rob led the way through the wet, spongy soil. "This looks like a guid place to stack them," he said. "We'll get an early start on Monday mornin."

⚓

The weather held and the roof was slated by Wednesday een.

Hugh walked into the yard just after Maggie joined Rob. "Will you look at that." He waved his hand. "I'm thinking this must set some sort of record for building, even on Innisbraw."

Maggie bounced Robbie on her hip. "This one needs a new hippen and some supper. Are you coming to the cottage, Hugh?"

"Of course. All the way up the fell, I've been thinking about the guid coffee you make."

She kissed Rob's cheek. "Show Hugh around. I'll start the coffee."

Rob walked Hugh around the outside before leading him through the entry and inside. "Mind how you go. The water's gone down but we haven't laid the floor yet. 'Tis still slippery in places."

Hugh looked up at the sloped ceiling. "How are you going to have an upstairs?"

Rob pointed to the back wall rising the full two storeys. "We'll have twa large bedrooms for guests up there, with a wide staircase for easy access. On the ground floor, the ceiling will be flat over the bairn's bedrooms, office and weaving room at the back of the house. The living room ceiling will go all the way to the roof, starting low, going higher and higher to where the first storey bedrooms start. The kitchen and bathing room and our bedroom will be on opposite sides of the living room, so they'll be coomceilt too."

"Och, I've never seen anything like it. It will take a verra large fireplace to heat such a home, but I see you've taken care of that."

"Aye, and there'll also be the heat from the kitchen stove. You can see the opening in the roof for the pipe. There won't be a wall separating the kitchen from the living room. 'Tis going to be one verra big room."

An impish grin lit Hugh's face. "I'm thinking your luve for our Maggie may have played a hand in this design. Couldn't stand having her tucked away in the kitchen out of your sight, could you?"

"That's me sorted then. 'Tis that obvious?"

"It is, and it warms my heart."

Wiring and plumbing the house required a lot of labour and inventiveness on Rob's part. He met with Dougal Stewart, who had helped when electricity had been brought to the harbour area. Together they contacted by shortwave radio one of Dougal's friends in Oban who phoned the company that supplied the electricity. After hours of awkward radio-to-phone-to-radio haggling, Rob was finally granted permission to tap into the main power source if he consented to use one of their company experts to install the wire at the construction site.

Because he had to go to Oban for pipe, interior electrical wire, and plumbing fittings, Rob agreed to stop by their office and make the arrangements. But first, he needed a list of all the things it would take to finish the house. Hours later, disheartened by its length, he sighed and shook his head.

This would be no pleasure trip. It meant leaving before Elspeth was strong enough to attend kirk. And how could he sleep without Maggie's body pressed to his, or their lad asleep in his cradle?

The crowded streets in Oban drove him to distraction. He'd grown accustomed to quiet island living. The throngs of folk, many in naval uniforms, all shouting to be heard, made his skin prickle. How could anyone bear to walk these streets when every other step involved a jog to one side or the other to avoid bumping into someone?

A stringy-haired busker stood on a corner plunking a battered guitar, his nasal voice almost as grating as the anti-war words he mouthed. Merchants hawked their meagre wares from doorways, and lines formed at every pub. Noxious fumes from military vehicles added to Rob's discomfort. Och, what he wouldn't do for a breath of clean, salted sea air—or a sniff of Maggie's heather.

His meeting with the electric authorities in Oban went smoothly, but it took four days of scavenging, bartering, and pawing through a junkyard to find what was needed for the house. Late on the fourth afternoon, he hung around the harbour, eventually hiring a large truck and three men who would pick up all of his purchases and take them to the dock by 0530 the following morning. He declined Malcolm's invitation to share a meal at his local howff and fell onto a cramped cot in a tiny bed sit-in, too exhausted to eat. He dreamed of Maggie that night and awoke with a longing, deep inside, melting the marrow in his bones.

⸙

Maggie, Robbie, and Shep waited on the dock when the *Sea Rouk* arrived.

Rob paced impatiently while Sim secured the mooring ropes, then thanked the skipper again, said guidbye to Sim, and put the gangplank in place. After racing to his family, he kissed Maggie so fervently she pulled back, gasping for breath. "How's Elspeth?" he asked.

"Her auld self again. She's back to working in her garden."

"Thank the Lord." He grabbed Robbie from her arms and held him high. "Here's my lad!" he exclaimed before hugging Maggie again. "Five days is twice as long as I can bear. Next time—if there is a next time—you're both going with me."

"We missed you too."

Rob squeezed Maggie's hand and put Robbie over his shoulder, nuzzling his neck. "I'll have to hire several of the crofters and their cairts to unload that pile on Malcolm's deck." He took a deep breath of clean, salt-laden air and grinned. "But since 'tis Friday, Malcolm said to wait till the morra since he'll be here till after the Sabbath services. "Let's go home."

She pulled on his elbow, eyeing the huge stack covering much of the *Sea Rouk*'s deck. "Och, Rob, did you buy everything in Oban?"

"I'll show you the list of construction items when we get home, but I'm on heckle-pins wanting to show you what I got for the inside of the house. I found an Aga for the kitchen. You're going to luve the stove. 'Tis used, of course, but kept well and twice the size of the one you have now."

"You'll have to cast and stack twice as much peat then." She panted as she trotted down the pier beside him.

"I ken that." He shortened his stride. "I'm sorry, lass. I keep forgetting how hard it is for you to keep up with me."

"In more ways than one, I fear. You're an impatient man."

He stopped and studied her face. "Are you fashed with me, then?"

She shook her head so her hair danced a jig on her back. "'Tis who you are and I luve it."

"Are you certain?"

Fingers fondled the back of his denims—and pinched. "Biddy certain. Let's go home. I've a skillet of beef collops and neeps and tatties to go with."

His empty stomach growled. "Guid. I'm gleg as gled." He called a greeting to Katag MacLeod, who was coming down the steps of the post office. "I forgot to tell you, I also got mattresses and several lamps."

"I hope you found a mattress big enough for that box-frame you made for our bedroom."

"We'll have to make do with one double mattress and one twin at the foot, but no more cold feet for me once we move in—though you will have to sew a couple of sheets together."

"I don't mind. It all sounds perfect." She stopped suddenly. "Och, there's something I disremembered to tell you. The *Scotsman* arrived. American and Soviet forces met at Torgau on the Elbe and Hitler's Army was cut in twa."

"That's guid news. It surely won't be long till the war's over in Europe. After the American Army and Marines took Okinawa twa weeks ago, even Japan is feeling the squeeze. Mebbe Truman taking over as President won't cause a fankle after all."

She hugged his arm. "Some Tommies came by yesterday to see the new house and they all said the war should be over soon." Her face fell and she took a moment to speak. "I hate to ruin your homecoming, but I'm afraid I have some bad news for you. 'Tis Martin, Colin and Ruth's lad—his merchant ship was sunk by a U-boat. A reconnaissance plane spotted some of the lads being plucked oot of the water by a German destroyer. They've released no names so the Red Cross isn't able to help."

Rob's stomach plummeted. "No' their only lad. Och, I'll have to see Colin as soon as I can."

"I'll go with you. Hugh held a prayer meeting last een and both Colin and Ruth are taking it so hard. Their lass, Betty, offered to come home from her Women's Land Army posting at the Borders but they told her to stay put until they had more news."

"This horrible war!" Another family torn apart, their lives in pieces, perhaps forever. Rob clasped Robbie to his chest, fighting panic at the thought of losing his lad. *Keep our bairnie safe, Faither, and if Martin survived, give him the strength to endure whatever he faces.*

Chapter Thirty-Seven

On Monday, Rob and a handful of somber men with plumbing experience gathered to tackle the piping required before the floors of the house could be laid. Rob told of his heartbreaking conversation with Colin on Saturday night, and they all bowed their heads for a silent prayer before beginning their work.

Eight and a half days later, the plumbing was finished and the wooden floors laid.

"I can see why you had to go with wood instead of stone flags," Angus said. "Like the infirmary, manse, and Elspeth's cottage, yours is too far off the ground to flag."

Rob heaved a sigh of relief that afternoon when the electrician from the power company arrived, along with twa helpers. They unloaded a spool of wire and a large pole, along with all the equipment they would need. Rob told the foreman payment would be posted the day the day the receipt for services was rendered, then left them to it.

⚓︎

Digging the hole for the digester, and trenches for the water pipes tying into those from the loch, proved a monumental task because of all the rocks they encountered. Though they all wore gloves, most went home with blisters pick and shovel use.

Now there was power to the site, Dougal Stewart arrived to help Rob wire the inside of the house. He and Rob worked several days running wire before the used, pieced, and patched wire mesh and lime slurry were added to the walls. The home was finally taking shape.

Angus laid a stone hearth, topped it with leftover roofing slate, and installed a large piece of rough-hewn driftwood above it for a mantel. "'Tis a wonder how you cut it to fit around the stones," he said to Rob.

"'Twas a lot of bother, but I think Maggie will like it. 'Tis your stonework that's a wonder. Every stone complements the one next to it, yet they're all different in size and colour. You're a true craftsman, Angus."

As usual, the crofter ducked his head.

Rob tackled the windows next. He carefully cut old panes into new, and installed the hardware that would allow the windows to be swung outward to be opened, then inward to be closed and locked.

This was one new innovation all of the men were driven to copy. "I've always wanted to be able to open the windows," Lachlan said, "especially at night."

Angus agreed. "That way you can take advantage of the wind in the simmer too."

"I'll help you any time you ask," Rob said, "unless 'tis when I'm building the rescue boat."

That een, the thirtieth of April, John radioed Rob and Maggie with the news that Adolf Hitler, Eva Braun, and Herman Goebbel and his wife had committed suicide in a bunker beneath the Reich Chancellery in Berlin. "I know you've been too busy to listen to the news broadcasts on your wireless and I didn't want you to have to wait for the newspaper for news like this," he told Rob. "It appears our Heavenly Faither heard our prayer for President Truman. The Soviets have almost reached Berlin. 'Tis definitely the beginning of the end for Nazi Germany."

The knots in Rob's chest slowly dissolved. "Aye, thank God, though I'm sorry Hitler took the coward's way out. I'd rather have seen him tried and hanged for all he did."

"There's many who feel the same, but at least this whole sorry midden will soon be over."

"Thanks for the heads-up. Be sure and call with any news of a surrender in case we miss it."

"You know I will. Give my luve to Maggie and Robbie and my best to all our folk."

"Before we sign off, have you been able to find any news about Martin?"

"Och, I've called in every last favour I could." A long sigh. "There's no news at all."

Rob and Maggie turned on their Pye wireless and listened to the late War Report following the news bulletins on the BBC General Forces Programme. Wynford Vaughan-Thomas, voice rising in excitement, announced the death of Hitler.

Rob turned the radio off and went into the spare bedroom, returning with the radiogram. He put on their only record, songs from Vera Lynn's radio program, *Sincerely Yours,* broadcast in 1941. After making sure Robbie slept soundly, he sat in his rocker.

Vera's first song, "We'll Meet Again," had been their favorite when they were facing a long separation before they were married, but now the second song, "The White Cliffs of Dover," brought tears to their eyes. *Peace ever after* seemed much closer than it had just the week before.

"Pray God it is the morra." Rob turned off the radiogram and carried Maggie to bed.

He lay awake a long time. That the war appeared to be coming to an end in Europe was something to celebrate, but the cost of the Allied victory was almost too horrible to contemplate.

And still no word on Martin's fate. Rob had lost countless crew members and friends, and Maggie had witnessed innumerable deaths and injuries. The toll in human suffering was almost more than he could bear.

He held her tightly, drawing comfort from her body pressed to his.

⚓

On the eighth of May, Rob asked Maggie to go to the howff with him to celebrate the third anniversary of the night they met. "We don't have to stay late, just dance a bit and relax."

She laughed and raised up on tiptoe to kiss his chin. "Let me change and get Robbie ready so we can go. We haven't danced since Hogmanay, and I'm told Paddy has changed the howff so much since he bought it. 'Tis a pleasant place to take the family now."

"'Tis that. And I agree with you—Hogmanay was much too

long ago."

They walked down the hill close together, Rob carrying Robbie in the crook of his right arm, his left around Maggie's shoulders.

A full moon, a "bomber's moon," rode low in the sky.

He drew Maggie nearer, blocking out memories of leaving SHAEF Headquarters in London to the distant wail of air raid sirens, of lights probing the sky for German Heinkle He 111 bombers, of the raw, deafening concussion of bombs raining destruction on homes, businesses, and dockyards.

That's all in the past, now. The war in Europe should end soon.

He parted Maggie's hair, caressed the back of her neck, and scanned the sky. "'Tis a bonnie night. That's one of the benefits of biding away from a large city during peacetime. There's no light to blot out the stars."

"Aye. The stars seem so much closer here than they did in London or Edenoaks, even with the blackout."

He kissed the top of her head. "They are," he said, voice soft. "For we're much closer to Heaven here."

Tears glazed her eyes when she looked up at him. "I'm thinking we may even be living in a wee corner of Heaven."

He stopped walking and looked down at her. The luve shining in her eyes almost more than he could bear, he bent down and kissed her tenderly.

Robbie kicked and arched his back.

"Och," Rob laughed. "Your bairnie doesn't like to stop."

"My bairnie?"

He tapped the tip of her nose and resumed walking. "If he's my bairnie when he's rouping or wet, he has to be your bairnie the rest of the time."

Her delighted laugh filled him with contentment.

When they reached the howff, Rob took off his A-2 jacket and helped Maggie out of her coat. They found an unoccupied table at the side of the room, close to a bench that would serve as a bed once Robbie decided to sleep.

Rob went to the bar where he and Jack Ferguson, the bartender, exchanged greetings. He ordered a bottle of ale for himself and a lemon skoosh for Maggie. Still suckling their lad, she wouldn't drink alcohol and found Irn-Bru too sweet.

✦✦✦

Maggie hugged herself. Such a glorious treat. She looked around the large, refurbished room, exchanging nods with the other patrons. It was amazing how much Paddy had been able to do with everything so heavily rationed. The original, ornately carved bar shone with several coats of varnish, and used, mismatched tables and chairs were scattered around the room, leaving in the centre a large area for dancing. Blackout curtains covered the two small windows, and the light fixtures, while obviously scrounged from different sources, had been fitted with small bulbs. A huge fireplace on the far wall, glowing with a peat fire, gave the room a cosy feel.

"Though I only keeked in once when I was a lass, I remember it being dark and dirty. Even the windows were never washed." She shivered at the memory. "Paddy's done a glorious turn."

"Indeed he has." Rob swigged his ale.

Graham and Rinait sat at a nearby table. They waved hello and resumed their conversation, heads close together, hands clasped tightly across the table.

"Were we ever so young?" Rob asked. "Though I ken I robbed the cradle myself."

Maggie felt a tease coming on. "You're only as auld as you feel, luve. So how auld are you the night?"

Green flecks danced in his hazel eyes. "About twenty, I'd say."

"Guid. That's how auld I feel."

He nodded at Robbie who had gone to sleep in his arms. "Do I dare put him down? The lads are about to start the music."

"Wait till they begin. If he stays asleep, we should be safe." She laid Rob's jacket and her coat on the bench and covered them with a small hap.

The skirl of the pipes filled the room. Soon the other instruments joined in. When Robbie didn't stir, Rob laid him down on his side and patted his back. "I'll put the chairs up now so he can't roll off when we dance."

Paddy McDonald announced the Eightsome Reel and the musicians upped the tempo.

Rob and Maggie joined three other couples as the dance began in a square, quickly changed to a circular formation, and then back to a square again. The dancers moved around the floor and Rob squeezed Maggie's hand every time they passed. Since this was one of the dances she had taught him at Edenoaks, he could keep up. She smiled as his shoulders relaxed. He had been working so hard he deserved a night of fun.

When the dance was over, he led her to the centre of the floor, nodding at Paddy who gave him a wink.

Before Maggie could ask what was happening, she heard a familiar tune. "The Nearness of You" may never have been played on the bodhran, button box, pipes, penny whistle, and guitar before, but to her, it sounded perfect.

He grasped her hand tightly as they danced around the room.

Oblivious to everybody else, she lost herself to memories. This was the first tune they had danced to. This was their song, the song which began with a dance and led to a luve which would last forever and ever and ever. *Aye, the nearness of you, my luve.* When the song finished, she ignored the folk's applause, too busy thanking Rob for the surprise.

They had just taken their seats when a Tommy burst through the door, leaving it wide open. His short hair stood on end and his grin was so wide his back molars glinted in the flickering light. "The Germans have surrendered! The war's over!"

Chapter Thirty-Eight

Rob knocked a chair over in his haste to reach Maggie.

Some men shouted questions at the Tommy.

The lad raised his hands and waved until he had everyone's attention. "All the allies involved are meeting now to go over the surrender conditions." He took a deep breath. "But we've heard from Stornoway that two U-boats have already surfaced in their harbour and surrendered their crews and boats." He raced to the windows and tore down the blackout curtains. "Go home and turn on your shortwaves, folk. Sometime tomorrow it should be official."

The noise of the following celebration awakened Robbie, his cries interrupting Rob and Maggie's long kiss.

"Let's get oot of here and go home!" Rob shouted to Maggie as he picked up their lad.

The bright moon lit the path beneath their feet as they walked quickly up the hill.

Rob looked down at their drowsy bairnie and squeezed Maggie's hand. "I hope that lad was right."

"He surely was. The military would be the first to know."

They listened to the wireless until after midnight. The news reporter confirmed the Tommy's announcement, adding that though there were a few spontaneous celebrations taking place in London and elsewhere in the United Kingdom, most people were waiting for the official proclamation before they would believe the war had really ended.

⚓

The following morning brought a change in the pleasant spring weather. A brisk, snell northwest wind blew spindrift high on Innis Fell and an ominous dark cloud obscured the top of Ben Innis. While Maggie hovered over the wireless in the cottage for news,

Rob moved his woodworking tools inside and covered any holes remaining in the exterior of the new house so rain could not blow indoors. The chill in the air did not bode well for the last of the lambing season. He decided to forgo his work after dinner and see if Angus needed help.

"If you're set on going, I've made a thermos of coffee," Maggie said as he slipped into his A-2 jacket. "And I've wrapped twa butteries for a piece in a napkin to put in your pocket."

"A crofter's work never stops, luve, even at a time like this." He patted her bottom. "Did anyone ever tell you what a bonnie lass you are?"

"Aye, just last night this braw man I was dancing with said those exact words."

"Smart man." He put the napkin in his pocket and nuzzled Robbie's rosy cheek. "I'm away then. I'll catch you up late unless you hear owt on the news. Be certain you let me know if you do."

"Don't work too hard." She blew him a kiss, turned the radio louder, and put Robbie on her hip so she could begin her chores. The following day was wash day, but gathering up all the dirty clothes and linens for Anna would have to wait until the bairnie went down for his nap. She sang as she worked, nonsensical ditties she'd learned as a small lass, heart so light her feet hardly brushed the floor. She was surely living a dream. Rob's tender, romantic gesture the night before touched her deeply. He must have asked Paddy weeks ago to prepare the Glenn Miller song. She couldn't think of another man who would plan so far ahead to please his wife.

She hummed a few bars of the tune as she wiped out the jawbox, smiling when she recalled how many times he apologized for not being able to put into words how much he luved her. Och, he said far more than most Scots men. And didn't he realize the luve shining in his hazel-brown eyes, the many times he held her hand or cuddled her on his lap, the thoughtful things he did, spoke more eloquently to her heart?

Reluctant to leave the radio, but anxious to see what the Edinburgh *Scotsman* had to say, she bundled Robbie in several sweaters, pulled a hap over his head, and put on her heavy coat. Despite her warm clothing, she shivered as she walked down the fell to pick up the post Malcolm had brought from Oban the een before.

The girse, green and tall, almost obscured the rocks littering the sides of the path, and a few early wildflowers bent in the wind, petals fluttering like wee birds' wings. The harbour, covered with vast herds of white wave horses, roared and pounded over the rocks at the base of the fell. Overhead, armies of clouds did battle in rolling, black hordes.

She hadn't found Rob staring up at the sky for several weeks. Was he saving his grief for those times when she wasn't around, or had his heart finally begun to heal? If the war in Europe was truly over, he shouldn't have too long to wait before he could begin building the rescue boat.

Breathing hard, she pushed open the post office door and sat Robbie on the counter.

Alice handed her their copy of the newspaper. "That's all for you the day." She plucked up Robbie and bounced him on her hip. "Och, he's a heavy lad, especially dressed in all these clothes. How do you carry him, as wee as you are?"

"On my hip, of course." Maggie discarded the first four pages of advertisements and editorials, turning to the fifth page where the news began. The headline disappointed her: "End Of The War In Europe Imminent." Och, she should have known any late news of the war being over would be in the day's edition, no' yesterday's.

"Do you think the war's really over?" Alice pried a stamping tool from Robbie's quick fingers. "When Morag passed on what that soldier said in the howff last een, I felt faint but I find myself afraid to hope 'tis true."

"I'm certain Hugh will ring the kirk bell the moment any news reaches him." A headline toward the bottom of the page caught Maggie's attention. "Trawler Sinks, Two Rescuers Killed." She scanned the words quickly, heart throbbing. A twenty-three-metre fishing trawler out of Inverness had capsized and two crewmen from a RNLI lifeboat were knocked into the sea and drowned attempting to save the trawler's crew.

Alice was talking about how the end of the war would change their lives, but the postie's words buzzed a muffled drone in Maggie's ears. Her stomach felt sick as the old fear she had battled when Rob flew bombing missions—that she would lose her precious husband—echoed in her mind. She had a dreadful vision of him sinking into the raging sea, waves washing over his head. *Och, dear Lord, please, not again.*

She tucked the newspaper beneath her arm and reached for Robbie. "We have to go." She ran out the door, ignoring Alice's open-mouthed stare. She prayed frantically all the way up the hill. Yes, she had always known rescues at sea were dangerous, but their lives had been so filled with luve and happiness and Rob's boat was so far in the future, she had shoved it to the back of her mind. Now … *Och, please, please, Heavenly Faither, take away my fear. The rescue boat is Your perfect plan, I know it. I just can't bear the thought of losing my Rob when it's in service.*

The moment she stepped into the cottage, she removed the hap and Robbie's heavy sweaters, sat him on the hearthrug, and told Shep to stand guard. Tossing a handful of spoons into the bairnie's lap, she shrugged out of her coat as she raced into the bedroom for her Gaelic Bible.

In her haste, she grabbed the one Hugh had given Rob. She leafed frantically through the pages to the fourth chapter of Philippians, to the verses that had helped her overcome her fear before. Though she knew the verses by heart, she needed to read them.

The passage was underlined and the page looked worn.

In nothing be anxious; but in everything by prayer and supplication with thanksgiving let your requests be made known unto God. And the peace of God, which passeth all understanding, shall guard your hearts and your thoughts in Christ Jesus.

Her eyes skipped down the page to the ninth verse, which Rob had also underlined.

The things which ye both learned and received and heard and saw in me, these things do: and the God of peace shall be with you.

She collapsed to her knees beside the bed, memories of the many times she had paced the corridors of the base hospital flooding her mind, praying for assurance that Rob would return from a mission. And, though he had been terribly injured in that last crash, he had lived. "Guard my heart, Faither. Don't let this fear take over. I know how it affected Rob when he was flying missions, and I can't burden him now when he has so much on his mind. Give me Your peace, please."

Fifteen minutes later, she thanked God for hearing her prayers as she scrubbed her tear-stained face and brushed the tangles from her hair. Why had Rob underlined that particular passage? Though he had numerous bad dreams, he hadn't awakened her with his thrashing and groaning for several weeks. Did he have fears he had not shared with her? Would he never learn that talking about fears or sorrows helped lighten his load?

Robbie had fallen asleep on the rug, head buried in Shep's soft flank. Rob would need a hot, filling supper no matter how late he worked, so she ran out to the cooling shed and returned with everything that she needed to make a haddie and vegetable bree. Too distracted to turn on the wireless, she chopped the fish and vegetables. Even if the war in Europe had ended, the fighting in the Eastern Theatre was still far from over. She should not be facing the danger of him drowning for a long time.

The shortwave radio chirped to life. She raced for it and turned up the volume.

"Maggie?"

Her faither!

279

Chapter Thirty-Nine

"The war in Europe is officially over! King George will offer a proclamation by radio in a few minutes and Churchill will speak sometime later the een."

"Och, Faither, what glorious news!"

"Aye, lass, at last we can get back to living normal lives, if we can even remember what that is. Is Rob there?"

"Our weather's taken a cold turn so he's helping Angus with the lambing."

"Then you'd best find a way to get the news to him. It was just three years ago the day he crashed his B-17 that first time. A bit of irony, if you ask me."

"I don't think he even remembered the date, though he should have. We celebrated the third anniversary of our meeting last een."

"He most likely didn't want to remind you. They're celebrating and dancing in the streets all over Edinburgh. Look him up and tell him the guid news."

"I will. Thank ye for calling, Faither." Maggie put on another sweater and her heavy coat, dressed Robbie warmly, and wrapped him in two blankets. Though she hated missing the King's proclamation, they would surely re-broadcast it later. She walked briskly down the hill, heart rejoicing. The war in Europe was really over!

Robbie caught her excitement and bounced up and down, babbling and waving his arms.

By the time she reached Angus's croft, her arms and back ached. Even balancing him on her hip, at eight months, Robbie was heavy. Out of breath, cheeks stinging, she didn't bother to stop at the cottage, but went directly out to the sheep fauld.

Angus was on his knees trying to coax a lamb to suckle.

Rob sat nearby, briskly rubbing another newborn lamb with a rough towel. He scrambled to his feet. "What is it, lass? Is there news?" He took Robbie from her as she fought for breath.

She patted her chest and panted. "The war's officially over!"

He hugged her, rocking her back and forth. "How did you hear—on the wireless?"

"Faither radioed a few minutes ago." She wiped at the tears trickling down her face. "Och, Rob, it's really over. No more bombs, no more battles, no more ghastly wounds or broken hearts."

Angus released the struggling lamb. "I'll harness up Feona. Rob, you drive over and tell Hugh. He needs to ring the kirk bell."

"But the lambs ..."

"Edert'll be back from his other turns in a minute. We need that bell rung."

Rob handed Robbie back to her. "Be back in a tick. Wait here." He fondled her shoulder, dimples dancing. "It's finally over—at least in Europe."

Minutes later, the nervous filly trotted down the narrow MacPhee path, eyes rolling, head tossing, Rob at the reins.

Flora ran into the fauld, clutching her shawl about her throat. "What's happened?" she asked, voice shrill. "Is there more news?"

Angus picked her up and twirled her around. "Aye, 'tis really over. Rob's gone to help Hugh ring the kirk bell."

She pulled her apron over her face, sobs racking her body.

After Flora quieted and wiped her cheeks, Maggie said, "Faither just radioed from Edinburgh. He told me they're dancing in the streets."

"Well, the least we can do is ring our bell." Flora hurried to the doorway. "I must tell Rinait and Graham. He's helping her warp her loom. On you come, Maggie. 'Tis too cold oot here for you and wee Robbie."

⁂

Strange hands controlled the reins, so Feona fought Rob the entire way. When he pulled the cairt up in front of the manse and set the brake, she lunged, trying to escape. He jumped down and tried to quiet the spirited filly.

Hugh appeared on the manse entry. "John just called me with the news," he shouted, smiling and weeping as he ran down the flagged steps.

"'Tis official, Hugh. The war in Europe's over!"

Hugh hugged Rob and pummeled his back. "'Tis finally over. I can't believe it."

"Me either. I knew it was coming, but now 'tis here, I find myself bumbazed."

Hugh wiped his face with his handkerchief. "Tie Feona to that post over there. It'll take the twa of us to ring the bell as many times as this calls for."

"Lead the way."

The two men climbed the narrow steps of the steeple until they reached a platform halfway up where a long rope dangled before them. Hugh grabbed it and gave a hard pull.

The bell rang out loud and clear.

He put his entire weight into it and the bell pealed its joyous message again and again.

When he tired, Rob took over. They took turns pulling until a large crowd gathered in the kirkyard. When they stopped, they were both sweating and out of breath.

"You're the shepherd of this flock," Rob said. "On you go. Give them the guid news."

The minister mounted the kirk steps, smile so broad his eyeglasses tilted. He raised his hands.

The excited chatter stopped as though everyone was suddenly struck dumb.

"Dear folk," he shouted. "We've cause to celebrate. The war is officially over!"

Stunned silence followed by pandemonium. Some folk laughed, others wept—most did both at the same time. Alec and Morag hugged each other, weeping wordlessly. As newcomers arrived, the news spread quickly.

"Has anyone thought to tell Elspeth?" Hugh asked Rob.

"Och, I disremembered. I have to get back to Angus's croft, so I'll go up the fell first and tell her."

Hugh leaned close so Rob could hear him. "We'll have a

service of thanksgiving the night at 1900 hours. Pass the word to all you see on the path."

Rob untied Feona and leaped onto the bench.

The filly caught the excitement and lunged in the traces, snorting and tossing her head.

When he released the brake, she tried to break into a gallop. He sawed on the reins until he had her under control, gave her some slack, and she trotted smartly up the path, still snorting.

The entire population of Innisbraw seemed to be on the path. Those islanders who were sheep crofters on the southwestern end of the island and had no cairts or cuddies were running down the path from the fell, faces bright with hopeful expectation.

Rob shouted the good news and they stopped, huddling in family groups, embracing.

When he reached Elspeth's cottage, she stood on her entry, leaning on her walking stick.

He set the brake, looped the reins around the handle, and leaped down.

She didn't call out a greeting, but waited, face serene.

He took the steps two at a time and grasped her hands. "The war in Europe's over. The Allies have accepted the terms of Germany's surrender."

When she raised her eyes to his, her expression caught him off-guard, the sadness in her eyes negating her smile. "But all the lads still in the fight won't be going home, will they?"

He let out a deep breath and squeezed her hands. "A lot may, but many, especially Americans, will be sent to the Pacific Theatre."

A contemplative nod. "'Tis as I thought." She walked slowly over to one of the rockers on the entry and sat, patting the other one. "Please take time to humour an auld woman."

What would she say? He eased into the rocker, grateful for the cushion.

Her steady gaze probed his. "We have reason to rejoice the day. Europe is finally freed from the ravages of war, but I'm thinking we need to pray even more diligently now. We thought the Germans a proud race, but the Japanese are even prouder. They won't give up easily and America, especially, will pay a dear price in men."

He closed his eyes, unwilling to allow her a glimpse of the hideous carnage running like a Technicolor picture show through his mind.

"Is Hugh having a service this een?"

Fingers pinching the bridge of his nose, he opened his eyes. This was a time to celebrate, not lose himself to grief over future horrors. "At 1900."

Gaze unwavering, she said, "I've been thinking about you all the day. I don't know why, but I've been saddened."

"Let's go inside. 'Tis too cold oot here for you."

"Don't try to change the subject. My shawl and coat are warm enough." She placed a hand on his knee. "Something's troubling you, though I don't know what. Care to share it with a nosy auld friend?"

He looked out at the wind-tossed waves, hoping to avoid an answer.

Her fingers tightened.

Maggie was right. It would help to share. "I wanted to be in on it. The whole thing. I feel like I've left a turn half done."

"If you were still in the American Air Forces, where would you be now?"

Her question caught him off guard. He'd asked himself the same question many times but never come up with a definitive answer. "I don't really know. I should have been sent to the Pacific months ago, but with so many sorties and missions under my belt that isn't a given." He stood and walked over to the railing and leaned against it, staring out at the turbulent waves. "More than likely, I'd be training new pilots in the States or pushing paper around on a desk."

"So why are you torturing yourself with feelings that you've somehow failed in your duty?"

"I don't know. Until you said it, I didn't even know that's what I was doing—but it is."

"Nobody appointed you to save all the unfortunates in the world."

284

"I ken that."

"Your head kens it, but your heart doesn't."

He studied the Minch, mind filled with all the what-ifs that plagued him when he let his vigilance slip. What if he'd tried to set the *Bonnie Maggie* down in the Channel? What if he'd nursed his fuel more carefully? What if he'd found a field sooner? What if— och, he couldn't change the past, no matter how hard he tried. "I still had something to contribute to this war, but they wouldn't let me."

"With guid reason. The war in Europe is over and the war with Japan will end someday, hopefully soon. Don't limit yourself to only fighting wars, Rob. There's a much larger picture. If you'd stayed in the Air Forces, once the war with Japan was over, you could have found yourself doing the one thing you hate—flying a desk, as you say. You've set a lofty goal for yourself right here on Innisbraw. No' just the rescue boat, which is a verra noble endeavor in itself, but bringing life to a dying island."

"But I can't start anything until the war with Japan's over. There's no way to get the supplies I need shipped here until then, and like you said, the Japs won't give up easily."

"And, as usual, you're chomping at the bit like Feona out there, impatient to get started."

He whirled around and met her gaze. "Of course."

Eslpeth stifled a gasp at the raw pain on his face.

"We'll have to go through another winter at least, even if the war in the Pacific ends soon."

"And what are you doing in the meantime? Tweedling your thumbs, or seeing that your own family is provided for? Which, I hope I don't need to remind you, is your God-given responsibility."

His shoulders slumped as though burdened with an unbearable weight. "What's wrong with me, Elspeth? Why do I feel so driven? Why can't I be like other men and just wait patiently for the time to be right?"

She pulled herself up and took his hands in hers. "Because it isn't who you are, dear heart, and thank the Lord for it. We need impatient people like you in this world to see that things get done as quickly as possible." So cold, his hands. "Stop feeling guilty, lad. Guilt can destroy you and that would be a tragedy, for you're guilty of nowt more than expecting the impossible from yourself."

"I've let our folk down."

"You're the only one who feels that way. If you can't get what you need to build the rescue boat, you can't get it. 'Tis that simple. Everyone here understands but you."

"Are you certain, or are you just saying that to make me feel better?"

"I've never lied to you, Rob, and I never will—even to make you feel better." She rubbed his hands briskly. "Somehow, we've managed to have this entire conversation and you've avoided telling me what's so special in your life about the day."

"Three years ago the day, my plane crash-landed on the runway at Edenoaks."

"When you got that shrapnel in your back, paralysing your legs?"

"Aye."

"And how do you feel about that? Angry that it happened, that you edured so much pain and feared you'd never walk again?"

"No, I'm grateful from the bottom of my heart. It brought me my Maggie."

"Och, and all the day I thought there was something wrong."

"There was, only it had nowt to do with that first crash and everything to do with my impatience."

Her hands tightened on his. "Just remember that impatience can defeat you if you don't keep your eyes on the Lord. Don't listen to the de'il's lies. Believe in your dream, Rob, and allow God time to work His perfect will."

A dark shadow passed over his eyes. "And what about Martin? There's still no word. Colin and Ruth are in agony. 'Twould be kinder all around if they knew he perished. 'Tis uncertainty that's hurting them most."

"Och, Rob, there are thousands of folk all over the world suffering the same uncertainty. All we can do is pray for that lad and his family. Our Lord will provide an answer when the time is right."

Chapter Forty

"'Tis Europe you fought for, Rob. You must wear your dress uniform for the thanksgiving service." Maggie laid freshly ironed uniform shirt and breeks on the bed and took his blouse from its peg, ignoring the bunched muscles in Rob's jaw. Let him grit his teeth. She was tired of his bouts of stubbornness. "All the Tommies will be there, and in uniform."

"That's why I don't want to wear the blasted thing."

"Stop swearing."

"I wasn't swearing."

"A rose by any other name ..." Cheeks burning, she threw a tie over the shirt and rummaged through the clothes-press for his skivvies and khaki hose. "You should be proud to represent America at a time like this. 'Tis unlikely we would have won the war without your help."

"Why rub the Brits' noses in it? They resent Americans enough as it is."

She whirled about and stared at him, planting her hands on her hips. "Resent Americans? What are you blethering about?"

"You never heard what they called us? 'Overpaid, over-sexed and over here'?"

She tossed his skivvies on the bed. "Och, they didn't mean all of you—only those few who took advantage of naïve country lasses."

"You said it. 'A rose by any other name would smell the same.'"

"Och, would smell as sweet, no' would smell the same. And here I was, thinking you had a grand education. They obviously didn't teach William Shakespeare at your university."

The fire smoldering in his eyes died to ashes. "I learned how to

287

fight a war at the Point, no' quote words from a play. You ken what I'm about—how to come up with the best plan for maiming and killing. I didn't get in on the finish, but ..."

His ragged whisper dowsed her pique more effectively than a dip in an icy burn. What was wrong with her? Aye, she was exhausted and dreading the walk, but this was a night for celebrating—no' exchanging hurtsome words with the man she luved. She stumbled into his arms.

⚓

Rob buried his face in her hair. Why couldn't he leave the past behind where it belonged? It wasn't Maggie's fault he'd been invalided out. "I'm sorry to gaw you, luve, especially on a night like this."

"Och, 'tis me who should be apologizing. So much has happened the day, I'm in a fair fash and I don't know why, unless 'tis dreading the long walk to kirk when I'm already so tired."

He picked her up and carried her to their bed, sitting with her in his lap. "Angus is taking us in his cairt."

"Thank the Lord for that."

He gave her a squeeze. "I'll wear my uniform—if you wear yours."

"But what about Robbie? I can't hold him wearing my dress uniform."

"We'll ask the MacPhees if we can sit with them and Flora can hold him. What say you?"

She jumped up with a teasing smile. "I'll have to pin my hair up and we both ken how you hate that."

"You have to promise I can take it down the tick we're home."

"'Tis a promise."

⚓

Rob and Maggie followed the MacPhees toward their pew, Flora cradling a sleepy Robbie in her arms.

Rob flinched under the stares of the parishioners. A little late to remember that only Malcolm, Sim, and Elspeth had seen him in full dress uniform. He narrowed his eyes and clamped his lips at the shocked looks on the faces of the Tommies who were crowded into

288

three pews.

One lad, sitting on the aisle, poked his companion and pointed to Rob's silver eagles, pilot wings, and rows of ribbons. Och, there would be a lot of blether about a Yank Air Force officer here on Innisbraw when the Tommies returned to their camp the night.

But not all of it would concern him.

Their attention quickly turned to Maggie. Her grey-blue RAF nurse's skirt and tunic hugged her tiny, perfect body. Her hair, black as a peaty loch at the turn o' night and pulled into a bun above her tunic collar, glinted in the soft light of flickering candles. Like him, she clutched her uniform cap beneath one arm.

Rob stood back and allowed her to slide in next to Flora and their lad before he took the aisle seat.

Maggie's cheeks blushed rosy-red and her violet-blue eyes were downcast as she pulled out their kneeler.

Och, my bonnie Maggie. You'll never realize how you make any lad's blood rise like sap in a willow bush come spring.

Prayers of thanksgiving offered, Rob settled back in the pew and clasped Maggie's hand.

No more fearing for her and Robbie's safety. No more U-boats rearing out of the sea like black monsters eager to devour their prey. No more—

A tap on the shoulder interrupted his thoughts. Alec stood beside him, holding a large American flag. "If you and Maggie will jyne me in the aisle, I have a request from Hugh."

Rob released Maggie's hand and stepped into the aisle.

She scooted closer, but remained seated.

A shiver of apprehension washed over Rob's body when he accepted the flag. But whatever Hugh wanted, it involved Maggie too.

"Hugh wants you to carry this flag up the aisle when it's your turn. Your Maggie will take the lead with The Saltire, followed by the sergeant in charge of the British platoon who will bear the Union Flag—and after him, you with your flag. The stands are in place on the dais."

Maggie pressed trembling fingers to her lips. Och, what was Hugh thinking? No' her—no' a woman! Ignoring the wicked gleam in Rob's eyes, she stepped slowly into the aisle.

Morag handed her the blue flag with its diagonal, white cross. "With pride, lass. With great pride."

The gentle reprimand dissolved her embarrassment. Of course. With pride. She held the flag high and, when Alec nodded, walked slowly up the aisle.

In the back of the sanctuary, a lone piper played "The Land of Gallant Hearts." Everyone stood as she passed. Tears pooled in her eyes as the words to the auld, haunting song echoed in her mind.

Ours is the land of gallant hearts, the land of lovely forms, the island of the mountain-harp, the torrents and the storms; the land that blooms with freeman's tread, and withers with the slave's, where far and deep the green woods spread, and wild the thistle waves.

How many lives had been lost or changed irrevocably by this ghastly war, not to mention the hardships endured by everyone? Three Innisbraw lads had paid the ultimate price and several more, including Graham, suffered agonizing wounds. And Martin ... would they ever know whether he was alive or dead?

She mounted the stairs to the dais and planted the Saltire's staff in the left stand, the remainder of the song bringing hen's flesh coursing over her body.

Ours is the land of gallant hearts, the land of honour'd graves, whose wreath of fame shall ne'er depart while yet the thistle waves.

She stood beside The Saltire as the British sergeant made his way up the aisle.

Rob's shoulders straightened as Sheila MacNab played "The Star-spangled Banner." Aye, he now considered Scotland home, but America was the land of his birth and he would never allow himself to forget it. Wasn't this why he had come to the UK?—to help see the war in Europe brought to an end?

The price of victory, though horrendous, was not in vain. Hitler was dead. His Army, Navy, and Air Forces beaten. The bright beacon of hope once again shone over their lands—pounded to rubble, but not defeated. The laughter of happy children would sweeten the air, church bells would ring again, and brave hearts would face a future filled with promise.

He placed Old Glory in the last stand as the kirk bell pealed out its message of freedom across the island. Once back in his seat with Maggie at his side, Rob listened intently to Hugh's scripture-laden message. Though long because of the repetition of translating the Gaelic into English to accommodate the Tommies, it lifted sorrowful hearts, calmed exuberant ones, and left everyone firmly grounded in the Word.

As they stood on the kirk entry, Rob and Maggie declined invitations to a ceilidh the islanders had planned for the night. "We need to spend some time alone," Rob explained.

"We're going to show the soldiers how to do some reels and jigs," Anna MacLeod said, voice breathless. "They're even bringing all the sweets they have in their supplies." Her cheeks flushed red. "Elam, a lad I met at the Hogmanay ceilidh, said he was bringing chocolate."

Her blush reminded Rob of the first time they had met, her a halflin with only a promise of the bonnie young woman she had become.

"Are you certain you don't want to go?" Rob asked Maggie as they stepped into their cottage.

"Biddy certain. We had our time last een. All I want to do is take down the blackout curtains, light the lamp, and change into my gown before smooriching with my husband."

After Maggie nursed Robbie, they put him between them on the bed and laughed when he flipped over, trying to wriggle off. "I'm thinking he's inherited your impatience," Maggie said, her smile so fond Rob's blood simmered.

He grabbed the lad up and kissed his bare belly, then his toes.

Robbie squealed with delight, his chin shiny with saliva, teeth gleaming like pearls in the lamplight.

When the bairnie fell asleep, Maggie settled him in his cradle, and cuddled next to Rob. Her breath caught when he revealed his conversation with Elspeth about his impatience. "She's right, you ken," she said, snuggling closer. "You can't do more than you already have."

He sighed. "I ken that, I really do, but sometimes I get lost in all that has yet to be done and I forget."

"Tell me whenever you feel fashed and I'll remind you."

"I will, if I even realize it myself."

She wanted to ask him about the verses he had underlined in his Bible and learn what he feared, but she couldn't do that without revealing her own fears for his safety. She stiffened. "I just remembered something. Faither reminded me today is the anniversary of your first airieplane crash. Are you no' feeling resentment about all your pain and suffering?"

He rose up on one elbow and looked down at her. "Elspeth asked the same thing, but all I feel is gratitude. It's been so long ago and so much has happened since, it's like that crash was only a bad dream." His fingers brushed her cheek. "And all I want to remember is how it brought us together. I'd go through it again in a heartbeat."

She read the truth in his eyes and her heart swelled with luve. How had such a man ever chosen her when there were all those sophisticated London women he could have fallen in luve with? She felt a moment of panic. With the war over in Europe, the building of the rescue boat loomed closer than she'd thought. "Hold me tighter," she said, hiding her face against his chest. "I luve you so much."

He gathered her close.

Chapter Forty-One

Rob stood on the shore and watched with pride as the rescue boat he had designed and built slid off her launching skids into the harbour. Crowds of celebrating islanders clapped and whistled.

Maggie bobbed for a moment, then quickly sank, until only the top foot of her deck showed above the water. Elation turned to horror.

He shouted a hoarse, "No!" and ran forward, wading into the water until it was up to his shoulders. He pushed against the side of the hull, pleading with the Lord to make her float.

Prayers unanswered, body shaking, he slumped against the boat, sobbing.

꧁꧂

Maggie shook Rob's shoulder. He'd kicked off the bedcovers and sweat poured down his face and body as he lay sobbing beside her. "Rob?" She grabbed his hand when he tried to pull away. "Wake up, Rob. Wake up!"

He finally opened his eyes.

She moaned at the agony in their depths. "'Twas a bad dream, luve."

"A dream?" He ran fingers through his wet hair. "Only a dream?"

She drew him down beside her, nestling her cheek against his wet chest, his heart pounding in her ears. "Aye, only a verra, verra bad dream." She shivered with relief when he let out a long sigh.

"Och, 'twas so real. I disremember what I dreamed about, but I'm left with the feeling I wouldn't want to live if it really happened."

"But it won't. Remember when I had that bad dream about your airieplane crashing and burning? You told me then dreams are

293

only that, and they never come true."

"I had bad dreams at Edenoaks, and I couldn't recall them, either. I only knew they happened after bombing strikes gone sour. But I don't have any idea what I dreamed the night—only that it felt like the end of everything."

"Then I'm grateful you've disremembered it. If you can, would you turn on the lamp so I can change the sheets? They're soaking wet and our lad is stirring."

⚜

The cold snap lingered. Rob put his work on the house on hold and continued to help with the lambing. The bad dreams didn't return and, though he feared giving in to sleep, he tried to push all thoughts of it from his mind by keeping busy.

He gained a healthy respect for these hard-working crofters who invested all they had in a flock of sheep, especially Colin who laboured on, an unbearable burden of grief stooping his shoulders. The ewes did not even have the good sense to seek shelter when they were about to give birth and he spent hours combing the girse for new or sick lambs. At least, with the war in Europe over, he could do his searching after dark with the aid of a paraffin Tilly lamp, though he used it judiciously. The island's supply of paraffin was low and it could be years before rationing ended. The only good thing about the weather was that the constantly threatening rain never materialized.

⚜

Just one week after the temperature plummeted, it rose to normal levels again. The soldiers dismantled their camp before being reassigned or de-mobbed. The cook gave their remaining food supplies to the islanders, and the sergeant even offered to leave the Nissen huts and barbed wire fences.

Several of the poorer crofters accepted the huts to replace deteriorating sheep faulds, and a few with crumbling capstones on top of the dykes around their crofts were eager to add posts and wire to the tops. Perhaps the most important gift to be left behind was over a dozen large drums of paraffin. Now those without electricity or plumbed water could use their Tilly lamps for trips outside to the watterie every night.

There were a few tearful lasses on the island, especially Anna MacLeod who was only consoled when the British lad she was smitten with promised to write often. Her mither and faither, Katag and Gordon, swallowed their dismay at such young luve and invited the lad to their cottage for supper the een before he was to leave. Their consternation was assuaged somewhat when Elam said—in a twangy Northern England accent difficult to understand—that he had been raised on a sheep croft without electricity or indoor water in a cottage very similar to theirs.

Most of the islanders, including Rob and Maggie and each member of the shore guard, turned out to see the soldiers off. Those islanders who had been schooled wrote down their addresses and asked the young men to write and let them know where they were to be based.

As the soldiers lined up to board their boat, Hugh offered a prayer asking God to bless and keep them and to help them realize how much all their hard work and sacrifice had been appreciated.

Rob paid his respect by standing at attention and saluting when the boat weighed anchor and departed.

With the lambing season over, late turnips were planted and those who had not already sowed their rye, barley, and oats did so. Rob returned to his work on the house. With Angus's help, he moved his heavier woodworking equipment from the shed up to the new house so he could build kitchen cabinets and doors.

Maggie often came over and watched him, voicing her surprise at how he could construct so bonnie a press from a few pieces of wood. Glad for her company, he occasionally had her reach as high as she could to be sure the shelf heights were serviceable.

"I'm putting one kitchen bunker lower than the others so you won't hurt your back when you're kneading bread," he told her one een after supper. "And though I'm making the presses go all the way to the ceiling, you can use the top shelves to store things you don't use often. I'll build you a sturdy stool to climb on."

"You're going to spoil me. I've gotten by this long without all these betterments you're building for me."

"You deserve them. I don't see how you accomplish so much every day. It makes me feel verra humble."

"Och, you never stop working yourself."

"But I get to do new things. You do the same washing and scrubbing and cooking day after day." He picked her up and sat her on the table so he could look straight into her eyes. "'Tis a guid thing God made women different, or we'd all be in a terrible muddle."

That bonnie smile again. "And 'tis a guid thing God made men different or we women would have no reason to live."

Robbie suddenly squealed. He had pulled himself to his feet by a chair and stood victorious, legs wobbling, tiny fingers grasping for a hold.

Rob lifted Maggie down from the table and they raced to their lad, who tottered back and forth, eyes wide.

Rob scooped him up and hugged him. "He stood up! He stood up all by himself!"

Robbie arched his back and squealed again, this time with indignation.

Maggie laughed. "He wants down. Our lad's like his faither. He wants to go places and do things."

Rob sat the lad on the floor and they watched. Would he do it again?

Smiling with glee, four front teeth flashing in the light, the lad looked at his faither, then at his mither. He scooted on his bottom to the leg of the chair and grasped it with both hands, face red with effort as he pulled himself up to his knees. One bare foot went to the floor, then the other. His hands inched up the legs to the edge of the seat and he pulled himself erect, crowing with delight.

Rob and Maggie looked at one another, their faces mirroring disbelief.

"Maggie, lass," Rob said, grin wide. "I'm thinking we're in trouble now."

She shook her head. "Och, those wee fingers will be into everything."

Chapter Forty-Two

Robbie's new mobility put a crimp in Maggie's daily routine. She could no longer place him on the hearthrug with a pile of spoons and pot lids and expect him to stay. The moment she turned her back, he scooted after her on one knee and one foot with amazing speed.

After two days of pounding on the hard stone flags, one look at his bruised knees sent her racing to her sewing basket. She fashioned several small cloth bags, stuffed each with a handful of precious eider down, and, using the last of her snaps, fastened them to the knees of his trews.

Her pleasure with Rob's compliments on her clever solution was short lived. She had just seen him off to work on the new house when Shep's frantic barks came from the bathing room. She rushed there.

Robbie leaned precariously over the watterie, splashing water everywhere, squealing with delight. Nightclothes drenched, water pooling on the floor, he lost his balance and slipped, headfirst, into the bowl.

She jerked him out, heart pounding.

Had he sucked in water?

Och, Lord, help him breathe!

He looked at her, eyes wide.

She jostled him.

He spat out a mouthful of water and laughed.

Knees on the verge of collapse, she held him tightly and sat on the side of the bathing tub while he squirmed to get down, sputtering and giggling. Grabbing a towel, she wrapped it around his wriggling body, trapping his arms. "Och, you wee skellum! Try to wriggle oot of this!"

297

From that moment on, the bathing room door remained firmly closed, and Shep followed on the bairnie's heels, watching every move.

Rob worked even harder to get the new house ready. He sanded the floors smooth and sealed them with several coats of varnish rather than shellac, which would not give with the natural swelling and shrinking of the wood. He built presses in each bedroom closet for storing folded clothing. and varnished the stairs to the first floor and all the interior window sills. Before he varnished the kitchen cabinets, he explained to Maggie, "Paint will chip and show every dirty fingerprint. Besides, the grain of the wood looks bonnie."

Because rationing was still in effect and no lace panels were available to buy, several friends gifted Maggie their hoarded ones.

She cut back on her baking so she could have more time to sew lace curtains for the new house. Though careful not to complain when there were no fresh scones or shortbread, Rob often caught her with a look of guilt.

The twentieth of June, Rob and several helpers used a rope cradle to lower the digester into the waiting hole. After it was placed, Rob sent the men home, insisting he could attach all the pipes and fill the hole himself. He turned the pipefitter until his palms burned beneath heavy gloves, then tested the unit by running the cold water tap in the kitchen and flushing the watterie several times.

No leaks.

He spent the rest of the afternoon filling and tamping soil down around the tank, leaving only the outlet plate exposed. He limped home at the gloaming, covered with dirt and sweat and so exhausted he almost fell asleep in the bath Maggie drew for him.

"I've fixed you a light bree," she said, bringing him his dressing gown. "I knew you would be too tired to eat owt heavy."

He choked down one bowl and gulped two cups of coffee before his drooping eyelids stirred Maggie into action. "Away to bed before you go to sleep and fall off your chair." She pulled him to his feet and steered him into the bedroom, pulling back the covers and plumping up his pillow.

"'Tis too early," he mumbled, slipping out of his robe, "and you still have to feed Robbie."

"I'll join you as soon as he's asleep." She pushed him onto the bed and pulled up the covers. "Off to sleep now."

The contrasting colours of dark blue sea and white sand almost blinded Rob as he stood on the shore watching his rescue boat leave the launching skids.

The islanders shouted with joy as she moved into deeper water—and gasped when it sank like a heavy building stone. Only the top of her cabin remained visible, a crushing reminder of shattered ambitions.

Sobbing, he fell to his knees.

The brightness slowly dissolved.

He pawed himself upright in bed, blinking in bewilderment until he realized where he was and what he had dreamed. This time, every part of the heartbreaking picture burned in his mind—the dark harbour water, the sun glinting off the sand, the boat gaining backward momentum as she floated free.

Then sank, releasing thousands of bubbles as her keel settled into the sandy seabed.

Och, Heavenly Faither. His hands trembled as he pulled up a corner of the tangled sheet to wipe his sweaty forehead. He must have been dreaming the same dream over and over, not as fully formed and not every night, but often enough to keep him in a constant state of unease.

He turned and reached for Maggie. Not there. Where was she? He grabbed his watch from the bedside table and squinted to read the illuminated hands. Only a little after 2200. But he'd just gone to bed.

She must be sitting in her rocker, nursing their lad, thank the Lord. He straightened the bedding and turned his pillow over to hide the wet spot. *Help me, Faither, please help me. I can't go on like this, dreading sleep, skeering my Maggie. I've prayed over and over and claimed Your promises, but the bad dreams keep coming.* He lay on his side, squeezing his eyelids closed. *If I've made a mistake in the design, show me where and I'll correct it.*

He feigned sleep when Maggie crawled into bed, then lay awake for hours praying. He would have to share the dream with her, if only to ease his own burden, he couldn't yet. Taking care not to disturb her, he crawled from bed, grabbed his watch, slipped into his dressing gown, and left the bedroom, closing the door softly. He turned on the kitchen light and checked the time. 0300.

With Robbie sleeping most of the night, he had at least two or three hours to check his plans and look for an error.

⚓

At 0600, Maggie found him at the kitchen table fast asleep, head resting on his arms. Drawings and scraps of paper covered with columns of numbers and small sketches littered the table, some so distorted she couldn't make out what he had been attempting to draw.

So he'd had another bad dream, and this time he must have remembered it. She should have known from the damp sheets and his sticky skin when she cuddled him.

She chewed her lower lip as she lifted Robbie from his cradle and laid him on the bed for a change from the skin out. Should she ask Rob what was troubling him? It always seemed to help, but she wasn't certain this time. She couldn't share her own fears about him drowning—not yet. Perhaps she should haud her wheesht until he felt free to bare his concerns.

Chapter Forty-Three

By the first week of July, the new house was ready and they started moving a few of the smaller things from the cottage. Rob borrowed Angus's cairt and brought up all of the furniture he'd made in the shed. With their new home so large, he would have to build a few more side tables, benches, and chairs. He also wanted to make Maggie a chest for the bedcovers and knitted haps she'd crafted over the years. And someday, when rationing ended, they would need a sofa for the living room.

Hugh stepped in with several large boxes of everyday dishes, glasses, teacups, heavy earthenware coffee mugs, tableware, and pots and pans. "They've been gathering dust in my attic since I moved in. Living alone, I've no use for a kitchen equipped to cook for an army."

"Och, you've saved me from a fair fankle." Maggie kissed his cheek. "Malcolm's been looking for kitchen things but he hasn't found any. With rationing still so tight, everybody's holding onto what they have, whether they use it or no'."

The kitchen equipped, Maggie decided it was time to bring all of the handsel to the new house. Gratitude welled up when she looked at Elspeth's detailed list—every item noted with the name of the giver. "Och, Rob," she exclaimed as she unfolded a large multicolour rug. "This will be perfect in front of the hearth. Ishbel braided it."

He fingered the soft wool. "That's a handsome gift. It must have taken her weeks to make."

All of the gifts were practical and thoughtfully made. Morag had sewn embroidered seat and back cushions that fit the rockers perfectly. The women must have consulted one another for they

301

didn't receive a single duplicate and all the colours matched. There were three delicate watercolours of wild flowers from Siobhan MacNab—who'd have guessed she had such a talent? There were sheets and pillowcases, edges embroidered with flowers. Many of the crofters' wives had canned jars of jellies and heather honey with a list of the contents printed on labels adorned with hand-drawn, coloured pictures of wildflowers.

Elspeth's present brought tears to her eyes. She had gifted them a large Gaelic family Bible with their names and the date of their marriage written in her old-fashioned script on the page after the ornate frontispiece. "We need to enter our Robbie's birth." She reached for Rob's hand. "And in about seven months we'll have another birth to enter."

He stared at her. "Did I just hear what I think I heard?"

"And what is it you think you heard?"

"Are we going to have another bairnie?"

She gave a coy smile and nodded.

He grabbed her and covered her face with kisses. "Och, my Maggie, you've just made me the happiest man alive."

The true move into the new home took only a day, thanks to the help of the MacPhees and MacDonalds. Flora and Morag helped Maggie box up all of their belongings, which the men moved next door in Angus's cairt. While Rinait and Graham kept Robbie entertained on the front entry, boxes were emptied, presses and drawers filled, the bed made, and Maggie's loom set up in her weaving room.

Hugh provided the only surprise of the day when he appeared in Alec's cairt with a large desk and matching chair.

"I'd disremembered it completely," Hugh told Rob, who rubbed his hand over the worn, polished desktop. "It belonged to the previous minister of the kirk. Since I had my own, I stored it away in the attic."

"Are you certain you've no need of it then?" Rob eyed the large drawers.

"Absolutely. Is it too big for your home office?"

"No' at all. I was planning to make do with a sheet of plywood on sawhorses. I can't thank ye enough."

"There are also twa bookcases, if you've room."

"I'll take anything you've no need of. All I have is a drafting table and stool I made out of lumber scraps."

The last thing moved was the large china aumrie Rob had made for Maggie's birthday. When it was finally in place, everyone went home and left the twa new homeowners to bask in their happiness.

Rob settled Maggie in her rocker and ordered Shep to watch Robbie.

"Where are you going?" Maggie lifted her chin. "Did you disremember something?"

"I understand there's a custom here on Innisbraw we need to observe. I'm going to go get Angus's cairt and pick up Elspeth. She has some embers from her fire she wants to bring us."

"Och, of course! I was so kittled up I'm the one who disremembered. How fitting to use Elspeth's fire to light our own."

"I asked her after Sabbath services last Sunday. She said she'd be honoured."

"She hasn't seen our home since it was finished. I'll make tea and coffee, and Rinait brought over some of her crème cookies so we can have a bit of sweet." Rob trotted down to the MacPhee's croft and harnessed up Jack.

A gentle summer breeze carried the salty scent of the sea inland. He inhaled deeply, looking out at the gently undulating surf and murmuring a prayer of gratitude as he drove up the path. Living on Innisbraw might be physically hard, but the benefits far outweighed the hardships. Where else could one have such unbroken vistas of sea and sky, the varying colours of blue and green so soothing to the eye? In summer, the sweet, warm-honey scent of heather filling the air?

He smiled, heart filled with contentment, when he pulled to a stop in front of Elspeth's cottage.

She knit as she sat in one of her rockers on the front entry.

He set the brake and leaped down. "Are you ready?" he called as he bounded up the steps.

She set her knitting on the table. "Aye." Her blue eyes sparkled with mischief. "I was thinking you'd disremembered."

"Never. Where's the bucket? I'll get the embers."

"They're already in yon bucket. Gathering the embers is an important part of the custom. 'Tis my gift to you and Maggie and wee Robbie."

He sat in the rocker next to her and took her hand. "You're the first to ken, other than John. Come sometime next February, we're going to have another bairnie's name to place below Robbie's in that bonnie Bible you gifted us."

"I was wondering when you'd get about telling me." Her laughter reminded him of the deep-throated bells ewes wore to help dog and crofter find the flock.

"But I just found out. Maggie told you then?"

"Of course no'. The lass has that look about her. I noticed it when I saw her at kirk the past several Sabbaths."

"Och, Elspeth, there's no keeping secrets from you."

She pulled herself up with her walking stick. "Auld age has its benefits. When you've seen that special glow as often as I have, 'tis hard to miss."

He helped her into the cairt, fetched the bucket, and clucked to Jack.

The old cuddy set off at a leisurely walk.

As they neared the house, Elspeth hugged his arm. "'Tis a fine home you've built, Rob. You should be proud."

"I couldn't have done it without our menfolk's help."

"Aye, but don't forget, 'twas your design that makes it your own—that and all your hard labour."

"I'm going to hire Angus to build a dry stone dyke around our croft. He does the finest work I've ever seen."

"Indeed."

They pulled up in front of the entry where Maggie waited, holding Robbie. "Elspeth," she cried, "you're our first visitor. Welcome to our new home."

Elspeth pointed to the broad, stone-flagged entry with its overhanging roof. "I'm thinking 'tis large enough to dance on," she said as Rob helped her down.

"No' large enough for a proper Eightsome Reel, but it could do for a couple's dance."

"And verra nicely."

He supported her elbow as they climbed the two stone steps, then took Robbie from Maggie and kissed her cheek. "Come away in." He stepped aside as Elspeth hobbled through the open doorway.

She stopped so suddenly he almost walked into her. Turning, eyes bright, she said, "'Tis a marvel." Her gaze swept over the gleaming wood floors and large windows. "An absolute marvel." She paced, walking stick tapping, as she toured the kitchen and living room. The large Aga, resplendent in its new coat of heat-cured stove-black was inspected, as were the tables and chairs. She ran twisted fingers over the satiny surfaces. "I'm thinking you're a born craftsman. No one could have done a better turn."

He chuckled. "Are you saying I've missed my calling in life?"

She looked at him, eyes snapping. "You know your calling, and 'tis much broader than this."

"Do I really? Sometimes I wonder if 'tis a plan much more ambitious than I'm capable of fulfilling. I've had dreams of the boat sinking when we launched her."

***

Maggie's breath caught. He was actually acknowledging he'd had bad dreams—and remembered them. Why hadn't he told her? She wanted to blurt out an accusation but this was no' the time. She'd wait until they were alone.

Elspeth's question to Rob interrupted her dark thoughts. "Did you ever imagine you could do all this?" Elspeth waved her hand.

"No, I don't suppose I did."

"Then stop all this blether. God spared your life twa times for a verra guid reason, so don't start questioning His wisdom now. Put down that braw lad and fetch the embers. We don't want them to die before we've lit your fires."

Maggie stood back, watching him sit Robbie on the hearthrug.

"Guard Robbie, Shep," he ordered as he went out the door.

Before anyone could react, the bairn was up on one knee and one foot, scooting toward the door.

In an instant, Shep blocked his path.

Though the lad squealed and pulled on his legs, the dog did not move.

"You have a real treasure in that dog," Elspeth said.

"Aye, I don't ken what I'd do without him," Maggie agreed coolly, resentment building. How could Rob act as if nothing were wrong? Didn't he sense her anger?

He brought in the bucket of embers and handed Elspeth the tongs. "The peat's already waiting. 'Tis time for you to do the honours."

Elspeth held up a hand. "But first, a wee prayer ... our precious Heavenly Faither, when we light these fires, fill this home with the fire of Your Holy Spirit, that these luved ones living here might always walk in Your ways and fulfill Your purpose in their lives. In Christ's name we pray, amen." She picked up an ember and dropped it into the kitchen stove, then added several more.

Rob carried the bucket into the living room where she repeated the process in the fireplace.

The peat caught fire, releasing its uniquely sweet, smoky aroma into the air.

"Now it smells like a home," Rob said.

"Like our home." Maggie forced herself to return his hug. She also made herself sip her tea, but could not bear the thought of eating any of the crème cookies, though they were her favorites. The flame of resentment grew until it threatened to ignite her insides.

"It's such a comfortable home," Elspeth said. "I'm thinking there are many folk on Innisbraw who will be tempted to copy this design."

"That's fine by me." Rob drained his coffee mug. "I just know it fits the way we want to live."

Robbie began to fuss and Maggie settled him to nurse, hoping her milk wasn't curdled. "I'm certain Rob's told you about the new bairn." Of course he had. He told Elspeth everything.

"Aye," Elspeth said. "I'll add the new one to my daily prayers."

By the time Rob returned from delivering Elspeth home and dropping off the cairt and cuddy, Maggie paced the floor, so filled with hurt and resentment she felt ready to explode.

"I thought you'd already be abed." He scooped her into his arms.

She jerked away and stood back, appalled when tears stung her eyes. Chin high, tear-filled eyes meant to be shooting daggers, she said coldly, "So you didn't disremember those bad dreams after all."

Chapter Forty-Four

Rob had never seen Maggie so angry. Och, he should have told her days ago, no' spit it oot to Elspeth like a lad with a hot secret scalding his tongue. "No' the first few dreams—just the last one."

"And once again you've chosen to keep it from me, but no' Elspeth."

Her scathing tone reminded him of the taunts he had heard so many times growing up. He wanted to run, to escape, to hide. He studied the floor, knowing he'd caused this muddle, and he'd forgotten how emotional Maggie became when she was biggen. "I ... I've been biding for the right time, but we've both been so busy it never seemed to come. I never meant to fash you."

She whirled away and turned her back, adding peats to the dying embers in the fireplace. Behind her came a long sigh and footsteps.

"What I did was wrong, and hurtsome to you." He brushed his fingers over her hot cheek. "I haven't had the dream since and realized a few days ago that it only happens when I'm verra tired—like at Edenoaks. I had bad dreams there when I was so exhausted I couldn't hold my head up—falling asleep at my desk with my face buried in a pile of papers that needed my attention. So I've been trying to pace myself better."

Arms encircled her shoulders. She'd seen him that tired at Edenoaks. The constant pressures of planning and flying missions, of arguing for more planes, of the grieving. Each loss etched into his face, into the dark depths of his eyes. She hardened herself against turning and clutching him close. "Why tell Elspeth?" A tortured whisper, but all she could manage.

"I don't know why, it just slipped oot." His arms tightened.

"Please forgive me, my Maggie. I'd never, ever hurt you a'purpose."

Everything he had done for her paraded before her blurred eyes, making a mockery of her hurt and anger: the cradle, her bonnie aumrie, the celebration at the howff on the anniversary of their meeting, the months of backbreaking labour on this home … The list was endless.

She turned in his arms and rested her cheek against his chest. "Then I want you to tell me everything. You're so exhausted, the dream could return the night." She nestled in his lap while he described his last bad dream. When he finished, she hugged his neck. "Your boat won't sink, luve. 'Tis only the de'il's way of trying to weaken your faith in God."

"It isn't my faith in the Lord that's weakened—but my faith in myself."

"Then my belief in you will have to be enough. And all I expect in return is your promise you'll never hide another bad dream from me."

He raised her chin, his steady gaze penetrating to her soul. "That's a promise I can give with all my heart."

As they spooned in their new bed that night Rob was too exhausted to sleep.

The night breeze wafted the new lace curtains, casting delicate, intricate shadows across the moonlit walls.

He chuckled. "I have enough room to stretch out my legs, but it's much nicer to coorie doun with you."

"Mmm, I agree."

He twisted a strand of her hair between his fingers. "It's hard to even say this, but what will we ever do when Elspeth's called home to Heaven? Hugh's teachings and her prayers are what hold this island together."

"They're an important part of that, but we can't think God's going to leave us without a prayer warrior."

"But who could it be? Elspeth's been the spiritual backbone of Innisbraw most of her life."

"There's always Auntie Mairit. Her arthritis almost keeps her housebound, so she has all the time in the world to hold us up before the Lord, as I'm certain she does."

"That's just the problem. She's so frail she can hardly go to kirk anymore, and her cottage is on the other side of the island."

She turned over, facing him. "Going to kirk isn't what's important, luve, nor where she bides. What matters is her commitment to prayer."

"As usual, I've got the wrong cuddy hitched to the cairt. You're fine right on both counts."

"Besides, our Elspeth's no' going to Heaven for a while. She's still amazingly healthy."

"Aye, she is that." He snuggled closer and buried his face in the hollow of her throat. "We've been so blessed. I just hope God knows I recognize it and thank Him for it."

"Of course He does. He has a divine knack for reading the intents of our hearts."

"The intent of my heart isn't always so noble." A deep sigh relieved the pressure growing in his chest. "I'm always running ahead, trying to make something happen before its time."

"That's why He chose you. You want to do the right thing so badly. You just push yourself too hard sometimes, but you're always ready to act and that's what's important. The world is full of people with lofty dreams. He knew what Innisbraw needed was a doer, no' a dreamer."

"Pray God I don't fail."

⁂

A pang of guilt.

Rob wasn't the only one who harbored secret fears. Was it her guilt that had made her so resentful earlier? Should she tell him how she feared for his safety once he launched the rescue boat?

No, not now when they were both so tired.

Despite his heartfelt promise, he would never learn to share all his fears instead of keeping them buried deeply within his heart—like he had when he was a lonely, desolate bairn—if she always shared hers in turn and made him feel worse.

"You will no' fail, Rob. The rescue boat will be perfect, for the

Lord directed your thoughts the entire time you were designing her."

Help him believe, Faither. Please take away his fears. Mine too.

❧

Maggie eyed the platters of sweets she and Flora had been baking for twa days. "Do you think this will be enough? I used honey when I could, but I used both of our sugar coupons for July and there's no' much sugar left."

Amusement warmed Flora's blue eyes. "There are sweets galore. The folk aren't coming to eat—they just want to see your home. 'Tis all they've been blethering about since you moved in."

Maggie poured twa cups of tea. "'Twill give us a chance to thank everybody for their wonderful handsel gifts." She spooned honey into both cups and added milk. "I know I've thanked you for the bonnie pressed flowers you framed, but I don't think I've shown you where I hung them."

"Och, 'twas my pleasure." Eyes downcast, Flora stirred her tea.

"Come away into our bedroom." Maggie led the way, critically eyeing the floor and furniture for any spot of dust she might have missed on her cleaning spree. She stood in the doorway and pointed.

Two large driftwood frames hung above the bed, their colorful pressed flowers complementing the bright quilt.

Flora's cheeks flushed. "They do look guid there."

"I'm thinking you knew which quilt I'd use and you made those bonnie pictures to match. I can't thank ye enough."

"It was nowt. I knew which was your largest quilt, and when I saw how verra tall Rob was, 'twas your only choice." Flora nodded at the platters of sweets as they returned to the kitchen. "Do you suppose you can keep that man of yours away from all that temptation till the morra then? I've never seen one who enjoys them more." She picked up her cup and sipped her tea.

"That will take some doing. When he's been working hard, as he has for so long now, he eats more than you can imagine."

"How does he stay so thin?"

"I have no idea. I suppose he just burns it all up by never

staying still for a single moment until after we've had our supper, and even then, he's always jumping up, getting another mug of coffee or adding peats to the fire or letting Shep in or oot."

Flora took off her apron. "He's a worker, that's a fact. I always thought my Angus was never one to sit, but I'm convinced Rob always gets his turns done." She looked out the window. "Speak of the de'il and up he pops. Angus is here with the cairt as we speak."

"Thank ye for all the help." Maggie hugged her. "I never could have done it without you."

"We were lucky, we were. Wee Robbie's taken a guid long nap or we couldn't have accomplished so much."

"That's a fact. He's into everything now." She accompanied Flora out to the entry and waved to Angus.

"Rob home?" he called.

She made her way out to the path. "He's down at the shed sanding the floor so he'll have a smooth place to draw his full-size plans for the rescue boat."

Angus puffed on his pipe. "Doesn't take much time to fauld his fit, does he?"

"That's biddy certain. But that's just Rob. He can't sit still if there's something to be done."

"We're lucky to have him as one of our own." Angus helped Flora into the cairt, tipped his bunnet, and picked up the reins. "See you at kirk on the morra, then."

Maggie smiled and waved as the cairt moved down the path. Her smile faded as she stepped into the house. She hadn't shared her concern with Flora. She put damp linens over the sweets and sat down in her rocker with her tepid tea.

Worry nagged. She had cooked Rob a large breakfast of sliced sausage, eggs, and tinned beans while he scanned the Edinburgh *Scotsman*, but he had only taken a few bites of beans on fried bread and hadn't even come home for dinner.

Either he was hurting or something was bothering him.

And she was sure it was the latter. As far as she could tell, he hadn't had any more bad dreams, so it could only be one thing; just two years ago on the morra, his life had almost ended in that dreadful crash outside of Canterbury. Even worse, at least in Rob's mind, was that date marked the end of his military career.

Robbie awoke jabbering, and she changed him.

Since he didn't act hungry, she took off her apron, threw a light shawl over her shoulders, picked him up from his new bed, and went out the door. Whether Rob was willing to admit it or no', he needed her. She propped Robbie on her hip, called Shep to follow, and set off down the path to the shed. Panting by the time she reached the shed, she put Robbie down and stood for a moment breathing deeply.

He was definitely getting too big for her to carry so far.

The door to the shed stood open and the whir of the electric sander echoed within.

She picked up her bairnie and stepped inside.

Rob had opened the huge door at the shore side and sunlight poured in, illuminating the motes of wood dust dancing in the air like swarming midges.

She took out her handkerchief and tied it over Robbie's nose and mouth, but he howled, shook his head, and pulled it off. She backed out the door, unwilling to expose him to so much dust.

"Maggie!" Rob called. He turned off the sander, stood, and rubbed his knees. Though he wore a heavy paper nose mask, his face, hair, and clothing wore a mantle of gray-brown dust. He removed the mask, brushed himself off vigorously, and came out the door with a welcoming smile. "Surely you didn't carry him all the way." He took the lad from her arms. "You'll hurt yourself."

She hugged his waist. "Is this the greeting I get, then?"

He leaned over to kiss her. "What brings you all the way down here?"

"I missed my husband."

"I'm sorry about dinner, lass. I didn't realize how late it was till a bit ago."

"You mean your stomach didn't ring any alarm bells?"

"The racket the sander makes must have drowned them oot."

She waited. Perhaps he would say more. When he didn't, she took a deep breath and held out her hand. "I'm here, luve. If you've a need to talk, I've a desire to listen."

His lips pressed together. "Let's go sit on the bench by the pier. There's too much wood dust here."

Robbie fussed and reached for his mither when they sat down. She unbuttoned her sweater, put him to her breast, and pulled her shawl over him.

"What gave me away?"

"You only picked at your breakfast, and missed dinner entirely."

"I thought so." He got up and paced in front of the bench. "I don't know what to say."

"Let me tell you what I've been thinking then." She took a minute to collect her thoughts. "I know the morra's the second anniversary of your last crash and I've been trying to think about something in my own life that could equal all you lost that day." At the look of pain on his face, she reached out and clasped his hand. "I realized it would be like me being told I can never have the bairns I want. It would break my heart."

He sat down beside her, shoulders dejected, head down. "I didn't even know the date till I saw it in the *Scotsman*. I thought I had put it all behind me—I really did."

"I know, luve."

"I never imagined how hard it would be to give it up."

When he raised his head, she stifled a gasp at the look of despair on his face.

"I have to give it up, Maggie, I know that. I just don't know how."

She lay Robbie against her shoulder and patted his back. "'Twill take time. More time than you've had."

"'Tis like trying to land a plane without full flaps. There's no going back and making different decisions that day and I know it, but I can't get it out of my mind. I keep going over the 'if onlys' but all it does is make me feel worse, no' better."

She put Robbie at the other breast and leaned her head against his shoulder. "Have you prayed about it?"

"It seems all I do is ask the Lord for help. Surely He expects me to take care of some things myself."

"This is no' 'some things.' 'Tis a verra, verra big hurt. You

314

know He specializes in big hurts but you also know He won't force Himself into your life. You have to ask Him."

He sat for a time, facing the harbour. "What makes you so smart, lass?"

"Experience." She read the question in his eyes. "I don't think I've ever told you how lonely I was before we met. I was twenty-twa years old, my mither gone, my faither away, apart from my brother, and hadn't met a single lad who interested me." She handed Robbie to Rob. "So I buried myself in my work, but nowt filled the void in my life."

"You're so bonnie and fine, I can't understand that."

"You'll just have to believe it, for 'tis true. Then I remembered Hugh telling us so often that the Word says to cast all your cares on Him, so I did."

"And?"

"The verra next night you asked me to dance."

"I've never told you this, but if Den Anderson ever pays us a visit, he's biddy certain to tell you." He put Robbie down and let him stand at the bench, holding onto the back of his trews. "I never would have had the nerve to ask you to dance if Den hadn't dared me."

Her smile turned to a laugh. "I wonder how he'd feel if he knew who really inspired that dare."

"Den? He'd probably deny it to the death—not being a believer."

"But we know different, don't we? He got a verra gentle, yet verra insistent prodding from the Holy Spirit to do exactly what he did."

"I'd like to tell him that someday just to see the look on his face." His palms framed her face.

So tender, that kiss.

He jumped up, whistled to Shep, put Robbie over his shoulder, and his hand beneath Maggie's elbow. "On you come, lass," he said with a broad grin. "I'm suddenly gleg as gled."

There was her Rob.

Though he didn't eat his usual three helpings of supper, he did eat twa. He raised a tea towel from one of the platters of sweets. "Off limits?"

"Since they're your favorite scones, you can have twa but that's all."

He helped himself to two and returned the cover. By the time he seated himself in his rocker, one scone was gone and the other soon followed. "They went down a treat and the house looks grand. You must have polished everything."

"No' everything, but most." She cuddled Robbie on her lap, kissing his chubby cheeks and bouncing him up and down on her knees.

"Our home couldn't look better. You've decorated it perfectly."

She felt her cheeks flush. "Thank ye."

He got up and put several slabs of peat on the fire. "'Tis a wee bit chilly the night considering how warm it was the day."

"Did you enjoy your shower?"

"You'll never ken how much. But I'm no' averse to bathing with you later. 'Tis said that 'cleanliness is next to godliness.'"

"You don't have to make excuses. I'd luve to have you bathe with me."

He laughed and took Robbie from her. "I'm thinking 'tis about time this lad learned how to walk. He's too big for you to carry."

"He isn't even a year auld."

"He's been pulling himself up for over twa months. He just needs a little confidence, don't you, lad?" He nuzzled the back of Robbie's neck.

The bairnie waved his arms and giggled, babbling his childish gibberish.

He stood Robbie and pressed the lad's hands around his index fingers. "Hold on tight now. We're going for a walk."

Robbie arched his back and refused to move.

"Och, he's too used to being carried." He stood the bairn at Maggie's side and moved a few feet away, holding out his hands. "On you come. Come to Faither."

The lad grinned up at him.

"On you come, lad," Rob urged.

Robbie sat down and scooted over to his faither.

"That's no' what I had in mind." Rob shook his head. He picked the lad up and nuzzled the nape of his neck again, inhaling his unique fragrance rivaled only by Maggie's.

She tickled the bairnie's bare toes. "He'll walk when he's ready and no' before."

"I wonder where he gets that stubborn streak."

"Aye, I wonder where," she said, smile sweet as honey from the comb.

Rob sat the lad on the hearthrug and called Shep to stand guard. He walked slowly toward Maggie. He took the barrette from her hair and ran his fingers through her long tresses.

"Sometimes I think all you luve about me is my hair."

He raised an eyebrow. "Surely you ken I luve everything about you," he said in a soft growl, pulling her into his arms. "Everything."

They stiffened as the sudden pealing of the kirk bell echoed through the open window.

"Och, what's happened?" Rob raced for his A-2 jacket and Maggie's heavy sweater while she scooped up their lad and bundled him with sweaters and blankets. He ordered Shep to stay and they dashed out the front door.

Rob anxiously scanned the harbour below. "No fire or anything I can see."

"But Ben Innis ... is in the way," Maggie panted. "We can't see the ... far side, where most of our folk live."

He slowed his steps so Maggie could keep up. "That sounded like a call to prayer, no' as fast as the danger signal."

"You're right. It did."

He stopped suddenly and gripped her shoulder. "Could it be Elspeth?"

Robbie arched his back and squealed.

Their eyes turned to the cottage on their left.

The light from a single lamp illuminated the flagged entry. Elspeth stood at the top of the steps, head bowed in prayer.

317

"Thank Ye, Faither," Rob breathed as they hurried up her walk.

"Have your heard owt?" Elspeth asked, voice taut.

"No' a word." Rob transferred their squirming lad to his right shoulder.

"I see Angus with his cairt coming up the path. Help me down the steps."

The cairt approached, made a wide turn, and pulled up in front of Elspeth's gate. Angus and Flora sat on the front bench with Edert and Rinait standing in back.

"Guid you're here, Rob," Angus hailed. "Save me a few minutes going up the fell." He dismounted and helped Elspeth onto the bench next to Flora while Rob boosted Maggie up into the back, handed her Robbie, and leaped in.

"Any idea why Hugh rang the bell?" Rob asked as Angus climbed up and flicked the reins.

"No' a word from Hugh. I tried his radio but he's no' answering."

⁂

Maggie cuddled Robbie in her lap and hugged Rob's back. "Whatever can it be? Surely Hugh would have radioed me if someone's sick."

Rob took their lad and wiped off the slobbers after Robbie planted a wet kiss on his cheek. "I don't know. 'Tisn't like Hugh to keep everyone on heckle-pins."

The cairt tore along the path, only slowing to make the turn to the west and to avoid a few folk hurrying toward the kirk.

The kirkyard was filled with throngs of people. Several cairts and cuddies lined the long pole off to one side of the entry. The lights in the sanctuary lit up the faces of the waiting folk, gazes anxious and filled with fear.

Angus pulled the cairt to a halt and helped Elspeth and Flora to the ground while Rob lifted Maggie from the back. "I'll be with you in a tick," the crofter shouted over his shoulder as he guided Feona toward an empty spot at the end of the pole.

Alec pushed his way through the crowd to Elspeth's side. "I'll help you to the front so you can see."

"Do you know what's happened?" Rob asked.

"No' a glimmer. Hugh's being most mysterious, he is." Maggie clung to Rob's arm, fighting to still her trembling legs. Someone needed prayer.

But who?

And why?

they were standing, Hugh was being more mysterious he... Maggie woke to her feet, fighting to still her trembling legs. Someone moaned.

Chapter Forty-Five

A loud murmur of conversation buzzed through the air as Hugh stepped from the narthex and stopped on the top step of the entry. He raised his hand.

Instant silence broken only by the snort of an impatient cuddy.

"Dear folk," he said, scanning the crowd. "I apologize for no' passing the word earlier, but this is the way Colin and Ruth wanted it."

Martin! Maggie's mind screamed. Her knees turned to jelly. Only Rob's firm grasp around her waist kept her from falling.

Colin and Ruth joined Hugh. Hands clasped tightly together, they raised tear-streaked faces, gazes traveling over the faces before them.

Maggie laid her head against Rob's arm.

The Stewarts both looked like they had aged twenty years in the past few weeks. Colin's body hunched forward, his weathered face lined, grey eyes haunted. Ruth, always thin, must have lost at least twa stone. Her dress draped over her gaunt body like a becalmed, collapsed sail. Her auburn hair, usually worn in a braid, caught no light, but lay in loose, limp strands over her shoulders.

Rob stiffened as Colin pulled a paper from his jacket pocket.

Colin cleared his throat and swallowed convulsively, shoved the paper back into his pocket, and straightened his shoulders. "Ruth and me, we received a ... a wire from the military this een. I was going to read it aloud, but I can't see that well right now and there's no reason to draw this oot."

Tears coursed down his chapped cheeks. He pulled Ruth close. She sobbed silently into a limp handkerchief.

Rob closed his eyes and braced himself. *Och, Faither, another*

family torn apart by war. Pictures paraded before his eyes.

Colin, grey eyes wide and serious, explaining how to fire a single-shot shotgun to a paralysed Yank flyboy sitting in a wheelchair. Colin, crouched behind a rock, his eyes pressed to binoculars. Colin slumped against the infirmary wall with his head bowed, calloused, bloody hands lax in his lap.

Help them, Lord. Please, please help them.

Colin leaned over and whispered something into Ruth's ear. She nodded and raised her head. A sudden, bright smile illuminated her face from within.

"Our Martin was found by the Red Cross in a German naval hospital. He suffered a broken arm and some burns on his body, but—" her soft voice rose to a shout of triumph "—he's on his way home!"

The liquid song of a laverlock trilled and bubbled over Rob's head as he ran up the fell toward home. The thought of having to spend the day showing folk around their new house had driven him out for a run before the sun keeked over the horizon, but perhaps the rare, wee bird augured a pleasant, though sleeperie day ahead. He and Maggie had been too kittled up to sleep well after the long prayer meeting filled with thanks and praises to the faithful Lord.

Pretend it's a parade inspection and bear up, man.

Maggie and Rob thanked each of the folk for their handsel gift and showed them where they were displayed. The women commented on the size of the large rooms, eyes shining with wonder, and the men ran calloused palms over the furniture, nodding approval at the workmanship.

Though his stomach cramped at being the centre of attention, Rob took his cue from Maggie and graciously thanked each person for his or her compliments. But whenever she was in another room, Rob pointed out how well Maggie had pulled everything together with her decorating skills.

Flora and Morag filled teacups and coffee mugs and passed around platters of sweets while Rinait and Graham kept the bairns on the flagged entry entertained with stories and funny songs. Hauflins congregated in the side yard, lasses flirting as lads pretended indifference while exchanging sly grins.

"Now see, that wasn't so hard, was it?" Maggie asked as the last guests took their leave late that afternoon.

Rob plonked himself into his rocker with a groan. "It was agonizing but at least 'tis over."

"Och, you're impossible. How would you feel if every time you complimented me I made light of it or gave the credit to someone else?"

"That's different."

"How?"

"What you do is truly amazing. I just do what has to be done."

"Aren't you proud of what you've built?"

"I repeat. That's different."

"And I repeat. You're impossible."

"I think we're at an impasse."

She swatted at him. "Listen, you verra tall, braw, loving, giving man, don't make light of your God-given talents."

He laughed. "You fight dirty, lass."

The following afternoon, Graham showed up at the shed using a walking stick instead of crutches. "Maggie wouldn't let me tell you yesterday. She wanted you to be surprised."

Rob gaped. "I'm dumfoondert. How does it feel to have so much more freedom?"

"You know how it feels—wonderful. And the next big one is walking on my own."

Rob clapped him on the back. "I remember well how it felt to finally get rid of those crutches."

Graham eyed the sanded floor with dark pencil marks outlining an enormous hull. "Looks like you're lofting your plans."

"Just a start. Had to keep oot of the way while Maggie redded the house after all the folk tromping in and oot. 'Twill take a long time to get it all down and make sure each measurement is exact."

"Need some help? I can't kneel, but I can call out the dimensions so you can check them."

"That would be a lifesaver. Certain you have the time?"

"After I do my workout on the parallel bars, I have nowt to do. 'Tis driving me daft."

"The *Maggie's* a big boat—I'll take the help gladly."

"You named her already?"

"She had a name before I ever put pencil to paper."

Graham looked at Rob intently. "I need to talk to you—about my future."

"Then, let's go over to Paddy's, get some coffee, and sit a spell." Rob dusted off his breeks. "My knees are already giving me fits."

They sat at a table, mugs of coffee wafting wisps of steam.

"So what's up?" Rob asked. "Have you come to a decision then?"

Graham nodded. "It wasn't easy, but I have." He was obviously stalling for time, blowing on coffee that was just right to drink. "When John finally declares me fit for duty, I'm going to resign my commission. I want to stay here."

Rob looked at him closely, eyes narrowed. "You're biddy certain that's what you want? You're no' trying to please your folk or Rinait?"

"I'm certain. I had John check for me. My unit's been assigned to permanent duty in England. The war's over for us."

"There could still be a future for you in the Army."

"I ken that. I just realize now how much being at war influenced my decision to join." Graham leaned forward, gaze intent. "I want to do something to help our folk. You of all men should understand that. You weren't even birthed here, yet this is your home and you want to help. I grew up with these folk, and I want to help you make Innisbraw the place it was intended to be. Mebbe you could use a partner."

Rob sat back in his chair, rubbing the side of his nose. "You're certain you'll no' regret it when 'tis too late?"

"I'm biddy certain."

A partner. Just what he needed. *Thank Ye, Lord.* "Then I'm thinking you'll make a guid partner."

"There's just one problem. I don't have any silver for a buy-in."

"Don't need silver. What I need is help with everything else." Rob extended his hand. "Welcome aboard."

They shook hands, grins wide.

Chapter Forty-Six

The war in the Pacific raged on. On the twenty-ninth of July, Japan formally rejected the United States' ultimatum to quit the war or face total destruction. On August sixth, the world was shocked when an American B-29, piloted by Brigadier General Paul Tibbets, dropped an atomic bomb on Hiroshima, Japan, killing and wounding thousands upon thousands.

⚓

Unable to comprehend the magnitude of such an explosive, Rob gasped when John radioed him with the news. "An atomic bomb? One bomb did all that?"

"One bomb. It was reported that the cloud of debris looked like a giant mushroom."

"Och, John, I can't believe it. How could they keep the development of such a weapon a secret?"

"I don't know, though I remember reading something in the *Scotsman* about President Truman telling Stalin at the Potsdam Conference that the United States had a new weapon of unusually destructive force."

"And the Japanese haven't surrendered?"

"No' yet. How do you feel about all of this? There are some who are condemning the Americans for using such a weapon."

Rob's reply was instantaneous and heartfelt. "We were forced into using it. America did nowt to provoke their brutal attack on Pearl Harbor. Japan started this bloodbath. If it brings the war to an end soon, it's worth it in the lives saved."

"That's exactly what I think."

"Let me know when the Japanese government responds."

"I'll radio you at once."

325

Everyone Rob talked to voiced the same conviction—that the new American President had acted justly.

"'Tis a frightful shame about the Japanese innocents killed or maimed," Elspeth said, "but that is the price you pay when your government declares war."

Maggie's fears about losing Rob to the sea returned with a vengeance. If the war with Japan ended soon, he would be that much closer to risking his life during a rescue. She plodded through a mist so thick everything and everyone were vague shadows somewhere in the distance. She cooked their meals and tended to Robbie's needs, but every spare moment, she prayed and read the same Scriptures. Her world narrowed to one consuming thought.

He'll die in that sea. My Rob will die.

On August 9, Rob received a radio message from the doctor that another atomic bomb had been dropped on Japan, this time on Nagasaki. "It didn't cause as many casualties, but the devastation was enormous."

"What's it going to take to drive that nation to its knees? Surely they surrendered immediately."

"There's been no word if they have."

Rob spent the next few days in almost constant prayer, beseeching God to end the carnage. He ate little and slept poorly.

Maggie didn't appear to notice. Only Robbie's squeals and constant babble brought life to their home.

Rob and Graham finished lofting the plans, talking only when necessary. Those folk he met on the path to the shed doffed their bunnets or raised their hands in greeting, but nobody stopped for a blether.

The harbour waters reflected the sun like a mirror, and even the wind softened to a light breeze as though nature held her breath for the awaited news. Each day the tension heightened.

This war had to end.

It had to.

When Martin Stewart arrived home on Innisbraw, the entire island turned out for the docking of Malcolm's *Sea Rouk*.

Rob and Maggie arrived at the pier early for a position at the front of the crowd.

"What a glorious day," Maggie said, her heart light for the first time in days. "There he is!"

His body gaunt and slightly stooped, the lad hesitated at the foot of the gangplank.

Colin and Ruth rushed forward, paused for a second, then pulled him into their arms, Colin grasping his shoulder and Ruth showering his face with kisses.

"He favors Colin," Rob said. "Same light hair, same grey eyes. He's thin, but his frame looks broad like his faither's. 'Tis too bad he's bent on jyning the Navy. Colin could use the help."

"But he's home, Rob."

"Aye, he made it home."

The United Kingdom erupted into pandemonium on August 15, when word of the Japanese formal surrender was broadcast over every radio and screamed from the headlines of extra editions rushed out by even the most obscure rag.

Once again Hugh and Rob rang the kirk bell. Tears mingled with sweat as Rob pulled the rope. Aye, he'd made a life for himself on a remote island off the coast of Scotland, but he was still a loyal American and rejoiced at the long-awaited victory.

When they were rushing to get ready for the thanksgiving service Hugh had scheduled for that een, Maggie grew more and more quiet.

Why wasn't she as jubilant as he? She had eaten only a few bites of supper, and her violet-blue eyes were as dark as the Minch on a winter's night.

He pulled her away from the jawbox and handed her a towel before taking her into his arms. "What's the matter, luve? You act like you've had news of a death."

She averted her eyes and tried to pull away. "Nowt."

Her hoarse whisper thrust a stab of fear into his chest. He picked her up and carried her into their bedroom, sitting on the bed with her in his lap. "You once made a promise never to lie to me, and I'm thinking you just broke that promise."

She laid her head against his chest, shoulders shaking, silent tears wetting his shirt.

"Och, Maggie, have I said something—done something?" When she shook her head, he pressed her gently onto the bed. He lay beside her, stroking her hair. "Talk to me, please. You're breaking my heart. I must have done something to have you in such a fash, especially on such a joyous day."

Her silent weeping turned to sobs. She clutched his hand so tightly, her short nails dug into his skin. "It isn't you," she cried. "'Tis me and my ... my lack of faith in the Lord."

His fingers tightened around hers. Her lack of faith? Not Maggie. He didn't know anyone with a stronger faith.

Shep nosed his arm and he pushed the dog away, grateful that their lad, tired from all the excitement of the day, was taking a late nap. He pulled a pillow from the head of the bed and placed it beneath both of their heads before burying his face in her hair. "Is it the new bairnie?" he asked, voice hoarse from the tears clogging his throat. "Are you worried about Alice no' getting here in time to help birth it?"

"No." A single choked word.

"Then what, luve? As you're always telling me, I can't help you if I don't ken what has you in such a fankle."

"I'm ... I'm afraid of losing you."

"Losing me?" Memories of her fears he could be killed on a bombing strike flooded his mind. "But I'm in no more danger than any other man on this island—or woman, if the truth be told."

She pulled away and sat up.

He offered his handkerchief.

She wiped her face and blew her nose before turning her gaze toward the window. "I've tried to lose my fears in the Word and prayer like I did when you were flying, but they won't leave me this time."

He sat up beside her and smoothed away tendrils of hair sticking to her forehead. "You'll have to tell me more for I still don't understand."

"'Tis the sea, Rob. The pounding, angry waves that haunt me day and night."

What could she mean?

She turned from the window and looked at him. "Someday, perhaps soon, you'll be out there, battling that sea, and no human—even one as strong as you—ever wins such a battle."

The impact of her words sent his thoughts reeling. The rescue boat. She feared he would drown. "Och, Maggie, I'm doing it to you again. It never occurred to me you'd be afraid of losing me on a rescue shout."

"That's why I said 'tis my lack of faith. I shouldn't be afraid. I ken you're doing the Lord's will and I ken He luves you even more than I do." She brushed at the tears beading on her lashes. "I never gave a thought about how dangerous rescue shouts are till I read in the *Scotsman* about twa men from a lifeboat being ... being ..." She fell silent, hands folded in her lap.

"Why haven't you told me? Once again you're doing the verra thing you're always accusing me of—hiding your fears—just like you did before we were merrit." He pried her trembling hands apart and laced the fingers of one hand through hers. "All I can say is what Hugh's told us so often. That our days on earth are numbered, and that number known only by God. Surely you can't think He'd pull me back from death the twa times we know of, only to allow me to drown on a shout He's mandated. It doesn't make sense, luve. And the Lord we both believe in with all of our hearts, always follows a plan. Even if I were to die, that would still be in His plan and would somehow make sense."

"But believing God's Word and putting it into practice can be as far apart as Heaven and Earth."

"Just keep practicing."

⚓

Rob, Graham, and other lads who had returned to Innisbraw during the previous weeks, including Elam Taylor, who was on the

329

island to ask Gordon MacLeod for Anna's hand in marriage, wore their full dress uniforms to the kirk thanksgiving service. Martin Stewart, clad in a cobbled-together uniform of black tunic and trousers and a crescent scar on his cheek, smiled broadly as he ushered his mither and faither to their pew.

Rob stood next to Maggie, knuckles white from gripping the pew in front of him. This was it—the final guidbye to all the dreams that had fueled his every thought, every action, for years—the last time he would ever don the uniform he had worn so proudly for so long.

He forced his selfish thoughts aside and stood tall as Graham MacKay piped "Amazing Grace" for all of their fallen comrades. Heartbreaking images paraded before his eyes, the faces of those he would never see again on this earth. So many young lads, so many lives cut short before they had been given a chance to finish their education, woo their childhood sweethearts, marry and have bairns.

Don't let us ever disremember them, Faither. They are the true heroes of this war.

He proudly carried Old Glory, following Martin with The Saltire, and Elam with the Union Jack. After placing the flags, Rob stepped between Elam and Martin. Tears flowed down his cheeks and dripped from his chin as he grasped their trembling shoulders. Two of his brothers—one already a friend, the other one of the fortunate who had made it home.

Hugh took his place at the lectern, clearing his throat as he mopped his face with his handkerchief.

The three men huddled together, shoulders shaking.

Och, so much grief, even on a day of rejoicing. He cleared his throat again before saying in the Gaelic, "This is a momentous day, an historic day, and a day filled with often tragic memories for those who wear their country's uniforms with pride—or those who have lost a luved one." He repeated his words in English for Elam's benefit. Hands shaking, he raised his arms to encompass the entire congregation. "Before I begin the lesson, I would like all of you to take a few minutes of quiet prayer and contemplation as you look forward to a life without war or the threat of attack." He repeated his

Gaelic in English before motioning the three uniformed lads on the dais to return to their seats.

Rob returned to their pew and pulled a sleepy Robbie onto his lap, lacing his fingers through Maggie's.

She handed him a handkerchief and squeezed his hand as he wiped his face.

Her smile, so filled with luve and understanding, cleansed his grief. This was his new life. Not a dream, but a reality.

And the war no longer threatened to take it away.

Someday soon he and Graham would start building the rescue boat. Robbie would continue to grow and thrive, and the new bairnie, lass or lad, would be welcomed into their family with luve and gratitude. And the folk of Innisbraw, his larger family, could face day and night, sunshine and gales, hard work and refreshing sleep, with hope and confidence.

Maggie squeezed his fingers again and he smiled into her violet-blue eyes.

The Lord would see them both through their fears. His bad dreams and her dread of losing him on a rescue shout were only wee, wispy clouds in an infinite blue sky illuminated by the face of God.

He raised Maggie's hand to his lips.

The abysmal war was finally over.

A frisson of joy rippled through his soul. Like the Selkie and her crofter, he and Maggie would be together forever and ever and ever.

Acknowledgments

My thanks again to my dear friend, Paddy MacKinnon who kept me well-fed and entertained while I paid my annual summer visit to the Isle of Barra in the Outer Hebrides of Scotland. Also, my continuing thanks to my daughter, Valerie, and her husband, Jim. To the Air Guard and Air Force pilots who made the flying scenes believable and accurate.

I can't forget to mention my editor, Christina Tarabochia, who not only caught my mistakes, but offered love, support, prayer, and a kick in the right direction when needed. And critique partners, Mary Hall, Jennifer Simon, Lindy Jacobs, and Julia Johnson, who provided insight into the reader's mind and understand why I treasure my time spent in that land of misty glens, tumbling burns, and towering bens.

True history buffs will note that I have taken liberties with some dates so they can fit the tale. Any mistakes are mine alone, but thank you to Kristen Johnson, John Ashcraft, Andrea Cox, and Tami Engle for attempting to find them all.

Remember, you will not find Innisbraw on any map. It exists only in the fertile imagination of this author's mind.

Bio

Dianne fell in love with writing at the age of five. Because her father was a barnstorming pilot, she was bitten early by the "flying bug" as well. She attended the University of California, Santa Barbara and met and married the man God had prepared for her—an aeronautical engineer. After their five children were in school, she burned the midnight oil and wrote three novels, all published by Zebra Press. When her husband died, only three years after he retired, she felt drawn to visit the Outer Hebrides Isles of Scotland, where her husband's clan (MacDonalds) and her own clan (Galbraiths) originated. Many yearly trips, gallons of tea, too little sleep, and a burst of insight birthed her *Thistle Series*.

PUBLISHER'S NOTE: Dianne, born August 1933, lived joyfully despite dealing with terminal cancer and died in August 2013, a mere week before the release date for the first book of this series, *Broken Wings*. Everyone involved with the production of this book and the next four has been blessed beyond measure to be part of giving readers a chance to meet Rob and Maggie and visit the beautiful, fictional isle of Innisbraw.

Leave a message for her family and sign up to hear the latest about her books at www.ashberrylane.com/dianneprice or www.facebook.com/authordianneprice.

Glossary

All words are Scots, unless otherwise noted.

aff the knot: off one's head, crazed.

auld: old.

aumrie: hutch or breakfront.

awn up: confess.

baffies: bedroom slippers.

Baile a' Mhanaich: Gaelic (pronounced *Ba-liv-a-nik*), an island off Benbecula.

bairn: child.

bairnie: baby.

bambazed: astounded.

bannock: oat griddle bread, similar to English muffins.

beannachd: Gaelic (pronounced *Ba-Nachg*), blessing, regards.

ben: mountain.

biddy certain: very sure.

biggen: pregnant.

blether: talk, visit. (In the plural, nonsense.)

blowsterie: gusty, windy.

bodhran: Gaelic (pronounced *bo-rahn*), one-sided drum.

bonnie: beautiful.

bowf: a dog's bark.

brae: hillside.

braw: handsome, a pleasing sight.

bree: soup or broth.

breeks: pants or trousers.

brose: creamy oat porridge, soaked overnight.

bubble: cry, sniffle.

bunker: counter, like in a kitchen.

buttery: biscuit made with butter.

button box: accordion using buttons instead of keys.

Cairistiona: Gaelic (from Latin Christiana), woman's name, Christina.

cairt: cart pulled by a horse.

cannie: shrewd, expert, skillful, or lucky.

capercailie: Gaelic, large game-bird, grouse.

casting peat: slicing off pieces of peat, digging peat used for
    fuel.

cat's lick: wash hands and face, short wash-up.

ceilidh: Gaelic (pronounced *kay-lee*), party with music, dancing,
    sharing of news.

chaumer: parlour or gathering room.

clootie dumpling: steamed, sweet dumpling served with clotted
cream.

clothes-press: dresser for clothing or bedding.

collops: beef strips browned in meat drippings, can be served
    with mushrooms.

coo: cow.

coo gang: pen for cows.

coorie doun: nestle together, back to front, spoon.

croft: piece of land.

crofter: farmer, or one who owns a croft used for agriculture.

cuddy: small, shaggy horse, usually used to pull a cart.

cuttie: clay pipe.

daft: insane.

danke shoen: German, thank you.

digester: UK, septic tank.

disremember: forget.

door flags: group of flat stones before door to a cottage.

dreich: dreary, dull, grey, usually describing weather.

dunt: a blow, or to deliver a blow.

eejit: idiot, fool.

een: evening, can be written e'en.

entry: porch, passage into house.

faither: father.

face flannel: UK, washcloth.

fald your fit: rest, sit down.

fankle: disorder, entanglement.

fash: worry, vex.

flag: piece of stone used as floor of a cottage.

first-footing: Hogmany custom of a stranger bearing whisky stepping over your door flags.

firstie: West Point 4th year or senior.

frieren: German, freeze, don't move.

fug: UK, American, stuffy, airless atmosphere.

gey few: Old Scots, very few.

girse: grass.

gleg as gled: starving.

girse: grass.

gloaming: twilight.

grandbairn: grandchild.

grandmither: grandmother.

greetin' match: a baby's cries when first born.

guid: (pronounced *gid*) good.

haddie: haddock, white-meated fish.

halflin: adolescent, teenager.

handsel: gift, usually handmade for a special occasion, like marriage.

hap: knitted blanket, afghan.

haud yer wheesht: hold your tongue.

head full o' mince: stupidity.

hippen: diaper.

howff: pub.

hoy: greeting.

incomer: outsider who comes to live on island.

infirmary: UK, hospital.

IP: American Air Force, Initial Point of bombing run.

Irisher: Irishman or woman.

Irn Bru: soda with a taste of tangerine, very sweet, national soft drink.

jawbox: kitchen sink.
joint: UK, roast.

kailyard: kitchen garden, or small garden in a cottage croft.
keek: look at, peek.
ken: know, understand.
kirk: church.
kittled up: excited, enlivened.

laverlock: skylark.
lemon skoosh: sparkling lemonade.
louring: dark, black, heavy clouds or sky.

machair: Gaelic (pronounced *ma-K-er*), alluvial plain, unique to
    Outer Hebrides.
maskin pat: a teapot.
mebbe: maybe.
medicaments: UK, medicine.
merrit: married.
midden: dirty, mess, untidy place.
Minch: arm of the Atlantic between Outer Hebrides and Scotland.
mither: mother.

natter: chat, talk, often nag.
neeps: turnips.
no': not.
Nollaig Chridheil: Gaelic (pronounced *Na-leg Kri-gil*), Merry
    Christmas.
nowt: nothing.

owt: anything.

partan: common crab.
PDI: American Air Forces, Pilots Directional Indicator, used when
    bombing.
piece: snack, usually a small sandwich or buttery.
pishing doon: hard rain, usually used by men.

ploutering: splashing, playing in water.
polis: police.
press: cabinet.

radiogram: UK, phonograph.
reekie: smelly, sometimes refers to smoke.
redd: clean up, organize, straighten up.
rouping: Scots, crying, usually a baby or small child.

sair heidie: Gaelic, iced sponge cake.
sark: shirt.
Sassenach: Englishman.
seconded: UK, on loan to another base or service.
Sellotape: UK, clear, one-sided tape, like American Scotch
    tape.
SHAEF: WWII military, Supreme Headquarters, Allied
Expeditionary Force.
shilpit: skinny.
Siobhan: Gaelic (pronounced *Shi-vahn)*, woman's name.
skailwind: heavy, driving wind.
skellum: little imp or misbehaving child.
skirlie: recipe made with raw oats and chopped onions browned in
meat fat.
slubber: slobber.
skite one's luf: box on the ears.
sleeperie: sleepy.
sma': small.
smoorich: cuddle.
snell: cold, if wind, usually from the north.
sooking: sucking.
stille: German, silence, be quiet.
strathspey: regal, gliding dance.
swither: bemused, perplexed.

tablet: UK, vanilla fudge.
tatties: potatoes.
the day: today.

The Lift: Outer Hebrides, bearers carry casket from kirk to
    grave after service.
the morra: tomorrow.
tick: a second, or very quickly.
trews: leggings, tight pants, worn by a male.
turns: jobs, chores.
twa: two.

uggit: upset, annoyed, disgusted.

verra: very.

watterie: toilet.
whittie-whattie: aimless, every which way.

BROKEN *Wings*

The Thistle SERIES
BOOK ONE

DIANNE PRICE

He lives to fly—until a piece of flak changes his life forever.

A tragic childhood has turned American Air Forces Colonel Rob Savage into an outwardly indifferent loner who is afraid to give his heart to anyone. RAF nurse Maggie McGrath has always dreamed of falling in love and settling down in a thatched cottage to raise a croftful of bairns, but the war has taken her far from Innisbraw, her tiny Scots island home.

Hitler's bloody quest to conquer Europe seems far away when Rob and Maggie are sent to an infirmary on Innisbraw to begin his rehabilitation from disabling injuries. Yet they find themselves caught in a battle between Rob's past, God's plan, and the evil some islanders harbor in their souls.

Which will triumph?

ASHBERRY
LANE
ASHBERRYLANE.COM

The Journey of Eleven Moons

Bonnie Leon

A successful walrus hunt means Anna and her beloved Kinauquak will soon be joined in marriage. But before they can seal their promise to one another, a tsunami wipes their village from the rugged shore … everyone except Anna and her little sister, Iya, who are left alone to face the Alaskan wilderness.

A stranger, a Civil War veteran with golden hair and blue eyes, wanders the untamed Aleutian Islands. He offers help, but can Anna trust him or his God? And if she doesn't, how will she and Iya survive?

ASHBERRY
LANE
ASHBERRYLANE.COM

On the Threshold

Sherrie Ashcraft &
Christina Berry Tarabochia

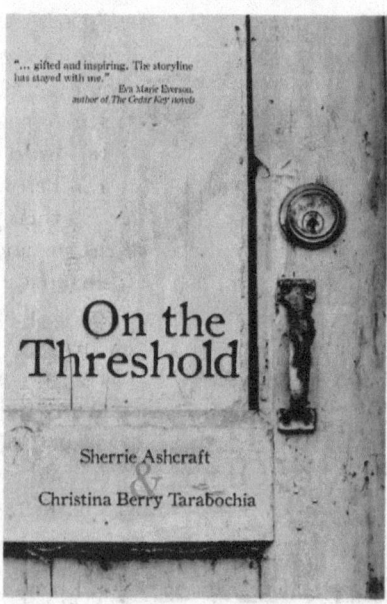

Suzanne ~
a mother with a
long-held secret

Tony ~
a police officer with
something to prove

Beth ~
a daughter with a
storybook future

When all they love
is lost, what's worth
living for?

ASHBERRY
LANE
ASHBERRYLANE.COM